The Lion Slayer

The Lion Slayer

A TALE OF ANCIENT PHOENICIA

DAVID LEE GIBBS

Primix Publishing
East Brunswick Office Evolution
1 Tower Center Boulevard, Ste 1510
East Brunswick, NJ 08816
www.primixpublishing.com
Phone: 1-800-538-5788

Published by Primix Publishing: 11/10/2025

ISBN: 979-8-89194-556-2(sc)
ISBN: 979-8-89194-557-9(e)

Library of Congress Control Number: 2025917405

Contents

*Long ago, at many times and in many ways, God spoke
to our fathers by the prophets, but in these last days he has
spoken to us by his Son, whom he appointed the heir of
all things, through whom also he created the world.*

— Hebrews 1:1-2 English Standard Version (ESV)

Chapter 1

The Maneater

Early spring, 1342 BC on the White Mountain

The morning sun broke over the top of the White Mountain. Its rays touched a long, brushy meadow on the western slope. Men and dogs moved slowly out of the forest at the meadow's far western end. They were spread out in a long, straight line. Their progress was accompanied by a cacophony of barking and shouting. Cymbals clashed, drums sounded, and horns blared, causing every creature in the meadow to flee before the riot of sound. Birds were the first to leave: quickly followed by deer, wild pigs, goats, rabbits, and all of the other animals that made their home in the meadow.

The meadow lay in a depression that had been scooped out of the mountain's side by a long-vanished glacier. It had slowly filled with fertile sediment that supported a rich variety of plants. Tall, steep, tree-covered ridges on the north and south sides hemmed the animals in, making it perfect for the type of hunt that was now taking place. The terrified animals could only go eastward to escape the advancing beaters and dogs.

Men armed with bows and javelins waited inside the tree line at the meadow's eastern edge. The still morning air hid their scent from the panicked creatures that rushed toward them. These huntsmen held their ground and did not molest the animals that ran past them to disappear in the forest beyond. They were waiting for one particular beast: a large, wounded lion that they believed was hiding in the tall brush.

The lion might run within range of the huntsmen's weapons at any moment, and their anticipation rose with each passing second. This was the third time in four days that the hunt brought them close to their quarry, and twice the lion had escaped. Today the huntsmen were determined to make the kill.

Hunting lions was fraught with danger, but was vital to maintaining the safety of the woodcutters who harvested the great cedar and fir trees that grew on the White Mountain. Timber from these trees was a major export for the people of the city-state of *Gebal*. The timber was a source of great wealth to the city's trading houses. Anything that threatened to disrupt the flow of timber from the mountain to the city's port was a threat that could not be ignored.

Leopards and bears also lived on the White Mountain, but they normally left humans alone unless provoked. Only lions posed a serious threat to anyone who entered the great forests. Lions were efficient killers that would actively stalk and attack humans. Only lions considered humans to be prey.

A new cutting season began at seedtime each year. The woodcutters would take their wives and children up the White Mountain, and return to their base camps. One of the largest camps had long been the spring and summer home of a company of Gebal's woodcutters and their families. Each member of this company: man, woman or child, was in the service of a great trading house, the House of Dan-El. Their master was a man named Ahinadab, son of Nat'n-el.

Ahinadab was a *shofet* and a member of the council of elders who, with their king, ruled the city, its port, and territories. He was also one of the wealthiest merchant-traders in the city, and the cedar and fir timber from the White Mountain was one of his most lucrative commodities.

When the woodcutters and their families had returned to their camp this year, they found everything just as they had left it the previous fall. Their huts required a few minor repairs, but everything was soon made ready for another working season. This same camp had witnessed the daily activities of these mostly mountain-born people for several generations. They were well compensated for their work, and life was good in the high country where they spent their summers.

Although they did not know it yet, this year would be very different. This time, a two-year old male lion was prowling on the mountain ahead of their arrival.

Unlike the lions of the plains east of the White Mountain, those that roamed its forested slopes did not hunt in prides. They were mostly solitary beasts that seldom met others of their kind except in the mating season. They hunted alone, each within its own territory, which they marked and defended against all rivals.

This young lion was big for his age. Almost fully grown, he weighed close to four hundred pounds. His mother made sure he had always been well-fed as a cub and taught him how to hunt as he grew. At two years old, he was well-equipped to fend for himself. This year, with the arrival of spring, his mother had driven him away. She was about to give birth to a new litter and would not tolerate him anywhere near her den when the cubs arrived.

Once the snow below the tree line had melted, he began to search the vast expanse of the White Mountain's forests for a hunting ground of his own. He arrived in the area surrounding the woodcutters' camp a few weeks before their return, and found it to be rich in wildlife. It was also empty of any other lions. After securing his new territory from other predators, he began to hunt its fifty square miles: ranging at least that widely in search of deer, elk, porcupines, wild pigs, and smaller game.

Unfamiliar scents reached the lion's nostrils the morning after the woodcutters reoccupied their camp. The smell of smoke and cooking, mingled with the familiar scent of goats, came from the slope below him. These combined scents triggered his hunger. But the air carried another scent that was not familiar, and it triggered his curiosity.

Following his nose to a spot above the woodcutters' camp, he watched from the cover of the surrounding forest. He saw humans for the first time in his life, and realized that they were the source of the unfamiliar scent. His senses quickened as he watched them move about the huts and pathways of the camp.

Cautious, though not from fear, he had learned to observe anything unfamiliar before interacting with it. He heard human voices, and saw a small herd of goats emerge from one of the huts. Two boys drove the herd down a path toward a nearby meadow. The goats' bleating made him salivate, but the presence of the boys kept him from moving to follow them. Goats were most certainly prey, and his instincts told him these new creatures might be as well. But the same instincts told him to wait before doing anything.

He remained perfectly still for over an hour, watching without giving away his presence. He saw the humans preparing and eating their first meal of the day. He saw the men gather their tools and leave the camp. They took a path that climbed toward his hiding place, but he didn't move a muscle as they passed nearby on their way to start harvesting cedars. Once the men were gone, he focused on the women working in the camp, and a group of small children playing under their mothers' watchful eyes.

The day grew warmer and the lion's position was exposed to the sun's direct rays. He silently retreated from its heat and worked back up the mountainside to a well-shaded spot. The remains of a deer he had killed the night before was there and his stomach rumbled as he began to feed. Unless forced to hunt in the daytime he was mostly nocturnal. He finished eating the deer and laid up to rest until dark.

The lion would leave these new creatures alone for now, but he would visit them again. Soon.

Chapter 2
The Death of Ariana

On the path below the woodcutters' camp

The lion hid in the brush bordering a well-traveled path below the camp. He had been watching the humans for five days, and had seen the females use this path each morning to reach a nearby creek. The sixth day, just after dawn, a group of women carrying water jars were chatting softly as they walked along the path, without paying much attention to the surrounding forest.

The lion caught their scent first, then heard their voices as they approached his hiding place. The women walked at an easy pace: enjoying the cool, crisp, morning air. They did not see or sense the danger lurking just off the path. None feared what was soon to happen.

The women reached the creek, filled their jars, and were preparing to walk back to camp when a girl of about fourteen years came running toward them. She was supposed to have gone for water with them, but was only now catching up to the others.

"Hah, ladies, see who has decided to join us! I believe it is Ariana, the lazy one," said Ja-rune, the matriarch in charge of the women of the camp.

She was becoming increasingly annoyed at this girl's tardiness. Today was not the first time she had scolded Ariana for what seemed to be habitual laziness.

"Perhaps I should beat you again to get you to do your work when it is time. Your laziness is disrespectful and must stop at once! Here we are, ready to return to camp, where the men must still be fed before they begin their day's work. Many other tasks also await our return, and only *now* you decide to join us! Ariana, you know we come for water at sunrise each day, yet you cannot be bothered to leave your bed to come with us!

I swear to *Ba'al Šāmēm*, this is the last time I will speak to you about your tardiness!"

Come ladies. We will return to camp and leave this lazy girl to fill her jars by herself. Let her catch up to us as best she can."

With that, the women lifted their water jars and followed their leader up the path, not realizing how true the elder woman's words were. This was indeed the last time anyone ever spoke to the girl again. About anything.

Ariana reacted to Ja-rune's scolding with the universal expression of childish disrespect. She stuck her tongue out and made a rude face behind the backs of the departing women and their leader.

She sat down on a large rock by the side of the creek and sulked. It was unfair that she had to rise before dawn, each and every day, to make the long, cold, and boring trek after water. This would be followed by a multitude of routine chores that never varied, and never seemed to be done.

She decided there was no reason to hurry back to camp. Ja-rune would be sure to punish her with extra work for her tardiness. This day was only going to get worse, and these brief moments alone, beside the creek, would be the only time she would have to herself.

The morning was gradually warming, but it was still pleasantly cool beside the creek. Ariana had run to catch up to the others, hoping Ja-rune would not notice her late arrival. She had worked up a good sweat by the time she reached them. It wouldn't hurt to rest a bit and catch her breath before filling the jars. Or so she thought.

Gazing into the clear waters of the creek, her mind drifted until her thoughts focused on Isba'al, the handsome son of Ja-rune. Ariana had certain romantic designs on Isba'al and fantasized about him often. What did it matter if he was six years older than her? He was very strong and good looking. His long, straight nose, his thick, curly beard, and matching hair made him the most handsome man she had ever seen. He sometimes used an expensive ointment on his hair and beard to make them shiny and fragrant. This luxuriant scent, mingled with his other natural smells, made her dizzy whenever he walked by or stood near her. The manly odor of his honest sweat, mixed with the resinous scent of cedar wood, aroused her.

She had spied on him once, when he went to bathe in a large pool downstream from the spot where the women filled their jars. She had followed him there, unseen, as he returned from cutting trees on the mountain side. She watched him slip out of his tunic and remove his loincloth. His slender build and bulging muscles gave her a thrill and she blushed now, remembering the sight of his fully naked form as he entered the water. He looked like the god, *Adon*, as he soaked away the aches in his back, legs, and shoulders. She longed to be held in those powerful arms, crushed against his perfect form. She was completely lost in her daydream and totally unaware of her surroundings.

The lion watched the girl from his hiding place and silently crept closer to where she sat, with her mind elsewhere and her back turned to the forest. The lion gathered his heavily muscled legs beneath his body and prepared to strike.

He launched himself from his cover without a sound and closed the last twenty paces to the girl in little more than a second: his great jaws opened wide and his forepaws spread left and right. His sandy-cinnamon colored, four-hundred-pound body was a blur as it crashed into her petite frame. The impact flattened her to the ground, knocking the breath from her lungs. The last thing she felt in life was her neck breaking as his heavy jaws clamped shut with crushing force.

With bigger prey the lion would have grabbed for the face, setting his jaws to cover the nose and mouth to cut off its breath. Or he might have crushed the animal's windpipe. In either case, death by suffocation would have been the outcome. But this slightly built human didn't require that much effort. She died almost instantly, without a sound and unaware of what had brought her short life to its end. One shake of his black-maned head was all it had taken to snap her neck.

The lion shook his victim once more, confirming that she was dead, then stood over her body to survey the forest around him. When he was sure there were no other predators lurking nearby to contest his kill, he lifted her corpse in his jaws and moved back into the forest's cover. About a hundred paces beyond the creek he settled down in heavy brush and began to feed.

Ariana was not missed at first. The women reached the camp with their water jars, set them in their places and turned to other tasks. Ariana was supposed to help gather downed wood for the cooking fires, and if the women thought of her at all, they assumed the girl was off doing just that.

It wasn't until work stopped for the noon meal that her absence was noticed. Ja-rune was the first to miss her.

"Where is that lazy girl now? Who has seen Ariana?"

When no one could answer her, Ja-rune began to sense that something was not right. She ordered the other women to search the camp. But the girl wasn't found and it was quickly determined that no one had seen her return from the creek. Ominously, her water jars were also missing. That was a clear sign that all was not well, and Ja-rune's initial irritation instantly turned into deep concern. Ariana was an orphan who had no one else to look after her, and in spite of her harsh words and stern manner, Ja-rune was very fond of her.

Ja-rune sent two women up the side of the mountain to summon help from where the men were working. She then led five of the other women down the path to look for Ariana. When they reached the creek where she had last been seen they were horrified by what they found. Next to the rock where Ariana had been sitting, her water jars lay broken, their pieces scattered. The disturbed ground, the crushed bracken, and the lion's great paw prints in the muddy soil at the water's edge, told the unmistakable story of what had happened.

A rush of adrenalin coursed through Ja-rune's body. She reacted with shock, overlaid by the primal fear that all humans feel when unexpected danger suddenly confronts them. Her heart was racing, her breathing was constricted, and a hard ball of dread began to grow in the pit of her stomach.

Her eyes darted back and forth from the scene of the attack to the surrounding forest. Clearly a lion had been there. Did it kill the girl? There was no blood. Had she somehow escaped and run away? Or was she lying injured somewhere nearby? What could they do? What should happen next? All of these thoughts flashed through her mind in seconds, until she reached a conclusion. She composed her thoughts and spoke.

"We must find Ariana! She may need our help!"

The other women were badly frightened, with some beginning to wail in fear and sorrow. It was clear to all that a lion had attacked one of their own. Would it attack again?

The women huddled together, peering into the forest around them. Collective terror was creeping over the group like a dark, heavy cloud. None were eager to go looking for the girl, and some seemed paralyzed by their fear. Those who could speak gave voice to that fear:

"We have no weapons!"

"When will the men get here?"

"It isn't safe. We should go back to camp!"

Ja-rune had great difficulty mastering her own emotions. Her sense of responsibility warred in her heart with the desire to flee and find safety. On top of that, she felt deep guilt for having left Ariana alone that morning.

But after a few moments, she summoned the courage to do what had to be done. She straightened her back, assumed an air of calm that she truly didn't feel, and spoke with all the authority her voice could command.

"Listen to me ladies! The men have been sent for, and they will be here soon. But if Ariana is injured, they may arrive too late to help her. We must search for her. If we stay together, we will be safe."

Some of the braver women began to rally under the influence of her words and tone. Ja-rune knew her next sentence would be critical.

"If it were one of you out there in the forest you would pray to the goddess, *Ba'alat-Gebal*, our Lady of the Well, that your sisters would find you quickly! Now let us begin. We will start in the direction these tracks lead."

With a show of more courage than she truly possessed, Ja-rune stepped off into the brush beside the path. She kept her eyes moving from side to side, peering into the forest between glances at the beast's tracks, and did not look back. She was greatly relieved when she heard the sounds of the other women begin to follow.

"Spread yourselves out to the sides," Ja-rune commanded, "and make as much noise as you can!"

She hoped the sounds might scare the lion off if it was near. Perhaps Ariana might hear them as well, and cry out for help. The women fanned out to the left and right of their leader, like a flight of geese behind the strongest flier.

"Ariana! Where are you?" Ja-rune called in her loudest voice. She kept repeating this as she walked. The others began to echo her calls, and soon the forest was ringing with their desperate pleas. But no answer came.

The brush was so thick that it took the women nearly half an hour to work their way from the scene of the attack to the patch of blood-soaked ground where they finally found what remained of Ariana.

As was his habit, the lion had first peeled most of the skin from her body, swallowing her bloody clothing along with it. He had then eaten her organs and entrails, followed by the larger muscle groups and bones. What was left was not pretty, and could barely be recognized as human. He had stripped the flesh from her head and face, leaving only one eyeball to stare, as if in horror, from a ruined socket. The back of her skull had been crushed and her brain matter devoured.

Then, having eaten his fill, the lion wandered a short way off and lay down in a thicket of bracken to clean himself and digest his meal. But as the women began searching, their voices and the sounds of their approach told him it was time to move. But feeling no need to hurry, he simply moved a bit further into the forest. He reached a more secluded spot, from which he could keep watch over the remains of his kill without being seen.

Shocked and horrified at what they found, several of the women began to weep with deep keening sounds and wails of grief, overlaid with an icy layer of fear. Most kept their eyes on the surrounding forest. Few had enough nerve to gaze on the body of their young friend. Those who did, felt their stomachs churn with nausea and several nearly fainted.

"Give me your cloak Saphara." Ja-rune said in a subdued and gentle voice. Saphara, one of the older women in the group, obeyed at once. Her eyes fell on the tragic sight of Ariana's remains and bile rushed up into her throat. She handed over her cloak and quickly turned aside to vomit. Ja-rune spread the cloak over the remains, tucking the fabric around the scattered body parts, and pulling everything together into a tight, pathetically small, bundle.

With weary sadness, Ja-rune said, "We must get back to the path, and take Ariana up to the camp."

All were eager to leave the forest and moved as fast as seemed safe. They followed their own tracks back the way they had come, with Ja-rune and Saphara leading; solemnly carrying their small burden between them. Without the need to search, the short hike back was accomplished quickly. Once back on the path, they hastened along it toward the camp, and were met on the way by a party of five men with the two women Ja-rune had sent to summon them.

At this point the lion, having silently followed a short distance behind the women, halted. He wasn't bothered by the loss of his kill. He had finished what he wanted from it and hadn't left much anyway. Rather, he was curious about what these humans would do with it.

He recognized the men, armed with their bronze axes and pruning hooks, who were talking animatedly with the women. He had no more fear of the men than he did of the women, which is to say he had none. He had seen them cutting down the great cedar trees and lopping off their branches. He didn't perceive them, or their activity, as any kind of threat. He watched two of them take his kill from Ja-rune and Saphara, and saw them carry it up the path, followed in haste by the women.

For a moment, the other men remained standing on the path, looking in the direction the women had come from, and staring into the surrounding forest. They did not see the lion, and after a few minutes, they turned and walked quickly after the others.

Chapter 3
Death Stalks the Camp

At the woodcutters' camp

The lion normally made a kill of average size about once or twice each week, but if all he could find was smaller prey he had to hunt more often. The girl he had killed and eaten didn't provide enough nourishment to satisfy his appetite for more than a day. So, over the next three days as his hunger grew, he became bolder regarding what he now considered a new and easy food source.

He began entering the woodcutters' camp at night, to prowl around between the low, bowl-shaped huts where the humans slept. He sniffed at their cooking pots and stole strips of goat meat from drying racks. The goat meat was tasty but there wasn't much of it, and all it did was whet his appetite.

The lion salivated at the thought of the easy pickings such helpless prey would be, penned up and unable to escape. If only he could reach them. He tried, unsuccessfully, to find a way to get at the humans inside their huts. But the huts, though small and meant only as temporary shelters, were too well-built for him to simply tear apart. The same was true of the larger hut that served as a fold for the camp's small herd of goats. All he accomplished was to terrify the humans and their animals.

Frustrated after failing to solve this puzzle several nights in a row, he left the area around the camp to seek his meals elsewhere. But as he ranged throughout his territory, his mind kept returning to the camp. He would be back soon—and often.

Year after year, the woodcutters returned to this same base camp. Their huts had been built long ago, out of stout cedar poles that were cut, shaped and raised to stand on end in a circle. The downward ends were buried to a depth of three *cubits*, or about four feet. This anchored them firmly in the ground, allowing the upper ends to be bent over toward the center of the circle and lashed together to form a strong framework. Each year, new layers of freshly cut cedar branches with their dense tufts of spiky green needles, were woven horizontally between the poles. The result was a sturdy, sweet-smelling structure. The resinous aroma of the cedar wood and needles repelled most insects, and kept the huts free from unwanted pests all summer.

An outer covering of thick ox hides was spread over the whole structure and lashed to the framework with heavy leather straps. This made the huts waterproof and able to withstand the strong winds that sometimes swept the forest. The huts were like overturned bowls about ten-to-fifteen paces in diameter. Each had a floor paved with flat stones.

A narrow door flap, always on the east side to face the rising sun, and a small smoke hole at the apex of the frame, were the only openings in each hut. The door flaps were usually left open during the day, but were blocked at night with a layer of dense, thorny brush on the outside. Each hut provided a family with safe shelter and a secure space to store personal items.

Since Ariana's death, extra layers of brush had been added at each door flap, with more piled all around the outside of the huts. After the lion's nocturnal visits began, heavy doors, made of thick branches bound with strong leather straps, were attached to the frames between the door flaps and the thorns. But even with these added measures, no one knew how long the huts could keep a determined maneater at bay.

The men stopped working and stayed in camp to guard their wives and children. No one went anywhere alone. The goats were kept in the fold and fed what grass could be gathered from near at hand. Children stayed close to their mothers and none were allowed to play or wander unattended. Groups of men went for water, carrying axes and other edged tools for protection.

Terror ruled every heart and mind, day and night. The woodcutters knew they needed help and held a meeting to determine what to do. Their choices were to send for aid, or abandon the camp and return to the city. They decided to send for help first.

Chapter 4
A Desperate Plea for Help

In the great hall of the House of Dan-El

A week later, in the city of Gebal, a messenger arrived at the House of Dan-El, bringing word of the lion's attack and its continuing threat to the camp. Arriving just as the sun was setting, the messenger was brought at once into the great hall of the house. He was ushered into the presence of his patron, the shofeṭ Ahinadab. As the messenger knelt before his lord, Ahinadab spoke.

"I know you, Ba'aldo, son of Ba'al-tazar. What brings you from your labors on the White Mountain? What report do you bring from my woodcutters' camp?"

Ba'aldo bent lower and touched his forehead to the floor three times before looking up to speak. His mouth was dry with anxiety. Overawed by his surroundings, he began by addressing his master in the most formal style he could manage.

"My great and gracious lord, Ahinadab, son of Nat'n-El, may you live forever. May the goddess, Ba'alat-Gebal, our Lady of The Well, pour out her blessings upon your great house and grant you success in all you do. May the goddess Ashtoreth make your women fertile and bless you with many sons and daughters. May the great god Ba'al Šāmēm protect you always and smite your enemies with his lightning bolts. May the high god, Almighty El—who in this magnificent house is worshiped before all other gods—grant you the desires of your heart."

Catching his breath, Ba'aldo hesitated for several heartbeats as sweat beaded on his forehead. Gathering his courage, he continued.

"Most merciful lord, do not be angry with your servant because of the message I bring you now. I was sent by those who labor for you on the White Mountain to beg for your help! Out of great fear, and in peril for our lives, we plead with you to save us!

A fierce and terrible lion has come to your woodcutters' camp and has taken a young servant girl for his prey. Now this lion stalks your people by night and day, so that none is safe. The danger is so great that no one dares walk about alone. It is not safe for the women to go for water, and they cannot cook for fear that the scent of food will bring the lion upon them. The men have been forced to stop all work, and keep watch in the daylight hours. At night, all must remain shut up in their huts, their doorways blocked with thorn bushes lest the lion should take them in their sleep.

Great lord, your people pray that you will send your huntsmen to rid us of this evil beast and enable us to return to our labors in safety. We urge you not to delay but rather come in haste to save your servants. We beg this of you, lord Ahinadab, for without your help we surely must leave the White Mountain or we will all perish!"

Ba'aldo bowed three more times, and remained with his forehead touching the floor, awaiting his lord's reply. Ahinadab turned to He-sham, his *rab-tamkari*, the chief administrator of the House of Dan-El.

"Summon my huntsmen, and tell them to gather their weapons and field gear. I will lead a hunting party to the woodcutters' camp myself, and deal with this lion. If it shall be the will of Almighty El, we will slay the beast, so that our people may be safe to return to their work. Do whatever is needed to make ready. We will depart for the White Mountain at daybreak tomorrow."

Turning his attention back to Ba'aldo, Ahinadab said, "Be assured, I will bring help to my people. Rest yourself in my house this night. My servants will prepare food to strengthen and refresh you. Then, in the morning, you will guide us to the camp on the White Mountain, where this beast was last seen."

To his scribe, sitting cross-legged on the floor nearby, Ahinadab said, "As I have spoken, so let it be recorded, and as it is recorded so it shall be." This last phrase signaled the end of the audience. All bowed as Ahinadab rose and left the hall. He-sham signaled for the house servants to guide Ba'aldo to the kitchen building, outside the house, as the others exited the room. Soon all had left the great hall to begin making preparations for the morning.

All that is, except one.

Hidden in a shadowed corner of the great hall, behind one of the massive, square pillars, a small figure had crouched throughout the audience. Gamil, the thirteen-year-old, son of the *ba'alat*, or noble lady, Nikkal, had been in his bedchamber preparing for sleep, but heard voices coming from the great hall. It was strange for the lord of the house to receive visitors so late in the evening, and although he wasn't summoned, the boy had been too curious to stay away.

Now his mind was whirling with excitement. There would be a lion hunt! Such a rare thing had only happened once in his short life, and he had been too young to have had much interest. He could barely remember it. But now he was surely old enough to join the hunting party! That is, *if* his father would allow it.

Father was always hesitant about letting Gamil do anything the least bit dangerous. He often looked at the boy with a strange mixture of pride and something else; something Gamil didn't understand. It was as if he was afraid of something that might happen at any moment.

To Gamil this was very odd. Throughout his entire life he had been surrounded by luxuries that most people in the world could only dream about. Except for the city's three great temples, in all of Gebal the House of Dan-El was exceeded in size and splendor by only two others, the House of Abdhamon and the palace of king Rib-Hadda himself. Who could blame Gamil for thinking that life held only adventures and glorious opportunities?

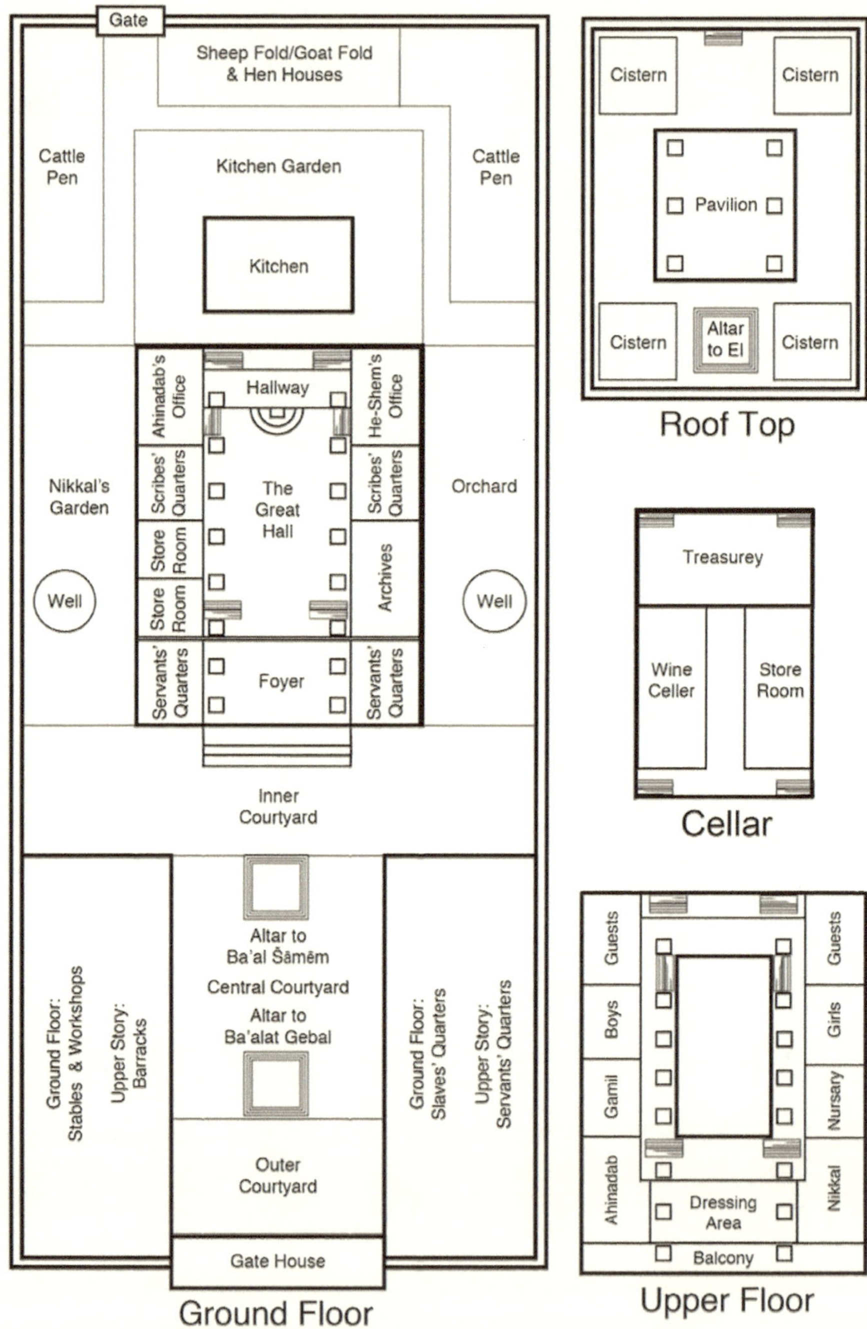

The House of Dan-El in the City of Gebal

Chapter 5

Council, King, and High Priest

Gebal in the days of king Rib-Hadda

By the time Gamil was born, the cities along the east coast of the Great Sea had developed a unique form of government. Gebal, its outlying villages, and farm lands, were governed by a council of elders and a king. In an age when most lands were ruled by tyrants, the *Kena'ani*, of Gebal were a peaceful, industrious people who had become incredibly wealthy from their trade with foreign lands. Their council of elders was formed to make their laws and regulate the commerce that was the city's life blood. The people of the city elected shofeṭim from among their wisest men, and gave them the authority to ensure that laws were obeyed and disputes were settled fairly. The city guard was created to maintain order, enforce the judgements of the shofeṭim and carry out the laws decreed by the council.

The king's powers were not absolute. His responsibilities primarily involved interaction with foreign heads of state. He served as a figurehead to satisfy the need of most foreign leaders to deal with the head man. His acts were subject to approval by the council, which had selected him from among its members, and could remove him if necessary.

This system had worked smoothly for centuries in the coastal city-states: first as independent governments; then as vassals of the pharaohs of *Kemet*. Kemet had long been their most important customer. In the reign of pharaoh Thutmose III, they were incorporated into the empire of Kemet as vassal city-states. They owed their allegiance to the succeeding pharaohs for over one hundred years when Rib-Hadda ruled in Gebal.

For all those years, little changed under Kemet's rule. Kemet derived great wealth from the taxes paid by these cities and it was not in their interest to run roughshod over their vassals. Their policy toward Gebal gave wide latitude to the council of elders, as long as the members remained loyal and pharaoh's taxes were paid.

But in Gebal, signs of internal unrest began to appear. By the time Gamil was born, factions had arisen that split the council along lines of competing interests. These factions sought less for the common good and more for their own advantage. Each faction attempted to sway the council's proceedings in its favor. The potential for real trouble was there, creating opportunities for unprincipled members to push for a greater power.

Rib-Hadda had been chosen to be the city's king, because the factions agreed that he was a safe choice. He was not the brightest among them, was somewhat weak-willed, and more than a bit paranoid at times. He could be counted on to side with whichever faction seemed to be prevailing on any issue. He was easily manipulated when necessary, and easily ignored when he wasn't needed.

Despite his flaws, Rib-Hadda was respected as a good business man whose own trading house had prospered before he was king. As king, he prospered even more, since he was entitled to a share of the profits from all the city's commerce. It wasn't long before he became the richest man in Gebal.

That should have satisfied anyone, but for Rib-Hadda it was not enough. Although he was careful not to show it, he secretly lusted for the power of the tyrant kings he dealt with, and he began to think hard about how he could gain it.

The people of Gebal were not warlike, and relied on the might of Kemet for protection from external enemies. Thus, the council saw no need for an army of their own, and knew that raising one would be an act of rebellion against the pharaoh. Thus, Rib-Hadda had no army to back him and could not simply force his will on the city. Instead, he tried subtle manipulation of the factions to control the council's deliberations. By selectively adding his support to whatever group best served his interests, he gained some control of the council. But merely influencing the council was not the kind of power that he craved. He dreamed of being a real king, unencumbered by the elders.

To achieve this, he needed leverage, in the form of information about individuals on the council members that they didn't want anyone to know. What he needed was a network of spies.

Servants and workers within the houses of the elites sometimes heard or saw things not meant to be shared with outsiders. But it was natural for them to gossip among themselves and their peers in the other houses. It was one of the few ways they had to entertain themselves. But if their masters were unusually harsh, or abused them, the inevitable resentment could undermine the most faithful servant's loyalty.

In time, Rib-Hadda learned which individuals were the disloyal ones. The information he wanted could be bought from some of these. Others were foolish enough to offer up their master's secrets without compensation. Over time, the king's network of spies and informants had penetrated most of Gebal's great houses. Much of the information they gathered was far from useful. Just simple gossip that was embarrassing perhaps, but not something that could be used for leverage. He needed better information.

Rib-Hadda's younger brother, Ili-Rapih, was the high priest of the two most powerful gods of the city: Ba'al Šāmēm, the god of fertility, lightning, and thunder; and *Yam-Nahar*, god of the sea, rivers, and lakes. As high priest, Ili-Rapih was only answerable to the gods, and he held total authority over two of the city's largest and most prominent temples. He had no vote in the council, but exercised great power over the spiritual life of the city, and was the principal advisor to the king and elders in spiritual matters.

Ili-Rapih was privy to many of the secret fears and dark desires of Gebal's common people, the elite citizens, and the council members. Most of the city's inhabitants were devout believers in their many gods, and earnestly sought to gain or keep the favor of these deities. They believed the intercession of the priests in the temples was vital, and came to them with their prayers and offerings. Many private matters, supposed to be held in strict confidence, found their way from lesser clerics to the ears of the high priest.

Ili-Rapih passed some of this information to his brother, but kept most of it to himself. By carefully sharing a few secrets with Rib-Hadda, he secured the king's support in matters before the council, and reinforced his brother's naive belief that he had the high priest's loyalty.

But Ili-Rapih had a covert agenda of his own. For him, it was not enough to control the great wealth of the two temples, and enjoy the considerable income from his own trading house. He used the secrets he hadn't shared with the king to campaign for his own goals. His ultimate desire being to take his brother's seat on the throne, with total control of the council.

To these ends, Ili-Rapih was constantly hatching new plots and manipulating the factions in the council right under his brother's nose. Behind the scenes, he had forged a small, but potent, faction, which he surreptitiously guided and inspired through intimidation or mutual greed.

As a servant of the gods, Ili-Rapih could not hold a voting seat on the council, nor was he free to act in secular matters without their approval. But he did have the right to attend council meetings. His voice was heard there as often, and sometimes more often, than the king's. His advice was always sought on all but the most minor issues, along with his intersession between the gods and the city. These were the tools he used to try and gain control of the council.

The shofeṭ Ahinadab was one member of the council that Ili-Rapih could not bend to his will. He was a leader of the merchant and trader faction, and one of the few men in Gebal who could act as a check on Ili-Rapih's scheming. He was wise enough to detect the hidden motives behind the high priest's words, even when they were coming from the mouths of others.

In his office as a shofeṭ, Ahinadab presided over all legal proceedings in the northern half of the city. He considered and passed judgment in criminal cases: and settled civil disputes between council members, merchants, traders, and other citizens. All judgments were final, and could only be overruled by the unanimous votes of the full council.

Shofeṭim were also charged with enforcing the laws of Gebal within its walls, and had the full complement of the city guard at their command. The shofeṭim could call upon the guards to keep order in the marketplace, the taverns and all quarters of the city except for the various temples and shrines dedicated to the gods.

There were three principal temples, and hundreds of minor shrines scattered around the city. Each of the major sites were protected by dedicated teams of temple guards, who served under the command of their high priests and most senior clerics. This led to occasional conflicts of jurisdiction between the city guards and the temple guards, and in the northern sector, between Ahinadab and Ili-Rapih.

Ahinadab was highly esteemed for his fairness and equitable judgments as a shofeṭ, and for his equally fair dealings as a business man and head of the House of Dan-El. In short, he was the exact opposite of the high priest in all things pertaining to morality and character. This made them natural competitors, if not enemies.

Ili-Rapih's conniving within the council frequently placed him in direct opposition to Ahinadab, and vice versa. The rivalry between the high priest's faction and the shofeṭ's was epic. Ili-Rapih acted as if the laws of Gebal did not apply to him; Ahinadab saw to it that they did. When someone objected to Ili-Rapih's high-handed treatment in business affairs, their usual recourse was to take their grievances to the shofeṭim, and if at all possible, most preferred to bring their issues to the court in the northern gate, where they believed impartial justice and fairness would be guaranteed by Ahinadab.

Whenever Ahinadab ruled against Ili-Rapih or his faction, the smoldering wrath of the high priest intensified. He looked forward to a day when he could somehow settle the score with the shofeṭ.

In the midst of this turbulent mixture of complex internal intrigue, Ahinadab prepared to depart for the White Mountain, in hope of rescuing his woodcutters from a dangerous lion.

Empires of the Eastern Mediterranean
in the Fourteenth Century BC

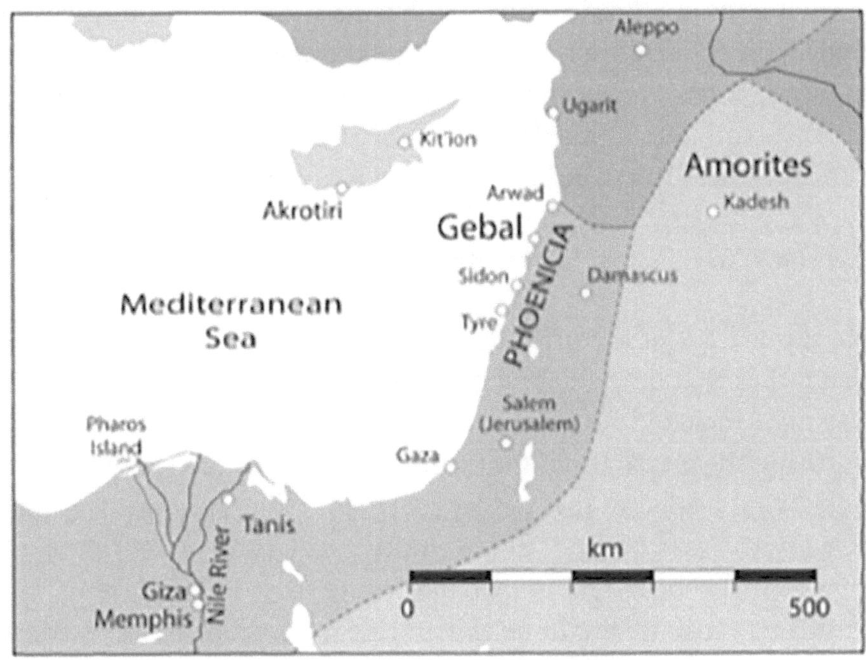

Gebal and Her Sister-Cities of Phoenicia
in the Fourteenth Century BC

Chapter 6
The Hunting Party

In the courtyard of the House of Dan-El

Growing up in a house where the business involved in all types of trade was conducted: a house where great wealth seemed as common as water, it was impossible for Gamil to conceive of anything bad ever happening to him or his family. So why were father and mother both such needless worriers? It seemed as if he was never allowed to have any fun at all. With the departure of the hunting party just a few short hours away, he was desperate to be included.

He slipped out of the great hall with his mind spinning. He knew that father would never agree to let him join the hunt. He needed a way to be included without asking permission. He wandered about, watching the preparations for the hunters' departure. Three ox carts were being loaded in the middle courtyard. The third one was half filled with sacks of food. Some empty grain sacks lay in that cart, giving him an idea. If he crawled into one of these sacks and remained completely still, he might be able to ride in that cart undetected, at least until they traveled too far to send him back. If he was discovered, father would surely punish him, but would soon forgive him. Then father would have to let him join the hunt, wouldn't he? It was an idea that just might work.

With all the frantic preparations, the children, except the babies, were up and excitedly roaming around. No one was paying any close attention to him. When the men loading the carts were busy elsewhere, Gamil made his move.

Daybreak found the hunting party assembled and waiting for their lord in the inner courtyard of the House of Dan-El, ready to start for the White Mountain. As promised, Ahinadab himself would the party. His horse stood ready, with his hunt master, Osiris of Kemet, and Ba'aldo the woodcutter mounted beside it.

Osiris's reputation as "the best hunter alive," in his own words, was "uncontested from Ugarit to the Nile Valley, and from *Karduniaš*, or Babylon, to the western seacoast." That was how he had presented himself a dozen years earlier, when he came seeking service among the great houses of Gebal.

Ahinadab had been skeptical of such extravagant claims, but took Osiris into his service none-the-less. That he was still serving the House of Dan-El twelve years later, in such a lofty position, testified of Ahinadab's complete satisfaction.

Osiris was a tall man by Kena'ani standards, standing slightly over four cubits, or almost six feet, in height. He stood out in a city where most full-grown men barely reached three-and-one-half cubits. He had the olive complexion of the Nile Valley people, with strong, weather-beaten limbs from an active, outdoor life. Age and good living had thickened his waist a bit, but had not diminish his sharp eye and canny tracking skills. At the advanced age of thirty-nine summers he was still a man of considerable strength and endurance.

Osiris selected four of the best hunters in Gebal for this trip. He also chose nine others who knew the mountain well, to serve as porters and beaters. They would do the work of setting up the hunting camp and other labor as needed. Once the hunt began these men would drive the lion to the hunters.

Ahinadab would also be attended by three body servants, and accompanied everywhere by two well-armed bodyguards. These last were trusted mercenary warriors from a tribe of men who lived north of the Black Sea. Trovorst and Hurark had served in his household guard for six years and would give their lives, if necessary, to save their lord.

Including himself, Ahinadab had designed his hunting party to consist of three times seven men in total, which was believed to be a very lucky number. Gathered in the courtyard of the House of Dan-El, none knew that the actual count, would be twenty plus two.

Ahinadab offered a sacrifice to almighty El on the altar atop his house, with a prayer for the safety of his woodcutters and the success of the hunt. As he surveyed the assembly below him, he was pleased with the efficiency and good order that he found in everything. Despite the haste with which it had all been brought together, He-sham had done his usual excellent job of organizing and provisioning the party. Three oxcarts stood loaded with supplies of food, water, tenting, and all the other baggage needed for an extended hunt on the White Mountain.

The first cart carried Ahinadab's great bronze armor and weapons, along with the huntsmen's gear and personal items. The second cart was filled with tenting, bedding, and other camp equipment. At the back it held cooking utensils, pots, spices and other essential ingredients for meal preparation, and medical supplies. The third cart held sacks of grain, baskets filled with small loaves of hard bread or dried fish, amphora filled with olive oil or *garum*, a popular, fermented fish condiment, and a supply of clean water. What Ahinadab could not see was that this last cart also held the uninvited member of the hunting party.

Ahinadab's armament consisted of his recurved bow, with two leopard-hide quivers full of bronze-tipped arrows, his favorite hunting spear, three javelins, and his *khopesh*, a wicked-looking sword. Shaped much like a sickle, this sword was designed for slashing at enemies, rather than stabbing, and it was very effective. Its mere presence on a battlefield inspired fear, and when properly used, it could cut through most light armor.

The heavy, bronze khopesh had an elaborately carved ivory and gold handle. Its jewel-encrusted pommel signified the high prestige of its owner, and was a source of great pride for Ahinadab. It was a gift presented to him by Akhmun-tar, the special emissary of pharaoh Akhenaten. Akhmun-tar had been sent north to Gebal to arrange the purchase of timber for his master, who was deeply engaged in the process of creating his new capital city at Akhena*tan*. But because there were no forests in Kemet, pharaoh Akhenaten had to rely on the cedars and firs of the White Mountain for the timber required to build the great pylons for the second temple of his god, *Aten*, the sun. Of the many projects that Akhenaten had launched since coming to the throne, this was the most important. He had given Akhmun-tar specific instructions to purchase the timber for this temple from the House of Dan-El.

That, and the gift of such a weapon demonstrated the high esteem and trust the pharaoh had in one who had served him well. That esteem was something Ahinadab worked hard to earn and maintain. Akhenaten recognized the excellent quality of the timber the House of Dan-el provided, and knew this was due to the efforts of Ahinadab.

The pharaoh had come to regard Ahinadab as a man of the highest integrity; one who could be trusted to charge a fair price for his goods, and who always kept his end of any bargain—even if it cut into his profits. The great sword was a symbol of pharaoh's trust and confidence.

Ahinadab doubted this fine weapon would see much use on a simple hunting trip, but if they met with thieves or Amurri raiders, the sight of this khopesh in Ahinadab's hand would make a real difference. Kemet's pharaoh did not bestow such weapons lightly, and any man so armed would be recognized as one who enjoyed the pharaoh's favor.

Fully satisfied with all he saw, Ahinadab descended from the rooftop and joined the others in the inner courtyard. He mounted his horse and gave the signal to depart. The huntsmen sounded their horns, and their pack of six half-wild hunting dogs barked loudly as the party began to move.

When the head of the party reached the middle of the outer courtyard, Ahinadab looked up and saw *ba'alat* Nikkal, his noble wife, standing on the upper level of the gatehouse. Their eyes fixed on each other as she called out to him.

"Go forth with the protection of Almighty El, my lord husband. May he watch over you and all your people and bring you safely home."

The household guards opened the gates and trumpets gave a salute to their departing lord.

Chapter 7
The Journey

The road to the woodcutters' camp

Men on foot or horseback could reach the woodcutters' camp in four days or less. But the plodding gait of oxen hauling heavily burdened carts up the steep grade of a rough, switch-back route, made the hunting party's progress much slower. With the unpredictable spring-time condition of the mountain trails, the party would do well to make about three leagues per day. They expected the trip to take eight or nine days, and as the first morning wore on, they still were within sight of the city walls.

They crossed the narrow plain between the city and the foothills of the White Mountain: bypassing fields and pastures that fed the city's population. Small villages dotted the landscape and people waved as they went by. They climbed into the foothills and planned to pause near mid-day at a place that Ba'aldo knew of. There a tree-shaded stream crossed the road. It was a good location to rest and water their animals, and eat their noon meal. After that they would press on until just before nightfall.

Gamil stayed completely still and hidden in his grain sack while the men finished loading the third oxcart. They never glanced at what seemed like just another sack of provisions. Baskets, amphora, and other sacks: filled with dried fish, dried fruit, or loaves of bread, were added until he was completely hidden.

Adrenaline pulsed through his veins, from fear that he might yet be discovered, but he calmed down once the cart was full and he had not been noticed. He stayed alert, however, as other preparations continued through the night. At daybreak the cart's wheels began to roll, and his excitement peaked. He heard the trumpets saluting the hunting party's departure, and the gates closing behind his cart. So far, his plan was working. He began to relax when they passed through the city gates. Just a little at first, then a little more, until the gentle rocking of the cart lulled him to sleep.

He awoke several hours into the journey. The day was bright and much warmer, with the sun's rays falling directly on Gamil's sack. He had been sweating profusely in his sleep, and his sack's rough fabric had become itchy, hot, and stifling. He could barely breathe, but didn't dare poke his head out. He had to remain hidden. He moved the sack's opening close to his face and opened it slightly. Just enough to let in some fresher air. He felt better after a minute, but was still very uncomfortable. His limbs were cramped and he itched all over from the dust of whatever his sack had previously held. Before long he was fidgeting and scratching like a dog with fleas. He desperately wanted to be free of the sack. But not yet. It was too soon.

Gamil could tell they were still close to Gebal. If he were discovered now, he might be sent home. That must be avoided at all costs, so in spite of his itching, he was determined to stay hidden. He tried to think of pleasant things to distract himself. His favorite pastimes were playing with his friends in the surf and along the shore near the city's harbor. He thought of the hours he spent at the great quay, watching the activities of the stevedores, and crewmen of the ships that were berthed along the wharves. But these thoughts only seemed to make him feel even hotter and stickier.

The party reached the resting place just before noon, and Gamil would have given anything to be able to stretch his legs. But he could tell that some of the men were moving around his cart, getting dried fish and bread to eat. He heard their voices and footsteps moving farther away, and he breathed a sigh of relief. Others came and went, drawing their rations for the noon meal. All moved to rest and eat in the shade of trees along the creek's bank. The six, Kena'ani hunting dogs worked from man to man, hoping to catch a few crumbs. The hunters tossed small pieces in the air and watched as the dogs leaped to catch them in their mouths.

These robust, mid-sized dogs were excellent at herding their masters' flocks and guarding their cattle. They were highly valued by hunters who trained them to find and drive game. They were especially useful when hunting lions.

Kena'ani dogs were bred from a race of wild canines that had shared these lands with humans for thousands of years. They had a wolf-like appearance, and many qualities inherited from their wolf ancestors. They had large, triangular-shaped heads, with forward tapering snouts. Their ears were firm, up-standing, and rounded where they joined the head, but tapered to blunt points at their ends.

Like wolves, they had a thick winter undercoat, which was shed during warm weather. Their outer coats were straight, coarse, and very dense; protecting them from thorns when scrambling through brush, and from the fangs and claws of the animals they hunted. With the acute survival instincts of wolves, they were alert and quick to react to movement, sound, and especially scents.

All morning the dogs were allowed to range ahead and on either flank of the hunting party, but stayed within earshot of the humans.

When the party stopped, they tended to roam a bit further off. But once the food came out, they all drew in close.

One dog wandered near the oxcarts, sniffing around for bits of food that might have been dropped. He was a big male the huntsmen called Khe-ahn. Older and larger than the other dogs, he was the uncontested pack leader. He had been with the hunters for four seasons, and knew what the humans expected of him, part of which was to keep the younger dogs in line.

His whole attention was focused on food at this moment. Drawn by the smell of dried fish and bread, his nose brought him close to the cart Gamil was hiding in. Something didn't seem quite right to Khe-ahn, and the closer he got to the cart the more his curiosity was aroused.

Just then, Gamil's nose began to tingle and burn with the onset of a sneeze. He tried hard to stifle it, but inevitably his body shook as he convulsed, and he let out a small, short, barely audible sneeze. He prayed that no one was near enough to have heard him. The dust in the sack was getting to him, and he knew that this sneeze would not be the last.

Khe-ahn's ears shot up as he came to full alert on hearing the muffled sneeze. He knew it had to have come from a human, and that the humans did not allow the dogs to get too close to their food. He had not sensed any human near the cart as he approached it, but the sound distinctly came from among the sacks of food. He froze, worried about being seen lurking so close to the food. Then the sound came again! This time he located its source. One of the sacks had moved just slightly. What or who was in that sack? It was too small to be a man, but concentrating, Khe-ahn could detect a human scent among the smells of fish, bread, oxen and axle grease. It was not the smell of the huntsmen, and it was not the smell of the porters. He needed to get closer to sort this out.

Gamil listened hard after his second sneeze, worried that someone might have heard. He heard a sound, but wasn't sure what it was. Is it footsteps?

"*Be still, be still!*" he screamed at himself inside his head. Then he heard a very low, unmistakable growl. Something was creeping up on him! He felt the cart shake slightly with the impact of a body climbing onboard. Gamil's hair stood on end, and was about to leap out of his skin. But just before he reached the breaking point, he heard one of the porters shouting from a short way off.

"Khe-ahn! Get away you flea-infested mongrel! There is no food there for you! Be gone!" A sharp sound rattled against the side of the cart as the porter threw a poorly aimed rock at Khe-ahn.

Khe-ahn jumped down from the cart immediately, and began to slink off with his tail between his legs; letting the porter know how sorry he was for this unthinkable breach of etiquette. From a safe distance he turned: standing straight-legged, staring hard at the rock-thrower, but still watching the cart. The porter, satisfied that he had driven the dog off, turned back to his own food, but moved to sit at an angle that let him keep his own eyes on the cart.

Inside his sack, Gamil breathed a silent sigh of relief that it was only one of the hunters' dogs that had almost discovered him. He had imagined all sorts of terrible things that may have been about to attack him. That seemed silly now, and he realized how close he'd come to giving himself away. He was determined to be even more careful and completely still in the future.

Gamil was suddenly aware of his own hunger. He had not eaten anything since the night before, and hadn't thought to bring any food with him before climbing into the sack. He noticed he was quite thirsty too. But there was nothing he could do about hunger or thirst from inside the sack. Reluctantly, he resolved to tough it out until the hunting party stopped for the night. Once it was dark and everyone was sleeping, he would see if he could help himself to some of the food and water around him.

Khe-ahn kept watch on the oxcart. He was restless and anxious about the human inside the sack. Normally he would have given alarm; barking to alert the humans and summon his pack. But having been ordered off and away from the food cart, he wasn't sure how to act. So, he watched and waited to see what the stranger in the sack might do. In a while, without any new movement or sounds, he lost interest and wandered over to where the porters were finishing their lunches. The other dogs were busy looking for scraps and he joined them.

After resting for one hour beside the creek, the porters began to repack the things they had taken from the oxcarts; preparing to continue the journey. The oxen were re-hitched to the carts and when all was ready, Ahinadab gave the command to press on.

As the cart began to move, Gamil became aware of something else he hadn't thought about. Despite a lack of water and his profuse sweating, he had not had a chance to relieve himself since before hiding in the sack. Now, more than seven hours later, his bladder felt near to bursting. He would have to do something about that very soon! He tried to ignore the urge, but that proved impossible. The jostling of the cart rolling over the uneven trail increased the pressure on his bladder, and the need to relieve himself was almost overwhelming. What to do? He could not think of any way to get out of the sack without being noticed. Maybe if he only exposed the part of himself that could take care of this business he might not be seen.

He felt along the seams on the inside of the sack until he found a spot where the stitching was loose and he worked at it with his fingers until he had made a small hole. He shoved his short tunic up over his hips and liberated his penis from his loincloth with a minimum of movement, hoping the porter guiding the oxen would not see anything. The hardest part was turning face-down in the cart, with his penis poking out through the hole in the sack.

The oxcart's body was wickerwork, really just an over-large basket mounted on a single axle with two large wheels. Gamil's urine would trickle through the bottom of the cart without forming a puddle. He hoped no one would notice the trail it left in the dust as the cart moved on. With everything arranged as well as it could be, Gamil relaxed and let go a strong stream.

No one noticed. Ahinadab, with his guards, Osiris, and Ba'aldo, rode at the head of the party. The huntsmen, porters and Ahinadab's servants, all followed on foot. The three oxcarts were last in line, where the dust they raised would not bother the rest of the party. The three porters guiding the oxen wore scarves to keep that dust out of their mouths and noses. Gamil was in the last oxcart, with no one following to see the evidence, and the constant creaking of the cart masked any sound he made. No one was aware of the boy's presence. No human, that is.

Khe-ahn had been ranging to the left flank of the party and had drifted back near the last oxcart when Gamil began to relieve himself. Khe-ahn picked up the scent of hot urine, and immediately located the source. It had to be coming from the human in that cart!

What a strange thing for a human to do. The other humans had relieved themselves earlier, in the brush near the creek, or had fallen out briefly as the party moved along. Khe-ahn had never seen a human pee inside an oxcart before. His curiosity peaked as his mind tried to process this.

He sniffed along the trail of urine as it sank into the dust and picked up several clues about the strange human inside the sack. He could immediately tell that this was a male and a young one at that. He could also tell that this human was probably not a threat, as the urine held none of the pheromones that would have signaled aggression. Why would a human boy mark his trail this way? The dog was thoroughly puzzled.

When the trail of urine finally ran out Khe-ahn paused and lifted his hind leg to cover the boy's scent with his own unique marker. Then, after kicking dust over it with his hind feet, he trotted on after the oxcart and its strange passenger.

Chapter 8
The Uninvited Traveler

The first night's campsite

The hunting party reached the point where the foothills gave way to the lower slopes of the White Mountain. Nightfall was soon approaching and Ahinadab informed Ba'aldo that he wished to stop as soon as a suitable campsite could be found.

Thieves were known to frequent the lower slopes, so it was wise to camp off the trail. Ba'aldo guided them to a spot near a natural spring and terrain that provided some degree of safety for the night. On a low hilltop, about one hundred paces from the trail, was a reasonably flat meadow of about one *uzalak* in area, roughly a quarter-mile square. They made camp and prepared to rest for the night.

The oxcarts were drawn into a loose, three-sided perimeter. The horses and oxen were hobbled and allowed to graze. Ahinadab's tent was pitched inside the perimeter and fires were lit for preparing the evening meal. The fires would be kept burning for warmth and light throughout the cool night to come. Ahinadab's servants set up a low table and cushions for their master and Osiris. Wine was brought forth and shared with everyone.

Two small deer were brought in by the hunters, quickly skinned, cleaned and set to roast on spits. Soon the aroma of cooking floated on top of the pungent smell of wood smoke. After proper courtesies to the gods were observed, and the meal was underway, Ahinadab began to question his master of hunters.

"How many do you think are out there?" he asked in a low voice, as his servants poured wine for them both.

"My men counted not less than seven and not more than twelve," came the answer. "They have been shadowing us since we stopped for the noon meal and their number has grown a bit as we progressed through the afternoon."

"Have you set a watch then?"

"Yes, my lord. At least two of my men will stand guard at all times, taking turns watching and sleeping. The others will keep their bows strung whether awake or asleep. We can also depend on the dogs to give alarm if anything is amiss."

"Good. I will have my bodyguards keep watch over my tent and the center of the camp in turns. My armor and weapons will be with me in case of any serious trouble."

"I don't think you will need them, my lord. No skulking band of *habiru* will dare attack a party as large and well-armed as ours." Habiru, literally meant "the dusty" or "dirty" ones. It was applied to any loosely organized group of outlaws, or thieves.

"No doubt, we shall all be safe, at least for tonight, as long as none of us strays outside the camp. However, if their number continues to increase, they might be tempted to test us. See to it that everyone is armed with hunting knives and javelins, at minimum. They are to sleep with the weapons at their sides, and be sure that no one drinks too deeply of the wine."

After they finished eating, Osiris left to attend to these matters, and Ahinadab sent one of his bodyguards to place his weapons inside his tent. The foothills of the White Mountain were a haven for bands of thieves. These were mostly men who had been displaced since the recent rash of raids by the Amurri. Though mainly a nomadic people, the Amurri sometimes attacked unwalled cities and small villages without warning, leaving little standing in their wake. Only the larger walled cities, like Gebal, were safe from these raids, and even these could be seriously threatened by larger, better organized assaults. The king and council of elders found it expedient to pay tribute to the Amurri leaders, to keep them from preying on their people and caravans.

But outside the walled cities, victims of the raids suffered greatly. Survivors of the attacks were in desperate circumstances, their lives almost entirely destroyed. Older children and women captives were sold as slaves, but infants and men were almost always killed outright. Any man lucky enough to escape was forced to flee to the hills, or beg for entry into a city, in hope of finding work. After decades of these raids the cities were full, so a growing number of men sought work as oarsmen aboard Gebal's fleet of merchant ships. Many failed to gain even this backbreaking work and were forced to sell themselves as slaves.

It wasn't hard to understand why many took to the hills, living off the land and forming themselves into bands of roving thieves, such as those now stalking the hunting party. It was a desperate option and the lives of the dusty ones tended to be short and brutal.

The fires burned brightly as the night wore on, and the stars were the only illumination in the moonless sky. All except those on watch were asleep when Gamil began to stir. Hearing only snoring and other sounds of slumber, he finally felt safe enough to poke his head and arms out of the sack. The cool evening had given way to a much colder night. His light tunic and kilt-like loincloth, though warm enough in the city, was woefully thin at this higher altitude.

Gamil was stiff and the sweat of the day had dried on his body, adding to the irritation caused by the dust and rough sackcloth. He looked around slowly, but saw no one. He moved away from the firelight to the side of the cart that was in shadow. There were a number of waterskins, one of which he drank deeply from.

The water was refreshing, but with the cold night air it sent a chill through his famished body. He longed for the warmth of his sack, but urgently needed food. He helped himself to several small loaves of bread and some dried fish, keeping his movements as quiet as possible. But he couldn't keep from making some noise as he moved about. He did not know that four sets of eyes silently watched him.

Khe-ahn lingered as close to the third cart as he could, after the party stopped for the night. Twice more the porters had to shoo him away, thinking his interest was in the food. But Khe-ahn was still confused and very intrigued by whatever the boy in the sack might do next. Under the star-lit sky, his keen eyes easily spotted Gamil as he rose up out of the sack.

Creeping closer for a better look, the big dog froze as his ears picked up other sounds coming from the edge of the camp. There, in shadows cast by light from the campfires, he saw three shapes approaching the third oxcart. Their movements were slow and cautious. To any but a dog's sharp ears they were almost undetectable. Khe-ahn heard their shallow breathing, soft footfalls, and the slight rustle of their garments as they moved to where the boy stood in the cart.

Khe-ahn caught their scent, which was not that of the porters, nor the hunters. They smelled like feral beasts from the forest. It was the unmistakable stink of unwashed men. The rough fur on the back of his neck stood straight up, and his legs stiffened as a low growl came through his bared fangs.

That sound caught Gamil's attention and he turned toward the source, seeing only two bright eyes reflecting the firelight. He sucked in a startled breath and was about to dive back toward his sack, as if it might offer protection. Suddenly he felt a hard, cold hand painfully gripping his arm as another hand was clamped roughly over his mouth.

Waiting in the bushes beyond the light from the fires, three thieves, armed with clubs and knives, slowly crept to the edge of their cover. Watching the camp for hours, they had seen the food in the third oxcart, and hoped to slip between the guards and quietly make off with several of the sacks.

This seemed like easy pickings, and could also tell them how alert the guards were. The trio had been sent by their leader as scouts. He needed to know what to expect before planning a full-on attack.

They had almost reached the oxcart when they saw a head rise within it, followed soon after by the neck and torso of a young boy. They froze and watched him drink before rummaging through the sacks and baskets in the cart.

"I'll grab the boy first, then you two get as much food as you can carry," whispered one who seemed to be in charge. The others nodded in agreement, then all three eased ahead. The improvised plan might have worked if not for a sequence of unexpected events.

The leader grabbed Gamil and jerked him out of the cart. Shocked and completely surprised, Gamil instinctively bit down as hard as he could on the hand over his mouth. He hit the ground hard and the thief's knee in his back knocked the wind out of him. A nearly silent curse left the thief's throat. His hand throbbed in pain, but he held on. He raised his club for a blow that would at least knock the boy unconscious, if it didn't kill him.

But before he could strike, the night rang with a rapid series of loud angry barks, very close and quickly getting closer. The thief turned his head in the direction of the sound to see a blur of pale fur, glowing eyes and flashing teeth. He let go of the boy and raised the arm with the bitten hand to fend off the charging dog. Too late, he aimed his club to hit the dog instead of the boy's skull. His reaction was too slow and the full weight of the dog crashed into him and knocked him flat.

Sharp fangs sank into the man's hand, just below the wrist, with a cracking sound as powerful jaws clamped down hard. The thief was swinging his club wildly, trying to drive the dog off, but couldn't land a blow as Khe-ahn danced nimbly around and around the fallen man, shaking his head from side to side and sinking his fangs deeper and deeper into the thief's flesh.

The man was screaming now and calling out to his companions for help. They had frozen when they heard the dog barking and seemed paralyzed by this furious assault. One came to his senses, but rather than help, he snatched a sack of bread from the cart and ran off into the night.

The third thief raised his club and a long dagger to strike the dog. But an arrow cut through the air and its bronze head struck him in the neck and penetrated until it stuck out the other side to almost half its length. He fell beside the cart wheel and lay there as blood spurted from a severed carotid artery. A moment later he was dead.

The thief on the ground had almost stopped fighting now, and his club arm was swinging feebly with slower and slower strokes. The dog's jaws had broken his wrist and now it had a grip on the last three fingers of the same hand. Khe-ahn bit down hard and with a final jerk three of the man's fingers came off in his teeth. The thief screamed in agony as he struggled to his feet and tried desperately to run off into the brush. Khe-ahn swallowed the fingers and was about to run after him when another arrow buried itself in the man's back. Struck through the heart, he was died almost instantly, with his forward momentum carrying his body into the brush beyond the firelight. The guard who had shot the two thieves moved quickly to the dark side of the oxcart, nocking another arrow as he did so.

"Drop your weapons and stand where I can see you with your hands above your head!" the guard shouted at Gamil's prostrate form. The guard assumed the boy was a fourth thief, and was ready to shoot him if he tried to run or made any threatening moves.

Khe-ahn had dashed after the dead thief, but hearing the guard's threatening tone, rushed back to stand between the boy and the arrow that was now aimed at his heart. The whole sequence of events had taken mere seconds, but all the noise aroused the entire company. The other dogs added their own barking to the mix as they ran to join their pack leader. Men who were sound asleep took up their weapons and rushed to the sound they feared was an all-out attack. A group of them surrounded the oxcart, and were pointing their knives and javelins in Gamil's direction.

Staying between the men and the boy, Khe-ahn circled with hackles raised, ears laid back and fangs bared. First facing the guard with the bow and then the others in turn, he was clearly there to protect the boy. No one recognized Gamil or knew where he had come from, so they didn't understand Khe-ahn's actions. The other dogs milled about, alert but confused and visibly agitated by their leader's strange behavior.

"Hold, Ish-nahan!" Osiris found his way to the source of the commotion, and quickly assessed the situation. He command was directed at the guard, but was meant for everyone. The men relaxed slightly and lowered their weapons, Khe-ahn stopped circling and ceased his growling and barking. But he kept himself between the boy and Ish-nahan's bow. Osiris stepped to the front and gestured to Khe-ahn. The dog relaxed and backed away, as he had been trained to do. He sat down just beyond the circle of men.

"What is all this about? What has happened?" Osiris asked Ish-nahan.

"A handful of those stinking Habiru tried to make off with our food supplies." I killed two, while a third managed to get away with a single sack. This one," pointing at Gamil, "they left behind. If we hurry, we can catch the one that ran. He can't be far off."

"No! Do not pursue him! This whole thing may be an attempt to lure us into a trap." Osiris said sharply. That thought sobered the men, who soon became more alert to what might be going on in the surrounding darkness.

"What should be done with this boy we captured?" Ish-nahan asked, as he and one of the others took hold of Gamil.

"Bring him to the center of the camp, where he can be questioned."

Gamil was too frightened to speak through all of this. He remained silent as he was raised to his feet and roughly pushed in the direction of the largest campfire.

Osiris turned to Ish-nahan, and said, "You have done well tonight, Ish-nahan. Return to your post and put two men where they can cover the food supplies. And for the gods' sake, get these dogs under control!" The dogs continued barking and milling about. Khe-ahn had relaxed and stopped his growling and barking, but still remained alert. The boy was no longer being threatened, and he moved out of the way as Gamil was led off.

Ahinadab had been awakened by all the noise. He grabbed his khopesh and bow, and met his two bodyguards by the door of his tent. He led them to the center of the camp, to a position from where he could command the defense. Osiris had joined him there briefly, but after making sure his lord was safe, hurried to the source of the disturbance.

Now, as the commotion died down, Ahinadab watched a captive being led toward him. His eyes grew wide in amazement as he beheld the dirt-smeared face of his first-born son.

"*Gamil!*" he shouted. "What are *you* doing here? How did you get here? *What is the meaning of this?*" All this was expressed in an increasingly loud, angry voice.

Ahinadab's reaction to what he saw went from shock and bewilderment, to seething anger, as his mind absorbed the impact of what was before him. Gamil was a sorry sight. His hair was disheveled, and his tunic torn and muddied by the struggle with the thief. He was filthy from head to toe after his sweat-soaked day inside the sack and now with blood from the thief's severed fingers all over the front of his clothing. It was a wonder Ahinadab could recognize him at all.

Gamil watched his father's face turn white and then red as his emotions played across it. This was not going to be the easy conversation the boy had imagined would follow once he revealed his presence. He expected his father would be angry at first, but also knew that Ahinadab was a practical man who seldom gave way to strong feelings.

The shofeṭ was rightfully praised by everyone in Gebal for his calm, steady and diplomatic demeanor. In any crisis he could be counted on to keep his head, and even the king looked to him for council in times of great stress. At this moment, however, he was anything but cool-headed. Gamil cringed as he waited for the storm he could see was coming.

But the storm didn't break. After staring, almost in horror at the boy, Ahinadab shook himself and seemed to gather his composure. Still quite angry, but with a measure of calm he looked into Gamil's eyes and said, as his face drew near, "I will deal with you in the morning." Then, catching a whiff of the pungent odor rising from Gamil's soiled clothing, he drew back and with wrinkled nostrils, turned to his body servants, saying, "Get this mess of a boy cleaned up, and don't let him into my tent until he is fit to be in my presence!"

With that, Ahinadab strode back into his tent and the servants led Gamil aside to begin the cleanup. They brought tubs of cold water from the spring below the hilltop, and warmed them by the fire. Fragrant soaps from Ahinadab's personal supplies were fetched. When all was ready, Gamil's garments were stripped from his body and carried off to be cleaned and repaired.

Once he had been washed thoroughly, Gamil was anointed with scented olive oil, and his shoulder-length hair was brushed to free it of tangles. His long locks were curled with a heated bronze rod until they hung from his head in princely ringlets. He was wrapped in a linen sheet, since his clothes would not be dry until morning, and in this condition, he was finally allowed to enter his father's tent for sleep.

But sleep did not come easily. His father's loud snoring, and fear of whatever punishment the morning might bring, conspired with his overwrought conscience to keep sleep at bay until very near dawn. He kept thinking about his father's words, "I'll deal with you in the morning!" He thought this must be how criminals brought for judgment before his father must feel while waiting to learn their fate. How would his father punish him?

Chapter 9
His Mother's Son

Morning at the campsite

The next morning Gamil awoke on a makeshift bed of furs and blanketing at the foot of his father's sleeping pallet, still wrapped in the linen sheet he had worn to sleep. After a fitful, nearly sleepless night, he took a few moments to realize where he was.

He could hear the sounds of cooking, and men moving about. Osiris's voice came from outside the tent, as he spoke with Ahinadab.

"What will you do about your wife's son, my lord?"

"By the gods, he should not be here! He is too young to be of any real use in the hunt, and his presence makes more work for all of us. My guards are not nursemaids, and now they have two of us to protect. The servants I brought are barely enough to attend to my needs, and they will have to care for the boy as well. His mother will be frantic, wondering where he is. She will tear the city apart, looking for him."

"If you wish to send him home my lord, some of my men could deliver him to his mother."

"I should put him in a sack, tie it to the back of an ass, and send him home at once. We made good progress yesterday, but are still close enough that he could be home by sundown. Unfortunately, we can't spare the men to get him there safely. Those Habiru were just testing us last night and are still a threat. We will need every man to keep them off our backs, and sending Gamil home with only one or two men would be sending them to their deaths. No, he shall have to stay with us at least until we reach the woodcutter's camp."

Gamil overheard this conversation with mixed emotions. His father's words stung him more than a little. All the more-so, as he knew they were well deserved. In the name of Almighty El, how had he not realized what his mother would think when she found him missing?

His cleaned and mended clothes lay folded next to his bed. He quickly dressed and left the tent. The cold morning air hit him and he realized how little protection his tunic and loincloth provided. He began to shiver, but the cold air was nothing compared to the icy look he saw in his father's eyes.

Ahinadab saw the tent flap open and looked hard at the shivering figure of his first-born. He was grateful there were no signs of any serious injuries from the late-night assault. But the expression on his face did not reveal how relieved he was to find the boy unhurt. All Gamil saw was barely suppressed anger.

"So, the uninvited traveler has finally risen! Do you feel refreshed and ready for a day of adventure?" Ahinadab's tone was thick with sarcasm.

Gamil halted in front of his father and tried to look as contrite as he felt. His teeth began to chatter slightly from the cold and his shivering grew turned into trembling at his father's words.

"Tell me, boy, how will you make yourself useful today? Can you guide us to the camp of the woodcutters? No, unfortunately you don't know the way. Well, perhaps you could help guard us from thieves? But you have no weapons, nor would you know how to use them if you had brought any.

Wait! I know! Maybe you could drive the oxen as they pull our carts. No, that's not it! You have never done anything like that in your life, and the oxen would scarcely notice one as small as you. They would tread right over you, grinding you into the dust of the trail.

Can you cook, build a fire, draw water, or do even the simplest tasks? Tell me, son of ba'alat Nikkal, what good are you on a journey such as this?"

It was the custom in Gebal to refer to a young boy as the son of his mother. Gamil was known as the son of the noble lady Nikkal. This would usually continue until he reached puberty and his beard began to show itself. At some point, usually between the ages of eleven and fifteen, when a boy achieved something that brought honor to his father's house, he would be formally recognized in a public ceremony as the son of his father. It was a rite of passage that all Kena'ani boys went through, and the first time a father referred to his child as "my son" or more formally as "son of _____" was an event to be celebrated.

If wealthy, the father would hold a banquet and make much of proudly acknowledging his son among gathered family and distinguished guests. Men of humbler means held simple family gatherings with a celebratory meal to serve the same purpose. The poorest of men would simply gather the attention of a crowd in the marketplace, and there publicly name their sons, saying a ritual phrase, "This is ____ my beloved son, who has pleased me greatly!"

From that day onward, fathers took a more active role in raising their sons, and the mothers' role diminished. A mother's influence on her children would always be strong, but once a boy was acknowledged by his father he was treated like an adult. He would be expected to act like an adult as well. Much more was expected of him thereafter. All of this was something Gamil craved. But with the phrase "… son of ba'alat Nikkal…" hanging in the morning air, Ahinadab was reminding Gamil that he still regarded him as a child.

Like every Kena'ani boy, Gamil longed for the day his father would acknowledge him as "my son" to signal his new status as a man. But for him it was more than that. Gamil desperately needed the love and acceptance of his father. And he knew that only by doing something extraordinary to win his father's approval would that need ever be met.

Some fathers saw this custom as a mere formality, requiring only minor achievements of their sons before acknowledging them. But not so Ahinadab. The shofeṭ had high standards, and Gamil knew a great deal would be expected of him. This was what compelled Gamil to seek ways of proving himself: why he took risks, and why he had to be part of this hunt, invited or not.

Since his face first began to sprout the beginnings of a beard, he looked for opportunities to earned the right to be known as a man in the eyes of the Kena'ani people. Yet now, as he stood trembling before his father's stern countenance, he felt very child-like, and very foolish.

"Have you nothing to say for yourself?" his father asked.

Gamil felt tears forming in his eyes, but held back the urge to cry and summoned his courage instead. He thought hard, knowing his next words would be critical.

"Forgive me, father! I was wrong to have come unbidden on this journey, and I was wrong to leave home without my mother's knowledge and permission. I did not mean to offend you, nor cause either of you any grief. But how am I ever to become a man if I am always treated like a child? I am ten and three years old, and will be ten and four in two more months! I am almost a man, and surely, I should not be sitting at home with the women and small children." Once he started, Gamil's words pour out in a torrent. He thought he saw his father's features soften a little as he continued.

"Please, father, I beg you to let me stay and join in the hunt. I promise to make you proud of me, and glad to have me with you. I will stay out of the way, and you won't have any more reason to be angry with me! I already know how to use a bow, and have had some training with sword and javelin. If nothing else, use me as one of the beaters! I will gather wood for the fire at night, and can help the cook to clean up after meals. Please, please, father, let me stay with you. Do not send me back to the city!"

That his first-born might be more than a child was a new idea for Ahinadab. But the shofeṭ began to notice unmistakable signs of growth and change. He saw that Gamil was taller, though still a head shorter than he would be when fully grown. His voice had deepened timbre and sometimes cracked into a higher register before settling back into its new, more masculine, tone. His face had lost its child-like shape and his features were more mature. His cheeks were covered in the downy promise of what would be a handsome beard. Ahinadab stroked his own luxuriant beard as Gamil wound down his appeal.

To himself, Ahinadab thought, *"When did these changes begin? Why have I not seen these things before? Indeed, the boy is growing into manhood. But he hasn't arrived there yet! There is still much for him to learn. Why have I not given him more of my attention? I have let my business and the affairs of the council take up too much of my time. I have neglected my duty as a father to raise up the son who will one day replace me."*

"ENOUGH!" he said in a loud, but less harsh voice, bringing a halt to his thoughts and the boy's pleas. "I will consider your request. You have spoken well, Gamil, but there are other things to consider. Hunting on the White Mountain is dangerous, and when the quarry is a lion, a maneater, it is all the more so. I am not sure the risk is something I am prepared to hazard. The chance of you being hurt, or of others being hurt on your account, is very real. We will speak no more of this for now."

With that, Ahinadab turned and spoke to Osiris. "It is time this boy became proficient with the bow, the sword, and the javelin. He should also learn to hunt and track game. I charge you, Osiris, with teaching him these things, or as much as you can while we travel and are at the woodcutters' camp. If he is going to insist on being a part of such things, with or without my blessing, then at least he should know what he is doing."

This last sentence Ahinadab directed at Gamil, turning his face toward the boy as he said it.

"I will teach him all I can, lord." Osiris answered, bowing as he spoke.

"Test him. See what he already knows, and report to me daily on his progress." Ahinadab said, bringing the conversation to an end.

Chapter 10

On the March

Morning at the campsite

Gamil ate a quick breakfast of barley mush and dried figs before the hunting party set out on the day's travel. Osiris gave him a javelin and a long hunting knife, saying, "Keep these weapons with you at all times. You must learn how to march bearing arms and get used to handling their weight. You will walk behind my huntsmen. Be sure to observe their ways as we go. I will test your skill with the bow when we stop for the noon meal."

Osiris also gave Gamil a spare cloak. It was a little too long for him. Osiris tucked it in at the waist and used the knife belt to secure it snugly to the boy's thin frame. He added a small pack and a water skin to Gamil's gear. The pack held a few necessities: a bit of soap, a small sharp knife for eating, a sharpening stone, three small biscuit-like loaves of hardened bread, and some dried figs. Warmer, Gamil stopped shivering and stood tall.

Osiris looked him over, clapped him on the back, and declared with a smile, "You'll do." These words of modest approval were a balm to Gamil's bruised ego, and were the beginning of a warm respect and appreciation for the tall hunter. Osiris mounted his horse and rode to the front of the party.

Ahinadab was already astride his horse, with Ba'aldo on his left and his bodyguards mounted a few paces behind him on either side. Osiris took his place at his lord's right hand, and when all the others were in marching order, Ahinadab gave the signal to begin. Gamil fell in behind the huntsmen, who were directly behind Ahinadab's bodyguards. Next came the servants, the porters, and the three oxcarts with their drivers at the rear.

The dogs were allowed to range free: their positions varying as the party progressed: sometimes they ran ahead, sometimes at the flanks, and sometimes they trailed the oxcarts. Khe-ahn bounded along parallel to Gamil, keeping an eye on the boy. He was confused to see Gamil walking, and not riding in the oxcart as before. He ranged back and forth, from flank to flank, but always stayed close to Gamil's position.

Before long, Gamil discovered that carrying his gear, though it didn't weigh much, was more difficult than he thought it would be. Despite his boasting about being "almost a man" he was soon forced to admit to himself that he wasn't as grown up as he thought. The pack, although actually quite light, began to feel like an enormous weight on his shoulders, and the knife in its scabbard kept sliding forward on the belt until it was hanging directly in front. There it would slap from side to side against the inside of his thighs as he walked; becoming first an annoyance, then an impediment as he struggled to keep pace with the huntsmen before him.

The javelin was also giving him problems. The one he was given was of an ancient design. It had a shaft of fire-hardened ash wood almost half a palm's width in diameter and five and a half cubits, or nearly eight feet, in length. It was tipped with a long leaf-shaped bronze head that was honed to razor sharpness along its cutting edges and attached to the shaft by a long tang riveted to the wood. To help balance it for throwing the other end had a small, pomegranate-shaped, bronze sphere, that ended with a long, sharp, butt-spike. Bronze bands circled the shaft just forward of the middle to move its balance point slightly ahead of its exact center.

Though considered a "light" weapon, Gamil's short stature made it necessary for him to reach above his own shoulder height to keep the javelin upright. If he gripped it lower it tipped toward the men in front of him. But gripping it higher, at the balance point, strained the muscles of his right arm. Soon they burned from shoulder to wrist. His arm grew numb and the butt-spike dug into the dirt at his feet causing him to stumble. Ish-nahan, the huntsmen who had saved him from the thief, took pity on the boy and showed him how to rest the shaft on his shoulder so he could grip it lower. That solved his problem.

Gamil also discovered that his soft sandals, which served well-enough on the smoothly paved streets of the city, were unsuited for walking long distances over a rough, sometimes steep, mountain trail. Sharp stones tried to push through the thin soles, and often rolled beneath his feet, causing his ankles to twist painfully. By the time they had put the first few stadia behind them, one stadion being about an eighth of a mile, he almost wished he was back inside the sack, riding in the gently rolling oxcart.

Gamil was determined not to embarrass himself by complaining, which he feared would be seen as childish behavior. He pressed on, pretending that he was having no more difficult than if he were walking the city streets in Gebal. He forced himself to concentrate on the huntsmen in front of him, as much to take his mind off his aches and pains as to observe what they did. He knew Osiris would question him on what he had seen when the party stopped for the noon meal.

At first the huntsmen didn't seem to do much of anything except walk. But Gamil began to pick up a few things. He noticed that those on the right would often glance to that side of the trail, and seemed to be watching out of the corners of their eyes for any unusual movement. Those on the left would do the same on their side of the trail. Gamil found himself trying to imitate them, though he didn't know what he was looking for.

The huntsmen also seemed to ignore any normal sounds, be it birds calling or trees sighing in the wind, but instantly reacted to sounds that seemed out of place. Their heads turned as one and all eyes focused in the direction that any unexpected noises came from. Obviously, these men were well acquainted with the mountain, and constantly alert for any danger. It gave Gamil a new appreciation for the risks he had taken in coming on this journey. He hadn't thought much about danger when his father chastised him earlier, thinking it was just more of his typical over-protectiveness. But walking behind the huntsmen, the reality that something truly bad could happen stirred up new thoughts in his mind. Especially after the attack of the night before.

He pushed those thoughts to the back of his mind, but continued to watch the men ahead of him. Gamil noticed they didn't stumble the way he did, and as they walked their feet seemed to fall into a natural rhythm that propelled them smoothly over even the roughest ground. They did this without seeming to watch where they stepped, as if they had extra eyes on their feet. Gradually he found that if he watched where they stepped and put his feet in their tracks, he had much less trouble with rocks and other obstacles. He had to stretch his legs to match their stride, but found this also helped him to keep up with the pace they set. Soon the rhythm of the march began to be more natural to him, and his aches and pains receded in his mind to where he barely noticed them. The march continued throughout the morning hours until they reached another spot Ba'aldo led them to. There Ahinadab called a halt for the noon meal.

Chapter 11
The Tree Fathers

In the forest on the White Mountain

They were higher on the mountain than where they stopped the day before. They had left the brush-covered foothills behind and passed through a mixed forest covered with oak, sycamore, wild fig, acacia, and myrtle trees. By noon they had entered the more heavily forested slopes and wide meadowlands of the middle elevations. Groves of fir, pine, juniper, and cypress trees had begun to appear, amid occasional stands of tall cedars.

They had passed through places where the forest suddenly opened into wide clearings, where old cedar stumps could be seen, peeping through a thick undergrowth of fern and bracken. Gamil was amazed at the sheer number of stumps he saw. They stood in silent witness to the thousands of trees that had been harvested. He realized that teams of woodcutters must have worked for generations to leave such massive clearings in their wake. This troubled him until he noticed scores of new cedars that were growing up to replace the harvested trees. In some cases, the replacements were so large they looked almost ready to be harvested themselves.

Here and there, much older and taller trees towered over the new-growth cedars like adults surrounded by scores of their children. These were called the Tree Fathers and were sacred to the gods of the White Mountain. By law the woodcutters were required to leave one tree in ten untouched, out of respect and as an offering to the gods. Over time the woodcutters learned that this was also an excellent way of ensuring that new cedars would eventually replace the harvested trees. The party halted beside a creek that bisected one of these meadows, near a stately pair of Tree Fathers.

The size of the Tree Fathers was awe-inspiring to Gamil. Some were almost one hundred cubits in height; as high as five and twenty men of average height would reach if they stood one on top of another in a long chain. He had often seen great rafts of cut and trimmed cedar logs floating in the waters of the southern harbor at Gebal, waiting to be towed along the coast to their buyers in Kemet. But this was the first time he had ever been among the uncut forest giants.

He marveled at their lofty stature, and at their huge branches all clothed in beautiful evergreen tufts of short, resinous needles. Their trunks were wrapped in dark gray-to-black bark, but in places where the trunks had split, he could see the rich, reddish, interior wood that made such beautiful furniture, ships or other useful things.

Gamil gazed upward and noticed that about one third of the way up their height the main trunks branched into six or more limbs, each as big in girth as the main trunks of lesser tree species. Lateral branches grew out of the sides of these huge limbs. These created a layered canopy that extended to a diameter nearly matching the tree's full height. Gloriously crowned with such majesty, Gamil could easily see why these forest giants were sacred to the gods.

The rugged beauty of the forest was so different than the familiar world inside the city walls that it gave Gamil a new perspective on his life. It dawned on him that things he had always taken for granted

were secured for him by the efforts of many other people. He sat
and pondered this while he ate his lunch, and his thoughts turned
to his present situation.

In some ways, things had worked out better than he had hoped.
Father had been angrier than expected, but now seemed willing to
give him a chance to prove himself. He had been trusted with real
weapons for the first time in his life, and even if handling them was
proving more difficult than he had imagined, that was a sign of his
father's trust. As a bonus he was going to be taught how to use those
weapons by the best hunter of them all! It was well worth the aching
in his arms and legs, and the blisters beginning to form on his feet.

Gamil's thoughts were interrupted when he became aware of the dog
that saved him from the thief. The big, buff-colored brut sat a short
way off, eying him in an intense, but friendly manner. "Khe-ahn,"
the huntsmen had called him.

Khe-ahn wagged his tail when he saw the boy was finally looking at
him. His eyes follow the movement of Gamil's hand to his mouth as
he ate. He licked his muzzle with his long tongue, silently signaling
that he was hungry and wanted Gamil to share his meal. The message
could not have been any clearer if the dog had spoken to him.

Gamil took a piece of dried fish from his bowl and tossed it in the
dog's direction. Khe-ahn dashed forward, caught the morsel in midair, and swallowed it whole without even taking a second to chew. He
sniffed the ground in front of him for a few seconds, on the chance
that he might have missed a fragment or two. Then he turned his
eyes back to the boy in anticipation of more.

He had moved much closer to catch the piece of fish, and now stood
just beyond arms distance, tail wagging with expectation. When
Gamil didn't seem to understand that more would be welcomed,

Khe-ahn lowered the front of his body and pawed the ground while letting out a soft "wuff."

Gamil smiled, "Ah, you liked that, did you? And now you want me to share my lunch with you?" Another "wuff" was the reply, accompanied by much tail wagging and prancing about. This time Gamil held out his hand, holding another piece of fish.

"Careful of that one" said the voice of Osiris from behind him, "he has a taste for human fingers."

Startled, Gamil turned his head toward the voice and in the same instant felt canine teeth gently graze his hand as Khe-ahn deftly grabbed the piece of fish and ran off toward the other side of the camp.

Gamil watched him leave, thinking *"I believe I just made myself a new friend."*

Chapter 12
The Making of an Archer

Lessons from the master

"If you have finished feeding that dog and still have all your fingers, it is time for us to see what you know about using a bow." Osiris said. Gamil scrambled to his feet and stood as tall as he could in front of the master of the hunt.

"Take your bowl back to the cook and return quickly."

Gamil did so with great haste, and when he reached the spot where Osiris stood, he saw that the master of the hunt had set up a large piece of firewood, with a prominent knot, atop one of the tree stumps about twenty and five paces away.

Osiris had a quiver of arrows and was holding three recurved bows of different lengths. These were sturdy hunting bows made from layers of acacia heartwood, glued together on the inside of the bow stock. A layer of ox horn was glued to the curved outer edge. Bowstrings made of animal gut, about four-fifths as long as the bow stocks, were attached at their ends by a loop at the bottom, tied tightly to notches at the tip of the lower limb, and another loop at the top was slipped down over the upper limb of each bow to hang loose against the inside of the bow stocks.

"We begin with stringing the bow. Here, take this one and place the end against the inside of your right foot." Osiris said as he handed the longest bow to the boy. When Gamil had done so, Osiris said, "Now hold the string in your right hand, and grip the bow with your left. Good, now bend the bow and slide the bowstring up the arm until the loop on the end slips into the notches at the upper tip."

Gamil did his best, using all his strength to try and bend the bow, but could not get it to yield much at all. Osiris watched him struggle, and after a moment he stopped him, took back the bow and exchanged it for the next lighter bow. This one was slightly easier for Gamil to bend, and he almost got the loop up to the notch before it refused to bend any further. Osiris took the bow back and handed him the third. This, the smallest, lightest one, Gamil was able to string with only a little effort.

"Well done!" said Osiris, as he handed Gamil an arrow.

This arrow was of the Kemet style, with a long, slender shaft measuring a little over one and a half cubits in length, about twenty-six and a half inches, and just under a finger-width in diameter. The shaft was made from a single length of reed, fire hardened and straightened by an arrow maker, using the flat surface and long, narrow groove of a shaping stone to perfect its form. The reed was forced back-and-forth through the groove until its outer surface was regular, smooth, and straight.

One end of the shaft was fitted with a hardwood fore-shaft about two palm-widths in length, to which the arrowhead was attached. Hunting arrows, like the one Gamil held in his hand, were tipped with flat, diamond-shaped bronze arrowheads, two finger-widths long and one finger-width wide. A thin tang about one and a half finger-widths long was used to fasten the arrowhead to the shaft.

The other end of the arrow was fletched with goose feathers, split along their shafts and trimmed to a uniform size and shape. Three fletchings were fastened with glue and gut at an equal distance from each other in a triangular arrangement, near the end of the arrow. Behind these fletchings, at its very end, the arrow was cut to form a deep notch, called a nock, where the bowstring would rest.

Completely assembled, the arrow weighed surprisingly little; only about as much as one qedet, or about nine and a half grams, with more than half that weight being the arrowhead.

"Watch and learn" Osiris said. Gamil studied the movements of the master of the hunt as he took a shoulder-wide stance, his left foot forward in the direction of the target. With his left hand, Osiris held the largest of the three bows parallel to the ground. He fitted the nock of an arrow around the bowstring, raising the bow while rotating it until it was perpendicular to the ground with his left arm fully extended.

With his right hand he drew the bowstring back to his right ear and when he had the bow fully drawn, he sighted down the length of the shaft. He elevated it slightly, drew in his breath and waited a second to steady his aim, then let the arrow fly.

With a slight whooshing sound, the arrow sped through the air and buried its bronze tip in the center of the knot; exactly where Osiris aimed it.

"Now you try." Osiris commanded.

Gamil repeated all the steps that he had seen Osiris take; drawing a breath, and holding it as he pulled back on his bowstring. He pulled as hard as he could, but could not bend the bow far enough to bring the string to his ear. Something was wrong. His left hand, holding the bow, began to shake and he had trouble keeping it pointed toward the target. The two fingers of his right hand, holding the bowstring and arrow, were sweating and shaking under the strain of trying to hold the arrow steady while he pulled. Worst of all it felt as if the bowstring was cutting into his fingers. When he knew he couldn't hold his draw any longer he aimed as best he could and let fly.

The bowstring came off his curled fingers with a jerk instead of the smooth release that Osiris had demonstrated. It snapped from his hand, propelling the arrow forward and slapping painfully against the inside of his left forearm, numbing his wrist and causing an angry, red, stinging welt to quickly rise. He lost his grip on the bow and it fell to the ground. He grabbed his injured arm with his right hand and hugged it to his chest.

The arrow, flying free, went exactly where it was aimed, a full four paces to the right of the target. Because Gamil's draw was short, there was only enough force to propel it two-thirds of the distance. As it fell to the ground it bounced up once and traveled another five paces before it was fully spent.

Behind him, a short distance away, two of the huntsmen had watched the archery lesson while finishing their own lunch. They burst into laughter, but cut their amusement off as Osiris shot them a withering glance.

"Not bad for a first attempt." he said to Gamil. "You will do better with practice, and will have to grow some muscles in your chest and arms, but we will work on your technique. It is not as simple as it looks, is it? Do you know what you did wrong?"

Gamil thought about it and as he rubbed the welt on his arm, he realized that he hadn't held the bow correctly. "I let my arm get in the way of the bowstring." he replied.

"That is right. You must not let your elbow lock when you draw the bow, or your arm will feel the rebuke of the bowstring every time. Here, until you gain some strength and improve your technique, you should wear this." With that, Osiris handed the boy a leather arm guard and showed him how to put it on, lacing it tightly so it covered the offended flesh of his arm. "What else did you do wrong?" he asked.

Gamil thought hard, then said, "My grip on the bowstring was wrong. I did not release the arrow smoothly, as you did. By jerking my hand away from the bowstring, I changed the path that the arrow took."

"Very good, Gamil." his mentor replied. "You also were a little off on your stance. Remember, the arrow will only go where you aim it, and your aim begins with where you point your left foot. It should be pointed slightly to the right of your target's center, and your right foot should point directly to the side of your left foot. Also, you must keep your weight balanced evenly between both feet. If your weight is on your forward foot, the arrow will tend to angle down; if your weight is on your rear foot, the arrow will angle upward. Both will throw your aim off, so make sure your weight is evenly distributed before you release. Remember all of these things and try again."

He handed Gamil another arrow, and watched as the boy readied himself for his second attempt. This time he was careful to position his feet exactly as instructed. He drew back the bowstring a little farther this time, and tried hard to keep his left elbow from locking. As he aimed, Osiris adjusted his left arm slightly, raising it to compensate for the short draw. Gamil sighted down the shaft, lined it up with the target and uncurled the fingers of his right hand, being careful not to jerk them as he let the arrow fly.

This time the bowstring did not slap his left arm, and the arrow left the bow smoothly. It was still under-powered, but struck the tree stump just below and to the left of the firewood target. Without enough force to penetrate, it bounced back and landed in the grass at the foot of the stump.

"Much better." Osiris proclaimed. "We will make an archer of you yet. It takes much practice to become proficient with the bow, and years before one can become a master archer. But you show promise. Now, go and retrieve the spent arrows and remember the things I have taught you. Keep practicing until it is time to resume our journey."

Osiris left to tend to his other duties, and Gamil did as he was told; hitting the target twice before the signal came to fall in. He gathered up the arrows he had been using and took them with the bow back to where Osiris stood, directing his huntsmen. Osiris noticed him and told one of the huntsmen to "Give him your spare quiver." He showed Gamil how to tie the quiver to his belt so that it did not drag the ground, and how to put his head and one shoulder into the unstrung bow between the bow stock and the string so that it could be carried while leaving his hands free.

"How are your feet? Osiris asked. "I noticed you limped a bit when you went to retrieve the arrows."

"They are fine, really!" Gamil answered, not wanting to admit the fact that he had developed several painful blisters during the morning's march. Osiris looked at him skeptically. "No, really!" Gamil insisted, fearing that his father might order him to ride in the oxcart again if he learned that his son was suffering. He did not want to show any sign of weakness.

"Sit." Osiris commanded. "Remove your sandals and let me see your 'fine' feet."

Gamil reluctantly did as he was bidden, and Osiris lifted up one foot, then the other, to inspect them carefully.

"Hmmm." he murmured. "I've seen worse. You have a few bruises on the soles and a cut on the right instep, but those blisters are the most serious problem. If not tended to they will keep getting worse until they fester and cause your feet to rot. You could end up a cripple for the rest of your life. Come with me to see the cook."

The cook kept all his kitchen wares, spices and other essentials in a pair of chests inside the second oxcart. Summoning him, Osiris told Gamil to show him his feet, and the cook shook his head at the boy's condition and had him sit down on a mid-size rock beside the trail. The cook brought a laving bowl and some soap and carefully washed Gamil's feet. After drying them he took a pot of honey from his stores and applied a generous amount to each blister and to the cut on his instep. Then he wrapped both feet in linen cloth strips, as carefully as if he were preparing a pharaoh's body for burial. Over this he slipped a pouch of soft doeskin on each foot, tying them on at the top by their leather drawstrings. Then noticing that Gamil's city sandals were already coming apart after only half a day's march, the cook produced an extra pair from his own clothing sack and adjusted them to fit the boy's feet.

"It's a good thing you have large feet for your age, young master." the cook said. "The honey and these bandages should keep out any infection. Come to me when we stop for the night and I will examine your wounds again and tend to any new ones."

Gamil stood up and walked a few steps, feeling awkward in the oversized sandals. But at least his feet didn't hurt like they had earlier. Osiris watched him, and satisfied that his lord's son was properly cared for, told Gamil to take his place behind the huntsmen, who were waiting along with everyone else for the signal to proceed.

Ahinadab had watched all of this from his place at the head of the party, and was secretly pleased that his first-born had done so well thus far. But he was a little annoyed that their departure had been delayed by the boy's needs, and hoped it wasn't a sign of how his presence might become a serious hindrance rather than just a nuisance.

He kept these thoughts to himself and as Osiris joined him, and when all was ready, he gave the signal to begin the march. An hour later the party passed completely out of the meadow lands and into the deep forest proper.

There the trees grew thicker and closer to the trail, which became much narrower, until it was just wide enough for the oxcarts to pass in single file. Above the trail the tree branches overlapped to form a complete canopy that shaded their path and shrouded them in a cool dusk-like gloaming.

The men had been singing as they marched to help them keep pace, but in this part of the forest their voices became hushed and finally stopped altogether. This was the part of the forest that was most sacred to the gods, and it was easy to imagine their unseen presence all around. As they passed along in solemn, almost reverent silence, their footfalls were muffled by the carpet of pine needles and cedar fronds that lay on the trail, and the only sounds the party made as it went were the squeak of oxcart wheels and the jangling of the horse and oxen harnesses.

The many different kinds of birds that filled the trees around them felt no such reverence, and kept up a noisy chatter as the human invaders passed through their territory. Gamil thought to himself that the gods must truly like birds, as they had made so many of them. He tried to identify the different kinds by their calls and, if he caught sight of them, by their plumage. Many were familiar from the area around Gebal, but others that dwelt only in the mountains he had never seen or heard before. It helped to concentrate on them as the march wore monotonously on.

Apart from an occasional glimpse of deer, wild goats and pigs, or other forest creatures, the birds were their only company. They had left the thieves behind once they entered the higher elevations, and saw no sign of any other humans as they continued on. At nightfall the party made camp in a clearing beside the trail where a fairly large stream flowed in a boisterous cascade over huge rocks. Some of the men took advantage of a large pool to strip off their clothing and wash away the dust of two days' marching. At his father's insistence Gamil joined them. The water was like ice, and none stayed in it for long. Gamil was used to swimming in the much warmer water of the Great Sea, and found that this mountain stream took his breath away as he quickly rinsed off.

As soon as he could he climbed out of the pool and was back on dry ground, shivering. His father's body servant, an *Achaean* slave named Linus, helped him dress in fresh clothes that had been re-tailored to his size out of some of Ahinadab's extra garments. The fit wasn't perfect, but served the purpose, and Gamil joined the others around the now blazing campfire to warm his flesh and eat his dinner.

The night passed quickly, without incident, and gave way to the dawn of a day that was mostly a repeat of the previous one. Seven more days passed in much the same way. On the fourth day, one of the oxcarts broke a wheel that had to be mended before they continued, but that was the only break in the monotony of the march.

At each day's noontime stop, Gamil practiced with his bow and was becoming a fairly decent shot. His arms, though they ached all the time, were growing stronger from the exercise, and he finally was able to draw the bowstring as far back as his ear. His arrows found the target more times than not, and with the power of a full draw behind them, they would stick, rather than bounce off.

Each evening Osiris reported Gamil's progress to Ahinadab, who was well pleased with his first-born. On the fifth day Ahinadab joined Gamil, carrying his own beautifully burnished, recurved bow. He allowed the boy to try it. But this formidable weapon was far too much for Gamil, who could hardly pull its bowstring more than a palm's width. Ahinadab demonstrated its power by driving an arrow half-way through the pockmarked wooden target, knocking the chunk of firewood completely off the rock it rested on. Gamil discovered a new level of respect for his father; knowing how much strength such a shot required.

"One day you will use this bow, or one like it, as you have seen me do." Ahinadab said to Gamil.

The boy was overjoyed with this sign of his father's approval, and he felt that Ahinadab was gradually forgiving him for his uninvited presence. As these thoughts warmed his heart, he glanced at Osiris and saw him smiling slightly. Osiris said nothing, but winked one eye at Gamil, signaling that he understood how much Ahinadab's words meant to the boy, and how badly Gamil needed to hear them.

Chapter 13
Help Arrives

At the woodcutters' camp

On the eleventh day of what should have been an eight- or nine-day journey, the hunting party finally reached the camp of the woodcutters. The people were still inside their huts although it was several hours past dawn. They heard the hunters' horns announcing the party's arrival and rushed out with their families to meet their rescuers. They welcomed their lord with happy shouts: their excited voices thanking him for coming, and praising the gods for sending him.

Ahinadab's first concern was to determine the current situation regarding the lion. He met with the leader of the woodcutters, Ja-rune's husband Ad-Haddad, who told him of the lion's recent activities.

Two more people had been attacked since Ba'aldo had left the camp. The first was a small boy who had strayed from his mother and was killed. His remains had not been found. The other was one of the men, a woodcutter who had left his ax near where he had been working. Needing it for his family's protection, he risked going alone to retrieve it. He encountered the lion a short distance from the camp as he returned. The lion rushed at him and was stunned by a glancing blow from the ax that struck the side of its massive skull. The blow landed just as the beast attacked, causing his strike to miss the man's head. Instead, the claws of one paw raked the man's abdomen, partially disemboweling him. The lion staggered off into the forest as his victim ran back to camp: one hand carrying his ax and the other holding his intestines inside his body. At the edge of the camp he collapsed from shock and loss of blood, and was carried into his hut. Despite the best care his family and friends could give, and constant prayer to *Eshmun*, the god of healing, the man died a day later.

"That was two days ago," Ad-Haddad said, "and since that time no one has left the huts. Not even to get water. During that time, we have not heard the lion in the camp, but I do not think he has gone far. We rejoice at your coming to help us, my lord!"

Ahinadab listened to this report with a solemn face, and after thanking Ad-Haddad he turned to all his people, hunters and woodcutters alike, and said, "Hear me now, people of the House of Dan-El. I have come to rid you of this lion who has dared to harm those who are under my protection. I have brought Gebal's best hunters, led by my master of the hunt, the mighty Osiris of Thebes. Tomorrow we will rise early to seek the lion and, if El the Almighty One is willing, we will end his wicked life. This I have spoken, and so it shall be."

The people responded with a great shout. The voices of fifty men, women and children of the camp were joined by those of the members of the hunting party. Someone began singing a hymn to El, and others joined in with dancing and leaping from the great relief that all shared. Their lord had spoken, and they knew he would fulfill his words.

The women quickly lit cooking fires that had been cold for two days, and the men built a huge bonfire in the center of the camp. Foodstuffs were brought out and nine goats were killed, butchered and set to roasting. People who had been cowering in their darkened huts for days now danced in the sunlight; their hearts filled with renewed confidence.

Musical instruments were brought forth and soon a lively melody accompanied the dancers. Gamil had never before seen such a display before. Not even during the high festivals and feasts of the gods back in the city. He marveled at the apparent power of his father, a man who could bring on such a display of jubilation with only his spoken words.

Osiris and Ahinadab stood together at the edge of the crowd, and spoke quietly to each other. "What do you make of the ax blow to the lion's head?" Ahinadab asked. "Do you think he was badly wounded? Could he already be dead or dying?"

Osiris answered, "It didn't sound to me as if the blow did any real damage. At best I think we can hope that it weakened him; making him easier to track and kill."

"One thing is certain," Ahinadab said, "A lion might attack a human once, and never bother anyone again. But a lion that attacks and kills repeatedly has become a maneater, and must be destroyed. If only wounded, he will be all the more likely to strike again and again."

"My huntsmen and I will find the lion, my lord. But unless he is lying up nearby, nursing his injury, it may take days to locate him."

"I know Osiris, I fear it may be weeks before we have him, but I spoke as I did for my people's sake. You saw how disheartened they were. Another day and I'm sure they would all have abandoned the camp and returned to the safety of the city. They might still flee unless we make sure my words come to pass very soon."

All of this Gamil heard as he sat nearby, gnawing on goat ribs and eating cheese and bread, a welcome change from the dried fish and hard bread of the journey. He thought about what had been said as he ate. He hadn't realized how urgent the need to quickly kill the lion was, or how difficult it might be to find him. But with the training he had received on the journey, and his father's approval of his progress, he was sure he would be included in the next day's hunt. What if he were the one to actually kill the lion? What would his father think of him then? Would that be enough to cause his father to proclaim him *"Gamil, son of Ahinadab of the House of Dan-El"*, letting all men know that he was no longer a mere boy. His heart soared at the thought of how near that all-important moment might be.

Around them as the people ate and danced and sang, something more like normal life was beginning to return to the camp. Ja-rune organized a party of the women to fetch water from the creek, guarded by two huntsmen with their javelins and bows, and accompanied by two of the dogs.

Water jars that had been empty for days were now full, and some of the woodcutters brought fresh fodder from a nearby meadow to feed the goats, horses and oxen. Others took time to repair some of the huts where the lion had tried to break in, and they brought more thorn bushes to add another layer of protection to their walls. Routine chores of all kinds, some neglected since the lion's first attack, were now tended to.

Osiris sent two of the huntsmen into the forest around the camp to inspect the areas where the young girl, the boy, and the woodcutter had been attacked. They were to look for signs of the lion's movements, and to see if a trail could be found. Khe-ahn and one other dog went with them to try and sniff out the lion's spoor. Gamil was about to ask if he could go with them, but Osiris forestalled that question with one of his own.

"So, young master, do you think you can do something with your javelin besides lugging it about in such a clumsy fashion? Bring it and follow me." Without waiting for a response, the master of the hunt began walking toward the outer edge of the camp. Gamil raced to fetch his javelin and followed him to an open space where Osiris had hung a wicker basket from a low tree branch. He marked a line in the dirt a reasonable distance away from this target and summoned Gamil.

"Watch and learn." Osiris said, and taking up his own javelin in his right hand, he hefted it to shoulder height and held it parallel to the ground, gripping it about a palm's breadth in front of its center at the balance point. His feet were spread, with his left foot forward in the direction of the target. He backed up five more paces, rebalanced his own weight, and steadied the horizontal javelin for a second. Then with three running steps toward the target, his right elbow cocked for the throw, he shot his arm forward in one fluid motion just as the toes of his left foot touched the line in the dirt. The instant the last third of the javelin passed his ear he released his grasp. The javelin flew straight and level, passing cleanly through the very center of the basket landing eight paces behind it with its head buried in the earth. The basket was still hanging in the tree as if it had not been disturbed at all.

"That is how it is done." Osiris said, "Now you try". Gamil did as instructed, and when he thought he was ready, Osiris said, "Lift your javelin in your right hand. Steady! Find its balance point and bring it up to your shoulder and hold it level. No! Wait. That is not quite right."

Osiris adjusted Gamil's position and corrected his grip on the javelin, then continued, "Now take five paces to the rear and stand with your weight balanced on both feet, left foot forward. Good! Now, keep your eye on the target, run to the line and throw."

Gamil took a breath and with his eyes on the target ran forward, trying to keep the Javelin balanced and parallel to the ground as Osiris had demonstrated. As his right foot touched the line, he snapped his arm forward, releasing the shaft as he did so. His timing was off, however, and the javelin went sailing high over the target to land some fifteen paces beyond it.

Disgusted, Gamil gave vent to his disappointment with an oath, "By the smoking thunderbolts of Ba'al Šāmēm! That is not how I saw it in my mind! Wretched *stick!*"

Osiris smiled, amused slightly at this display of temper and said, "That was good for your first attempt. But just like the bow, it takes practice to drive the javelin's point where you want it to go. Calm yourself. You will learn. Do you know what you did wrong?"

Gamil shook his head and Osiris explained his faulty stance, grip and release in detail. "Now, go retrieve your javelin and practice throwing it until you have hit the target ten times."

Osiris left to make preparations for the next day's hunt, as Gamil continued to practice. On his fourth throw he hit the target for the first time. He made a single straight line in the dirt to mark his score and after two hours he had placed three groups of three marks each in the dust. This was how a tally was figured; ||| ||| ||| (3+3+3=9). When he struck the target the tenth time, he erased all the vertical marks with his foot and made a single horizontal mark instead. This was the way his people wrote the number ten. For twenty he would have made a pair of horizontal marks with one above the other,

Throwing the javelin was harder than archery and his right arm felt like it would fall off at the shoulder, but he had gained a feel for what the javelin required from him before it could properly do its work. Quite satisfied with himself, Gamil went looking for his father.

The hunters' camp was set up a short distance from that of the woodcutters. Gamil found where Ahinadab's tent had been pitched, and saw his father sitting in front of it with Ad-Haddad. They were going over the woodcutter's records of the season's work so far. Gamil put away his javelin and sat quietly just inside the door of the tent, listening to their conversation. They discussed things Ahinadab had observed as he toured the camp earlier.

"This lion has cost me several weeks of my woodcutters' time and labor already. You will all have to work hard to make up the loss. Do you think you can still fill our portion of the order for the great temple of Aten on time?" Ahinadab asked.

"My lord, it depends on how soon we can return to our work. We made good progress before the attacks began, and our portion of the order is about one-sixth filled already. But until the lion is killed who can say. If, in say two or three days, then we can safely work from dawn until dark. We would be able to make up the lost time in the twelve weeks left until this year's cutting season ends." Ad-Haddad answered.

Ahinadab said, "You will still need two weeks to bring the logs down the mountain and into the port. If the other cutting teams have their logs ready, we can add ours to the great rafts that will be towed to the mouth of the River Nile. I will have kept my promise to the great pharaoh. He will have his cedar wood as the high heat of summer fades into the fall season. Our best customer will be pleased.

But if it takes longer to kill the lion, or if some other delay occurs, I may have to hire more men to be sure the order is filled on time. As you know, Ad-Haddad, all of my woodcutters share equally in the profits gained from their work, with an extra portion going to you as their leader. If I add more men to the work it lessens everyone's share. Be sure to remind your men of this and use it to encourage them to work hard.

Remind them that if we fall short in delivering our portion of the order our competitors: the House of Mahar-ba'al, the House of Abdeshmun, or even worse, the House of Ili-Rapih, will leap at the opportunity to fill the shortage. Any one of them would like nothing better than to take the great pharaoh's business away from us."

"I understand, my lord. Please be assured that my men and I will do our utmost to complete our part of the order. If Almighty El and the lion permit it, we will not disappoint you, nor give you cause to hire others for the work."

"Good! Your assurances are pleasing to me, Ad-Haddad. Still, I have seen some things here that need attention if your men are to do their best work. Before I name them, tell me what your needs are, and I will see that you have all you require."

"Very well, my lord." Ad-Haddad answered. "As my lord has seen, we use our supplies wisely and have plenty of food at present. But some grain was spoiled by the recent rain and must be replaced. We also need goats to replace those that we have eaten. The lion's presence has driven most of the small game away, and we haven't been able to trap or hunt to feed ourselves. Of the thirty goats we brought with us, half have been used for food, including those we ate to celebrate your arrival today. If you send us another thirty goats we will have enough for milking and slaughter until the end of the season. We also need..."

Ad-Haddad went on to catalog the other supplies and sundry items that would keep the camp running smoothly as Ahinadab listened carefully.

From inside his father's tent, Gamil listened to all that was said. He had never understood how much was required to equip and sustain a single camp of woodcutters. He was awed by his father's depth of understanding and powers of observation. Ahinadab seemed to know everything about the needs of his people and the ways in which they lived and worked. It made Gamil realize just how much he would have to learn before he could ever hope to measure up to his father's example.

Chapter 14
A Hero in His Own Mind

Gamil's rising expectations

The conversation ended and Gamil's mind turned to the coming hunt. From his father's words he could now see the urgent need to kill the lion as soon as possible. Ahinadab's position as a shofeṭ, and his seat on the council of elders, rested as much on his reputation as on the wealth of the House of Dan-El. If the woodcutters could not fill the pharaoh's order on time, Ahinadab's reputation would suffer, and the House of Dan-El could be weakened. Clearly, there were implications to this hunt that Gamil could not have imagined. He had been oblivious to the adult world that surrounded him. It was sobering to see just how much responsibility rested on his father's shoulders.

Gamil had never seen a living lion, and only knew them from stories and from one old, moth-eaten hide that used to serve as a rug in the great hall of king Rib-Hadda's palace. But he was certain that he would be able to kill this one. He could imagine himself playing a hero's role in the hunt, ending the lion's reign of terror with a well-placed throw of his javelin, or a deadly accurate shot from his bow.

His father's reputation would be saved, and his gratitude would surely move him to name Gamil as his son.

Bring on the beast! In his imagination he was ready to defeat it and claim his rightful place as his father's son. He saw himself as the protector of the woodcutters and the savior of the entire House of Dan-El. After all, how hard could it be to kill one lion? It almost seemed like a thing that was already accomplished.

One who killed a man-eating lion would be a hero indeed! All of Gebal would hear of such a great feat, and his friends among the children of the other great houses would be envious of him. Their respect for him would be magnified to the highest!

To Gamil this last point was a sore one. His playmates, all from the wealthiest houses in Gebal, loved to tease him. Especially the older boys. They taunted him because of his name.

"Gam*il*" literally meant "handsome" in the native tongue of the Kena'ani. But that meaning was at odds with its root *"gimel,"* the third letter in the Kena'ani alphabet. When written the gimel was a mark that resembled the head and neck of a camel. "Gimel" was also their word for a camel, a beast not usually thought of as being handsome. This ironic play on words was great fodder for his friends. Some only teased him in fun, but the older boys used it cruelly, as a way to knock him down a peg in their pecking order.

Shouts of *"Gam-il-the-Cam-el"*, were thrown at him mercilessly by the older boys. Aderba'al, in particular, took great delight in taunting Gamil this way. Aderba'al had been "named" by his father, the high priest Ili-Rapih, and was no longer known merely as the son of his mother.

It felt grossly unfair to Gamil that the fat, pimple-faced Aderba'al had been publicly recognized by his father almost four years earlier, when he was only nine years old! And not for any great merit that he had exhibited before, or since then! Ili-Rapih had acknowledged Aderba'al as his son for merely acting as an acolyte at the Feast of Ba'al Šāmēm. Pimple-face had done little more than hold a bowl to catch some blood from a sacrificed bull. From that day on, Aderba'al had used his elevated status to lord it over his playmates, much as he had seen his father, the high priest, treat the heads of the other great houses. Gamil relished the thought that all of this would change when he returned to the city in triumph after killing the lion.

These fantasies reinforced his determination to be the beast's killer. He left the tent of his father and took up his bow and arrows for another round of practice

Gamil was unaware that Aderba'al's hostility toward him was a reflection of the rivalry between Ili-Rapih and Ahinadab. That rivalry involved a long-running political feud between the two men. Ili-Rapih was jealous of Ahinadab's popularity, and he hated the shofeṭ for opposing his attempts to manipulate the council of the elders. Only the power and prestige of the lord of the House of Dan-El kept the high priest's animosity in check. Ili-Rapih would take revenge on Ahinadab and his family if any opportunity occurred.

Sons naturally look up to their fathers, and are shaped by their fathers' character for both good and bad. Ili-Rapih's bitterness toward Ahinadab colored Aderba'al's behavior toward Gamil. Gamil, in turn, grew to resent and reciprocate Aderba'al's misbehavior. Each had his own set of friends, and the two groups didn't join in the others' games. On a few occasions Aderba'al and Gamil had even fought each other, with neither one able to claim a victory as their scuffles were quickly broken up by their guardians. This left them both with a smoldering hatred for each other.

The boys weren't aware of what lay behind their mutual animosity.

For them it was only clear that they were enemies. The intricacies of their fathers' rivalry were beyond their grasp, but over time the city's complicated politics would be significant in the events of all their lives.

Chapter 15
The Lion Returns

The night before the first hunt

The afternoon op fires were lit for the evening meal. Gamil ended his archery practice and sought his place by Ahinadab's side. During the meal some of the men brought out their musical instruments again, while women danced for the entertainment of their lord and his huntsmen. The dancers' confident movements reflected the relief everyone felt from the terror of the lion's attacks. Beer and wine flowed freely and was consumed with the meal. But Ahinadab forbade any of his hunting party from over-indulging. He wanted them alert while on guard during the night, and needed them to be refreshed and clear-headed for the hunt in the morning.

Ahinadab and Osiris heard the report of the two huntsmen who had scouted for signs of the lion at the sites of his kills, and made plans for the next day's hunt. Gamil was sent to bed early, and except for those standing the first watch, all the hunters followed suit, once they finished eating. The long march from the city, followed by a second heavy meal, made a good night's sleep necessary for all.

As it was on the march, two of the huntsmen kept the early watch and the other two had the late watch, each with a pair of dogs close by. Ahinadab's bodyguards took turns watching over his tent and the center of the hunters' encampment. But now none worried about skulking thieves. Their concern was focused on the lion. If the beast appeared before morning, they might not need to hunt him down. A quick kill would be the best of luck for everyone.

But the night passed uneventfully, with only one small disturbance in the second watch, a few hours before dawn. The dogs with the huntsman on the south side of the encampment suddenly raised their heads. Their ears pointed straight up and the hackles on the back of their necks were erect.

A random breeze carried a scent that caught their attention, and both stood stiff-legged, staring into the dark forest. Low growls issued from their throats, and the huntsman readied his bow for action. Three pairs of eyes strained to pierce the blackness beyond the light of the campfire, but nothing was seen. After a minute or two the wind changed and the dogs began to relax. After sniffing the air a few more times they settled into a resting posture, with their legs extended in front of their bodies in a sphinx-like pose. *"Must have been a passing deer, or wild boar."* the huntsman thought as he lowered his bow and leaned back on the rock he had been resting against before the dogs alerted him.

Beyond the light from the fire, and now downwind of the encampment, the lion circled in frustration and confusion. After the ax smashed into his head, he had to lay up in the forest for days: dizzy, nauseated, and with throbbing pain where the blow had struck. He had been unable to hunt, and this evening a grinding hunger goaded him into action. Testing his legs that morning proved that the dizziness was almost gone and the nausea had left him completely. His senses were able to pick up all the clues from his surroundings that he needed to hunt.

His nose had picked up the aroma of roasting goat coming from the woodcutters' camp, and his mouth watered. So, as the sun was setting, he reached a place where he could observe the camp from a safe distance. He saw more humans than before, and that they now had dogs with them.

He hated dogs. Whether domestic or wild, they hunted in packs, and more than once wild dogs had driven him off of a fresh kill. He had no real fear of them, but knew that although they were no match for him, they could inflict serious injuries in a fight. He had seen what happened to older lions that became injured. They lost their ability to hunt, grew weak from hunger, and were either driven out or killed by healthy lions. Either way death came to them very soon. This lion knew that it was always best to avoid dogs.

Late in the night he heard the two dogs growling and realized that the errant breeze had betrayed him. His hiding place was no longer safe. But he had seen enough to convince him there was no way he could get to the goats, or to any of the humans without a fight, and the ax blow had taught him that humans could seriously hurt him if he wasn't careful. He decided to look elsewhere for tonight's dinner, and moved off into the darkness to search for an easier meal.

Chapter 16

Tracking the Lion

The next morning at the huntsmen's encampment

At dawn the hunters, beaters, and dogs prepared to find and kill the lion. The sun was rising in the east, but the encampment would remain in the shadow of the White Mountain's peak for another three hours. The air was cold, but no fires were lit. The heat would have been welcome, but there was no time to enjoy it, or to cook. What breakfast there was, hard bread and dried fish, would be eaten on the move.

The dogs were the first to venture out, roaming in wider and wider circles until they picked up the lion's scent at the place where he had spied on them in the night. The dogs' excitement made them hard to control, but the master of hounds gave a few crisp commands to Khe-ahn, who barked loudly and sharply to his pack. That, plus a well-placed nip here and there, soon got the other dogs to settle down. They still whimpered with nervous excitement and were on full alert, but they quickly focused and paid attention to the voice of the master of hounds, who shouted the command, "Trail!"

That command released them, and all six dogs instantly set off, following the scent and tracks left by the lion. They barked, howled, and goaded each other on, outdistancing the men who followed behind at a deliberately unhurried pace. They knew the dogs would follow the lion's trail until they cornered him and brought him to bay. That was their job: to locate and hold the lion until the men caught up. They were trained to surround their quarry at a safe distance and worry him to wear him down. When the men arrived, the lion would be dispatched with arrows or javelins. At least that was the plan.

The lion made a kill at a spot near where he hid the night before. A wild sow had led her litter of shoats to drink from the creek below the woodcutter's camp, close to where the women drew their water. The lion caught them unaware. He sprang from the brush, the sow bolted, and her young ones scattered in all directions. But one was too slow. It wasn't much of a meal, but that small piglet had dulled the edge of the lion's hunger. Unfortunately, the effort caused his head to ache again and his dizziness intensified. He devoured the shoat and moved to a rocky ledge a safe distance from the humans. He needed to rest there and allow his pain and dizziness to pass.

The barking of the dogs in the early morning woke the lion from a sound sleep. He knew they were still far off, but were moving in his direction rapidly. From months of roaming through his territory he knew these woods better than the dogs did. He could tell almost exactly where they were by all the racket they made.

Lions never gave their location away like these foolish dogs were doing. Success in stalking depended on silence, and success was the difference between life and death. He knew he could keep away from them, and as long as he did there was nothing to fear.

He left his ledge and moved into a canyon on the mountainside that ended in a steep ravine with sheer sides rising to a great height. He had often hunted here for wild goats, and had seen where they climbed up and out of the ravine with their nimble feet. He was no wild goat, but following their example, he reached a place where a fallen pine tree lay with its trunk leaning from the bottom to the top of the ravine. The angle was steep, but not too steep for the lion to climb.

And climb he did. At the top he turned and listened for the dogs. He couldn't see them, but judging from their barking, they were approaching the mouth of the canyon. He turned away and vanished into the dense forest above the ravine.

When the dogs reached the fallen tree, the lion was long gone, and by the time the men arrived he was far away. The dogs milled about and barked in frustration and confusion; giving the impression that they had cornered the lion. But it took only a minute for the hunters to realize that wasn't the case. The hunters could see where the lion's claws had scored the tree's bark as he climbed, and they quickly figured out how the lion had escaped.

Osiris noted where the tree trunk touched the top of the ravine. He knew it would take most of an hour to go back to the mouth of the canyon, and hours more before they reached the spot where the lion had emerged. By then, unless the gods favored them, it would be much too late to catch up to him. But they had to try.

At the top of the ravine, the dogs circled around and picked up the lion's trail again, following it until they reached a place where he had entered a shallow stream. He left no tracks on the opposite bank, so the huntsmen knew he must have traveled in the bed of the stream some distance.

Osiris cursed under his breath. Not knowing the direction, the lion had taken, he divided their party in half, with some, led by Ahinadab, going downstream and the rest, with Osiris, going upstream. Both groups were watching for tracks or other traces that would reveal where their quarry had exited the water.

Half an hour later, the upstream hunters finally found the lion's exit point beside a large pool that lay below a long waterfall. He had scrambled up the rocks to the top of the waterfall, but the way was too steep and dangerous for the dogs to follow. Osiris cursed again. He had his huntsmen sound their hunting horns to signal the downstream party to join them at the pool.

Ahinadab and his group reached the pool two hours later and quickly realized the opportunity to catch the lion was gone. The day was growing old, and the men and dogs had been on the hunt for ten hours without rest. Tracking the lion had taken them almost a league from their camp, and if they wanted to reach it before dark the time to start back was now. Everyone was disappointed and felt defeated. Osiris most of all. He was not a man who was used to failure. His respect for the cleverness of this lion had grown greater as the day grew older. It might be the most intelligent, and therefore the most dangerous, animal he had ever hunted. He silently vowed that he would not fail again. Ahinadab ordered the return to camp. They would try again tomorrow.

Chapter 17
Left Behind

At the hunters' encampment

Gamil awoke late in the morning. He had been dreaming of his hero's parade through the streets of Gebal. He was beside himself with frustration when he learned the hunters had left him behind. How had he slept through the sounds of their leaving? The rest of that day he wandered about the encampment, sulking and in a bad temper.

He anxiously watched for the hunters return, expecting them to march into camp bearing the body of the lion on a pole. He was sure that he had missed his one chance to be a hero in the eyes of his father. He was too dejected to even think about practicing with his javelin or the bow. Mentally beating himself, over and over again, it occurred to him that perhaps he was wrong to think he was ready to take his place as a man. Perhaps he *was* still just a boy, a silly boy who couldn't open his eyes before dawn even on the most important day of his life!

He brooded on as the long day passed. Eventually the fires were lit for the evening meal and the smells of food began to fill the air. He had been too angry to eat anything all day and had no appetite even now. He sat on a log beside the trail, throwing small rocks at the trees, while the woodcutters and their families finished their meal. Night was coming on when, at last, he heard the hunters approaching.

The first to come into view was Khe-ahn. The big dog spotted Gamil and bounded over to him, tail wagging and eyes glowing. He was tired, but happy to see the boy. For reasons only he could understand, a bond had developed between him and the boy. Gamil, however, was not so glad to see Khe-ahn. The dog's upbeat mood seemed to confirm his worst fear. All his anger, disappointment, and self-loathing came to a head as Gamil believed the dog's upbeat attitude was a sign that the hunt had been successful.

Khe-ahn sensed the boy's distress, and nuzzled his arm, hoping for a reassuring scratch behind the ears. When that didn't happen, he licked Gamil's hand and face as if to say, "What's wrong?"

Gamil pushed him aside and jumped to his feet. He rushed down the trail toward the hunting party, with Khe-ahn shadowing his steps. His eyes darted about, searching for the lion's corpse. But it was not there among the weary, downcast hunters. Then he saw the faces of his father and Osiris. The marks of stress and frustration from the fruitless day's efforts told a different story than the one Gamil had expected. Hope was suddenly rekindled in his heart. The lion must still be alive! There was still a chance for him!

The mood in the woodcutters' camp reflected the hunters' disappointment. Fear began to creep back into everyone's heart, and the excitement that had prevailed since the hunting party's arrival was gone. The women quietly prepared a hot meal for the hunters, who had not eaten since their cold breakfast. The men ate in silence, with their spirits so low that even beer and wine could not raise them. There was no music, singing, or dancing this night.

In contrast, Gamil ate lustily, happily sharing scraps with Khe-ahn.

He pestered the men for details of all that had happened during the day. There were few answers at first, but he persisted and the day's events gradually came forth.

Satisfied that he still had a chance to kill the lion, he went to bed that night with his mind racing. He was certain about one thing; he was not going to sleep through tomorrow's hunt if he had to stay up all night!

Chapter 18
A Change of Plans

Below the woodcutters' camp

The second day of the hunt dawned with an overcast sky and a chilling drizzle. The dense canopy of trees kept the light rain from reaching the camp directly, but couldn't stop it from running down the tree trunks or dripping from branches and needles. It fell on everything in an unpredictable and unavoidable manner. Everyone moved about wrapped in blankets or woolen cloaks, dodging raindrops and trying to dodge puddles that grew larger as the morning progressed. What fires could be lit were small, smoldering affairs that gave little warmth and were constantly on the verge of being extinguished. Breakfast consisted of cold mush and dried goat meat with a few handfuls of dried fruit, all washed down with goat's milk.

Gamil was awake before dawn, having hardly slept. He was too keyed-up to stay in bed and was already dressed by the time the sky began to lighten. He got his breakfast and moved to join his father and Osiris beneath a huge pine tree that was keeping most of the rain off them. They were discussing the weather and what the huntsmen might be able to accomplish in spite of it.

"The dogs will not be of much use in all of this, my lord." Osiris said. "They won't be able to pick up a scent, nor follow a trail until the weather clears and the ground is dryer."

"I'm afraid you are right Osiris." Ahinadab replied. "The lion will have moved in the night and could be leagues from here by now. We won't have much chance of locating him, let alone killing him today. We chased him for more than a league yesterday and came back empty-handed. It could take weeks to chase him down. Weeks that I can ill afford. What advice can you give?"

The master of the hunt felt the need to redeem himself in his lord's eyes after the previous day's failure. He suggested an alternative that had worked in similar circumstances before.

"My lord, if we cannot find the lion, we may be able to draw him to us."

"And how do we do that?"

"If it pleases you my lord, we can tie a goat in the forest beyond the camp as bait. Two of my archers can keep watch from a perch in a tree with a clear view of the goat. They can stay there as long as necessary. If the lion is near, he will catch the goat's scent or hear its cries. That should draw him within range of the archers, who can kill him before he knows they are there."

"Ah!" Ahinadab mused. "I like this plan, but if the archers miss, the lion will escape, and this lion has proven to be a wary one. I expect he would wait until dark before making any move on the goat. If the archers miss, the lion will be gone as quick as one of Ba'al Šāmēm's lightning bolts. We will have lost him again, and it may be a long time before we get another chance. I'd rather not take that risk. Is there some way to make sure the lion cannot escape?"

Osiris thought for a moment, then said, "I have seen how the men of *Assuwa*, in western Anatolia, hunt bears in their mountains. They dig a pit too deep for a bear to climb or jump out of, and cover it over with branches and leaves until no trace can be seen. They hang a freshly killed deer above the pit where a bear must try to reach it. His weight causes him to crash through the leaves and branches, and he falls into the pit. The hunters stand above the pit and kill him in safety. It seemed to work well with bears, but I don't know if it has ever been used to kill lions."

"Then, if Almighty El blesses us, we shall be the first." Ahinadab said. "I want you to pick a likely spot and have the porters start digging. Set your archers in the trees when the pit is ready and have a live goat tied up over it by sundown."

"As my lord, wishes." Osiris responded. Bowing low he backed away from his master's presence before hurrying to where the hunting party was already assembled.

Sensing this as a likely moment, Gamil caught his father's attention and said, "Father, I have been practicing with my bow and I am ready to help you kill the lion. Please father, let me stand watch with the archers! Please?" he begged.

Ahinadab had been aware of Gamil's presence while the two leaders made their plans. He considered it important for the boy to understand how such things were decided. If Gamil was ever to become the head of the House of Dan-El, he must learn what that position involved. How better to learn than by observing his father dealing with day-to-day affairs, or solving problems like this one. But this was one time when he wished his son had not been listening.

"Gamil," he said to the boy, "Osiris has kept me informed of your progress with the bow and the javelin. I have also seen with my own eyes that you have some skill with both already. However, there is a great difference between shooting at a standing target that can do you no harm, and shooting at a living, roaring lion that will certainly kill and eat you if it has half a chance.

You say you are ready to help me kill this beast, but I know, in truth, that you are *not* ready. Should anything go wrong, if you were harmed in any way, I would have no words to explain to your mother why I was so foolish as to risk even one hair of your head. Someday, perhaps soon, you will be ready to hunt lions. But that is not *this* day."

Gamil answered, "I understand your concern for me. But father I will be high in a tree with two of your best huntsmen beside me. What could go wrong?"

"I'll tell you what could go wrong," Ahinadab said, with rising irritation in his voice. "Lions can climb trees! The men will be up there under miserable conditions in hope of getting a chance to kill the beast. For that chance they must keep watch throughout the night, with little or no sleep. They should not have to play nursemaid to you as well. If the lion doesn't snatch you from your perch, or you don't fall from it by yourself, and if you aren't eaten up by insects, you still risk taking a fever or might even catch the drowning lung. Speak no more of this! My word is fixed!"

Gamil's heart sank. He was sure that if a scribe had been with the hunting party his father would have ended by saying, "So let it be written. So it shall be." He knew it was of no use to beg further. The finality of this last phrase left no room for argument. His frustration overflowed as tears began to sting his eyes.

But he stifled his despair before his emotions could betray him. Tears would only add to his father's reasons for his decision. If his father saw even one tear, he would say there was no place for a bawling baby on a hunting trip. He must show him that he was not a child. So, he hardened his thoughts and let his frustration boil up into barely suppressed anger. Bowing stiffly, he said in a firm, quiet voice, "As you wish my lord." With that he backed away and out of Ahinadab's presence.

Chapter 19
The Pit

Below the hunters' encampment

The porters and woodcutters worked on the pit all day, lifting basket after basket of soft mountain loam out of the deepening hole and spreading it over the forest floor. The rain continued, increasing at times from mere drizzle to a mild but steady downfall. The soft ground soaked up the water like a sponge, adding its weight to each basket of earth and puddling around the feet of the workers in the hole. All of the men were splattered with mud up to their waists, with their arms coated from fingertips to elbow. The air was chilled by the cold front that had brought on the rain, adding to the misery of the workers. Only their strenuous labors kept them warm.

By noon the pit was as deep as a tall man and about ten paces in diameter. The men changed places frequently, taking turns at digging or hauling away the muddy soil. There were only two mattocks and one hoe in the woodcutters' camp, which were used to cultivate a small vegetable garden. This limited the number of diggers to just three at a time, leaving the rest to do the lifting and hauling. By mid-day everyone was exhausted, and Ahinadab called a halt for the noon meal.

While work on the pit had progressed, the archers prepared their platform in a tall tree about fifteen paces from it. They cut away all of the lower branches to a height of two and ten cubits. The cut branches would serve as part of the covering for the pit. They chose two large, high branches and built a crude, but stable base by piling some larger cut branches into something that looked like a huge bird's nest. On top of that they laid short lengths of small logs to make a fairly level floor, tying everything together with thin ropes. Above that they hung a sail-cloth tarp to keep the rain off. When finished there was just enough space for two men, with room for one to lay down while the other sat and kept watch. It was hardly a comfortable perch, but one that would serve its purpose. Using a sturdy rope to climb up and down, they did one more thing to secure their position. They cut away any branches between them and the pit that might interfere with their arrows.

Some of these branches were then cut and shaped into long spikes, sharpened on one end. These were driven into the trunk of their tree to point at a downward angle. The exposed ends were then sharpened to form a girdle of needle-like stakes that they hoped would prevent the lion from climbing up after them.

After an hour of rest, and a cold but sustaining lunch, the men returned to their work on the pit. By late afternoon it reached a depth of about ten cubits. The rain stopped as they neared the bottom, and the late afternoon sun finally appeared below the few remaining clouds.

The men laid thick, then thinner branches over the pit, covering it all with fallen pine needles and other detritus until it was completely hidden. When everything was ready, all of the men except the two archers cleared away their tools and went to wash up in the stream.

The archers took a small goat, trussed it up and suspended it from a tripod of logs above the center of the pit. The lion would have to step onto the flimsy covering to reach it. As they took their positions on the platform, the weary footsteps of the others faded as everyone left the area. Only the goat and the two archers remained.

At first the young goat had objected loudly to its situation, but as the light began to fade its frightened cries became frantic pleas for its mother.

 When she did not come to the rescue, the little goat gradually stopped struggling against its bindings and settled into a stupor; bleating intermittently as the sun set and darkness closed in. The archers in the tree also settled in, remaining quiet and absolutely still.

Slowly the nocturnal forest dwellers began to move about, seeking whatever type of food their kind required. Mice and other small rodents scampered to and fro, and bats flew out to hunt for insects on the damp night air. An owl floated silently through the trees with only a soft whoosh as its wings folded into a talon-first dive on a small rabbit. Far off in the distance came the cry of a leopard that had just made a kill. But as the first five hours passed there was no sign of the lion.

Midnight came and went, and the hunters in the tree quietly traded places; the one who had been napping now took over the watch while his partner stretched out to sleep. Half an hour later the moon set beyond the western horizon, leaving the site in a dense darkness. The few stars not blocked by patchy clouds provided very little light, and the night grew very still. Nothing moved below the archers except the occasional struggles of the young goat.

But then, an hour before dawn, the goat began to bleat again; softly at first, then with a growing sense of panic as its nose caught the feral scent of the lion on the night air. There was no other sound except for the creaking of tree branches and the sighing of the wind passing through the cedar fronds. Sensing something, the watching archer tapped his partner on the back to wake him. He sat up quickly without making a sound and both men raised their bows, with arrows knocked and ready as they peered into the darkness.

After silently circling the area for most of an hour, the lion was well aware of the goat's location from its cries and its reek of fear. With caution he studied his surroundings before moving closer. He sensed some things that seemed unnatural. The earth had been disturbed, and the scent of many men and their dogs lingered faintly in the area. But he didn't detect the two men in the tree. Whatever the humans had been doing their faded scent was cold in his nostrils, and reassured him that they were no longer near.

But something else was odd. The goat was before him, bleating desperately now, but did not run away as it should have as he came closer. It seemed to be caught or tangled in a strange bush with three trunks and long, vine-like branches. He had never seen such an odd bush before but it reminded him of other things he had seen in the camp of the humans. Something was definitely not right here, and the cautious part of his brain made him remain hidden.

With his senses on full alert the lion circled the strange bush and the goat stuck in its branches. When he didn't detect anything amiss, his growing hunger and the bleating of the goat triggered his most primitive instincts. His focus narrowed down so much that he could almost feel the goat's heart hammering in its chest and hear the adrenalin-flooded blood rushing through its veins. It was more than he could resist. Putting caution aside, he gathered his legs beneath him and with every muscle tensed he attacked.

He exploded out of the brush and closed the distance in an instant. But before he reached the goat the ground suddenly opened up beneath him. He crashed to a hard stop as he hit the bottom of the pit in a cascade of branches and cedar fronds, his fall ending with a muddy splash. The strange bush that still held the goat captive, teetered for a second before falling into the pit on top of him. One of its legs was leaning against the side of the pit, another was laying across his back. The third struck him on his head near the bruise left by the woodcutter's ax.

Stunned by this, his vision swam and he shook his head to clear it. He didn't know what had happened or where he was. But, as he tried to rise, an arrow followed quickly by another, flew toward him from above. One grazed his shoulder, carving a stinging furrow across the hide of his upper back before burying itself in the earth behind him. The second arrow, with a loud "thunk", embedded itself in the leg of the tripod that lay across his back.

In a flash, the lion's brain went from "attack" to "escape". His vision cleared and he realized where he was. He had fallen into a large hole in the ground. He had to find a way to get out of it quickly. 'Thunk", came another arrow as it struck a large branch that had fallen beside him, then "Thwack" went another, accompanied by a burning sensation in his right hindquarter. This last arrow had struck true and the pain both angered and terrified the lion. He couldn't see where the arrows were coming from, but knew they could only mean one thing. Humans were close, dangerously close. He had to escape.

He sprang upward as high as he could with his forelegs thrust forward as far as they could reach. But the pit was so deep he barely managed to catch the edge. For an instant his huge claws raked the ground until gravity and his weight combined to pull him down. This probably saved his life, as he landed in the darkest part of the pit, temporarily out of the archers' line of sight.

They couldn't see him, but could hear as he furiously scratched and clawed at the earthen walls of the pit, trying to gain a purchase that would let him climb up and out. But the soft ground defeated him, crumbling away wherever his claws touched it. He would never be able to leap out of the pit.

More arrows flew, but the archers were shooting blind and none did any harm to the lion. He was still in the darkest shadows and hidden from them, but they shot their arrows in hopes of a lucky hit.

The lion's eye fell on the leg of the tripod that leaned against the side of the pit. With a short leap he reached it, climbed as far up as he could, and was able to scramble high enough that another shorter leap brought him up and out of the pit.

As his head emerged above the edge an arrow flew past his ear, followed quickly by another that narrowly missed his back. He ran off into the night, and in the darkness the huntsmen could hear him crashing through the undergrowth in a total panic. They both grabbed their hunting horns and blew three short notes in a sequence of three blasts. This signaled the camp to let everyone know, "Quarry sighted…All come quickly".

Chapter 20
Blood Trail

At the pit

The dogs immediately responded to the horns with a chorus of barking and whining. Anyone in the encampment who had been asleep was instantly awake. The huntsmen on watch raised their own horns to answer the archers. A few moments after the lion's escape all members of the hunting party were fully alert, had grabbed their weapons, and were rushing toward the pit. They hoped to find the lion's body lying in it.

The dogs were tied up during the night to keep them away from the pit, but were quickly released. All six dashed down the trail toward the sound of the horns. Khe-ahn reached the site well ahead of the others. He saw the open pit, drew up short, and turned to face the others. His stiff-legged stance at the edge of the opening and loud, sharp commands brought three of the older dogs to a skittering halt. The two youngest did not stop and flashed past to suddenly find themselves suspended in midair above the yawning opening. Loud crashes and yelps of pain came a second later, as they landed on the branches and litter at the bottom.

Khe-ahn paced back and forth at the edge of the pit, concerned about the two that had fallen in, but at the same time he could smell the lion's scent everywhere. Seeing that the two in the pit were not injured or in danger, he stopped worrying about them and concentrated on finding the lion. He followed the scent from the place where the great cat had emerged from the pit, to where it had dashed into the underbrush. His keen nose picked up the strong scent of blood. He gave a loud howl, calling the pack to join him. The three dogs not in the pit quickly did so, and followed the blood trail into the underbrush, barking and howling as they went.

The archers came down from their tree and the others from the encampment arrived with torches. Osiris took charge of the site and quickly assessed the situation. His men retrieved the dogs from the pit, but it was too dangerous to go chasing after a wounded lion through the darkness and dense underbrush. Osiris held everyone back and ordered the master of hounds to call for the dogs to return.

Khe-ahn was intent on following the blood trail, but reluctantly broke off the pursuit when he heard the signal horn. Frustrated and confused, he led the others back to the pit. It took some time before the dogs finally settled down. The master of hounds rewarded the dogs with scraps of dried goat meat and checked the two youngest for injuries.

Many of the people from the woodcutters' camp arrived to see the lion's dead corpse. They joined the hunters who were gathered in front of the pit. Everyone was disappointed that the plan had not succeeded. Especially those who had worked so hard to prepare the pit. But none was as disappointed as Ahinadab who questioned the two archers.

"How serious are the lion's wounds?" he asked Elon, the archer whose arrow had grazed the lion's shoulder.

Elon replied, "We struck him twice my lord. One of my arrows hit him above the right shoulder. It was a glancing blow that caused no great harm. But Semiel's arrow struck his left hip. That was a solid hit and I believe it was still in his body when he jumped from the pit. But he climbed out of the pit and was able to run off so quickly that I don't think the arrow hit anything vital. Still, it was no small wound, and he will lose much blood from it."

"That will weaken and slow him down" said Osiris. "He will look for a safe place to lay up and nurse his wounds. If he is able to pull the arrow free its barbs will rip more of his flesh and increase the bleeding. This is very good, my lord. He will not go far, and when the sun is up, we will catch him for certain this time."

Ahinadab realized there was nothing more that could be done for the moment. He kept his disappointment to himself, and tried to put the best face on the situation. After all, a partial success was better than no success at all.

"I am well pleased," Ahinadab told the two archers, "I wish your arrows had killed him, but in such darkness, it is a wonder that you hit him at all. I am satisfied that you both did as much as could be expected. Had the lion not escaped from the pit you could have climbed down and killed him at will from the pit's edge. You both will be rewarded when we return to Gebal."

To the people gathered around he said, "Let us return to camp and make everything ready. Once the sun is risen, we will go after the lion and this time he *will* die. I vow it by the sacred beard of Almighty El!" He turned and led the way back up the trail toward the woodcutters' camp.

At the camp he offered a sacrifice of incense to El, thanking him for his help and praying for success in the coming hunt. Fires were lit and a hearty breakfast was prepared for the hunters and porters.

They ate quickly and hurried their preparations for what everyone hoped would be the last day of the hunt.

Gamil had been kept away from the pit during the action there, and was frantic to know what had occurred. He quickly learned the details of the lion's escape, and rejoiced that a chance remained for him to be a hero. Perhaps his last chance. His father *must* let him join in the hunt this time!

Ahinadab was busier than Gamil had ever seen him, giving orders and looking after all the preparations with Osiris at his side. It took several minutes before Gamil could catch his eye. Bowing low before his father, then standing as straight and tall as he could, Gamil spoke in a voice as deep, calm and formal as he could manage.

"My lord Ahinadab, I have come before you to request your blessing, praying that if I have ever found any favor in your sight you might permit me to join your hunters this day, as they seek to kill this evil lion."

Ahinadab could spare only a scant portion of his attention for Gamil, but the uncharacteristic formality of his request, and the obvious intensity of his desire, compelled him to stop and listen. Amused and amazed, Ahinadab thought, "*This is no longer a mere boy, but a son a father could be proud to name as his own.*" But at the same time, he knew the danger in what his son was asking.

"You *have* found favor in my eyes, Gamil," Ahinadab said softly, "You need never doubt that. But I cannot let you take part in the hunt."

"But, my lord..." Gamil started, only to be cut off as his father's brow furrowed and his eyes hardened.

"Do not *beg*, boy!" Ahinadab said with his voice rising. "That lion has been wounded, which makes him seven times more dangerous than before. He may have been driven mad with pain and anger. Have you ever seen what a wounded lion can do to strong, well-armed men? I have, and I fear this lion. He is by far the cleverest animal I have ever hunted.

What do you imagine you could do if I included you in the hunt? Do you believe you have the skill to slay a full-grown lion, wounded or not? Can you even keep up with the huntsmen, or do the work of the beaters, who will face the greatest danger if he turns on them? Or perhaps you could act as bait, like the goat last night?

No Gamil, I *forbid* it! You shall not go with the huntsmen, and you will not speak to me of it anymore!"

"Please father..." Gamil started again, only to be stopped by his father's final declaration.

"I have *spoken*!" Ahinadab pronounced in a loud voice freighted with the awesome authority of a loving father. Gamil's heart sank, knowing this was his father's final judgment on the matter. He knew if he pressed Ahinadab any further the next judgment would include severe punishment. The thought made Gamil's eyes begin to swim, and he fought hard to retain his composure. He made a formal bow before slowly backing out of his father's presence. His heart seethed with frustration that quickly gave way to anger and thoughts of rebellion.

"I should have joined the hunters without asking for permission. Like I did to come here. There must be a way." he thought

Chapter 21
Left Behind Again

The third day of the hunt

Osiris finished preparing for the day's hunt, and drew near to his lord, overhearing this exchange between father and son. "We are ready, my lord" he said. "The sun is breaking above the mountain's crest, and the lion's blood trail leads down into a large meadow below the camp. Command us and we will begin."

Ahinadab was upset about the unpleasant exchange with Gamil. He had spoken harshly, when patience would have been wiser. He heard Osiris, but did not react immediately. Osiris sensed his mood and waited.

After a moment, Ahinadab collected his thoughts and said, "I have broken the boy's heart."

"My lord?" Osiris asked, not letting on how much he had overheard.

"I forbade him from joining the hunt today." Ahinadab said, somberly.

"A wise decision my lord," Osiris said. "Gamil is doing well with bow and javelin, but as you have seen, he is far from ready. The danger to him is great, and his presence would cause you worry. He would be in the huntsmen's way. He is a good lad, and will get over his disappointment soon. By this time next year, I believe he will be ready to stand next to you on a hunt like this."

"I know you are right. But he is headstrong and often acts without considering the consequences. His anger toward me burns over this. I can feel it! I fear he might disobey me and find some way to join the hunt. I would have one of my bodyguards stay behind and take charge of him, but no one can be spared if we are to catch this gods-cursed lion. The best I can do is give him over to Ad-Haddad for safe-keeping until we return."

"Then let us pray for early success and be done with this business." Osiris replied.

The two men went into the heart of the woodcutters' camp, and there Ahinadab offered another sacrifice to El, praying for the god's blessing and protection for Gamil. When he was satisfied that he had secured the god's favor for the boy, Ahinadab summoned Ad-Haddad and charged him with Gamil's safe-keeping. That done, he led the hunting party down the trail to the pit, where the lion's blood trail began.

Chapter 22
Beating the Brush

Following the blood trail

Once clear of the pit, and certain he wasn't followed, the lion stopped to catch his breath and deal with the arrow in his left hindquarter. He was able to lick at the wound, and managed to get his teeth around the arrow shaft. He tried to pull it free, but a wave of pain and dizziness swept over him. The arrowhead was stuck fast, buried in the bone of his pelvis, just above the hip joint. He could not budge it. He bit at the shaft until it broke off, close to where it entered his body, with enough still in place to partly plug the hole in his flesh and slow the bleeding. After a few minutes it had almost stopped.

Weakened by blood loss, and with the arrow in his hip causing intense agony, all the lion wanted to do was stay still. But instinct told him that he could not stay this close to the pit. The dogs and the men would be coming soon. So, limping, and in great pain, he pressed on through the meadow. The blood trail ended where he had stopped to rest.

The lion reached a rocky ledge on the northern ridge just as the sun appeared over the crest of the mountain's peak. He rested again and brooded on his pain, growing more and more furious at his human and canine tormentors as time passed.

In the growing daylight, he saw the dogs and men come down the southern slope, following his blood trail to its stopping point at the place where he had first rested. The blood trail ended there, but the dogs picked up his scent leading off into the denser vegetation. The lion expected them to follow his scent, but the men stopped them and led the dogs back up the slope until they disappeared in the trees near the pit. He lost sight of them, but soon heard sounds of movement and loud barking off to the west.

A little later, he saw the men and dogs slowly emerge from the forest at the meadow's western end. They spread out in a long line from north to south, and moved eastward into the brush, making as much noise as possible.

While he watched them, the lion did *not* see the group of hunters that crept silently through the forest at the western end of the meadow, to form a thinner north-south line just inside the trees.

The beaters continued eastward, driving every living thing before them. Birds of all sort took to the air and flew off into the surrounding forest. Wild pigs, deer, rabbits, goats and other creatures fled from the beaters. The panicked creatures rushed toward the hunters, who held their ground and did not molest the animals that ran past them to disappear in the forest beyond. They were waiting for the lion, but their wait would be in vain.

If the lion had stayed in the meadow, he would have been driven straight toward the hunters. But once the beaters began their drive, he left his ledge and climbed to the crest of the northern ridge. He limped away from the noise below and silently passed beyond the hunters' ambush without knowing they were there. He followed the ridge until he had circled around and was back on the slope above the woodcutters' unprotected camp. He stopped and rested where the woodcutters had been working. No scent of the men or their dogs remained there, so he was safe for the moment. He licked at the wound again, tasting his own blood. It made him aware of how hungry he had become. He would have to eat soon.

Chapter 23
The Solitary Hunter

Above the woodcutters' camp

An hour after the hunting party left camp, Gamil was still sulking and brooding under the watchful eye of Ad-Haddad. Everyone else was still excited about the events of the night before. The workers stood about in small groups, gossiping about the progress of the hunt, and speculating on the odds of success. No one felt like doing any of the normal chores.

Gamil found their chatter very annoying. It reminded him of what he was missing and his mood grew even darker. He wanted to run away from the camp and its people. If he couldn't be with the hunters, he wanted to be alone. He definitely did not want to be stuck at the camp, watched over by an old man. But if he ran away to join the hunters, his father's wrath would fall on him like never before.

But then he thought, *"Exactly what was it that my father had forbidden? He said, 'I forbid you to go with the huntsmen!' But he didn't say not to go on the hunt! What if I were to hunt for the lion by myself?"*

"Yes!" Gamil thought, *"That might work!"* But he knew his father

would never accept such an obvious ploy as justification, and would never forgive such a blatant breach of his instructions. *"Unless I succeed in killing the lion."*

He convinced himself that he could do so, but how could he leave the camp unnoticed? Old Ad-Haddad was very watchful, and would surely see him if he tried to leave. He and the other woodcutters could easily prevent his escape, and certainly would.

"Hmmm." Gamil thought, *"What if I take my javelin and my bow to the edge of the camp to practice? Seeing me doing the same things I have done every day since coming here might cause his attention to slacken, and give me a chance to slip away unnoticed."*

With this in mind, Gamil pretended to be bored, kicked at some pebbles on the ground, and slowly walked to his father's tent where he gathered up his weapons. Breathing a heavy sigh of apparent resignation, he started walking toward the edge of the camp where his targets were set.

"Wait, young master," Ad-Haddad's voice followed him. "Your father has ordered me to make sure you do not leave the camp."

"I know, I know!" Gamil snapped. "I'm just going to do some target practice to pass the time."

"I will accompany you then!" came the reply.

"As you *wish*!" Gamil said with a note of disrespect and another sigh that he hoped would be received as his surrender to the unavoidable.

They reached the targets and Gamil began by stringing his bow and taking a few practice shots. He was consistently hitting the target now, and the more he practiced, the more his skill increased. He could hit the bullseye about a third of the time, and today he was able to improve on that. He hit the center of the knot four out of nine times. For each hit on the target he made a mark in the dust and for every bullseye he drew the letter *"Ayin,"* which was a circle representing an eye.

Ad-Haddad watched the boy with interest at first, noting how much his archery had improved since the hunting party had arrived. He saw Gamil mark his score, and noted how he retrieved his arrows each time, after the ninth was loosed. Ad-Haddad sat on the ground, resting his back against a tree trunk, as Gamil continued to practice with his bow. But after half an hour, the woodcutter's thoughts began to wander and other concerns crept to the front of his mind. Ten minutes later something changed and brought his full attention back to the boy.

Gamil had retrieved his arrows and set aside his quiver and bow. He had picked up his javelin and began to limber up his arm, taking some false running steps to loosen up his legs. These actions are what had caught Ad-Haddad's eye. When Gamil was ready, Ad-Haddad saw him hurl his javelin at the wicker basket hanging from a low tree branch. His first throw narrowly missed the target, and Gamil ran to retrieve the javelin. He threw and fetched the javelin twice more, striking the target both times. After a dozen throws, the old man's thoughts drifted again. This time his head began to nod as the warm sunshine and cool mountain breeze relaxed his body. No one had slept enough the night before, so it was inevitable that he would doze off, despite his best intentions.

Gamil continued to hurl his javelin, stealing a glance at his guardian each time he retrieved it. He saw the drooping head, and when he was sure Ad-Haddad was really asleep, he made one more throw. This time he deliberately released early, causing the javelin to sail far over and beyond the target. It landed in some thicker trees and as he went to fetch it, he saw that he was hidden from Ad-Haddad's view. He paused for a moment, listening to hear if the old man was still asleep. The sound of gentle snoring gave him the answer. Then, certain that his absence would not be noticed anytime soon, Gamil scrambled deeper into the woods and up the slope above the camp, carrying his javelin with him.

Fifteen minutes later, the lack of sounds from the javelin practice awoke Ad-Haddad with a start. He shook his head and looked around. What had happened? Where was his young charge? His heart began to race, and he felt a cold shock of fear as he realized what the answer might be. If the boy had run off, Ad-Haddad dreaded what might befall him for the lapse in his guardianship. But with a man-eating lion on the loose, a greater fear clutched at his heart. If something bad had happened to Gamil, it might be something very bad indeed.

"Young master?" he called as loud as he could, but got no answer. "My lord Gamil, where are you?" he cried. There was no reply. Only silence.

The pounding of his racing heart drummed in his ears. He was on the edge of panic, but forced himself to collect his thoughts. He ran past the target, seeing no sign of the boy or his javelin, and the gods be praised, no indication of any accident. Only the boy's tracks, leading there and back, again and again, as he retrieved his javelin, showed where he had been.

Ad-Haddad ran back down into the camp and gathered the other men to help him to quickly search the camp. When they didn't find the missing boy anywhere, they grabbed axes and knives, and hurried to the target tree. From there, they began searching the forest, worried as much for Gamil's safety as for their own.

Chapter 24
From Hunter to Hunted

On the slope above the woodcutters' camp

The lion rested among the stumps of recently felled trees, with the taste of his own blood making his stomach rumble. A breeze carried the smells of cooking from the camp below, and they caught his attention. He needed food and knew where he could find it, so he followed his nose down the mountain.

He had not gone far before he noticed another scent, this one closer than the smells from the camp. His ears detected the sound of something small that was carelessly pushing its way toward him through the forest. This scent was human and he immediately thought of the hunters. But he couldn't detect any scent of the dogs, just a single, small human. Here was the solution to his hunger. His predator's instincts took control, and his pain was forgotten. He crouched low and began to stalk his way toward this new target.

At first Gamil had run as fast as he could to get away from the camp. He wanted to put as much distance between himself and Ad-Haddad as he could before the old man woke up. When he didn't hear any sounds of pursuit, he slowed down and rested for a moment to catch his breath. His lungs were not used to such exercise in the thinner air at this elevation.

He also needed to think about what he was doing. He had never been hunting before, and didn't really know how to begin. But he remembered the few things he had heard the huntsmen say, and tried to fill the gaps in his knowledge by imagining what they would do. He knew animals could be hunted by following their tracks, and once his breathing became more regular, he started walking uphill, searching the ground for lion tracks. He had never seen a lion's track, but was certain that he would know one when he saw it, and that he would soon find the trail that would lead to his quarry.

Little did he know that the lion had already found him.

The noise Gamil made as he pushed his way through the undergrowth beneath the trees, and the strong scent of his sweating body, led the lion to him quickly. He observed the boy carefully, and would only attack when he was sure of success. Gamil continued to pick his way up the slope, completely unaware of the danger he was walking into.

The lion crouched into his attack stance, poised to launch himself down the hill at his approaching prey. He was all instinct now, intent on making a quick kill. The panic of the night before and the pain in his hip faded away. The dogs and men pursuing him were gone from his mind. Every muscle was tensed and ready to launch him forward like an arrow from its bow. He just needed the boy to come a little bit closer.

Forty paces away, Gamil entered the lion's optimum striking range. His eyes were focused on the ground, searching for lion tracks, and he was completely oblivious to the surrounding forest. He moved to step over a clump of fern, but tripped on a hidden tree root, and fell face-first into a low hollow. The fall dropped him out of the lion's view for a moment. He pushed himself to his knees, groping for his javelin, and heard a loud crashing and heavy footfalls charging from the brush above him.

The lion was startled by the boy's sudden disappearance, but launched his attack toward where he had last seen his prey. His four-hundred-pound, cinnamon-brown body flew across the space between them in an instant, leaping the last few feet with his jaws wide open and his claws out.

Gamil looked up to see death bearing down on him. The flashing eyes, yellowed fangs and wide-spread claws paralyzed him for an instant. But as if something or someone else was doing it, his left arm came up to shield his face. His groping right hand found the shaft of the javelin and gripped it tightly, bringing it up at an angle with the point aimed at the on-rushing lion. He closed his eyes and felt a tremendous shock as its huge body crashed into him, knocking him backward several feet and forcing the breath from his lungs.

The lion meant to strike a killing blow on the boy's head, but as his right front paw swung forward a strange thing happened. Instead of making solid contact his claws came up short of the target, and only cut through empty air.

Something was pressing against the lion's sternum, halting his forward movement. The javelin's butt-spike had been jammed against the same tree root that had tripped the boy just seconds before, preventing the weapon from moving backward. The lion felt a stabbing pain where the head of the javelin cut through the muscle, cartilage, and bone of his ribcage. His momentum forced the tip of the javelin's head deeper into his chest until it passed directly through his heart and emerged through the muscles of his back.

The result was instantaneous, and the lion could feel strength draining from his limbs. Life was leaving him quickly, but he swung his massive right paw one last time in the direction of the boy. The blow barely reached its target, glancing across the left side of Gamil's chest; cracking several ribs and opening three great gashes that began to bleed profusely.

With that final effort the lion gave a great shudder and died. His great weight snapped the fire-hardened ash-wood shaft of the javelin like a reed, and his lifeless body collapsed on top of the wounded boy.

Gamil fell flat on his back, striking the back of his head on the ground as he went down. He was barely conscious as the lion's final stroke tore into his body. He was aware of being hit hard on his left side, and felt the sensation of his flesh being hooked and torn, but strangely, there was no immediate pain.

When the lion's great weight broke the javelin's shaft, its lifeless body pinned Gamil below it, making it hard for him to draw breath. His injured flesh began to burn and he felt the warm flow of his own blood, mixed with the lion's, pouring down his sides. The weight of the lion's carcass compressed the wounds on his chest, staunching most of his bleeding. But the combined effects of searing pain, blood loss, and his stifled breath overwhelmed him. Almost at once, he went into shock and his vision faded until blackness engulfed him.

Chapter 25

A Desperate Search

On the slope above the woodcutters' camp

Ad-Haddad and his woodcutters searched franticly for most of an hour before they found Gamil's footprints and followed them up the slope. His tracks wandered toward the site of their recent tree cutting. Nearing it, they came upon the lion. When they first spotted it, they were unable to tell that it was dead. They stopped; afraid to approach too closely, even though the beast lay completely still in an unnatural pose. Then Ad-Haddad saw the bloody tip of the javelin protruding ,from the lion's back, and realized it had been killed. But by whom? The hunters clearly weren't there. Where was Gamil?

There was no sign of the boy, until the old man saw what appeared to be movement from the lion. The men jumped back and got ready to defend themselves. But when no attack came, Ad-Haddad crept forward, watching for any signs of life from the beast. Instead he saw a small hand reach from under the lion's carcass, and heard a low, muffled groan.

He shouted, "It is the boy! He is underneath the lion! Quick, we must help him!"

The men dropped their axes and pruning hooks and sprang into action. Together they quickly rolled the lion's carcass away from their master's son. Ad-Haddad's heart nearly stopped when he saw the boy was almost completely covered in blood. He could see more blood beginning to ooze from three great chest wounds. The heavy weight of the lion's body had compressed those wounds and kept the boy alive until now. Ad-Haddad prayed that most of the blood he saw was from the lion and not from Gamil.

"Lift him up! We must bind his wounds and bear him to the camp as fast as we can. Life is still in him, but he will not last long unless we can stop this bleeding!"

Two men ran to the camp to spread the word and prepare to treat Gamil's wounds. The others used some of their garments as makeshift bandages to slow the bleeding. They started to carry him down the mountain as quickly and gently as possible, but had not gone far when they heard dogs howling on the mountain above.

When the beaters failed to drive the lion from the meadow, they were sent back to the camp, and the dogs were put to work. They picked up the lion's trail and followed it to the ridge top. Howling and barking, the pack followed his scent along the ridge, with the hunters coming on behind them as fast as they could.

The dogs reached the place where the lion's dead body lay, and went into a frenzy: snarling, snapping and attacking the lifeless carcass. They savaged it with their teeth, shaking their heads from side-to-side, as they sought to tear the dead lion apart.

Khe-ahn was in the thick of it, but with no response from the beast, he quickly realized it was dead. He paused to catch his breath and began to calm down; satisfied that the beast was no longer a threat. The other dogs soon caught on and quieted, but were still focused on the carcass.

Khe-ahn circled it, licking at the blood that had pooled beside it. He recognized the lion's blood, but there was other blood. Human blood! His brain registered a familiar scent that was all but masked by the lion's reek. Gamil was somewhere nearby.

He cast about the area for the source of the scent, and found a fresh blood trail that was a mix of lion and human blood. Confused and alarmed, he started to follow this new trail, but stopped as he heard the blaring of hunting horns coming down from the mountain above.

A few minutes later the hunters caught up with the dogs and were just as confused by what they found as the woodcutters had been. The lion was dead. Of that there could be no doubt, but who had killed it? Osiris was the first to solve the mystery.

He pulled the broken shaft of the javelin from the lion's body and looked closely at it. The other half was still wedged against the tree root and Osiris pulled it free as well. He immediately recognized the butt-spike with its antique styling and rushed to Ahinadab with both parts in his hands.

"My lord!" he shouted. "Here is the javelin that killed the lion. It is the one I gave to Gamil!"

"*What!*" Ahinadab said, with alarm. "Gamil should be at the camp. How does his javelin come to be here in the body of this lion? *Where is he?*"

Khe-ahn was barking and running back and forth, obviously trying to get the hunters' attention. Elon followed him to see what the dog had found, and called out, "My lord, here is a blood trail leading down the mountain!"

Ahinadab and Osiris hurried to the spot and studied the stained soil. They saw a mass of sandal tracks alongside the blood trail, all leading down the mountainside. Ahinadab and Osiris started to follow when they heard Ad-Haddad calling to them from below.

"My lord, Ahinadab, come at once!" Hearing the hunters' horns, the old woodcutter had left Gamil with his other men and hurried back the way he had come. He was breathless from running and halted when he saw the hunting party. "Your son has been wounded and my men are carrying him to your camp!"

The woodcutters carried Gamil to his father's tent, where the shofeṭ's body servants flew into action and took charge of his unconscious form. They gently laid him on his father's sleeping pallet and cut away his bloody clothing. He was washed from head to foot with fresh water. Wine was poured onto his wounds to clean and purify them.

Ja-rune joined them: bringing a jar of honey, wheat flour, and fresh linen bandages. She gently probed his wounds to be sure there was no dirt or other debris contaminating them. She checked to be sure the lion's claws had not gone deep enough to puncture his lungs or to hit anything vital. The wounds were still oozing blood, which she knew was a sign that no major artery had been touched. She felt his sides and chest, finding the place where his ribs were cracked and noted that they weren't broken. They would heal without any intervention.

She used a silver needle and linen thread to close up his wounds, covering them over with a thick poultice of the wheat flour and honey. Then, with two of the body servants propping him upright, she bound up his entire chest: winding several layers of bandages around his body, crossing them over his shoulders, and tying everything off. She had just finished as Ahinadab reached the center of the hunters' encampment. He had to push his way through the crowd of onlookers to reach the tent's opening.

"*Where is Gamil?*" he roared as he burst inside!

Chapter 26
A Hero Awakens

In Ahinadab's tent

Three days later, Gamil opened his eyes. He had lapsed in and out of consciousness several times as he lay in a high fever on Ahinadab's sleeping pallet. The fever broke a few hours before he woke up. He had been visited by strange, very vivid dreams that he did not understand. Coming to his full senses, he struggled to recall the details.

He remembered the sky opened and in the midst of a blinding light he saw the great god, El, seated on a golden throne and surrounded by clouds of glory. The god had beckoned to him, and he felt as if his body was lifted up and soared through the air a great distance. He flew far to the north, to the peak of Mount Zaphon. There, the Almighty One, the Rider of Clouds, the Lord of all things, made his dwelling.

Gamil was terrified and trembled; falling on his face before the throne. Then El stretched forth his hand and blessed Gamil saying, *"Do not be afraid. You are safe. Your father loves you and has been praying to me for your sake. I have heard his prayers. You will not die from the wounds of the lion. I have plans for your life and I will be with you to see them fulfilled."*

There was much more, but as Gamil slowly regained his senses, the god's voice grew fainter and he could only remember part of the words El had spoken to him, *"...I will be with you..."* as he came to full consciousness.

He tried to sit up, but stopped and let out a gasp of pain as his movements put a strain on his stitched-up wounds and his cracked ribs flexed painfully. He groaned.

"Easy young lord," Ja-rune cautioned. "Do not try to move without help. Your wounds could open up again, and your cracked ribs might break if you move suddenly." Ja-rune had remained at Gamil's side the last three days, tending him and gently bathing his fevered body with cold water. Ahinadab's body servants also remained with him, relieving Ja-rune at times, and always following her instructions.

The servants gently helped Gamil to rise into a sitting position. His head was swimming and his heart pounding from the effort. Ja-rune lifted a bowl of water to his lips and he drank thirstily. When he had emptied the bowl, he spoke for the first time.

"I'm hungry," was all he said.

One of the body servants went to fetch food, and the other went to alert Ahinadab. He had spent the last three days and nights praying that El would spare Gamil's life. Three times each day, at sunrise, noon and sunset, sacrifices were offered to Ba'al Šāmēm, to Eshmun, the god of healing, and most of all to El, the Almighty One. When he learned that his son was awake, Ahinadab rose from his knees, left the altar , and rushed to his tent.

"Gods be praised!" he shouted to the whole camp as he went, "My son lives! *My Son lives!"*

Chapter 27
Ba'alat Nikkal

In the city of Gebal at the House of Dan-El

The *ba'alat* Nikkal was frantic the day the hunting party departed from the House of Dan-El. Her son, Gamil, was missing. She had been totally immersed in last-minute preparations for the hunters' journey, and did not notice the boy's absence until an hour after their departure.

The entire household had been up and working all night. Nikkal's children, except for the infants, were too excited to sleep and had been scampering about, and generally getting in everyone's way. Nikkal assumed Gamil had been doing the same.

Before departing, Ahinadab had embraced his wife, sharing a deep, meaningful farewell kiss, and lingering as long as he could. His words of love and devotion brought a lump to her throat. Both knew this would be a long separation, a perilous journey, and an uncertain outcome. This might be the last time they would ever see each other.

Neither of them had spoken of the possible danger, nor had they shown the fear that lay heavily on their hearts. He had climbed the staircase to the roof of the house and had made a sacrifice on the altar of El, the patron god of his house. She had pronounced the blessing of the goddess over him and he had invoked the blessing of El for her and the whole house. Then they descended from the roof to join the assembled hunting party in the courtyard below.

Nikkal had followed to the outer gates of the great house. She had climbed to the top of the gatehouse and stood on its parapet, watching as her husband led the rest of the hunting party through the gates, past the houses of the elite district and out of her view.

The gates had been closed and secured as the sun rose. Nikkal descended from the gatehouse with a deep sigh, and return to the house proper to begin the day's routine. She had not noticed Gamil's absence until it was time for the morning meal. When he hadn't joined his siblings in the great hall, she sent a servant to rouse him from his bedchamber. The servant reported that Gamil was not in his chamber and his sleeping pallet did not appear to have been used.

Annoyed, Nikkal ordered the servants to search the entire house. She entered Gamil's bedchamber to inspect it with her own eyes. When she found his pallet untouched, her annoyance became concern, but not worry. She sent for He-sham and Artros, the chief of the household guards. She directed He-sham to take the servants and search the house again, from top to bottom, thinking Gamil had fallen asleep somewhere else. She ordered Artros to have his men search the grounds and outbuildings of the house.

This was done, but the boy was not found. Nikkal was alarmed, and sent a message to Zimredda, commander of the city guards, requesting in the name of her husband, the shofeṭ Ahinadab, that a search be made of the entire city for her missing child. Artros and his guards were told to search the grounds again, carefully and thoroughly this time, looking for any sign that could provide a hint of where he might be.

By noon neither the city guards, nor the household guards had found the slightest trace of Gamil. Commander Zimredda, He-sham and Artros met with Nikkal in the great hall of the House of Dan-El.

"Are you certain?" she asked, "None of you has anything to tell me regarding my son's whereabouts?"

"My lady," Zimredda replied, "My men scoured the city from the door of this great house to the sea, and from the Northern Gate to the Southern Gate. They have searched everywhere except for the temple grounds, where they are not permitted entrance. But the temple guards said he had not entered their precincts and they did not find him when they did their own searches.

He could not have left the city or he would have been spotted by the gate watch. The only place left to search is the harbor district. I have a dozen of my men there now. It will take them another three hours to finish searching every ship, boathouse, warehouse, and all the shops, taverns, whorehouses, and other businesses in that district. If the boy is there he will be found, I vow it by the mighty thunderbolts of Ba'al Šāmēm."

"And you, Artros," she asked, turning to him, "Have you searched the house, the grounds, the servants' quarters, gardens, and stables?"

"Yes, great lady," Artros replied, "we searched everywhere, but we did not find the young master. Only some tracks that might be from his sandals in the garden by the kitchen door. These lead to the courtyard, but go no further. I think he may have gone that way."

"Show me these tracks Artros, and please accompany us Commander Zimredda." Nikkal said. She was beginning to suspect what Gamil had done.

The tall *Lukka* warrior led the way through the rear door of the house that faced the kitchen building and the garden. It was a large garden with almonds, pistachios, figs, apples, peaches, apricots, pomegranates and other fruit trees forming a mixed orchard at one end. Nearest to the kitchen, the orchard gave way to the growing of grapes, melons, cucumbers, gourds, pumpkins, turnips, carrots, radishes and other vegetables. Sage, rosemary, lavender, rue, wormwood and herbs prized for their medicinal properties, were also grown close to the kitchen.

The sandal tracks followed the path from the kitchen to the side of the house. Ahinadab had provided the space along this side of the house for Nikkal's beloved flower garden. There her gardeners had planted fragrant jasmine and honeysuckle, which vined their way up the outer walls. Dense carpets of mountain gold, red and white vinca, and blue stars covered the foreground in alternating bands of bright color. Beds of begonias in many hues, zinnia, poppies, and dahlia flourished beyond the creepers, up to the Jasmine and honeysuckle vines. All were carefully tended and nurtured by her gardeners. This group of young slaves competed with each other to be the one who most pleased their lady.

This garden was her retreat, where she spent as many hours each day as possible, refreshing herself by a large fountain that stood in the shade of two olive trees. Here she often entertained the other ladies of the city. But today she did not linger there. Her mind was fixed on the search for her son.

The tracks were little more than scuff marks in the smooth, packed sand of the pathway. But it was clear that someone had walked from the foot of the outer staircase, past the kitchen, and toward the inner courtyard. They followed the tracks along the side of the house, past the flower garden, to where they entered the inner courtyard and disappeared where the paving stones began.

"Did he do what I suspect?" Nikkal thought. Her motherly intuition

in play now. She knew very well the kind of foolishness her son was capable of.

"You are right, Artros, I believe he did come this way. The oxcarts stood near here this morning, just before my husband led the hunting party out. That boy of mine worships my husband and is always wanting to be with him. Especially when there is something exciting happening. I am certain he found a way to sneak off with the hunting party.

If he did, he will be safe enough for now. But he won't be when he gets home! If his father doesn't beat him, I certainly will. He won't be able to sit for a month! Just *wait* until I get my hands on him!"

Both men took a mental step backward at this display of anger, thankful that her wrath wasn't directed at them. Such an outburst was most unusual for her. Nikkal was normally calm and serene, but not today. They were unsure about what to do or say. Finally, Zimredda spoke, "Do you wish me to call off the search of the harbor district, my lady?"

"No," she responded, somewhat calmer, "I might be wrong, and if he is somewhere, hurt and alone, he must be found. If anyone has harmed him or taken him, they must be caught and prevented from doing any further harm. Keep searching until you are sure he is not there."

Turning to Artros she said, "Please have your men resume their regular duties. My husband was to meet with two of his master mariners and several important *tagari* after the noon meal. In his absence I must take his place. I will need four of your guardsmen to stand watch in the great hall for that meeting. The rest can return to their other duties."

Feeling suddenly pressed for time she looked up to the sky and exclaimed, "Oh, that *boy*!" His foolishness had already taken up far too much of her time this morning, and the noon hour was approaching.

Dismissed, the two men bowed low, and backed away before turning and hastening from her presence. Both were thinking how they would not want to be in Gamil's sandals when she next saw him.

Alone in the courtyard, Nikkal experienced a full range of emotion, from anger to frustration, from shock to fearful despair. *"What was Gamil thinking! Does he have any idea of the danger he is in? Oh gods, will I ever see my son again?"* These thoughts would not leave her.

Tears of frustration and fear swam in her eyes. She struggled with her emotions, finally getting a grip on herself by pushing all this to the back of her mind. There was nothing she could do for now, and worrying was a waste of energy. She had to compose herself before going back inside the house. It would not do for the servants or her children to see her in such a state.

She would need all her energy to project a calm, rational mindset during the meetings with her husband's master mariners and the tagari. So, after a silent prayer to the goddess, Ba'alat Gebal, she breathed a heavy sigh, wiped her tears and fixed her countenance with a tranquility that she really did not feel. With renewed poise and composure, Nikkal reentered the house.

Chapter 28

Two Ships and
Two Masters

At the northern harbor of Gebal

Gebal's northern harbor consisted of sixteen stone wharves that extended from a massive limestone quay, which followed the curve of a natural cove. Five of these wharves were reserved for ships belonging to the fleet of the House of Dan-El. The day the hunting party departed, two merchant ships belonging to the shofeṭ Ahinadab were tied up near each other along the first of these wharves. The smaller vessel, named *Shapash* had arrived that morning and was unloading a cargo of olive oil and grain from Kemet. The other ship, the *Cabax* had been in port for a week, awaiting the resolution of a dispute between the owners of its cargo and the buyers in Gebal.

The master of, a man named Abirami, saw to it that his cargo was being properly off-loaded and left the ship to make his mandatory appearance before the chief customs clerk at the palace of king Rib-Haddad. There he submitted the three wax-on-wood tablets that recorded the log of his journey and cargo manifest. These were given by the chief customs clerk to the royal scribes to be copied on papyrus. Abirami then made arrangements for the weighing and counting of the cargo.

Once this business was taken care of, he went to the House of Dan-El to pay his respects to his master, the shofeṭ Ahinadab who owned the *Shapash*. In this case, he had learned that Ahinadab was away, so he would meet with his wife the ba'alat Nikkal.

Abirami left the customs house and climbed the grand staircase to the city proper. At the top of the staircase he paused and looked back at the scene in the harbor below. He watched the stevedores off-loading the cargo from the *Shapash*, then his eyes drifted to where the *Cabax* was moored. She was a fine ship, he thought. It was twice the size and had one and a half times the cargo capacity of the *Shapash*. Just for a moment, Abirami envied her master.

He knew the master of the *Cabax*. His name was Barakba'al and the two of them had been shipmates on another vessel when they were just common sailors. There was something about the man that troubled Abirami, but he never figured out what it was. It was just a vague feeling that Barakba'al was not to be trusted.

Four years later, both were in command of their own ships; two small *gauloi*. the smallest ships in any of the fleets of Gebal. Abirami commanded the *Tanis* and Barakba'al was in command of the *Ishat*. Both ships were part of the fleet belonging to the House of Dan-El. In time both men came to command their current ships, but seldom met.

Abirami glanced at the *Cabax* again, and envied Barakba'al for a moment. But it was an idle thought, already dismissed as he turned and continued up the street leading to the House of Dan-El. A short walk found him standing before the gates of his employer's home.

He looked up at the bronzed and gilded, cedar-wood gates and was impressed anew with the greatness of this luxuriant estate. After being recognized by the guards he was allowed to pass through into the outer courtyard. There he was met by Han-nu, the assistant of He-sham, the rab-tamkari of the House of Dan-El, who ushered him through the outer courtyard, central courtyard, inner courtyard and into the foyer of the great hall.

Chapter 29
The House of Dan-El

In the home of Ahinadab and Nikkal

The home of the shofeṭ and his wife was built according to the plan of many of the better estates in Gebal. Cities in other lands were often poorly laid-out collections of one-room houses and shops, scattered around a few temples and larger public buildings. But the elite citizens of Gebal had the wealth to construct substantial estates that could only be compared to palaces.

The House of Dan-El, with its grounds, was one of the largest estates in the city. Surrounded by walls almost nine cubits high and over a cubit thick, it dominated the city's elite district. Three stone-paved, rectilinear courtyards covered a combined area of about twenty-four *semed*. Another twelve *semed* was taken up for the house proper, the kitchen building, outbuildings, livestock pens, and gardens. More space would have been desirable, but land inside the city walls was limited by the size of the peninsula on which it stood. The demand for space inside the city walls was high, and what land was available came at a premium.

Access to the estate was through two entrances. The main entrance, with its massive cedarwood gates and stone gatehouse, faced the northern gate of the city. The smaller, rear gateway, was used for removing rubbish, resupplying the kitchen, livestock pens, and other minor needs. It faced south, toward the temple district.

Nearest the gatehouse, a pair of two-story outbuildings lined the walls in the outer courtyard. To the left of the gatehouse one building held servants' quarters on the upper floor and slave quarters on the ground floor. The upper floor of the building to the right housed the armory and barracks for the household guards; a twenty-man unit of *Lukka* warriors, who were mercenaries that provided protection for the family and guarded Ahinadab's treasury. The ground floor consisted of stables, workshops, a forge, and blacksmith's quarters.

The central courtyard held two large altars: one for sacrifices to Ba'alat Gebal, which stood closest to the gates, and one for sacrifices to Ba'al Šāmēm, her consort, which was closest to the house proper. A third, much smaller altar, not dedicated to a particular god or goddess, stood in a small shrine near the eastern wall. It was used for sacrifices to other deities worshiped by foreign visitors.

Beyond the central courtyard, an inner courtyard ran the full width of the compound, with wells of pure water at both sides. Stone steps led up from the pavement to the front doors of the two-storied house proper. Entrance to the house was through a pair of massive cedarwood doors, bound with heavy bronze bands, and set on solid gold hinges with gold rings for handles.

The outer surfaces of the doors were intricately carved and inlaid with mother of pearl, turquoise, and other brightly colored gemstones in patterns that depicted figures of the goddess, Ba'alat Gebal, the god Ba'al Šāmēm and above them, almighty El. El was the father of Ba'alat Gebal and on these doors he was shown in the act of handing her the city as a gift. She was the patroness and protector of the city and its lands.

A large foyer, just inside these doors, served as a pleasant space where guests and those whose business brought them to the House of Dan-El were greeted and cared for while they waited for an audience with the rab-tamkari, He-sham, or with the shofeṭ Ahinadab himself.

Beyond the foyer, the interior of the house was divided into three parts. At the center was the great hall, running almost the entire length of the building, from front to back. This spacious room was open all the way to the ceiling above. Down each side of the hall on the ground floor were galleries, framed by great square cedar-wood pillars that supported the weight of the upper floor and the roof. A series of rectangular doors in the walls of the galleries gave access to rooms that made up the other two thirds of the ground floor.

The ground floor rooms nearest the front of the house were the quarters of the house servants. Nearest to the back were two large private chambers that served as the offices of Ahinadab on the right and He-sham on the left. In these offices much of the work of administering the wide-spread interests of the house took place. They were also used for more intimate business meetings or for other meetings concerned with private matters.

Also, along the sides of the great hall, between the servants' quarters and the offices, were storerooms for various supplies and extra furnishings. Identical rooms on both sides, immediately in front of the offices, served as the scribes' quarters and on the left side, nearer to the foyer stood the household archives, a large repository where all of the documents of the House of Dan-El were kept, along with ample supplies of papyrus and ink. All together these documents recorded seventy-five years of the history and business dealings of the House of Dan-El.

At the front, just behind the foyer on both sides of the great hall, stairways led to landings on the upper floor, where the chambers of the family members stood, and also led down into the cellars below.

The cellars were carved out of the limestone bedrock foundation of the house and stayed cool and at an even temperature year-round. Those at the bottom of the stairways held fine wines imported from all over the eastern shores of the Great Sea and supplies of other rare or exotic delicacies.

The back half of the cellar space held the treasury of The House of Dan-El. A guard was stationed in front of the treasury door at all times. Two other stairways located just in front of Ahinadab and He-sham's offices led to the chambers above, and to the cellar below.

Outside the house, a second set of stairways led to the upper floor chambers of the family members, with a last flight of stairs leading to the roof with its sun decks, pleasure garden, pavilion and water cisterns.

On the roof, facing the front of the house, was the altar of sacrifice to El, the patron god of the House of Dan-El. Sacrificial offerings of incense were made there each morning and evening. Then, if the weather permitted, the family would retire to the roof after the evening meal, to enjoy the cool breezes from the sea and share each other's company.

Ahinadab would sometimes pass on whatever interesting news he had heard that day: news of the council's deliberations, cases that came before him as shofeṭ, and sometimes details of the house's business dealings.

But to his children's delight, he often shared stories about his adventures at sea, of visiting far off lands and the people who inhabited those places. Sometimes the stories involved the gods and how they intervened in the affairs of men, and sometimes the stories were about the family's forefathers, and how they left their ancient homes and journeyed to the city of Ugarit, and eventually to Gebal. At these times Gamil and his siblings learned many things that would be important for them to remember when they grew older and took their places in the world.

A balcony ran across the full width the upper floor directly in front of the private chambers of the lord Ahinadab and the lady Nikkal. Large windows let light and fresh air into their chambers. Doors from the chambers opened onto the balcony, while other doors opened into a sitting room on the lord's side and a lavish dressing area on the lady's side. Nikkal's dressing area was complete with a highly decorated ceramic hip-bath and a fully functioning toilet. A system of fired-clay pipes provided fresh water from the cisterns on the roof and drainage connected to the city's sewers outside the estate.

Next to the lord's and his lady's chambers were the nursery on the left side, adjoining the lady's chamber, and the bed chamber shared by the two daughters of Ahinadab and Nikkal. On the right side, next to Ahinadab's chamber, were two bed chambers occupied by three of the couple's five sons. Gamil, as the eldest son occupied the larger room closest to Ahinadab's chamber. A second chamber next to Gamil's was shared by his two younger brothers. Two infant sons, a year apart in age, were kept near their mother in the nursery.

On both sides of the house, at the far end of the upper floor, were a pair of identical chambers that were reserved for guests. These two rooms once were occupied by Ahinadab's father, the shofeṭ Nat'an-El and his consort, the ba'alat Bet'tala. Both had died in the fullness of their years five summers prior. As they advanced in age and infirmity the time came for Nat'an-el to surrender his responsibilities as the head of the House of Dan-El and so he had entrusted all things to the care of his eldest son, Ahinadab. It was then that Nat'an-El and his wife vacated the rooms at the front of the house and retired to those at the back. Since the deaths of Ahinadab's parents these two chambers were reserved for honored guests.

Ahinadab had spent most of his adult life at sea, or at the many outposts his family maintained to serve their business interests in other lands. He returned to Gebal to assume the headship of the House of Dan-El when summoned by his father. There he reconnected with his parents and his wife, and took his place as a member of the council of elders. In time he gained a reputation for sound, sober judgment and was chosen by the other council members to be a shofeṭ of the northern quarter of the city.

Ahinadab and Nikkal had married in their youth, and while he was at sea learning the arts of a mariner and merchant-trader, she lived in the home of his parents as their daughter. From them she learned the intricacies of the family's business and their involvement in the politics of the city. With both of Ahinadab's parents as her mentors she developed the knowledge and skill to become a highly respected and important citizen of Gebal in her own right.

By the time Nat'an-El could no longer lead the family Nikkal had become an ideal partner for Ahinadab in life and in business. Their first child, Gamil, had been born nine moons after Ahinadab's return.

Close by the rear wall of the house was the separate kitchen building with its two huge brick ovens, large fireplace, larder and pantries. It was surrounded by orchards and vegetable gardens. The cattle pens, a fold for sheep and goats, and a hen house were located at the far end of the property, to keep the sounds and smells of domestic animals away from the house. The House of Dan-El provided comfort, security and maintained a significant degree of self-sufficiency. It served its occupants well.

The estate was a close second in size to the House of Abdhamon, the home of Gebal's wealthiest financier, Paltiba'al, the son of Itthoba'al. Paltiba'al was Ahinadab's friend and close associate, with whom he often partnered in business ventures. Paltiba'al, like Ahinadab, was a member of the council of elders, and the two men usually stood together in the council regarding governmental issues city.

Chapter 30
Nikkal's Judgement

In the great hall of the House of Dan-El

Abirami was offered the full courtesy of the house with all the honor and respect due him as a master mariner. A basin of water was brought to him in the foyer by a young slave, who loosened and removed his sandals before washing his feet with warm, perfumed water and drying them with a heated linen towel. Abirami was made comfortable on one of the low cushioned couches that stood against the walls of the foyer for the ease of guests while they waited to be announced.

From somewhere near the foyer the soothing strains of harp music drifted on the air. Abirami was offered wine, goat cheese and fresh grapes with melon slices while he waited. He was told that he would be announced as soon as the group of men ahead of him concluded their meeting with the ba'alat Nikkal.

Nikkal sat at the head of the great hall, on a richly decorated cedarwood demi-throne that rested on a raised dais. This was a shofeṭ's judgement seat that her husband occupied when hearing legal issues. Ahinadab would normally take his seat there at the fourth hour of the morning to open his daily court. But in his absence, Nikkal took his place, and was using the hall to hear a complaint that was a business concern for the House of Dan-El. As his wife, she had the right and the power to act for her husband, and by using the shofeṭ's seat she underscored her authority

Nikkal was dressed formally, in a gown of fine white linen. Brightly colored geometric patterns were woven into the fabric from shoulder to hem, leaving the upper portion and sleeves a spotless white. The sleeves were short and tight-fitting; covering her arms from shoulder to elbow with a thin band of the same geometric patterns at the open ends.

Her arms were bare below the elbows, but at each wrist she wore a number of fine gold bracelets encrusted with dazzling gemstones that sparkled in the light. These matched a three-strand gold necklace at her throat. Today she had chosen to wear a pair of large, golden hoops for earrings, each with three strands of fine gold chain hanging in their centers. Each chain was set with a cascade of matching, blood-red rubies, alternating with white pearls

Crowning her ensemble was a bejeweled golden tiara with two feathers of hammered gold pointing straight up above her ears, in imitation of the crown of the goddess Ba'alat Gebal. Her servants had worked the tiara into her densely curled, jet-black hair. Small strands had been pulled through a row of tiny openings across the bottom of the tiara to fall softly across her forehead, framing her face. Behind the tiara, her hair was curled and braided in rows running from front to back. These were caught up into a loose bun where her neck joined her head.

Her hands were painted from fingertips to wrists with henna in intricate designs that had been applied by a pair of priestesses from the temple of Ba'alat Gebal. Symbols among the designs invoked the goddess's power and blessing. Although not a priestess, these marked Nikkal as a person of immense spiritual power, with close ties to the high priestess herself.

Her facial makeup had been carefully applied to accentuate her eyes in the style popular in Kemet. Her upper eyes were shadowed with lavender and her eyelids were outlined with kohl. Her arms above the wrists, her face, ears, neck, and chest were all painted a stark white. Her lips, cheeks, and the nipples of her bared breasts were all painted a delicate shade of pink.

This fashion was popular among the high-born ladies of Gebal, and was copied from the style worn for centuries by the elite Kena'ani colonists on the Island of *Kaptara*. The top of the gown was cut to fully cover her sides, back, and shoulders, but the front was open from neck to navel. She wore a sleeveless vest of brightly colored wool over her gown. The vest was cut to scoop below her bare breasts to enhance them and provide support. A wide sash was wrapped around her abdomen, from the bottom of the vest to the top of her hips, completing the look.

This fashion was especially popular with younger women, but as years of childbearing and the effects of gravity took their toll, most women added a thinly woven, semi-transparent blouse under their vests. The blouses would become less and less transparent as the years passed. Nikkal had been sixteen years old when her first child, Gamil, was born. Now, almost fifteen years and six more children later, she still had no need to hide the attributes of motherhood the gods had blessed her with. Her ensemble this day was one that any high-born lady of Gebal would have been proud to wear, and was totally appropriate for her status and this occasion. She was radiant as she sat in her husband's place on the judgment seat.

Facing her this morning on her right stood three gentlemen of Gebal who held interests in the cargo of Ahinadab's ship, the *Cabax*, which was docked in the northern harbor at the wharf reserved for the ships of the House of Dan-El.

Two of these men were tagari. The noble Abiba'al, son of Ba'aliahon, and Urumilki, son of Sikarba'al. They were partners in the venture under discussion. Together they had purchased and shipped a cargo of wine that was carried by the *Cabax* from Kit'ion on the island of *Alashiya* to Gebal. Abiba'al had traveled with the cargo, to keep an eye on their investment. The third man, who by his dress and demeanor was clearly most important, was the man who had financed their venture. He was Paltiba'al, son of Itthoba'al of the House of Abdhamon. Paltiba'al was the city's most prosperous financier, and was often the financial backer of the House of Dan-El's many business ventures. Paltiba'al and Ahinadab were close friends, and due to their common interests, they were natural allies in the politics of the city. Together with the heads of two other noble houses of Gebal they formed a powerful *kàrum* that operated in circles very close to the palace of the king, but with complete autonomy.

The group to the left of Nikkal included two men from the wine buyers' guild: the wine merchant Bōdashtart, son of Ahirom of Gebal, and the tagari, Melqart-sha'ma, another buyer from the nearby city of *Be'erot*. The two merchants had contracted with Abiba'al and Urumilki to purchase their cargo when it reached Gebal. The third member of this group was master mariner Barakba'al, son of Ahumm, who commanded the *Cabax* for his lord Ahinadab. He had been assigned to carry the cargo of wine and deliver it to Gebal.

King Rib-Hadda was represented by his chief customs clerk, the worthy scribe Abiba'al, who stood before ba'alat Nikkal, reading from the log of the *Cabax* on her latest voyage. He had read aloud the record of the ship's departure from Kit'ion on the southeast coast of the island of Alashiya on the 15th day of the month of *Rekh-wer*. He had also shown Nikkal and the others the ship's manifest, notarized and sealed by the master of the harbor, declaring that she carried a mixed cargo of 400 copper ingots and 900 amphorae of wine. The log noted that the ship made only one stop at the island port of *Athar* to take on fresh water. Barakba'al had recorded his reason for stopping was to replace the ship's drinking water, because it had become foul. This was done on the ten and sixth day of Rekh-wer. She made port at Athar in the early evening and left with the high tide on the next morning. The rest of the trip was uneventful, and as he concluded his reading, Abiba'al bowed to Nikkal and stepped back three paces.

"Is there anyone who can add to what we have now heard on this matter?" Nikkal asked the two groups. She looked around the hall to see if there was any response from the small audience. After a moment had passed, she spoke again.

"I have learned, from one who witnessed it, that on the sixteenth day of Rekh-wer only one ship put into port at Athar. This witness, whose name will not be spoken here, is employed by the House of Dan-El at that port and his word is to be trusted. He is a reliable man who swears to me, by the thunderbolts of Ba'al Šāmēm, that what he says is true. I will now read to you his report of certain events that occurred while the *Cabax* was in port at Athar. I will skip his lengthy preamble, as it is not relevant to the matter at hand, and will now read the portion that is."

> 'May it please my lord Ahinadab, on the sixteenth day of Rekh-wer, I received word that your ship, the *Cabax*, made an unexpected visit to our island, stopping at the port for what was said to be resupply of fresh water. As you have ordered me to do when one of your ships makes port here, I went to the harbor and there did see the *Cabax* moored and her crew in the process of unloading six large amphorae. These I assumed were for the ship's supply of drinking water, and I waited to see what else might happen.

The sun had gone down and the men worked by torchlight, so I positioned myself as close to the ship as possible. I stood in the shadows where none could see me. After one hour passed, I saw the crewmen who had taken the amphorae to be refilled returning to the ship, bringing six amphorae, presumably refilled with fresh water.

I stayed where I was and continued to watch. Just after the night watchmen had made their rounds, I saw three small boats pull quietly up to the ship on its seaward side and out of my line of vision. I could see crewmen on the deck, working without torches or any other light. These men seemed to be lowering something over the side of the ship to where the small boats must have been waiting. It appeared that some of the cargo was being passed over to the small boats. The boats pulled away, and made two more trips to and from the *Cabax* before the sky began to lighten with the coming of day. I saw no more activity until the ship departed before dawn the next morning and I saw no other comings or goings from the crewmen, or any other person.'

Finishing her reading, Nikkal spoke to the two groups before her and the spectators in the hall.

"As we have heard, when the ship arrived at the harbor in Gebal, and her cargo was unloaded, the shipment of nine hundred amphorae of wine belonging to Abiba'al and Urumilki was short by fifty amphorae."

"Master mariner Barakba'al, you have already stated that you do not know how the shortage occurred. You suggested that the count may have been wrong when the cargo was loaded at Kit'ion, but that hardly seems possible. We have the manifest that was properly notarized and sealed by the master of the harbor at Kit'ion, and we have the sworn statement of the tagari, Abiba'al, which confirms the count as being the full 900 when the ship sailed. Now we have this report from Athar. What do you say about all this?"

Barakba'al stepped forward three paces and went down on one knee before Nikkal. He held his arms crossed over his chest in the proper posture of respect and submission. His eyes had gone wide in surprise as the report from Ahinadab's agent was read, but now they narrowed into crafty slits as his mind quickly framed an answer that he hoped would satisfy the lady. Suspicion had grown as the agent's report was read, and Barakba'al heard murmurs behind his back. He had to sow seeds of doubt in the minds of those assembled in the hall, before their suspicions hardened into anger.

"May it please you, noble lady," he began, addressing Nikkal but hoping to sway the others. "I did send some of my crew ashore on Athar to replenish our drinking water on that night, but I know nothing about any small boats coming near the ship. If it happened as the report from my lord's agent at the port states, it must have been while I was ashore, refreshing myself at the tavern of the red star on the street of the fish mongers. I was there from the time my men went for water until an hour before we set sail the next morning. Your agent can verify that. Many who were there saw me and can confirm what I say."

"I wonder," he continued, "if the worthy merchant Abiba'al could enlighten us. He traveled with us from Kit'ion to keep watch on his cargo. I invited him to go ashore with me for whatever entertainment and refreshment we might find, but he declined. I assume he was aboard all night."

"Liar!" Abiba'al exclaimed. "You did not invite me to go ashore, and you know I would have declined if you had. I was sickened by that fouled water for three days, beginning the day before we arrived on Athar. I was sleeping below deck while we were in the port. How dare you suggest that I had anything to do with the missing wine."

"My lady," Abiba'al said, turning to Nikkal, "I have dealt with the House of Dan-El for many years, and you know that my reputation is spotless. I always pay my debts on time and in full. I have never had any unexplained shortages in the cargoes I was responsible for. Why would I stoop to stealing a portion of my own goods!"

"He speaks the truth," said Urumilki, coming to the defense of his partner. "Abiba'al was still so sick when the *Cabax* made port here that he had to be helped from the ship. And he was still ill for three more days. It wasn't until I took possession of our wine that either of us knew of the shortage."

"My lady," Barakba'al said, "it seems clear to me that these two partners arranged this between them. It would not surprise me if Abiba'al fouled our drinking water himself, and pretended to be sickened by it so that we would have to put in at Athar. It would have been easy for Urumilki to be waiting with men and boats to steal part of our cargo!"

Voices in the hall were rising and accusations were flying back and forth between the master mariner and the merchants, with almost everyone taking sides one way or the other. Nikkal glanced at Paltiba'al, who stood in stony silence amid the uproar. He nodded to her to indicate that it was time to end this.

"Enough!" her voice rang out over the clamor. "Be silent!"

Her words had an immediate effect and the angry voices softened and hushed.

"I can find no fault with the noble merchants Abiba'al and Urumilki.

They are well known to be honest men. Master mariner Barakba'al has cast suspicion on them, but offers no real proof of any wrongdoing on their part.

As for the suggestion that Urumilki had men and boats to receive the stolen cargo at Athar, I find it is without merit. If Abiba'al fouled the drinking water he could not predict which port the *Cabax* would stop at for a fresh supply. Only the commander of the ship has the authority to decide where the vessel goes. There are two other ports less than a day's sailing from Kit'ion that could have provided fresh water. Only Barakba'al knew which port would be chosen.

It is also true that master mariner Barakba'al does not enjoy a reputation as spotless as our noble merchants." Her eyes were fixed on Barakba'al, who cringed at the mention of his reputation.

"For three years he has been the master of the *Cabax*. The records show that cargo has gone missing on five of the nine voyages he has made in those years. These shortages never amount to much in value, but go beyond what might be normal spoilage, or tribute paid to enemies for safe passage. The shortages are always hard to explain. His is by far the poorest record of all the ship masters of the Dan-El fleet, and his honesty has been in doubt before this.

Therefore, though clear proof of his guilt is lacking in this case, I find there is enough circumstantial evidence for me to reach a logical conclusion. It is my judgement that he is responsible for the current loss."

She had addressed this to everyone in the hall and had to pause a moment for the crowd's murmurs to subside. Turning to the men on her right she spoke further.

"The House of Dan-El will compensate the noble tagari, Abiba'al and Urumilki, for their losses on this voyage, up to the full value of the missing amphorae of wine. From this compensation, and the proceeds from sale of the rest of their cargo, they will repay their loan from my lord Paltiba'al with the interest due him.

The wine merchants Bōdashtart and Melqart-sha'ma', will also be compensated by the House of Dan-El for the loss of the profit they would have gained from selling the missing amphorae of wine at the fair market price. In exchange, they will pay the full price of nine hundred amphorae to the noble Abiba'al and Urumilki. In this way, I trust we are all satisfied that all those with a financial interest in this matter will be made whole, as if there had been no loss of cargo."

This was said as both a statement and a question. Looking at each one in turn as she spoke, she could see them nodding and bowing in evident satisfaction. Everyone knew she had gone far beyond what was required of the House of Dan-El under the laws of Gebal. But anything less would have left a stain on the house's reputation and would have cost far more in the long run than the missing cargo was worth. After a brief pause in which a murmur of approval was heard in the hall, she turned her eyes back on Barakba'al who was still on one knee before her.

"Master mariner Barakba'al" she went on, "I judge you to be at fault in this matter. If not by conspiracy to commit this theft, then by negligence in failing to safeguard the cargo entrusted to you. Therefore, you are dismissed from our service, and henceforth you are no longer master of the *Cabax*. Furthermore, you shall never again sail on any ship of the Dan-El fleet."

She was about to conclude the meeting by directing the scribe "Let it so be written, let it be so done," when she was rudely interrupted by the only person there who was not satisfied.

Chapter 31
The Curse of Barakba'al

Before the seat of judgement in the House of Dan-El

"Mercy, great lady! Have mercy on me!" came the loud, desperate cry from Barakba'al who had gone from kneeling before her to full prostration in front of Nikkal. "If you dismiss me like this, no house in any Kena'ani city will ever give me command of a vessel again! I beg you, please let me redeem myself!"

"Mercy you say?" Nikkal responded sharply. "I have already shown you mercy! By law I can have you put in chains until you repay the full value of the cargoes you have plundered. If you cannot pay, I can have you sold into slavery for whatever price your wretched self will bring. Be thankful that I only dismissed you!"

Suddenly, Barakba'al dropped all pretense of humility. He ceased his groveling and rose to his feet, taking on a threatening posture. The two Lukka guards that stood on either side of Nikkal stepped forward to block any move he might make against her. His face was a bright crimson mask of hatred, but he held his ground and spat out an angry retort.

"You call that mercy? I call it gross injustice! I have been proven guilty of nothing, and yet you have ruined me! I should demand a proper trial by the full council of elders, but I see there is no justice for me in this city. Your consort and his cronies hold too much power!" He said this while looking directly at Paltiba'al and the rest of the assembled citizens. "They will sway the other elders against me no matter what is true."

"I *spit* on your mercy," he continued, "and I curse this House! May your women be childless forever, may all your ships be destroyed by *Yam-Nahar*, and may you all fall from your high positions in this city and be utterly cast out into wild, barren places!"

Shocked silence fell over the hall. Gebal's people were highly superstitious. They believed their many gods held enormous power to do good or harm. Few of the elite citizens believed in all of their gods, but most played it safe by giving offerings to the major temples and making sacrifices to their own patron gods. They looked to them for blessing and protection from misfortune. No one wanted to risk the displeasure of any of the gods.

To place a curse like this on someone was believed to be the same as doing violence to them with your own hands, and to invoke a powerful god like Yam-Nahar to cause someone's destruction was tantamount to murder. Unless something was done to immediately counteract the curse, anything bad that happened to Ahinadab, Nikkal or any member of the House of Dan-El from this day forward would be believed to be a result of Barakba'al's curse.

The two guards next to Nikkal moved to lay hands on Barakba'al, but he turned before they could reach him and bolted out of the hall, shoving his way through the others there, and dashing out of the house through the foyer. The guards started after him, but Nikkal stopped them.

"Let him go! He can do us no further harm." She ordered, little knowing how wrong these words would turn out to be.

The voices around her rose to near panic, and Nikkal knew that something had to be done at once. She could not allow this meeting to end on such a sinister note. With Barakba'al's curse still hanging in the air, she rose from her seat and spread her arms wide. When they reached shoulder height, she held them straight out to her sides with her palms opened to the air above and called out in her loudest voice.

"Almighty El, my lord and my god, protector of the House of Dan-El, hear the cries of this woman, your humble servant. Curses have been called down upon me, and upon all the House of Dan-El. Yam-Nahar has been invoked against me and mine by an evil-doer who seeks our destruction. I pray to you, divine El, our shield and protector, to turn this curse aside and keep us safe from all harm."

At that moment the sky outside darkened as thin clouds moved in from the sea to partially blocked the sun. Light from windows above the foyer, which had illuminated the great hall, dimmed except for a single beam of sunlight that shown through to catch the figure of Nikkal, illuminating her head, shoulders and upraised arms.

The air in the hall seemed to grow heavy, and the people sensed a powerful presence settling there. Everyone was filled with awe. All went to their knees and bowed low toward the dais without having been ordered to do so.

Nikkal alone remained standing and with her upraised arms she continued her prayer. "We thank you Almighty El, for showing us your favor, we thank you for lifting this curse from us before any harm could find us. We thank you for restoring peace to our House. We acknowledge you as the source of the many blessings we have received throughout the years, and praise you for your mighty works.

We praise you for your goodness, wisdom and great strength. No god is like you, oh El. None is worthy to stand beside you."

As she ended this prayer, with its powerful counter-spell, the clouds that veiled the sun passed on and the shaft of sunlight that had illuminated Nikkal merged into the ambient daylight in the room. Everyone in the great hall felt a calm, peaceful spirit descending like a father's caress on the House of Dan-El.

All believed that the curse of Barakba'al had been forestalled. They rose from their knees and looked at each other with wonder at the power of Nikkal and her god. Nikkal raised her voice a final time, saying to the scribe, "Make a complete copy of all that has been said and done here and send it to the palace of the king. Let it so be written; let it be so done!"

Chapter 32
Abirami's Report

In Ahinadab's office in the House of Dan-el

Abirami was startled when Barakba'al burst through the inner doors of the foyer and dashed past him into the courtyard. He jumped to his feet and called out a greeting to his fellow master mariner. No reply came from the visibly enraged Barakba'al.

"Very strange behavior," Abirami thought, *"and unbelievably rude too."* The two men had never been friends, but whenever their paths had crossed in the past Barakba'al had never been so discourteous to Abirami. *"Most strange, indeed."*

His thoughts were interrupted as the great hall began to empty at the conclusion of the meeting. He bowed in greeting to each of the merchants and traders as they filed out, and they responded in kind to him. A few pleasantries were exchanged as these men excused themselves and quickly moved out of the house. The sky outside had cleared of clouds as quickly as they had appeared.

Abirami wanted to know what had happened in the meeting, but he had not been asked to join the others and it would have been impolite for him to ask about it. What had caused Barakba'al's odd behavior? He had been able to hear a few muted voices through the heavy doors to the hall, but could not make out any words. Perhaps he would have a chance to ask the lady Nikkal when he had his audience with her.

As the last of the principals and their aides were ushered from the house by Han-nu, He-sham turned to Abirami with a bow and said, "Peace be upon you, master mariner Abirami, son of Maharba'al. Welcome to the House of Dan-El. I must apologize for not greeting you at the gates, but as you saw there was a prior meeting in progress. Have you been offered the courtesy of the house?"

"Peace be upon you, rab-tamkari He-sham, and upon this great house. Yes, thank you, I have been well cared for and I want for nothing."

"Excellent," the chief administrator replied "then if you are ready, I shall announce you to my mistress."

With that He-sham bowed at the waist and made a sweeping gesture with his right hand to usher the master mariner into the great hall. The two men advanced toward the judgment seat at the back of the hall, and Abirami was surprised to see that the lady Nikkal was not there. He looked around the hall, but did not see her. They approached the judgement seat, where he usually met Ahinadab after a voyage, but He-sham led the way to the door of the shofeṭ's private office instead. He knocked three times before opening the door and leading Abirami inside. Then he stood to the side, bowed and said, "My lady, I am honored to present master mariner Abirami, son of Maharba'al and commander of my lord Ahinadab's ship, the *Shapash*." Nikkal nodded her head, and He-sham stepped away to exit the room, closing the door as he went.

Abirami stepped forward a pace and bowed very low before the great lady. He quickly noticed that she was not alone. Standing at the side of the room was the lord Paltiba'al, who had remained with Nikkal after the prior meeting ended.

"Peace and the blessings of El, the Almighty, be upon you my lady." Abirami knelt before her, touching his forehead to the floor three times.

"Peace and the blessings of Almighty El be upon you as well, master mariner," Nikkal responded, "Was your voyage profitable?"

"*Very* profitable, great lady. My cargo of olive oil and grain from Kemet is being unloaded at the wharf even as we speak. I have already filed my log and the manifest with the assistant to the chief customs clerk and the fees have all been paid. Once the crew has been paid, I expect your profit to be close to four-and-one-half talents of gold."

"Well done then! That is an excellent profit!" Nikkal said, "Especially so as the *Shapash* is one of our smaller ships. Tell me about the voyage."

Abirami did so, talking for more than an hour and covering every detail of the voyage, beginning with its departure from Gebal with a mixed cargo of trade goods and amphorae filled with garum, the fermented fish sauce that was favored as a condiment throughout the Great Sea region.

The *Shapash* had followed the eastern coastal currents northward to the island of Athar. There they stopped and unloaded some of the cargo and took on thirty amphorae filled with atar—the fragrant oil of the abundant flowers that grew in the local valleys. This oil was used to make a sweet perfume that was popular among the ladies of Gebal, and all the other cities on the Kena'ani trade routes.

From Athar they sailed further north to Arwad, Gebal's northern most trading outpost on the eastern coast of the Great Sea. There they took on a shipment of figurines of the goddesses and gods that were turned out in the shops of the craftsmen and women of Gebal for trade with the people of Ugarit. The majority of these figures were made of bronze, but almost one in four were made from solid gold or bronze with gold leaf. A few images of the goddess Ashtoreth were carved from ivory imported from Kemet. These last were special order items that were being sent to the temple of the goddess in Ugarit, but most of the other figures would be purchased for use in household shrines in that city.

From Arwad the *Shapash* sailed to Ugarit, the last stop along the eastern coast before turning to follow the westward currents to the port of Kit'ion on the island of Alashiya. There they unloaded all of the images and a large quantity of the garum sauce. They took on two hundred "ox-hide" shaped ingots of copper and 20,000 *shekels* of tin. The copper and tin would be delivered to Gebal where the smiths would melt and mingle the two metals to make bronze, a much more valuable commodity.

Leaving the port of Kit'ion the *Shapash* followed the southern coast of Alashiya westward to catch the southward currents. Driven by fair winds all the way to the north coast of Kemet, she arrived at the island of Pharos, the Kena'ani port that had been built by the seafaring men of Gebal just a short distance from the western side of the Nile delta. There they unloaded most of their remaining cargo of manufactured goods, including a shipment of gold and silver goblets, and two large *kraters*.

The kraters were gifts from king Rib-Hadda to the pharaoh Akhenaten, and were made of finely wrought silver, inlaid with gold figures of the Aten, the official god of Kemet, represented as a sun disk. The pharaoh was depicted in the act of worshiping the god, with everything done in a manner that imitated the royal Kemet style and form. Although they had been crafted in the workshops of Gebal by the city's most talented artisans and would be sent up the Nile river to the pharaoh's new palace at his capital city of Akhenatan.

"It was an easy voyage my lady. We were blessed by smooth sailing under clear skies most of the way. On the southward leg the winds favored us and we made good time, bettering our record for the passage from Kit'ion to Pharos by two days. We saw several other ships on that passage, but only once did we encounter any problem.

On the second day out from Kit'ion, we were sailing along the southern shore of Alashiya. We had just passed the tip of the peninsula at the western end of Akrotiri Bay when sails appeared on the northwestern horizon. As we rounded the point, I saw that they were Achaean craft, with their black bows and long, slim lines. These pirates had been lurking there, hidden by the land, and waiting to catch whatever ships might come that way.

The currents favored us and we had a strong wind in our sail, but I ordered the crew to man the oars to maximize our speed. The pirates gave chase and followed us far out to sea, and beyond sight of the land. Their sleek hulls were made for speed, and our gauloi-type ship was slow in comparison. But with the lead we had, and help from the gods, by late afternoon it was clear that we remained beyond their reach and would escape in the oncoming night. When they realized this, the pirates gave up the chase.

After that we continued south-by-southwest without any further danger until we reached the Kemet coast just half a league to the west of the great Nile delta. From there the current carried us eastward to the port on the island of Pharos."

"And our king's gifts for the pharaoh? What disposition did you make of them?" Paltiba'al asked.

"My lord, as soon as we docked, I sent a messenger to lord Aperel, the *tjati* of the north at his palace in Thebes, announcing the arrival of these gifts for Akhenaten. I had my men off-load them to our king's well-secured warehouse at the port. There, with the help of Yehomilk, the overseer of Pharos Island, I saw to it that extra guards were set to watch over the gifts. Two days later Aperel's royal barge arrived and the great tjati was welcomed with all proper ceremony by Yehomilk and the other port officials. The Kemet gods were invoked with sacrifices and the gifts were presented with king Rib-Hadda's letter to the tjati on behalf of our Kena'ani people and the lords of Gebal."

"Well said, and well done, master Abirami." Paltiba'al said, "You have served the shofeṭ Ahinadab most faithfully and done a great service to your city as well! That is exactly the news I stayed to hear, and now I will leave you to her.

Ba'alat Nikkal, I thank you most sincerely, for your hospitality and for your generosity in resolving the *Cabax* affair."

Paltiba'al bowed deeply to Nikkal and turned to the door; but before he started for it, he paused, looked squarely at Abirami who was himself in mid-bow to the departing lord, and said, "Farewell and may blessings be upon you, Abirami, son of Maharba'al. I believe the ba'alat Nikkal has another matter to discuss with you."

Abirami was puzzled to see a smile on the financier's lips with an overall look of great satisfaction. The door closed behind him and Abirami returned his attention to lady Nikkal. He wanted to ask if she had any new instructions for him before he took his own leave and returned to the *Shapash*.

But Nikkal spoke first, saying, "Lord Paltiba'al thinks very highly of you, master mariner. I value his judgment and invited him to stay while you gave your report. I am glad that he confirms my own opinion of you."

Abirami wasn't sure if this was good or not. The great lady seemed pleased, but he realized that he had been tested the whole time he was in her presence. He had been weighed and measured, and evidently was not found to be less than expected. But what was the reason for such a test?

"I hope, my lady, that I may always earn your good opinion." he said. "I strive to give you and lord Ahinadab the best service my humble talents can produce, and have done my utmost to be a profitable servant. If I have done anything to diminish your confidence in me, you need only to express it and I will amend any deficiency immediately. It is my heart's desire to be worthy of your highest confidence at all times."

This was as close as Abirami could come to asking her if he still had a job. Now that his present voyage was concluded, he was anxious to receive his next orders as quickly as possible. This was always a major concern for any master mariner. His position depended on the pleasure of his patron. If his ship's owner lost confidence in him, or especially if his voyages weren't sufficiently profitable, the owner could dismiss him at any time. Thus, the end of a voyage raised a special apprehension in any master's heart, even when a voyage was successful.

"Will you always be worthy of my highest confidence?" Nikkal asked. "Will you faithfully perform whatever I ask of you, even if I tell you I think your four seasons of sailing the *Shapash* may have been too many?" She wore a smile and had a twinkle in her eye when she said this, but her words cause Abirami's heart to leap into his throat. He was suddenly confused and discomfort must have shown on his face. *"Where have I failed her?"* he thought.

She quickly laughed, breaking the tension.

"I'm sorry. Good master Abirami, I have kept you twisting on a hook for longer than I should. Forgive me for amusing myself at your expense."

"I...I don't understand, great lady! How have I failed you?" Abirami asked.

"No, no, no! You have not failed in anything." Nikkal replied. "Quite the opposite in fact. I listened carefully to your report, expecting you to do what so many mariners are prone to do. Most exaggerate their accomplishments, or slant their reports to accentuate good outcomes and minimize any less successful events. But your report was straightforward and unvarnished. Such honesty is refreshing and much appreciated.

I meant only that we have kept you on one of our smallest ships much too long. We have been wasting your considerable talents."

The relief on Abirami's face was comical. Nikkal almost laughed out loud again. His face had worn a range of expressions, from alarmed, to relieved, to puzzled, and he still did not understand what the lady meant.

"My lady?" was all he managed to say. His question showed how profoundly lost he was.

"You have served my husband and the House of Dan-El magnificently, master Abirami, and it is just and right that you should be rewarded over and above the share of the profits you have already earned. It is in my mind to promote you to a higher position than the one you have held thus far. My husband and I have discussed this before, and I know that he agrees.

It just so happens," she continued, "that one of the ships in our fleet needs a new master. The *Cabax*, which I believe is twice the size of the *Shapash*, is here in port, and if you are willing to serve the House of Dan-El as her master, the job is yours."

Abirami too overwhelmed to respond as his mistress' offer sank into his mind. He had not expected a promotion. Least of all to a ship as fine as the *Cabax*, which was known to be the best ship in the Dan-El fleet. It was one of the fastest of its class in the eastern Mediterranean. He fell to his knees with gratitude, and with his right hand over his heart, he bowed down to Nikkal until his forehead touched the stone floor of the chamber. He repeated this twice more, overwhelmed with amazement and sincere gratitude. Then, at her insistence, he rose to his feet again.

"My lady, this is most generous, and completely unexpected!" Abirami said. "I am overwhelmed by this great honor and opportunity to serve this noble house. Thank you, a thousand times! You may rest assured that I will continue to perform my duties to guard your ship, crew, and cargo with my very life."

"Of that I have no doubt, master mariner Abirami, but haven't you forgotten something?" Nikkal replied. The puzzled look came over Abirami's face again, causing her to spell it out for him. "You haven't accepted the position yet."

"OH!" Abirami exclaimed, "Of course, of course. How stupid of me! I most certainly do accept, my lady. You do me an honor that no man could ever refuse!"

"Good." she said. "That settles the matter then. Here is your letter of commission, which I had He-sham prepare in expectation of your acceptance." She handed him the papyrus document that was rolled up inside a protective leather outer wrap. "You will note that it bears the seal of my husband, the shofeṭ Ahinadab, which makes it official. Take it and go forth with the blessings of the gods upon you, and with the blessing of the lord of this house. I have sent word to the *Shapash* for your men to carry on without you. They will see to the rest of the unloading, and will have leave to go ashore until their new master mariner summons them. Your personal items will be brought to your house this afternoon."

"Now I command you to hurry to your own house at once, and share this news with your wife. I am sure she is eager to see her husband after a long voyage." She said this last with a twinkle in her eye, and a wink.

"In the morning go to the port and visit the office of our chief agent there. He will have instructions for you, and a manifest of the cargo for your first voyage as master of the *Cabax*. But be sure, master Abirami, that you do not leave your house *too* early."

This last she said with a knowing smile and an arched eyebrow that would have made her meaning clear to any but a blind man.

Once again, Abirami went to his knees and repeated his triple-bow. As he rose, his right hand, holding the scroll of his commission, was still over his heart. Bowing from the waist he stepped back three paces before bowing lower one more time for good measure, then turned to exit through the chamber door.

Outside the chamber, in the great hall, He-sham handed him another document, saying, "master mariner Abirami, here is a letter of instruction to the treasurer at the palace. It provides for you to be paid your share of the profits from the last voyage of the *Shapash*, with the shares to be distributed by you to your crew.

I recommend that you go there in the morning and take care of this before seeing our agent at the port. Congratulations on your promotion. Go with the blessing of this house and of almighty El. May his peace be upon you and may he bring you the same success in your voyages on the *Cabax* as he has aboard the *Shapash*."

The two men exchanged bows, and Abirami departed from the Great Hall. "*So*, he thought, *"that is why Barakba'al had been so angry!"* He passed through the courtyards and out through the main gate into the street with his head held high, his chest thrust forward, and his shoulders squared. There was a spring in his steps and a wide smile on his face as he headed toward his own house, carrying the scroll of his commission like a baton.

Chapter 33

Melita, the Bitter and the Sweet

At the warehouse of ba'alat Tallayba'al

Melita was bored. So bored, in fact, that she was ready to scream! As the youngest daughter of the lord Paltiba'al, she had been forced to endure a long morning of waiting on her mother, the ba'alat Tallayba'al. Tallayba'al was the wife of lord Paltiba'al, the wealthiest financier in the city. She was also the head of a kàrum of weavers, whose looms produced great quantities of fine linen and other fabrics that made up a major part of Gebal's manufactured exports. It was not unusual for the women of Gebal and other Kena'ani coastal cities to have their own business interests apart from those of their husbands. In fact, it was the norm, especially among the elite.

The men and women of Gebal had always been equals, and the women took part in every aspect of trade, business and the social activities of the city. No woman was regarded as the property of her father or husband, and never was inferior to men.

Only the council of elders was closed to women, due to the expectations of customers from other places where such equality was not the norm. The Kena'ani of Gebal owed much of their success to convincing outsiders that they were just like those all around them, with a king and council of elders ruling them. But, in fact, the women were deeply involved in the city's government. Among their own people the women of Gebal were held in high esteem and enjoyed a degree of equality and influence not seen in other cultures. That and many other things about their way of life were carefully guarded secrets.

Tallayba'al had taken Melita with her on this particular morning, as she made her rounds of two dozen small shops where her looms were worked by men and women of the weaver's guild. Just now she was finishing up an inspection of her warehouse near the port, where great racks and shelves of finished linen and woolen cloth was stored until shipped abroad to fill customer orders. The air smelled of wool and the heavy scent of freshly dyed linen. Tallayba'al was reviewing the records of the previous week's production and receipts for the goods sold. Yutpan, the overseer of her warehouse was working with his mistress, droning on and on about the details, while Melita wished to be anywhere else in the city except at her mother's side.

Melita's name in the Kena'ani dialect of Gebal meant, "sweet", but also had the opposite meaning, "bitter", in some of the other dialects of the surrounding lands. Bestowed on her at birth by her mother, the name had proven to be very appropriate as she grew older, and now at eleven years old, she was a mixture of things both bitter and sweet.

Even as a baby, all who saw her noted her remarkable beauty. She was gifted with the classic features preferred by the high-born Kena'ani ladies of Gebal. A long, narrow nose with deep-set brown eyes that were so dark they appeared to be almost black; a smooth, round pale-skinned face, framed with long, straight, jet-black hair that was curled and coiffed into neat braided rows running front-to-back and cut longer in the back to hang in gleaming raven strands that just brushed her shoulders.

Now, as adolescence began to refine her limbs and add curves to her slender torso, she showed great promise of becoming an amazingly beautiful woman. She was growing up pampered, somewhat spoiled, and very headstrong. As she became aware of her budding beauty, she developed more than a little vanity and her high-born status imparted more than a little arrogance to her personality. This was the bitter part of her otherwise sweet nature.

She was also gifted with significant musical talent and a keen intellect. Her mother began to notice this at an early age, and hired tutors to teach her how to play the lyre and flute, and a voice coach to teach her how to sing. This coach was a young priest from the temple of Adonis, who delighted in guiding her in the use of her rich, strong voice. She loved to sing the hymns to the gods that were a part of the worship life of the city and such was her talent that by her ninth summer she had even composed several hymns of her own. On the other hand, she also picked up more than a few of the saltier songs favored by the sailors down at the harbor, where she and her friends like to play much of the time.

Melita was also inclined to be athletic and was a keen competitor in the games she played with the other girls and boys her age. This made her the target of resentment from the boys whenever she bested them, especially since she loved to rub it in. That was another way the bitter side of her nature showed itself.

When Melita and Gamil were infants her parents, Paltiba'al and Tallayba'al with Gamil's parents, Ahinadab and Nikkal, had made a covenant to wed their children to each other when they reached the proper age. The parents saw this as a means of uniting their houses in a way that was mutually advantageous to both; elevating their relationship beyond a simple business connection.

From Ahinadab's perspective this alliance would secure a rich source for future business financing. For Paltiba'al the House of Abdhamon united in marriage with the House of Dan-El would create the most powerful of all the elite houses, greater than the houses of the king and the high-priest combined. Gamil would one day inherit his parents' huge fortune and expansive network of trade and other businesses. The boy was a perfect choice for a son-in-law. There could be no better way to secure the financial future of both houses than through such a favorable marriage. It was a sound business consideration. Besides that, the four parents had been fast friends throughout their own childhood days.

As infants, Melita and Gamil were unaware of this perfectly reasonable arrangement, but as they grew older and the adults around them spoke more often of their eventual marriage, the impact of this covenant gradually worked its way into their minds. Children of the elite houses of Gebal were encouraged to play together and form friendships, so Gamil and Melita, with other children their ages, were often together.

Gamil knew Melita as the annoying younger girl who somehow always outran, out-swam and out-did him in just about everything. He developed a deep dislike toward her and was terrified at the idea of marrying her.

His dislike stemmed from the way she delighted in teasing him and the other boys; taunting them when they couldn't measure up to her superior athletic ability. She was always the first one to start the name-calling whenever Gamil came up short in a contest. Her chiding voice would lead the others in endless singsong choruses of "Gam-il the Cam-el, Gam-il the Cam-el...", until he would grow so angry that his ears turned red and his face burned with shame. His reaction always delighted Melita, prompting her to chant even louder until he reached his limit and ran away. Even then she would follow after him, continuing to chant that insulting trope.

Only once, instead of running away, he had tried to force her to stop.

He rushed at her, grabbed her around the middle and knocked her over onto the sandy beach that was their playground. They rolled around and tussled for a few seconds, with Melita laughing so hard she could barely defend herself. But soon enough she twisted free and flipped him onto his back. Then, after pinning his shoulders down she had taken a handful of sand and slowly trickled it onto his face, saying "Eat it Camel-boy! Eat!" Now he had to bear the added shame of having been out-wrestled by a girl, and one a year younger than him at that. Needless to say, he never tried that again.

From that point on he gave up any attempts to compete with her. Instead He developed a studied indifference toward her. He learned to ignore her jibes and insults and after a while she grew tired of taunting him. Failing to find any new way to get under his skin, she left him alone for the most part. Gamil could not imagine a worse fate than being married to this tormentor. Their betrothal was one thing, but a wedding seemed far off in the future, and Gamil was sure that something would happen between today and that dreaded day to save him from such a fate.

As for Melita, since she wasn't able to get Gamil's goat so easily anymore there was little fun in trying. She developed her own indifference toward him. Not that she completely stopped trying to provoke him from time to time, but these were always half-hearted attempts. She had no trouble finding other playmates and other things to do that were more enjoyable. As for marrying him? *We'll see about that!* she thought. This is how things stood between them as their childhood days passed and their teenage years came upon them.

Part of Melita's personality demanded that she be the center of attention wherever she was. Her arrogant and somewhat imperious manner with the other high-born children, and especially with her siblings kept her from forming any truly close bonds to all but a few of her peers. But she was the exact opposite with those who were her social inferiors. She always regarded them as equals, even when they obviously were not.

Her two older sisters called her "princess" and "little queen" behind her back. As the youngest child in her family, and with the gifts that she possessed, she developed an exaggerated need to control the things happening around her; especially things that directly affected her. She wasn't always successful at this, but that didn't stop her from trying, even with the adults in her life. She was certain that the marriage her father and Gamil's father had agreed on would never happen. Not if she could find any way to escape it.

Finally! The last receipt and the last of the shipping orders had been reviewed and approved by Tallayba'al. The papyrus scrolls containing the records were re-rolled and sealed, signaling that the day's business was done. Melita had been sulking on a stool beside the table that served as the overseer's desk. She perked up as her mother concluded her last instructions to Yutpan.

Yutpan was a man who began his work for Tallayba'al as a young slave, but who had earned her trust and respect for his good service. So much so that, in time, he was given his freedom. Then, by his own free choice, Yutpan, "took the ring" in his left earlobe as a sign of his willingness to continue in her service. A freedman, but one who was bound to her and to the House of Abdhamon for life.

This was done by a ritual, in which Yutpan stood before the gate of the House of Abdhamon with his mistress, Tallayba'al while the Lord Paltiba'al pierced his left earlobe with an awl, driving it through the flesh and into the gate post. A gold ring was then placed through the hole in the earlobe. Thereafter, anyone who saw that ring knew he was not just a freedman, but had been adopted into the household of his mistress and master.

A slave for fifteen years of his life, Yutpan went on to serve the

House of Abdhamon as a freedman for another fifteen years and had risen to the position of overseer of Tallayba'al's warehouse at the northern harbor of Gebal. In all those long years he had become more like a family member than a servant and like a loving uncle to Tallayba'al's children.

"*Mother*!" Melita said, pulling on Tallayba'al's sleeve, "May I please go and play now? I have been good all morning, and my friends are waiting for me by the temple gardens. *Please*, mother, please..."

"Hmmm," Tallayba'al said, pondering for a moment, "You think you have been good, eh? Honestly child, I don't think you paid the least bit of attention to anything we have done this morning. You know the reason I bring you with me on my rounds is so that you can observe and see how my business is done. You are the brightest of all my children, and I intend that you will take my place one day. That means I need you to pay close attention and learn how to run all my businesses. But all you want to do is play with your friends."

"Oh no mother," the girl replied, "I was paying attention. Really, I was! I saw how you corrected Oelah the weaver when she had the design wrong. I watched how you weighed the bolts of yard goods at the warehouse, and how you gave instructions to Yutpan about paying the workers. I think you must be the wisest and busiest woman in the entire city to keep all of this going so smoothly all the time. Please may I go?"

"Flattery," her mother said, "will not help you child! This old heart of mine is as hard as *shamir* when it comes to business, and teaching you how it is done is my most important task. But...perhaps you *were* paying some attention after all."

This last was said with a softer tone, and a slight smile played on Tallayba'al's lips. "Very well Melita, you may go and play, but stay away from the docks! I don't want you listening to those fishermen's bawdy songs! It embarrasses me to hear you waste your lovely voice by singing such trash. One would think you were a fishmonger's daughter instead of the daughter of the city's wealthiest financier."

"Oh, thank you, Mother, thank you, Melita said. "I won't go near the docks, I promise."

"Yes, yes! I have heard that promise before, and yet you still come home with new and nastier songs all the time. Go! Run along now, and be sure you are home in time for the evening meal." As she finished these last instructions, Tallayba'al was speaking to the back of Melita's head as the girl dashed out through the warehouse door and into the main street of the port district.

Tallayba'al stepped just outside the door and watched with pleasure how the long dark curls on her daughter's head bounced and flew as she ran down the street. Her eyes followed Melita's progress in the direction of the grand staircase.

The port district with its twin harbors straddled a low promontory that lay below the plateau on which the city proper stood. The staircase was the primary pathway that provided access from the sea to the city above. Five score plus seven stair steps were hewed from the limestone cliff as it climbed to the top of the plateau and entered the city through its western gate. It was a long climb, and many businesses had grown up into what had become the harbor district. This made it possible to avoid having to make that climb burdened with heavy loads unless it was absolutely necessary. All along the great quay at the northern harbor, and the lesser quay at the south harbor where the fishing boats tied up, a dozen warehouses stood, including Tallayba'al's fabric warehouse.

Melita turned the corner of the neighboring warehouse to continue toward the grand staircase. This quickly took her out of her mother's sight. Tallayba'al's pride in her daughter welled up in her heart, bringing with it a deep sigh. Of all her children this one, her youngest, gave her the most pleasure, and the most frustration.

For a moment Tallayba'al wondered if the gods had guided her choice of names, or if she had seen some glimpse of the child's future when her youngest was born. Melita. The name that could mean both the bitter *and* the sweet.

Chapter 34
Friends and Enemies

At the north beach

Melita did not look back as she left her mother in the warehouse. Stepping through the doorway and into the noonday sun her eyes adjusted quickly to the brightness of the scene around her. Already her mind had forgotten the morning's boring routine, as she noted the bustling throngs of slaves and workers that filled the Street of Warehouses. This was the main road running just above the great quay to hug the shore of the natural cove that formed the northern harbor of the city.

Seagulls soared overhead on a light, on-shore breeze that carried the tangy smells of salt and fish. Their cries seemed to echo the joy she felt as her mind shed the stifling effects of the morning's drudgery. The fragrance of the Great Sea revived all her senses and elevated her mood higher and higher. She was *free* and in control of her day! What pleasure!

Her thoughts quickly focused on finding her friends, and enjoying the games she loved to play with them. She knew they weren't really waiting for her in the temple gardens. She would find them where they always were; at the beach or down by the docks.

Of course, it was important to let her mother see her heading in the direction of the grand staircase, but she knew that rounding the corner of that warehouse would take her out of her mother's view. As soon as she could safely do so she stopped, then began walking slower, taking a side street that led past shops and houses as it curved back toward the north side of the port. She would keep her promise to stay away from the docks on the *south side*, where the fishing boats tied up, but she hadn't promised to stay away from the great quay, on the *north side*, where the large merchant ships tied up.

Despite her parent's encouragement to befriend other elite children, she had developed many friends among the children of the fishermen, and almost as many among the children of the laborers who loaded and unloaded the merchant ships. Actually, the beach to the north of the great quay was the best for swimming anyway, and after the stifling morning in her mother's warehouse, Melita fancied a swim in the cool waters of the Great Sea. Maybe she could get some of the other girls to go with her.

She reached the end of the street and could see the quay, with its wharves extending outward. A dozen ships were moored there in various stages of loading or unloading. She saw a face she recognized among the laborers. It belonged to a giant of a man who smiled and greeted her as she approached.

"Hello, Melita! May the gods bless you this day." the man said, "What brings you down here among the low-born?" His tone was light, gently mocking, and omitted the respectful phrases that were required when one of lesser status addressed one of the high-born; even the child of a high-born. But as a well-known visitor to the port, a greater degree of familiarity was permissible in her case. At least as long as she did not object, and as long as no high-born adults were present.

"Greetings Azra'al," she cheerfully answered. "I'm looking for Shema and Zephratha. Have you seen them today?" Azra'al was an overseer of slaves who worked for the shofeṭ Ahinadab,". He managed several crews of stevedores who labored at the great quay.

"Hmmm," Azra'al said, "Let me think. Have you looked over by the beach on the north side of the quay? I saw them headed that way earlier."

"Ah," said Melita, "That is right where I expected to find them. Thank you for that, Azra'al!" she said, flashing a bright smile at the man as she hurried down the street to join her friends. He sighed as he watched her go, remembering what it was like to be young and free to go wherever you wanted to, without a care in the world. *What a beautiful child*", he thought as she hurried away.

Melita quickly reached the point in the street where the sun-baked sand from the beach rose up to meet it. She stopped and put her right hand up to shade her eyes and scanned the shore for the two girls. This late in the day there were only a few people using the water and sand; some swimming or lounging, or walking along its clean, bright length. A group of boys kicked at an inflated pig's bladder, and two young men were casting nets for fish. It wasn't hard to spot her friends and soon she was running over the hot sand to where she saw them bobbing in the gentle waves.

"Zephratha! Shema!" she called out "Here I am at last!" She waved both arms over her head to catch their attention and heard them squeal with delight as they saw her on the shore.

"Melita! Come join us!" Shema said. The water is perfect for swimming today!"

Melita wasted no time in shedding the long, multi-layered, brightly colored skirt her mother had insisted she wear as they made their business rounds. "You must learn that dressing according to your station is required of you when you are responsible for such a large enterprise." Tallayba'al had said.

Next to go was the bright purple, tight-fitting, scooped-front vest, followed by the short-sleeved, sheer linen blouse that she wore under it. Melita kicked off her sandals and stood for a moment with her toes flexing in the hot sand, reveling in the feel of the sun's rays washing over her body. Then she waded out into the surf, clad only in her undergarment of white linen, which was wrapped around her hips, covering her loins and buttocks.

Like all the Kena'ani children she swam completely naked as a young child. This was perfectly acceptable for both sexes until they entered adolescence. Boys her age still swam naked, but girls were expected to behave more modestly as they passed from childhood into their early teenage years. At eleven years old Melita was beginning to show signs of the physical development that is typical for girls as they become women. But her figure was still a long way from what it would be when fully mature. Her breasts were barely starting to show and her hips were still slim and boy-like. Yet in subtle ways the early signs of change were there if you looked for them.

Melita and the other girls had been swimming together since they were six years old and were very much at home in the warm water off the beach where it was sheltered by the breakwater. They raced each other up and down along the sand, and searched the shallows for shells, starfish and other creatures that had been brought near the shore by the tides.

There was an outcropping of large rocks about four score paces offshore that they could reach by swimming or wading at low tide. Usually, after playing in the surf for a while, this was where they headed. The seaward side of the rocks offered greater seclusion than the open beach, and held some of the best tide-pools. The girls liked the privacy this afforded them while they scoured the shallow pools for small treasures the sea had given up.

The largest rock had a hollow with a large shelf at the bottom that the waves had scooped out over centuries to create a spot the girls had come to consider their own hideaway. It was an excellent place to lay out and sun themselves. In the rock's shelter they could stretch out across the wave-smoothed, sun-warmed shelf at its base and relax while talking and sharing secrets. That is exactly what they were doing as the early afternoon passed, until their privacy was unexpectedly, and quite rudely, interrupted.

Aderba'al, the son of the high priest Ili-Rapih, with two of his cronies, Bodo and Radmanu, had seen the girls swim out to the rocks from further down the beach. On a whim he decided to have some fun at the girls' expense.

The boys had been playing with a pig's bladder that they inflated and kicked back and forth in their games. Seeing the girls heading out to the rocks, they followed along, but angled toward the landward side of the big rock, and hid where they could spy on the girls without being seen. For a short while the boys listened to the girls' chatter, snickering quietly to themselves at what they heard. Then Aderba'al took the pig's bladder that he had deflated and filled it with seawater. He and his friends quietly climbed to the top of the rock, directly above where the girls lay stretched out in the sun.

The girls were unaware that they were being observed until they heard a voice calling out from above. "Ho, girls! You look like your skin is about to burn up! This will cool you off!" Aderba'al squeezed the pig's bladder hard, forcing the seawater out in a long, arching stream that sprayed down onto the backs of his three unprotected victims. The shock of the cold seawater hitting their bare, sun-warmed skin was intense, and all three jumped up immediately with shrieks of surprise mixed with shouts of anger!

"What are you doing?" Melita shouted at the three boys, as the pig's bladder emptied out and the stream slowed to a halt. The boys were laughing so hard they could hardly breathe. She stood there with water trickling down from her hair and scanned the faces of the trio of tormentors. Her surprise had quickly flashed into hot anger as she focused on Aderba'al who waved the now empty bladder at his victims. The sight of his taunting figure made Melita see red! Stooping, she quickly picked up a small smooth stone from a tide pool at the foot of the big rock, and with a perfect throw she smacked Aderba'al squarely on the nose with it.

No one was laughing now, as Aderba'al's nose began to bleed profusely. Melita bent down to pick up another stone and the other girls followed her example. Aderba'al was stunned, and dropped the bladder so he could use both hands to stem the flow of blood from his injured nose. Melita's second stone came whizzing in to strike his right shoulder hard. The other two boys had ducked down behind the top of the rock when the first stone hit its target, and now they reached up to pull their wounded leader down and out of the line of fire.

"Jackals!" Melita shouted. "What are you doing here? This is our rock and you are not permitted to come here unless we say you can. Get out of here now if you know what's good for you!" Her declaration and threats were followed by a shower of stones from the girls that arched over the top of the rock. Not many hit their unseen targets, but as all three girls scooped up handfuls of small, gravel-sized stones and hurled them up and over the top the desired effect was achieved.

Melita scaled the weathered surface of the big rock until she reached its top. She wanted to see if the boys were still there or if the bombardment had driven them off. The other two girls were still throwing stones and shouting at the boys. The noise from their catcalls and insults plus the pounding of the surf made it hard to hear, but Melita's ears could still hear Aderba'al wailing, and an occasional cry of pain from one of the two other boys as a stone found its mark.

From her position on the high ground she was able to take better aim at her targets and after a few well-placed throws she watched the three boys jump off the rock into the surf. Once they swam to a safe distance Aderba'al turned and shouted back at Melita. "You don't own that rock any more than you own the beach or the sea! You broke my nose! I owe you for this Melita. You're an ugly cow! I'll get even. Just you wait!"

"Oh, dear me! I'm so afraid!" Melita said in her most mocking tone. "Just try it, pimple-face, your nothing but a fat pig!" The other girls had worked their way around the rock to the side where the boys had been and were still throwing stones at their retreating forms. They only stopped when it was clear that the boys were out of range, and were not coming back.

"Victory!" Melita shouted, as her friends laughed and cheered. "Oh, that was fun!" Shema said. "Did you see how Aderba'al's nose was bleeding? That was a great throw, Melita."

"Yes!" Zephratha, added. "I think his eye will be black as well. But do you think he'll really try to get even, Melita?" Zephratha was timid, and more introverted than the other two girls, and threats like that made her anxious.

"He may try, but I don't care." Melita answered, "The worst he might do doesn't scare me. I'll serve him up another bloody nose and blacken both eyes if he doesn't behave himself. Come on, I'm tired of laying around. Let's go for a swim, and then I want to go over to the wharfs where the big ships tie up. There are more tide-pools there and that's where the best shells are found. Maybe we can find some to trade at the market."

With that she jumped off the rock and swam a short distance before turning to watch the other two girls follow her into the water. Together they swam a short race up, then down, the beach. Melita, as always, won, but she had to work especially hard to beat Shema today. Shema was becoming a strong swimmer, and was like a fish in the water.

After the race, the girls ran up onto the beach and rested a few moments to catch their breath. The muscles in their arms and legs were heavy from all the exercise and they stretched out on the soft sand to recover.

The sun was going lower in the sky, and Melita realized she hadn't eaten anything since early that morning. She thought maybe they should leave the beach and go a few streets up to the Street of the Rope Makers, where she knew there were vendors selling all kinds of delicious food to the men who worked at the docks. Just thinking about food made her stomach rumble.

"Come on girls!" Melita said, "Lets rinse off this sand and go get something to eat. I will pay for everything today." She jumped up and led the way to the water where they all waded in, splashing each other to remove the sand from their bodies. They continued to wade along the shore, parallel to the beach to where the great quay began.

Melita retrieved her dress, vest, blouse and sandals when they reached the place where she had left them. She didn't want to put on the skirt over her wet undergarment, so she tied it around her waist and tucked the vest, blouse and her sandals into it as well. She was about to turn and leave the beach when she heard Shema calling from the water's edge.

"Melita, Zephratha!" Shema cried, "Look at this!" She was standing beside a small tide-pool and pointing at something in the water. "What is this creature?"

The other two girls quickly joined her and were amazed at what they saw. There, inside the shallow pool, a large mollusk with a bright red, almost scarlet, shell, was twisting and turning on top of a large clam. The clam's shell was tightly closed, but the girls saw that the mollusk was biting into the outer edge of the clam's shell with a hard, beak-like lip. A half dozen particles of clam shell littered the bottom of the pool, and it looked like the mollusk would break through to the soft animal inside at any minute.

"That red one is called the *Trumpet of Yam*." Melita exclaimed excitedly as she invoked the name of the god who reigned over the sea. "Those have great value! That is what the cloth dyers use to make their red, purple and dark blue dyes.

"Let's grab it. We can take it to the dyer's street and sell it." said Shema.

"I have a better idea!" Melita said. "Let's take it to old Aqhat, the vendor who sells roasted snails on sticks up by the docks. We can trade it for some of his tasty treats. That way I won't have to pay him anything." Melita never left her home without at least two or three copper rings that she wore around her upper arms. These rings were used as a type of money, and could be traded whole or broken into pieces to pay for just about anything that was for sale in Gebal.

"But isn't it worth more than a mouthful or two of his dried-up snail meats?" Shema replied. "I think we should sell it. Then we could buy something nice at the market."

"Shema found it," added Zephratha, "so she should be the one who gets to choose what we do with it. That's only fair."

"Oh, do you think so?" Melita said, "Then she must catch it and carry it to the dyers. Go ahead, Shema. Pick it up."

"Eeeww, no, no, no!" Shema declined. "Snails are slimy, and it might bite me. I can't touch it. I shudder to even think about it."

"Zephratha! You do it." Melita commanded. "You're not afraid, are you?"

Zephratha's reply was to lean down and grab the mollusk by its seven-spiraled shell. She pulled, but as soon as the creature felt her hand begin to tug, it gripped the clamshell tighter and held on for dear life. The hunter sensed that it had now become the hunted, and it squirted out a small amount of dark purple fluid that floated in the tide-pool like an evil cloud. Zephratha had not expected that. She let go of the bright red shell with a shriek and jerked her hand back as if she had touched something hot.

Shema shrieked too, caught up by Zephratha's fearful reaction. Only Melita was able to maintain her composure. She reached down into the inky cloud and grabbed onto the creature's shell, giving it a twist while pulling with a slow, steady pressure. The mollusk sensed that it was now under a serious attack, so it let go its grip on the clam and withdrew into is shell completely. Melita's hand came up out of the water holding the bright red shell and waved it triumphantly in her friend's faces.

"So," she said, "since I was the one to catch it, I get to choose what we do with it, and I say we are going to take it to Aqhat!" With those words she turned and marched across the beach to the street above with her friends following. They walked briskly down the street to the quay where the merchant ships tied up. Her friends were still not certain that Melita was being fair, but they continued to follow her, half out of curiosity and half because they were hungry too. They wanted to see what old Aqhat would offer them for their find.

Aqhat was, at that moment, working the far end of the quay and had just sold two of his skewered delicacies to a couple of stevedores when the girls approached. He plied his trade from the back of a small, two-wheeled cart that he pulled from place to place.

Along with other supplies and cooking utensils the cart held a small terracotta oven, in which Aqhat kept a low charcoal fire burning. The oven was open on top and had a fluted edge molded into the clay. He toasted his skewered snails by laying the sticks they were impaled on across the fluted opening of the oven, turning them frequently and basting them with a mixture of olive oil and garlic until they were crispy and brown all over.

"Hello, Aqhat." Melita said in greeting, "The blessings of Our Lady be upon you."

"And upon you as well, little one," the old man replied. "What brings you three so far from the beach? As if I didn't know." He smiled at the girls as he said this, for he knew well their fondness for his cooking. Aqhat was a kindly man, who had known the girls from their earliest childhood days. He often gave Shema and Zephratha small samples of his wares, knowing that their father and mother had limited means and could not spare the girls the small amount of copper or silver that would cover the cost of his delicacies. As for Melita, she also loved Aqhat's wares. But he knew she was high-born and could afford to buy whatever she wanted or needed. With her, he usually dealt in hard metal, though his soft heart could be relied on to offer her a bargain. In return, Melita made sure he got the better of the bargain, knowing how hard he worked to make his meager living. She was quite fond of him too.

Melita got right to business. "If you're thinking we are hungry, you are correct!" she said. "I have something I'd like to trade for our lunches." She held out her hand and showed him the mollusk. Aqhat's eyes lit up as he beheld her small treasure. He noted its bright red shell, and knew at once that what she had was easily worth more than he normally earned in a week. Melita knew it too, but pretended it was nothing special. *"Today,"* she thought, *"it is my turn to do him a kindness."*

"Ah, you have a red triton, one of Yam's trumpets still in its shell. Where did you get it, and when was it last in the water?" He knew that a live triton was worth more than a dead one. With live ones the dyers could extract more of the purple fluid from their glands, keeping them alive in pools of seawater so they could secrete more of their ink. With the dead ones you could only extract the fluid their bodies retained, along with some additional color that could be leached out of their crushed shells.

"I just caught it a few minutes ago, in the tide-pool at the other end of the quay." She answered.

"Really," Aqhat replied, his interest growing stronger. "Are there any more? These red ones are really rare this far north. Around here we usually see only the black banded tritons. You are very lucky!"

"I'm the one who found it." Shema said indignantly. "But I couldn't catch it."

"Then you are a very lucky girl as well," Aqhat said. "First for making such a find, and second for having such a good friend as Melita to catch it for you." Aqhat knew that if Azra'al's daughters weren't befriended by a high-born girl like Melita, they likely would have gone hungry until their evening meal. Melita always paid for their lunches and hers when they were together. He would weigh her copper rings and smaller bits and pieces in a set of scales he carried in his cart, and when the weight was right, he would serve up their choices from his limited menu. Today, he knew that she could buy his entire stock of food and the cart too, for the triton was easily worth more than all of it.

"So, what will you ladies have today." he asked.

"I think we will each have two skewers and two slices of your fresh wheaten bread—not the day-old kind, and not that oat bread either—with olive oil to dip it in and one red apple apiece." Melita told him.

"My, oh my! You must be hungry to order so much!" Aqhat said, "I have pomegranate juice as well, if you are thirsty." He suggested.

"Yes, that would be nice," Melita replied. Aqhat pulled a large loaf of the wheaten bread from his cart and sliced off the six pieces for the girls. He took the skewered snails off the fire and laid them on top of the bread. Then he poured olive oil into a small bowl for them to share. He handed out the bread and skewers to the girls, then selected three small red apples from a sack of fruits and gave them to Melita. Next, he poured three small ceramic cups full of pomegranate juice and, since their hands were full, he set them on a side board of his cart, along with their olive oil.

"Is everything as you wish?" Aqhat asked Melita.

"Yes, thank you, Aqhat." She handed him the triton in payment. He bowed to her and turned to place the mollusk in a *situla*, or bucket, of seawater at the side of his cart to keep it alive until his young customers finished eating. Then he could take the mollusk up to the street of the dye makers.

The girls sat down on the low wooden curb of the quay, beside the cart and ate their meal. Despite the disparaging remarks Zephratha had made about the "...dried up snail meat," the skewered treats were really very tasty; lightly roasted on the outside and moist and flavorful inside. They were devoured rapidly. The bread went just as fast, with the girls licking their fingers as the olive oil dripped onto their hands between bites. Melita handed out the apples and these were soon stripped down to their cores. They finished up with the pomegranate juice and returned the empty cups and bowl to Aqhat, bowing to him and he to them.

Feeling very satisfied now, the girls were ready to run off and return to their play. Aqhat thanked them as they departed, then hastily extinguished his fire by dumping the oven's coals over the side of the quay into the water. He quickly closed up his cart and, lifting it by its handles, he began to pull it away from the quay, heading as fast as he could go toward the street of the dye makers. There he would turn the triton into silver. Then he would be able to go home to his wife early, with his work finished for this day thanks to the generosity of Melita. He silently offered up a prayer to the gods, thanking them for his good fortune and invoking their blessing on Melita and her friends.

Chapter 35
Melita's Hopes

The afternoon turned into early evening, and Zephratha and Shema headed home to help their mother prepare the evening meal. Melita knew she would soon have to leave as well. But she was reluctant to leave the beach just yet. It was always good to be away from her older sisters, her brother, and her mother's watchful eye, and she enjoyed being by herself. The food she had eaten earlier killed her appetite, so she wasn't thinking about eating again.

The sun was starting to set while she sat on the beach, thinking about the way this day had gone. She pondered her mother's intention to turn the fabric business over to her one day. She wasn't sure she like the idea very much. It seemed like such an endless bore, with day after day of checking and rechecking the records and invoices and all of that. She dreamed of a more exciting future.

A year earlier, a troupe of acrobats had come to Gebal from the city of Ugarit. They were from the city of Knossos on the island of Kaptara, but had journeyed from city to city around the eastern shores and islands of the Great Sea performing feats of strength and skill, and doing things that seemed impossible to Melita.

Most excited to her was a very thrilling and dangerous exhibition performed inside a stockade of stout poles erected on flat, sandy ground near the beach. A huge bull with long, curving horns, was brought into the fenced area and the acrobats, both young men and young women, took turns provoking the bull into charging at them!

To everyone's amazement, instead of running away the acrobats would run directly at the charging beast, grasping the ends of its horns and vaulting onto its back; somersaulting along its spine to land on their feet in the sand behind it. Sometimes the bull would jerk its head upward and the one grasping its horns would be tossed high in the air, seeming to fly end-over-end in a high arch. Melita was astonished to see that, no matter how high they flew, they always landed lightly on their feet.

Since that day, Melita had wondered what it felt like to fly through the air the way they did. What a thrill it would be to face a rampaging bull like the girls and boys of Kaptara. They were fearless and everyone admired them, cheering their exploits and showering them with silver and even gold pieces when the bull finally gave up trying to gore and crush his tormentors. The people of Gebal were still talking about them weeks after the troupe had left. These bull jumpers were heroes in everyone's eyes, and Melita wished that their sport would become one of Gebal's permanent entertainments. But more than anything else in the world, she wished that she could be one of them.

Thinking of all this, she stood up on the sand, dropped her clothes and took a running start, then twisted her body into a cartwheel that ended in a somersault that brought her to a perfect landing on her feet. Three times she did this same maneuver until she was satisfied that she could match whatever the bull leapers had done. *"Well…probably,"* she thought. After all, she didn't have a bull, or even a calf, to practice on. But still, in her mind she could believe herself able to do anything she set her heart on.

Maybe, when she was older and could start a business of her own, she just might be the one to bring this sport to Gebal on a permanent basis. Instead of a temporary stockade of wood she would build an arena of stone, where other sports and contests could be held as well. The more she thought about it, the more she liked this idea.

But, while she yearned for these things, the practical part of her mind knew that her parents would never allow her to deviate from their plans for her. In fact, she suddenly remembered, they had even planned whom she would marry! That thought completely ruined her mood.

If they had their way, she would marry Gamil in a few years, and would inherit her mother's fabric businesses. Her only brother should inherit his father's financial empire, but sadly lacked the mind for it. Father had tried to teach him, but even the basics were beyond his only son's grasp. Her brother would become a priest of the god Adon, instead.

Her sisters would marry into other elite families. Generous dowries would allow them to start their own new businesses. Melita knew her parent's plans were wise, but the idea of her marrying "Gamil-the-Camel". *Really?*

Gamil seemed entirely unsuitable in her young mind, and her heart sank at the thought of going through life yoked to such a fool. On the other hand, Gamil *would* inherit his father's wealth, his fleet of ships, and trading businesses. It was certain that she and Gamil would stand tall in the highest circle of Gebal society. He would join the council of elders, and in time he might even be elected by the citizens to serve the city as a shofeṭ like his father before him. She pondered that thought and reconsidered it. He was probably too big a fool for that. But whatever the future held; she was certain that it would include enough wealth to provide funds for building her arena and other plans.

The kind of wealth that would be required to make her dream a reality would never come from the looms of her mother's fabric business alone. But if she married Gamil she wouldn't need her mother's business. Let one of her older sisters have it.

Surely, she could control the kind of weak husband Gamil would be, and his wealth would be hers to use as she saw fit. She definitely could see the benefit of such a future. Anyway, who knew what the gods might decree. Perhaps with her ambition to push him, Gamil would rise higher than shofeṭ, and be chosen one day to serve as king! As his wife she would be at his side and rise along with him, however high that might be. The thought pleased her greatly.

If Gamil did become king one day, the possibilities would be very interesting.

Yet even as these new thoughts entered her head, something told Melita that she was being too hard on Gamil. She couldn't quite put her finger on it, but there was something about him beyond his family's wealth and status that made her want to be around him. She couldn't accept that she might be attracted to him, but something about him was drawing her to him. She thought it might be that he was such an easy target for her teasing, or maybe she was just curious about how far she could go before his feigned indifference to her jibes cracked. Or was it something more?

Her thoughts turned to Gamil's appearance. She pictured him in her mind as he looked when she last saw him. She remembered his youthful frame with its slim, straight arms and legs. A good runner's build, but not up to her level. His feet were long and narrow, with well-formed toes; a little too large perhaps, but he would grow into them, wouldn't he?

He was shorter than her by half a head, even though he was a year older. Was she just tall for her years, or was he undersized for his? His parents were certainly tall enough, both being better than average height. She wouldn't like it if she had to look down on him all their lives.

He had no unpleasant blemishes or moles, no warts or imperfections of the skin that she had noticed, except a few spots of acne. Overall his skin was a pleasing shade of tawny amber that shown like polished bronze when exposed long enough to the sun's rays. Not as dark as his father, more like his mother. All of these things made for a not unpleasing total appearance.

As she dwelt on all this, his face came to mind. His features were well-formed, and still softened by youth. He had a strong chin, wide cheek bones and a prominent but narrow nose. His lips were full and firm, framing a mouth that was perhaps a little wide. His teeth were like the whitest ivory, with those on the lower jaw being just a little crooked. That slight imperfection gave his smile a charming quality that would have been missing if they were straighter. Too bad he seldom smiled at her. Her fault perhaps, she admitted to herself.

His cheeks and jaw were graced with a downy fur that held the promise of the beard he would have in time, and his hair was dark and always well curled, tied back and hanging to his shoulders. She recalled its fragrance when freshly anointed with scented oils that made it glisten in the sun.

But perhaps his best features were his eyes. Dark brown, almost black. Not unlike her own. But his were like the well of Ba'alat Gebal, deep and unfathomable. The well was the source of the city's water, and therefore of its life. Is that what she saw in his eyes? Life, or just a life. Thinking of this she realized that those eyes were the thing about him that drew her. But why? And for what?

She shook her head to clear it of this strangely disturbing notion. Her thoughts had stirred up a new awareness of Gamil. What was that about? When did she ever take such detailed notice of him? Some undefinable, but disquieting favorable, new feeling was emerging that was completely at odds with her former judgment of him. It confused her greatly.

Chapter 36
Barakba'al's Revenge

At the wharf of the Dan-El fleet in the northern harbor

The sun was almost down now, and twilight was falling upon the city as Melita snapped out of her musing. With a start, she realized she would have to run home quickly to be in time for dinner. Mother would be furious at her! *"A lady must always be punctual, Melita!"* She could hear Tallayba'al's voice scolding her. That was not the way she wanted this day to end.

The sun slipped below the western horizon, and she rose off the beach; quickly slipping back into her skirt, blouse, and vest. As she stepped into her sandals she was already moving from the beach. She reached the road above the quay and started to run along it, passing the end of the first wharf where the trading ships were berthed.

But passing one of the larger ships, she saw something that made her slow down and even halt in her tracks. A tiny moving light had caught her eye and she saw two dark figures silhouetted against the rapidly fading light as they stealthily climbed aboard the ship. One was carrying a small oil lamp with a single flaming wick and a large situla. The burning wick is what had caught her eye. The other, a tall man who looked around nervously, held a naked bronze sword in his hand. Both clearly showed by their behavior that they were up to no good.

Melita crept nearer and hid in the shadow of the ship. She heard the sound of liquid splashing and smelled the pungent odor of turpentine. Then, to her horror, flames burst out above the deck of the ship and quickly spread to the mast and side boards. The two men had started a fire! They ran to the side and jumped from the deck to the wharf. They rushed toward the quay to make their get-away, but stopped when they spotted Melita. The shadows were gone and she stood there in the light of the growing flames. The larger man with the sword in his hand, looked hard at her and quickly checked to see if she was alone. Seeing no one else, his wary look gave way to a malignant grin as he started toward her. She immediately saw the danger she was in. Clearly this man couldn't leave her alive after what she had witnessed.

She turned and ran as fast as she could into the darkened streets of the harbor district. The man with the sword chased after her. She looked back and saw that he was gaining on her rapidly. As fast as she was, she knew she couldn't outrun him for long. She had to find another way to escape.

Melita dodged into the first alleyway she came to and found herself in a familiar narrow passage in a poorly laid out section of the district. The passage zig-zagged around buildings, narrowing even more due to piles of refuse, cast-off furniture, and other debris. Her nimbleness and knowledge of the area gave her an advantage. She scrambled quickly past the clutter and put a little more space between herself and her pursuer. She knew exactly where she was despite the darkness, having often played hounds-and-hunted with friends in this neighborhood. Even in darkness she had no trouble finding her way.

Knowing the passage would come to a dead end a shortly, Melita darted to her right, into a gap between two houses. She knew this was a shortcut into the Street of the Fishmongers. From there she could reach the grand staircase. But in the gloom, she didn't see an upturned cart in her path, with a broken axle sticking out. She managed to dodge it, but her skirt caught on the axle and a large piece of it was ripped loose. With no time to lose, she ran on, leaving the torn cloth hanging there like a flag.

On the Street of the Fishmongers she turned toward the grand staircase and ran past shops that were closed and shut up for the night. There was no chance of finding shelter or anyone who might help her. She was about fifty paces away from where she entered the street when her pursuer burst from the alleyway and started after her. He had passed her turn and didn't realize his mistake until he reached the dead end. He knew she must have turned somewhere and retraced his steps, looking for where she left the alleyway.

At the gap between the two houses he saw the torn cloth from her skirt hanging on the cart's axle. The blaze at the harbor was growing and threw just enough light for him to recognize the piece of her skirt, and expose her escape route. He entered the gap between the houses, avoided the cart, and hurried after her. As he emerged into the Street of the Fishmongers, he heard Melita's sandaled footfalls ahead of him and rushed in her direction.

The night sky above the houses, shops and other buildings was aglow with the light of a false dawn. The fire had spread quickly to engulf other ships, and they were burning furiously. The quay was made of huge stone blocks, but decked with a curbed boardwalk of wood, and covered by a thick coating of hardened pitch. The wharves were built completely of wood with the same overall coating of hardened pitch. All of this, and the berthed ships, made excellent fuel for the blaze. The flames quickly jumped from one wharf to another, and from ship to ship, until almost the entire harbor was an alight.

The night watch of the city guard took notice and sounded trumpets of alarm. The citizens living closest to the harbor were rushing to the harbor, where the conflagration was beginning to spread to the buildings along the quay. Several warehouses were already burning. There was little that anyone could do.

The city guard organizing the people into long chains from the water to the forward edge of the fire. Smoke and burning ash filled the air as the people passed situlas and other vessels filled with seawater from hand-to-hand. Those closest to the fire pitched the water onto the fires while others beat back the flames with lengths of water-soaked canvas. These desperate efforts to keep the fire from spreading began to take effect, as men and women from all parts of the city joined battle.

Moments after the first alarms the people of Gebal began to respond. The deserted streets were filled with men and women hurrying to the harbor district. The growing crowds were an advantage to Melita. She dodged between people, using them to shield her from her pursuer's view. She was hoping to find a city guard or an adult to protect her. But all the guards were too busy fighting the fire to pay her any heed, and everyone's attention was fixed on getting to the harbor. Moving along the street was like swimming against a strong tide. Melita had to slow her pace to avoid being knocked to the ground. She had completely lost track of her pursuer, and hoped that he had lost sight of her as well. Taking no chances, she kept moving as fast as she could, until she turned a corner onto the Street of the Rope Makers and headed toward the foot of the grand staircase.

Few people were in this street and she was able to start running again. She looked back over her shoulder to check for her pursuer, but didn't see him. She almost reached the first steps of the staircase, and hoped the big man had lost her at last. However, she did not see the small, dark figure that came out of an alleyway directly in her path.

The second man who helped set the fire had guessed that she would try to escape up the grand staircase, and managed to get there ahead of Melita as she maneuvered to escape from the man with the sword. She reached the alleyway the second man was hiding in and he knocked her off her feet, pinning her body to the rough paving stones with a knee in her back. He grabbed her by the hair with one hand, jerking her head back and clamping his other hand over her mouth before she could scream for help.

"Don't make a sound, if you want to live!" the man hissed in her ear. She was completely at his mercy and so terrified at what was happening that she could do nothing. His hands were filthy, calloused and work-roughened as he jerked her to her feet. He glanced up and down the street and pulled her back into the alleyway. There in the dark he pressed her up against a wall of a shop and ran his hands all over her body, feeling for any weapons she might have. Finding her unarmed, he let out a low, animal-like laugh, saying, "Thought you could get away, did you? Well, the gods weren't looking after you today, little one. Too bad you had to see that bit of business at the wharf."

At that moment the large man with the sword came running up to the bottom of the staircase. He looked up, expecting to see her fleeing up the stairs. He cursed when he didn't see her and wondered where she had gone. "Down here master," his partner called softly. "I've caught the little gutter rat for you!"

Her captor's "master" had put away his sword as the streets began to fill with people. An armed man running around would have been noticed and this was no time to be calling attention to himself. He had placed it back in its scabbard and kept it concealed inside his cloak as he followed the girl through the crowd. He lost sight of her briefly, but glimpsed her out of the corner of his eye as she broke from the crowd to dart into the Street of the Rope Makers. He pushed his way through the mass of panicky citizens as quickly as he could, but would have still been far behind her if his partner hadn't intercepted her.

The big man's face took on its wicked grin once more as he stepped into the alleyway and drew his sword from its scabbard. Light from the fire reflected off the adjacent buildings, providing a weak and flickering illumination. Melita's eyes grew wide as she saw the edge of his sword gleam in the dim light. It was clear that her life was in danger!

The man holding her had a sailor's knife pressed tightly against Melita's throat. "Let me do the honor, master!" he said. He held her pinned against the wall with his body, and she could feel his hot breath on her face. It stank of garlic, garum sauce, fish and rotten teeth. She almost gagged from the stench. But the knife at her throat kept her immobile.

"Shall we have some fun with her before I cut her throat, master? You can go first if you like." With his body pinning hers to the wall she could feel something hard between his legs that pressed against her stomach.

"Keep your voice down, fool!." the Master hissed, "There's no time for that. Besides, she is high-born. Can't you see from her clothes? Tell me whose brat you are, girl!"

Melita was too terrified to cry out for help, but when she heard this question, she thought there might be some hope. Perhaps these men would let her go if they knew who her parents were.

"My name is Melita," she said, "daughter of the ba'alat Tallayba'al and my father is the lord Paltiba'al of the House of Abdhamon!" As she spoke their names her voice held an air of confidence, courage, and an undertone of arrogance. "How dare you treat me like this?" she demanded.

"Paltiba'al!" the large man shouted, forgetting the need to keep his voice down. "Paltiba'al, the high and mighty financier? How excellent is that?"

Although Melita didn't know him, this man was the master mariner Barakba'al, who had that same morning been judged by the lady Nikkal in the house of Dan-El and dismissed for his corrupt dealings.

"Paltiba'al", he thought, *"the swine who stood there silently while I was stripped of my commission, and cast out into the street."*

"Paltiba'al who is one of the richest men in Gebal? Is that the man you call your father?"

"Yes, and you would be wise to let me go and flee as fast as you can, because when he finds out what you have done, and how you have treated me, he will have you beaten, and sold into slavery." Melita almost shouted at her tormentor. Her voice grew louder with each word. "Or perhaps he will have you dragged before the court of the Shofeṭim and you will face the judgment of the entire city. You'll be lucky if they execute you quickly!"

"Ha!" the master replied. "If you really are his brat, I am sure he will pay a princely sum to have you back, safe and sound in his fancy house." Turning to his henchman he said, "Tie her up and gag her. We will keep her until her father pays for her return. Or maybe we'll sell her back to him in pieces!"

The sailor reluctantly eased his body away from the girl and was spinning her around to bind her arms when a voice came echoing down the alleyway, "You two there, what are you doing?" It was one of the city guardsmen who had been sent to round up more men to help fight the fire. He heard Melita's voice and followed it to the alleyway.

"Stop what you're doing and get down to the harbor at once. Don't you know there is a raging fire there. Every man is needed to help fight it."

The guardsman stepped into the alleyway to goad the men on, and his eyes grew wide when he saw the child they were accosting. "What is this? "What are you do..."

His words were cut off as Barakba'al's razor-sharp sword was shoved deep into his stomach. The guardsman's leather armor was no match for the keen-edged blade. The full force of the tall man's strong right arm could have penetrated even a breastplate of bronze. He twisted his sword free and pulled back for another thrust, angled this time for the guardsman's heart.

The smaller man took his eyes off his captive to watch his master's sword-work play out. Melita spun back around and brought her knee up into her captor's groin as hard as she could. With a cry, he let go of her and grabbed his loins, doubled up in pain. she bolted from the alleyway and ran down the street, away from the grand staircase, screaming at the top of her voice.

Pulling his sword free of the guardsman's dead body, Barakba'al saw the girl escape and started after her, but quickly realized that he had blood on his hands up to his elbows and there was no way that would go unnoticed. They needed to get away. Fast!

He ducked back into the alleyway, bent over the corpse and wiped his sword clean on the dead man's cloak. Thrusting it back in its scabbard, he helped his companion to his feet and led him, hobbling, through the alleyway until they came out on the Street of the Tanners. They followed it down to the beach where they had hidden a small boat earlier. In this way the pair had planned to escape from the stricken harbor after setting the fire, but the light and all the activity of the citizens fighting the inferno made it impossible to reach their craft.

The south harbor had not been affected by the fire, so they abandoned their plan and moved clear of the north harbor. Above the high tide mark, they found a small fishing boat laying upside down on the beach. They turned the boat over and dragged it into the water. They manned the oars and rowed hard through the gap in the breakwater and headed south along the coast to disappear on the night-darkened sea.

Melita ran back to the Street of the Fishmongers, still screaming. Two women who were exiting their shop heard her cries and called out to her. She ran to them and threw herself into their arms. They took her inside their shop and barred the door.

"What is the matter child?" one of the women asked, holding Melita tightly to calm and comfort her. Her partner re-lit a small oil lamp that cast a weak light over baskets of salted, dried fish that filled the shop's interior. Catching her breath between sobs and collecting her strength, Melita told the ladies what had happened. Once she started her words tumbled forth in a torrent. She told them what she had seen at the harbor, how the two men had chased and caught her, what they tried to do to her, and how they had killed the guardsman. Hearing all this, the women were shocked, but quickly decided that one should stay at the shop with Melita, while the other went to summon help from the House of Abdhamon.

Reaching that noble house, the woman spoke to the guards at the gate and explained the situation. She was shown in to where Tallayba'al was organizing the household servants. Paltiba'al had taken half his household guards and a dozen servants down to the harbor after the first alarms, leaving his wife with the rest.

Tallayba'al reacted to the news of her daughter's peril the way a mother bear reacts when her cubs are threatened. She immediately took six of the remaining household guards and rushed down to the fishmongers' shop.

Tallayba'al's eyes radiated the rage in her heart as she crossed the shop's threshold, and scanned the room for her daughter. She carried a large cudgel and looked ready to do battle with anyone who might dare come between her and her child. She spotted Melita in the arms of the shop owner at the same time Melita saw her enter the room. They rushed together, with tears of relief and deep emotion.

Tallayba'al's fierce expression changed immediately to one of tender concern, as she looked her daughter over from head to toe, noting her torn skirt and the numerous small scrapes and bruises from her encounter with the two men. All things considered, Melita had come away with relatively minor injuries; the worst being from her fall in the street when the smaller man had tripped and held her down.

Yet even such minor hurts caused Tallayba'al to act as if the girl had lost a limb instead of just a little skin. She was cooing and clucking like a mother hen over her injured chick. She clutched her daughter to her bosom and gave thanks to the gods. Melita's last reserves of courage and strength melted away in her mother's arms and she began to weep uncontrollably, her whole body wracked with sobs and shaking from released tension.

Slowly and gently her mother was able to coax Melita into sharing what had happened. Her anger rose again as she learned the full story. She was outraged and loudly demanded that the gods take revenge on these men who dared to lay hands on her daughter. At the same time, she knew how urgent it was to get Melita home where she could be properly tended to and recover from her ordeal.

She sent word for her servants to bring a covered litter to bear Melita home. Waiting for it to arrive, she spoke to the two women who owned the fish shop, repeatedly thanking them for rescuing her daughter, and insisting that they must call upon her at the House of Abdhamon in a few days. She wanted to see to it that they were properly thanked and appropriately rewarded for rescuing and protecting Melita.

The women protested that they had done no more than any decent person would, but Tallayba'al would not hear of it. They simply must call on her, and she would not accept their denials. She didn't tell them at that moment, but as a reward, theirs was to be the only shop that would supply fish for the House of Abdhamon for the next five years, and they would be paid the best prices for whatever they provided.

When the litter arrived, Melita was carefully placed in it and the slaves set off with her, led by Tallayba'al and surrounded by four of the five household guards. The fifth had been sent to find Zimredda, the guards' commander, to report the murder of his guardsman and the circumstances involved. There was little that Zimredda could do for the moment, with all his guardsmen busy fighting the fire. But he himself took two men with him to the scene of the murder, where they saw there was no way to track the murderers down.

When Melita's litter arrived at the house, all of the remaining servants met her at the gates. They rushed to her and gently carried her inside. Tallayba'al's own handmaids led the girl into the bath chamber, where she was undressed and bathed thoroughly. Her disheveled hair was washed with fragrant soaps and brushed out with perfumed oil, after which her braids were redone. Ointments were applied to her injuries and the worst of these were bandaged with strips of clean linen. She was dressed in a silk sleeping tunic from her mother's own wardrobe and gently put to bed.

She was completely exhausted from the events of the day and every muscle in her body ached. But in spite of all that, Melita could not fall asleep. She kept thinking about the men who had tried to kill or abduct her and how close they came to succeeding. If only she hadn't stayed so long at the beach, she might never have seen them. If she hadn't been so distracted by her thoughts of Gamil she wouldn't have lost track of the time. This was all his fault! That awful boy! She couldn't even remember what had been going on in her mind. What had she been thinking?

She tossed about in her bed trying to find a more comfortable position, but no matter how she lay she found no relief. At last, exhaustion won out over her pain and unsettled mind. She fell asleep with the walls of her bed chamber glowing in the reflected light of the fire raging at the harbor and with the smell of smoke hanging in the air. She dreamed then of a pair of dark, unfathomable eyes. Gamil's eyes.

Chapter 37
After the Fire

In the harbor district

The fire raged for three days while the people prayed and fought the flames until they were exhausted. The priests offered sacrifices, cut themselves with knives, tore their robes, and cried out to Yam-Nahar for mercy. Their prayers were answered, or so it seemed, on the fourth day. A series of storms blew in from the Great Sea, bringing heavy rains that stopped the fire's spread. A day later the last remaining hot spots were finally extinguished. Soot and ashes were everywhere and on everything, especially in the northern quarter. The smell of smoke lingered throughout the city.

The priests claimed full credit for saving the city from further destruction, but almost everyone was skeptical. Most believed the fire was a result of Barakba'al's curse, and some even claimed to have seen a thunderbolt streaking from the sky to strike the *Cabax* to start the fire. Most thought it unlikely that the god was finished with the House of Dan-El. Three ships of the Dan-El fleet had been the first to burn, and the Dan-El wharves and warehouses were the first to be destroyed, but other parts of the curse remained to be fulfilled.

Rumors of more disaster to come spread almost as fast as the fire had. Only a very few knew the real cause of the fire.

The *Cabax* had been berthed at the landward end of the Dan-El wharf, next to the great quay, and the fire quickly spread from there all along the quay, blocking access to the other wharves. The moored ships could only be reached by water and in the frantic first hour, as flames spread ship-to-ship, brave crewmen and sailors had risked their lives; swimming around and beyond the flames to reach their vessels. Once aboard, these brave men raced to cut the mooring lines and move their ships out of harm's way. But there simply wasn't enough room to maneuver safely.

In the complete chaos that followed, a number of ships collided. Some received only minor damage and managed to clear the jetty and get away. Half a dozen others had run aground or were deliberately beached. Ships with serious damage barely stayed afloat. These and the ships that had run aground would not sail again without extensive repairs.

The ships that couldn't escape were trapped at their berths. Many were scarred by the fire, and others had burned to their waterlines. The remains of their hulls settled to the bottom, effectively blocking the north harbor until all of the wreckage could be cleared and the facilities rebuilt.

Fortunately, the nightly offshore winds were enough to keep the fire away from the southern harbor and it remained open. For the next year or more its limited capacity would have to serve ships from the northern routes along with the fishing fleets.

The losses were even more devastating along the shoreline, where the fire had gutted the heart of the harbor district. Close to a hundred buildings, shops, and warehouses had been damaged or completely destroyed. Here and there, the ruined walls of stone buildings remained as hollow shells, stripped of their roofing, wooden beams, flooring, doors and anything else that could burn. The goods contained in these buildings were completely destroyed. The combined value of these lost goods was astronomical. No one could calculate the total, and many merchants and investors were completely wiped out. It would be years before the city's economic base fully recovered.

The warehouse Melita had visited with her mother the morning before the fire was gone. The racks, bins, and shelves that had held scores of thick bolts of colored cloth and sacks stuffed with untreated wool had been reduced to blackened, rain-soaked ashes.

Fortunately, the loss of life was minimal for a disaster of this magnitude. Apart from the murdered guardsman just four men had died from burns or smoke inhalation while fighting the fire. Three more were killed in the process of moving their ships away from the fire. Dozens of others had been injured. Some had burns, some had cuts or broken bones, and one man was recovering from nearly drowning. Nearly a hundred others suffered various, less serious harm while attempting to save as much of their merchandise, property, and valuables as they could.

Those most severely injured were taken to the temple of Eshmun, the god of healing, where they were tended by the priests and their acolytes. Most of these would recover over time, though their lives would be forever changed. Some would lose limbs, some would bear deep burn scars, and others would be crippled. A few would linger near death before finally succumbing to their injuries or to infections.

One who died from burns was Yutpan, the overseer of Tallayba'al's fabric warehouse. He had been found, barely alive, in the courtyard behind the warehouse, next to a half-loaded oxcart. His sense of duty would not let him abandon the goods and records that had been entrusted to him. As the fire approached, he tried to save as many of the papyrus scrolls and records of his mistress' enterprise as possible. He succeeded in rescuing most of these and was trying to save some of the most expensive bolts of cloth. But as flames were consuming the warehouse, a section of the back wall had collapsed on him. Some of those fighting the fire saw this happen and beat back the flames to pull him out of the rubble. Yutpan languished in the temple of Eshmun for three days, but despite the priests' best efforts, he died. His skin was blistered or burned completely off in places and his lungs had been seared beyond recovery.

When first told of his injuries Tallayba'al and Paltiba'al acted swiftly to invoke the aid of the gods on his behalf. Gifts were brought to his caregivers at the temple of Eshmun, and a votive stela was inscribed and raised within the temple precinct. They hoped these measures would move the god to heal their servant. Other sacrifices were made to all the gods and goddesses of the city. Everything that could be done was made to happen for Yutpan.

When word of his death came their grief was immense. "Yutpan was in our service for twenty and ten years" Paltiba'al said with a heavy heart, "and was always an honest and faithful servant. We will not find another like him. He gave his life to us and suffered death for us."

"He left behind a widow and two adult sons, who are also in service to the House of Abdhamon." his wife replied. "This is a great blow to them as well. We must see to it that he is properly honored."

"My personal guardsmen will bear his body home from the temple." Paltiba'al responded. "He shall be accompanied by no less than three of the city's most prestigious mourners, dressed in sackcloth with ashes on their heads. They will stay to lament his death while the women of his house wash and anoint his body, and wrap it with the finest linen for his burial."

"I will go myself, to take myrrh and bdellium to his house for the anointing," Tallayba'al said, "and a shroud of purple linen for his burial. Beneath his shroud he shall be dressed with two new tunics; one of fine linen from Kemet and over that, one of silk from the eastern lands beyond Karduniaš. He shall have gold rings for his fingers, and his eyes and lips will be covered in gold foil."

"When all this is done", Paltiba'al said, "he will rest in his house for three nights, as is proper. At dawn on the fourth day my guardsmen will take up his bier and carry him outside the city to the old burial ground. There he will rest in a place prepared for him within the tomb reserved for the people of the House of Abdhamon. In that way his shade may continue to serve the *rephaites* of our house in the kingdom of *Mot* as faithfully as he has served us in this life."

The Kena'ani of Gebal firmly believed in an afterlife, in which the spirits of their revered deceased ancestors existed as shades that dwelt with Mot, the god of death. It was vital that these shades be kept happy, otherwise they might cause trouble for the living. Paltiba'al and Tallayba'al believed it was critical to properly honor this servant who had taken the ring; binding himself to the House of Abdhamon for life. His lord and lady not only thought of him as a beloved member of their household, but held a certain apprehension about what mischief his shade might do if they failed to give him the respect he so clearly deserved.

Chapter 38
The Funeral of Yutpan

At the tomb of the House of Abdhamon

On the morning of the fourth day after his death, and the ninth day after the fire started, Paltiba'al's Lukka guardsmen arrived at the house of Yutpan to take him on his last earthly journey. It was a cloudy morning, with fog shrouding the lower half of the city as if in sympathy for the somber nature of the funeral about to commence.

The guards were preceded by the lord Paltiba'al, his wife and children, and followed by all of the senior servants of the House of Abdhamon. The mourners were well paid by Paltiba'al to accompany his body home, and had maintained their vigil with wailing and mourning for the customary three days and nights. They followed his bier and continued to wail as the procession left the city through the southern gate and took the road to the old cemetery. There, on a spur of the White Mountain, less than a league from the city walls, the Kena'ani people of Gebal buried their dead. The road wandered away from the city, twisting and turning into a deep, narrow valley and crossing a small creek before climbing the opposite slope.

As they passed the entrance to the cemetery, the members of Yutpan's funeral procession first began to see many grave markers of the poor and less well-off lining the road on either side. These simple stones grew thicker as the road rose, until they gradually gave way to numerous small votive stelae that marked the graves of the wealthier citizens. These stelae were engraved with symbols pertaining to the gods, and occasionally had the names of the graves' occupants carved in the Kena'ani language and script.

They drew close to the top of the slope, below a steep cliff of limestone. Here the stelae gave way to more elaborate tombs, some built above ground and others with steps or ramps leading to stone-lined chambers dug below the ground. The entrances to these tombs were elaborately decorated with carvings of animals, human figures, and other living things, all engaged in scenes from everyday life.

The tomb entrances were sealed with large stone doors, which were richly engraved. These were multi-roomed tombs, belonging to the wealthiest and most distinguished families of Gebal. In these the remains of generations rested for eternity. Invariably, the posts and lintels surrounding the doors to these tombs were engraved with the name of the house and usually the stone doors themselves were engraved with extensive texts that recorded the deeds of the earliest ancestors. Most also included texts containing dire warnings to anyone who might be tempted to break in and rob the dead. The warnings described the horrific consequences of such disrespectful acts and contained dreadful curses on would-be robbers and their children's children.

This was the first time Melita had been included in a funeral. Everything was fascinating to her, and somewhat scary. As she walked with her family in the procession, she noticed that none of the tombs they passed seemed to have been disturbed in any way. But curiously, most seemed to have large amounts of broken ceramic cups, plates and other dishes scattered all around their entrances. Who, she wondered, would dump trash on their ancestors' graves?

At last the procession reached the foot of the limestone cliff at the top of the slope. There, carved into the rock, were the entrances to dozens of tombs belonging to the first families of Gebal. The one directly before the procession was open, and above its door Melita read the carved name of the House of Abdhamon.

Seven paces to the left of the tomb's entrance a small shrine dedicated to Ba'al Šāmēm was carved into the limestone cliff. Light from oil lamps glowed within the shrine, illuminating a small gold statue of the god, which could be seen through the open doorway. Outside the shrine's entrance a low altar of finely dressed stone stood. Fresh wood lay ready on its top and two acolytes from the temple of Ba'al Šāmēm stood on either side.

The acolytes raised large bronze cymbals above their heads, and brought them together with a loud clash that reverberated through the valley below and echoed off the western slope. They began a sing-song chant, calling on the god Ba'al Šāmēm and praising him for his many virtues.

A figure emerged from the shrine. His head was completely shaved from crown to neck and his eyebrows were completely plucked out. The only facial hair he wore was his dark black beard cut short, tightly curled, and groomed to a sharp point below his chin. His face was painted a bright red with the sockets of his eyes blackened with Kohl. This was Adoniba'al, a junior priest from the temple of Ba'al Šāmēm in the city.

Paltiba'al's face grew red, almost matching the painted face of the priest. For an instant his expression was that of a man ready to burst with anger. But he quickly regained his composure. He had expected the high priest, Ili-Rapih, to preside over the funeral, and had personally invited the high priest to perform the funeral rites. It seemed Ili-Rapih's absence was, at best, a show of disrespect for

Paltiba'al's servant and former slave. At worst, it was a snubbing of the financier and his entire household.

Paltiba'al felt it was the latter, and that was something he could not ignore. He would confront Ili-Rapih as soon as he could to determine what the high priest meant by this insult. But unforeseen events would take priority and postpone this reckoning for a later time.

As the priest made his entrance, the women mourners threw themselves to the ground; continuing their wailing and lamentations. They gathered dust and cold ashes, from the ash pit by the altar, to smear on their faces and rub into their hair. Then they literally ripped and tore the clothing from their bodies and rolled across the ground, naked. Their leader was an old woman, and a professional mourner all her life. She grabbed fistfuls of her hair with both hands and yanked hard until the hair was torn out by its roots. Blood from her wounded scalp ran down her head and onto her face, adding to the mess made by the tears, ashes and dirt already there. She kept up a loud, high-pitched ululation and the other women mourners produced small bronze knives and began cutting straight, parallel gashes on their arms and thighs that crossed over old scars from previous funerals.

Melita moved to her mother's side and hid behind her skirt. She was frightened by this shocking display of grief and the eeriness of the open tomb before them. The whole event had taken on a weird, unearthly quality that was deepened by the low clouds hanging over the cemetery.

Her mother put her arm around Melita to calm her daughter's fearful trembling. Melita half expected to see the shades of the ancestors emerge from the tomb to punish the living for disturbing their rest. She hoped the hired mourners had shown enough grief to convince the rephaites to forgive the disruption of their sacred sleep. She prayed they would accept the shade of Yutpan into their company and not do any harm to his family or to the others present.

Adoniba'al came forward to stand behind the altar, flanked by the two acolytes who stopped chanting and silenced their cymbals as he halted there. The hired mourners instantly ceased their antics and withdrew to the fringes of the crowd.

A fire had been kindled on the altar and was burning vigorously. One acolyte came forward to receive a young goat brought for sacrifice by the wife of Yutpan. He carried it to the altar, laying it on a shelf below the fire where he bound its legs so it could not move. Adoniba'al raised a ceremonial bronze knife over his head, and looked to the clouded sky. His eyes followed the smoke rising from the flames while he chanted an invocation to Ba'al Šāmēm. He paused for a moment when his chant ended and lowered the knife in one swift move to slit the goat's throat.

An acolyte caught the gushing blood in a large ceramic ewer that was decorated with images of Ba'al Šāmēm in black and red. When the ewer was full the priest raised it high with both hands before slowly pouring it onto the fire. The flames guttered and smoked as the blood boiled, then overflowed; running down the sides of the altar to become a blackened, gummy mass that disappeared into the dust at the altar's base.

The priest cut the belly of the goat open, removed its entrails and peered intently into them. After several minutes he seemed satisfied with whatever he read there. Then he threw the entrails into the fire. While these sizzled and steamed, a great smoke rose and hung above the crowd. The acolytes took up their cymbals again, clashing them together until the surrounding hills rang. The goat's entrails soon burned to ash, and the priest cut the animal's body into halves, then quarters. These he threw, one after another, into the fire. He began to chant again and continued until the goat's body was consumed.

While the priest chanted, the cymbals crashed, and the goat burned, the guards took up the bier again. Paltiba'al led the way as they carried the corpse of Yutpan down a short flight of carved steps and into the tomb. With a small lamp he lighted their way through two low chambers, and passed the coffins of his ancestors to reach a new chamber that would be his own resting place one day. There Yutpan's corpse, in its purple shroud, was placed inside a cedar wood coffin that rested in a niche carved into the chamber's side.

Yutpan's wife and sons had followed the bier and placed a number of small items with the corpse. These included an alabaster scarab, an Ankh, and other amulets to protect him in the afterlife. These joined other more utilitarian items that he would need as he journeyed to the underworld kingdom of Mot.

Once these last tokens of love and divine protection were placed beside his body, the coffin was closed and sealed along all its edges with melted wax that cooled and hardened quickly. When the wax had set, lengths of braided bronze wire were passed through holes in the coffin lid and body on all four sides; emerging through corresponding holes in the sides of the coffin. The ends of the braided wires were brought together and twisted to join them, and each was sealed with a lump of fresh clay. These were stamped with Paltiba'al's own signet, marking the coffin and the its contents as being under his protection. The coffin could not be opened without breaking the seals, and anyone who dared to do so faced the threat of serious legal consequences. Paltiba'al could also inflict his own private vengeance as well. But above all, they would have to face the wrath of the gods and the ancestors.

Satisfied that everything necessary had been done to secure the safety and peace of Yutpan's resting place, Paltiba'al led the party from the tomb and back into the world of the living. The torch was extinguished and the guardsmen lifted the stone slab that formed the tomb's door into place. Once it was properly seated, the edges of the door were sealed shut with molten wax and another clay seal was set at its top and impressed with Paltiba'al's signet.

Once the tomb was sealed, the funeral took on an entirely different aspect. Food was brought forth and laid on low tables that had been set up while the burial party was inside the tomb. With the ashes of the goat's body still smoldering on the altar, a trio of musicians began to play a lively tune, and the mourners, having fulfilled their function, faded away. They would return to the city quietly and call on Itthoba'al the rab-tamkari of the House of Abdhamon to collect their final payment.

People began to mill about and many pleasant conversations started up. Plates were filled with food and cups of wine were imbibed. To Melita, this abrupt change from solemn mourning into feasting seemed very odd, and she didn't know what she should do.

Her mother came to her rescue, saying, "Help yourself to anything from the tables, dear one. Ba'al Šāmēm has eaten from the sacrifice and now we must join him in honoring Yutpan with this feast."

Lowering her voice to a conspiratorial tone she whispered in Melita's ear, "You wouldn't want his shade to be angry with you. Eat a little something, even if you don't feel like it. There are two kraters on the first table, one is filled with wine mixed with water and has slices of fruit floating in it. That is for you and your sisters and brother. Help yourself to that. The other is unmixed wine for the adults, which you children are too young for."

The skies above began to take on a brighter, more cheerful aspect as the clouds parted and the sun was able to shine down on the cemetery. The eeriness that had frightened Melita seemed to evaporate and her mood began to reflect her normal confidence. She took up one of the red-glazed ceramic plates that had been provided for the feast, and walked among the banquet tables.

As was customary for funeral days no one had eaten anything all morning. Now that it was nearing noon, Melita was hungrier than she would have expected. But in spite of that she felt shy about enjoying herself on such a sad occasion. She half-heartedly selected a few tidbits of fruit and meat that looked good to her, hoping she would be able to eat enough to please the shade of Yutpan. That thought was banished from her mind as she came to a table spread with her favorite honey cakes and other delicacies. Her eyes lit up and all misgivings vanished as she loaded up her plate with the delectable sweets.

Finding a place to sit and eat among the graves and tombs of the dead was still a little disquieting to Melita. It would have been easier if some of her friends were there, but the only others in attendance who were close to her age were her older sisters and her brother. These children huddled together and nibbled at their food while gazing with apprehension at the graves around them.

Melita was halfway through a thick honey cake loaded with raisins when she heard a loud crash. Startled, she turned her head in the direction of the sound and saw a woman flinging an empty plate at the door of the tomb. It struck the stone with great force and shattered; its many pieces falling amid older broken pieces that littered the ground in front of the tomb. Melita was shocked, but then remembered seeing all the broken pottery surrounding the other graves, and realized this must be a part of the funeral rites. Other plates and cups soon began to fly through the air and crash against the tomb, creating a growing pile of broken shards in front of the entrance stone.

As the crockery smashed and the fragments fell to the ground those who threw them cried out in loud voices, "Blessings be upon you, Yutpan!" Men and women raised their filled cups and tipped them slightly, pouring out a small amount of wine onto the ground in front of the tomb as a libation to the shade of Yutpan. Then they drained their cups and cast them at the tomb. As soon as they threw a cup, they reached for another and filled it from the krater of unmixed wine. Not surprisingly, some of the people began to get quite drunk after several cups of this strong wine. Plates and cups were crashing against the entrance in an almost continuous hail now.

The musicians continued to play their liveliest tunes and some of the men and women began to dance in the space in front of the tombs. As the wine loosened their inhibitions, some of the dancers paired up into couples, and their dancing took on a more and more erotic character. Some of the women were shedding their clothing, and Melita was shocked to see one of the scribes who served her father cast off his tunic and throw aside his kilt as he danced closer and closer to one of the servant girls. Melita saw the girl smile and flutter her eyelids at the man as she looked down from his face to below his waist.

Melita's gaze followed the girl's eyes and was shocked to see the scribe's penis standing out from his body, hard and straight, with its tip a bright red color. It wasn't the first time she had seen an adult penis, but this was different. She had never before seen one as big or as strangely fascinating as the one her wide eyes were now locked on. The scribe and the serving girl were dancing close to each other now, with their naked bodies bumping and rubbing against each other in time to the music. Melita was fascinated and had never seen such a display before. The scribe wrapped his arms around the girl and lifted her as she locked her legs around his hips.

"MELITA!" Her mother's voice crashed in on her thoughts like one of the plates smashing against the tomb. "Come away from there, and stop staring. You are too young to see such behavior, and it is time for all you children to leave for home."

Melita's face turned bright scarlet, and though she couldn't have explained why, she felt embarrassed and was suddenly ashamed. "But mother," she started, "What are they doing?"

"Never mind," Tallayba'al replied, firmly, "You'll know one day, but that day is not *this* day! Now you go and get your brother and sisters. I will have your nurse, and one of the guards, escort you home.

As the children of lord Paltiba'al and lady Tallayba'al were being escorted back to their home under the care of a nursemaid and guarded by one of their father's Lukka warriors, Melita could not get her mind off of the things she had seen at the cemetery. Especially the dancing! She had never seen anyone dance like *that* before, and had certainly not seen *naked* couples together like that!

Except for the male and female slaves displayed for sale in the slave market and the weird women mourners at the funeral she had never seen adults unclothed before. She was shocked that a man and woman would behave like those dancers. She wondered what else she might have seen if her mother hadn't intervened when she did.

That thought angered Melita. Why had mother treated her like a little child? Surely at eleven years old she was old enough to have stayed. Instead, mother had dismissed her to the care of a nursemaid! It was humiliating. Melita could feel her face growing flush with anger at these thoughts. But she couldn't get the image of the naked dancers out of her mind and her angry flush turned to a blush of embarrassment.

"What are you thinking about, Melita?" her sister Arshut asked in a teasing voice as they walked along the road back to the city.

"Yes, Melita, tell us what's on your mind." Izabel, her other sister, said in the same teasing tone. Both of the older girls giggled and tittered behind Melita's back as they saw her ears turn red. Melita enjoyed teasing others but hated to be teased herself, especially by her older sisters.

"Stop it!" Melita shouted at them, "Don't talk to me like that! You two think you know everything, but you're really stupid, foolish, and mean!" She had turned to face her sisters as she said this, and stood in front of them blocking their way with her feet planted firmly and her fists clenched at her sides.

The older girls knew how to get a rise out of Melita, but they also knew not to push her too far. Unlike them, Melita had a fiery temper when angry and was not averse to hitting, kicking, or throwing things at her siblings when she had her fill of their tormenting. They decided to drop the subject for now, but still continued to snicker and whisper behind her back. Melita could tell that she was still the subject of their amusement, but she returned to her own thoughts and ignored her siblings.

"I must discuss this with mother tonight!" She decided.

At that moment, on a ridge overlooking the cemetery road, two men watched as the children and their escorts approached. They were not seen by those on the road.

Chapter 39
Barakba'al Returns

In the City of Gebal

The night of the fire Barakba'al and his henchman, Sakarba'al, rowed their stolen boat south along the coast and away from the city. They escaped from the city's southern harbor without being spotted. The moonless night provided perfect cover as they reached a sheltered cove where they could put ashore unseen and at a safe distance from the two harbors. They abandoned the boat and quickly moved inland to hide themselves in a wooded area near the road that ran south from Gebal to the other Kena'ani coastal cities.

Days after the fires were finally extinguished and order was restored, the two men had been cautiously gathering news of the disaster and its aftermath while hiding in a small village below the city's southern gate. They listened to the gossip in the village tavern and on the streets, trying to pick up the latest news. They especially hoped to find out if anyone had seen how the fire had started.

They were afraid that the girl might have reported what she saw and were eager to know if anyone was searching for the murderer of the guardsman. But they learned nothing they didn't know already and realized they would have to go back to Gebal for answers to those questions. Despite the very real risks returning to the city entailed, that is what Barakba'al decided to do.

Once the fires were out and the ashes had time to cool the two waited one more day to be sure they could safely reenter the city. When the gates were opened on the morning of the fifth day after the fire, they mingled with a crowd of travelers and caravanners who had spent the night encamped near the south gate. The two men were able to slip past the guards without incident by mingling with the crowd passing into the city. They stayed among others and headed toward the marketplace.

The marketplace was a good location to gather gossip, but a little too public. Barakba'al had a different plan in mind. They drifted away from the crowd of merchants and customers, to turn down the Street of the Tailors, which they followed to the grand staircase. There they paused at the top and surveyed the destruction they had caused. The sight shocked them at first, because they only intended to harm the House of Dan-El. But after a few moments of reflection on the crumbled ruins of buildings, wharves and ships Barakba'al began to feel a certain pride and satisfaction in how effective his revenge had been. They continued down the grand staircase toward the harbor district, careful to avoid anyone who might recognize them.

Their goal was an establishment known as the Inn of the Seventh Siren that catered to the needs of sailors who were in port for short layovers between voyages. This establishment consisted of a tavern and bordello, with a few upper apartments that were rented to mariners who could afford to make the inn their onshore residence.

To reach the inn, the two men left the grand staircase and turned to the south, away from the charred wreckage of the northern harbor. They entered the undamaged southern harbor district, where they reached the inn near the waterfront and entered its front door.

"Blessings be upon you, master mariner Barakba'al," the innkeeper said, greeting the larger of the two men, whom he recognized as the former master of the *Cabax*, who was one of the inn's semi-permanent residents. Barakba'al had been at sea more than on land in the last several years, but it was important to him to maintain a residence in the city befitting his status as a ship's master. He paid well for the small suite of rooms he occupied, even though he mainly used it during the off-season when no ships risked putting to sea unless the need was critical.

The inn's reputation was only marginally better than that of dozens of similar establishments along the waterfront, but it made a pretense of seedy elegance that may have done a little to enhance its clients' status. To Barakba'al it offered him an appearance of some solidity; of having strong ties to the city, and an implied trustworthiness. He knew that traits like these helped ease the minds of investors and ship owners, and thus might help keep him afloat, literally.

Two other attributes of the inn appealed to Barakba'al. First, the room and board were both economical and conveniently close to the port. Second, it was also home to several of his favorite whores, so it served all of his on-shore needs nicely.

"Blessings be upon you and this worthy house, Ba'aliahon," Barakba'al replied to his landlord. "How is your wine this day? My friend and I have just returned from a long journey, and our throats are as dry as the sands of Kemet."

"I shall have my best wine, with bread and fresh fish brought to you at once. Please, allow my servants to wash your feet and tend to your every need. Will you take your food and drink in the public room of my tavern, or do you prefer to dine in the privacy of your own quarters?" the innkeeper asked.

Something in the innkeeper's manner did not seem quite right to

Barakba'al. He couldn't identify the problem at first, but whatever it was raised an alarm in the back of his mind. He noticed when he introduced his "friend" that the innkeeper's eyes widened as if he had suddenly realized something. After that Ba'aliahon's attitude seemed to change. Barakba'al thought the man should not have been quite so eager to please a tenant who was currently a month behind in his rent.

If he hadn't had the urgent need for more information, the main reason for coming to the inn, the master mariner would have left the place right then. They also needed food, drink and a safe place to lay low while they gathered that information. Barakba'al expected to find all of this at the Inn of the Seven Sirens. But now the innkeeper's overly friendly attitude made him think it was a mistake to come there. What was behind all of that? Was Ba'aliahon up to something, or was Barakba'al just imagining things that weren't real?

Could the young girl who witnessed everything have shared what she heard in the alley with her father? What did he say about her father? Was it that Paltiba'al had helped ruin him? Did the financier put two and two together from what she told him? Did Paltiba'al figure out that the master mariner was the man who started the fire, killed the guardsman, and threatened his daughter? He needed the answers to all these questions!

"Curse that girl!" he thought, *"I should have slit her throat immediately. If that guardsman hadn't come along when he did, we could have gotten away clean."*

"We'll dine here in the public room," he told the innkeeper. "As we came down the grand staircase, I saw there has been a fire at the northern harbor. The damage seemed to be tremendous! I'd like to learn more about that. Perhaps your other guests might be able to tell us something."

"Oh, yes!" the innkeeper said, "A great disaster! Six merchant ships were burned and more than a dozen others damaged or destroyed in the confusion. After the fire reached the buildings along the waterfront it raged for three days! Many of the warehouses were destroyed, along with all the goods they contained. That is all the people of the city have been talking about.

One who died was Yutpan, the servant of the lady Tallayba'al, wife of lord Paltiba'al. They will be holding a funeral for him tomorrow, and he will be laid to rest in Paltiba'al's own family tomb. Along with the aftermath of the fire, this funeral is the talk of the city. You'll learn a great deal, I am certain, if you are here this evening.

Sadly, we don't have many customers at this hour of the morning, as you can see. Please seat yourselves anywhere, while I go and look after your meal."

With that the innkeeper made as if to scurry off, but was stopped by Barakba'al who said, "On second thought, I think we will just take a wineskin and a sack with some bread and cheese. I can learn more by going to the north harbor. I want to see the damage for myself. We can return for the evening meal, when you have more guests about."

"Oh! Of course, if that is your pleasure." A note of disappointment crept into the innkeeper voice. "I will have my servants pack a lunch for you right away." He bowed, then quickly turned to leave the public room and entered the kitchen.

As soon as the innkeeper left the room, Barakba'al turned to Sakarba'al and said, "Something is not right. You wait here for the wine and food and watch for trouble. I'll try to find out more."

With that he moved to the far side of the public room and climbed a set of stairs leading to rooms on the second floor.

Chapter 40

Ibqet the Harlot

At the Inn of the Seventh Siren

Barakba'al moved down the landing on the upper floor and stopped at the door to the third room and listened. Hearing nothing, he opened the door and slipped inside, softly closing the door behind him. The room was dark except for a sliver of light shining through a gap in curtains draping the room's single window. In the dim light, a naked woman, half covered with bed linens, lay on her stomach across a sleeping pallet. She was alone and snoring lightly.

Barakba'al crossed to the side of the pallet and looked down on the unconscious figure. The woman was one of the harlots who worked for Ba'aliahon. Her name was Ibqet, and Barakba'al was a frequent customer of hers whenever his ship was in port. In fact, she was one of his favorites during the winter off-season. For those months she entertained him at least three nights a week.

He watched as she snored softly into her bedclothes and let his eye trace a path from her head to her toes, admiring her shapely form. Part of him wished he had the time to enjoy her company, but knew he couldn't linger. He reached down and clamped his right hand firmly over her mouth and pinned her down with his other hand grasping her by the wrist.

She woke with a start and a scream that was muffled by his hand. She struggled, not knowing who was assaulting her or why. "Quiet!" Barakba'al breathed into her ear. "Don't make a sound and I'll let you up."

Ibqet recognized his voice immediately and relaxed. She shook her head in agreement, and Barakba'al let her up. She turned to face him, making no effort to cover herself. "My love! What brings you here at this hour? You know this is my sleeping time. My door is never open for business before noon."

"Keep your voice down." Barakba'al whispered. "These walls are thin and I don't wish to be overheard. I need to know what has happened since the fire. Quickly, tell me everything you know."

"I know that the city guard is on watch for two men who attacked the daughter of the lord Paltiba'al and ba'alat Tallayba'al. The child was at the harbor when the fire started and barely escaped with her life! The same men killed one of the city guards, and the others are sharpening their swords for when they catch them."

"Did she tell them who these men were?" Barakba'al asked.

"She didn't know their names, but one was a common sailor who called the other one 'master.' She was badly frightened, but is sure she will recognize them when they are captured."

This was bad. Barakba'al weighed his chances if the guardsmen captured him, and he didn't like the result. It all came down to that smart-mouthed, gods-cursed girl! He needed a way to silence her forever. Fear would not do it. He knew this from their brief encounter in the alleyway. She was not easily intimidated. No, he would have to kill her before she exposed him.

"What else have you heard?" he asked.

"It is said all over the waterfront that you were dismissed by ba'alat Nikkal, and that you are forbidden to even ride aboard any ship in the Dan-El fleet. Most of the other Houses have also banned you from their ships as well. You should never have placed a curse on a powerful noble house the way you did. Least of all, the House of Dan-El. But because you did so on the very day the fire started, many believe it was your curse that caused it.

Your very own ship, the *Cabax*, and the *Shapash* among others were completely destroyed, and suspicious minds are beginning to think that it wasn't the curse, but that you, yourself, started the fire! In fact, the commander of the city guards wants to question you about that! They came looking for you here. You should not have come!"

Barakba'al's face grew dark as he heard this. It was worse than he had expected. "I need a place to hide until I can get out of the city later tonight".

"Well you can't hide here!" Ibqet said. "Customers will begin knocking at my door soon! I cannot let them find you here."

"They won't see me if I buy your time for the full day. I have silver, and you won't have to work *too* hard for it." he said with a grin.

"Ha!" she laughed, "Don't lie to me. No sailor, not even a master mariner, ever stays a full day or night with a girl of my status. They just use us for their pleasure and forget us as quickly as they can. No one will believe I could keep a man like you occupied for a full day."

"There must be some way. What if you were too sick to work?" Barakba'al suggested. "I've seen the tokens you girls hang on your doors during your moon days. If you hang yours on the door pull no one will bother you."

"That might work," Ibqet said, thinking about it, "but I can't remember if I've already used that excuse this month. Ba'aliahon, old goat that he is, keeps track of such things. He won't be fooled. He charges us double rent for our rooms on days we don't work."

To Barakba'al it sounded like Ibqet was running out of excuses and was holding out for a bigger payment. He thought about haggling with her, but if the guardsmen were looking for him there wasn't time for that. He wondered if he could trust her to hide him until dark. She might take his silver and still turn him over to the guard. She hadn't mentioned it, but there was probably a reward for his capture, and she might be thinking about that as well.

The more he thought about it the more perilous his situation seemed. She was right when she said he shouldn't have come there. If what he now suspected of her was true, then he couldn't afford to take any risk with her.

"Very well," he said in an exasperated voice as he rolled his eyes, "I will pay you double your normal day's earnings and pay your rent at double the daily rate for hiding me and my crewman until dark. But quickly, hang out your token before anyone comes along."

"You said nothing about any crewman! Wait! There were two men who started the fire. So, it *was* you then!" Ibqet said. "Now you want me to hide you both in this little room of mine? And just what is it worth to hide his vile carcass too?"

Barakba'al was not surprised at her bargaining tactics. He needed her to think she was getting the best of him.

"Alright, alright!" he said. I'll pay whatever you ask for both of us, just hurry. Put out your token!"

The token he spoke of was a red silk scarf with the image of the goddess Anath painted on it. Anyone seeing it tied to the brass ring that served as a door pull would know that the woman inside was not available for sexual services.

Ibqet was already counting the things she could buy at the market with so much silver. There was also a fat reward for the killer of the guardsman that might be hers as well. Once the two men were settled in, she would give them drugged wine so she could slip away and summon the guard.

With a smile on her face, she rose from her pallet and reached for a tunic that lay on the floor nearby. She slipped it over her head and smoothed it along her body, then walked across the room with a gait that was part swagger and part seductive strut.

A large chest stood in a corner near the curtained window. She opened it and retrieved her token then turned and began walking toward the door. She had to pass close to Barakba'al and as she did, he grabbed her by the hair with his left hand, pulling hard and forcing her head back to expose her throat. His right hand flashed forward and before she had time to cry out, he slashed his razor-sharp sailor's knife across her bared throat, severing her windpipe and carotid artery.

Her eyelids fluttered spasmodically and she struggled at first. One hand reached for the fingers in her hair. Her other hand dropped the token and clutched at the gaping wound in her throat. Barakba'al let go of her hair, allowing her dying body to collapse at his feet. Blood continued to spurt across the room to stain the walls a bright crimson that looked black in the dim light. He pulled a linen sheet from the pallet and threw it over her body. Then he gathered the rest of the bedclothes and used them to wipe the worst of the blood spatter off the walls and sop up the growing puddle on the floor. With that done, he tossed the blood-stained bedclothes into a corner and dragged her corpse between the sleeping pallet and the wall. He made sure it couldn't be seen from the door and wiped his bloody hands and knife as clean as he could on her tunic. He opened the door, just a crack, and listened a moment before sticking his head out to look both directions along the landing. Seeing no one, he picked up Ibqet's token from the floor, tied it to the brass ring and closed the door.

Chapter 41
A Narrow Escape

At the Inn of the Seventh Siren

Sakarba'al was still standing near the entrance to the tavern's public room, wondering what his master was doing in the harlot's room for so long. The innkeeper had not returned with their lunch, and Sakarba'al suspected that Ba'aliahon was stalling while one of his servants went to fetch the guardsmen. Several of the slaves had been in and out of the public room, but no one came to wash his feet, or offer any other kind of comfort. They eyed him with guarded expressions, as if they had been told to keep an eye on the two visitors. Sakarba'al was beginning to worry.

He kept glancing at the door to the harlot's room, and finally noticed the red token. Had it been there before? He couldn't remember. But then he wasn't much of a man for details like that. He pondered the question, and saw the door open a bit. His master was standing there, signaling him to come up.

Sakarba'al crossed the room and quickly climbed the stairs, nervously glancing around, hoping that no one would see him. "What is he up to?" the sailor thought. "We should be getting ourselves lost in the crowds at the market, or finding some way to get out of the city." When he reached Ibqet's door it opened to receive him and quickly closed behind him.

"Watch your step." Barakba'al said in warning. Sakarba'al looked to the floor and saw a large pool of blood, and then noticed the blackened spray on the walls.

"Had to kill 'er did ya!" he said, approvingly. He lifted the sheet that covered Ibqet's corpse to admire his master's handiwork. "What a shame! That's a terrible waste of a prime harlot." Her tunic was still bunched above her waist from Barakba'al's attempt to clean his hands and knife. "What a waste!" The sailor said again as he eyed her exposed body.

"Enough of that." Barakba'al scolded. "I asked her if we could hide here, but she was planning to betray us. It had to be done." He jerked the sheet from Sakarba'al's hand and covered the body again.

"Master," the sailor said, "I think that gods-cursed innkeeper sent for the guard. We should get away from here while we still can!"

"I know! I know!" Barakba'al replied. But we will be safe here for a short while. I learned we are wanted for questioning in connection with the fire, and there is a reward for the capture of the men who murdered the guardsman that night. They don't know it was us for certain, but if that girl you let escape recognizes our faces, we are doomed."

"All the more reason to leave now!" Sakarba'al said, with rising urgency. "And I didn't let her escape..."

"Enough!" Barakba'al answered. "Use your wits! I know the man all too well. If Ba'aliahon had sent for the guard they would already be here. It is more likely he has gone to the harbor to round up some sailors to help him capture us. He'll think merely summoning the guard won't guarantee a reward for his trouble. He'll want to hand us over to the guardsmen himself. But, to catch and hold us until they arrive will require more than his servants alone can provide. That's something my pretty one here didn't think of.

No, Ba'aliahon thinks his servants can keep us occupied while he rounds up his gang, and knowing him, he will haggle over the cost of their services, so we have some time yet before he returns. That token I hung on the door will keep everyone away for now."

"Will we have time to get some food and drink?" Sakarba'al asked. "The scum never had his servants bring anything, and I'm starving."

"There is a crust of bread and some dried fish that smells like it has been sitting out since last night, over there on the table by the window." Barakba'al said. "If you can stomach that you may have it. There is water in the ewer next to it, but no wine as far as I could see. Just keep your voice down."

Sakarba'al ate the stale bread crust and sniffed at the dried fish. It had an overripe smell but he ate all of it as well. He took a drink of the water, but quickly spit it out. A look of disgust came over his features and he said, "Tastes like she used it to wash her backside!"

Barakba'al grabbed him by the back of his neck and drew his face close to the sailor's ear. In an angry, threatening whisper he said, "I told you to keep your voice down! Stop wasting time and look into that chest to see if you can find us something else to wear. I can't leave in these blood-soaked clothes. Look for something that will cover our faces. Do it now!" He shoved Sakarba'al in the direction of the chest.

After a few minutes of digging through the dead harlot's clothing, Sakarba'al found what was needed. She had pathetically few clothes of her own, but her occupation didn't require many. Underneath a few silken tunics and some better clothing worn to attract customers was a single casual woman's tunic and beneath that several men's tunics and other garments.

In addition to her sexual talents, Ibqet had been a fairly good seamstress and offered that service to the sailors and shopkeepers who were her regular clientele. Some of the sailors left clothing with her to be mended between voyages and planned to pick them up when they returned. But some might be lost at sea or never returned to claim their mended clothes for other reasons. Ibqet supplemented her income by selling the unclaimed garments along with other items that she could steal without being caught.

"Here master! These will do the trick." Sakarba'al said. He had come up with two cloaks, some slightly worn kilts, a pair of tunics and several of the knitted wool caps sailors wore at sea. The caps would cover their heads and could be pulled low to help mask their features. Barakba'al shed his bloody clothes and quickly dressed again, choosing the best of the tunics, kilts and cloaks for himself. Sakarba'al followed his example with the second best. Now they were ready to escape as soon as the time was right.

The morning wore on, the tavern filled with a noisy crowd of sailors and laborers who came for their noon meal. The hub-bub grew and the servants were all kept busy waiting on these customers. Ba'aliahon still had not returned.

The two in Ibqet's room could hear sounds from the tavern below and footsteps on the stairs. Customers were beginning to arrive, and some had more than lunch on their minds. This is what Barakba'al was counting on. He knew the more activity in the building, the easier it would be to slip away unnoticed. As customers became engaged with the harlots, or were busy eating and drinking, the chance to escape would come.

A little after noon, Barakba'al opened the door carefully and looked both ways along the landing. At the far end a man was just entering one of the harlots' rooms and as he shut the door behind him Barakba'al led the way out of Ibqet's room and the two men quickly went down the stairs.

They stayed close to the walls of the public room and kept out of the dim light of the ceiling lamp. As much as possible they kept their faces turned away from the noisy patrons and the bustling servants. At one point a slave bearing a large tray with bowls of fish stew and loaves of bread bumped into Sakarba'al. In the confusion the crafty sailor managed to snag a loaf and hid it in his cloak without being noticed.

Reaching the door, they exited past one of the servants that had been keeping a none-too-subtle eye on Sakarba'al, but he didn't seem to recognize them. He bowed to them as they exited through the tavern door to emerge in the Street of the Tailors.

At this hour the street was filled with people going about their business, but there was no sign of Ba'aliahon or any guardsmen. They crossed the street and walked several doors down to a small shop that provided food and drink to the working men and women of the harbor district. They seated themselves at a small table where they could not be seen from the street, but could watch the entrance to the Inn of the Seventh Siren.

They ordered two bowls of hot fish stew, a loaf of bread, and olive oil to dip it in. Wine was brought while they waited. Sakarba'al had already eaten the stolen bread, but was still starving. Barakba'al had not eaten anything since the evening before, and his stomach was growling. They ate quickly and were sopping up the last of the stew when they spotted Ba'aliahon and three burly sailors marching up the street and into the Inn of the Seventh Siren.

"Ha!" Barakba'al said in a low voice. "Just as I thought! That scum wants to capture us himself. By the thundering farts of Ba'al Šāmēm, I swear I will cut his throat the next time I lay eyes on him! Come, it is time for us to leave."

Barakba'al paid for their meal and the two men walked out of the shop. They turned down the street toward the south harbor and away from the Inn of the Seventh Siren. The harbor was deserted at this hour while the fishermen took their noon meal in nearby taverns and shops. They were able to steal another small boat that was carelessly left on the beach and used it to make their second escape from the city.

Chapter 42
Ambushed

On the road from the old cemetery

A day later, as the two men looked down on the cemetery road, Barakba'al could not believe his luck. He easily recognized the youngest girl, who was leading the others toward the city. It was the brat that saw them set the fire! She had separated herself a good distance ahead of the group for some reason.

Ba'aliahon had tipped them off about the funeral of Paltiba'al's servant, and they had been waiting on the ridge above the cemetery road in hopes that an opportunity to kill the girl might occur. This looked like exactly that.

From his vantage point Barakba'al could see that the road followed the course of a small creek that ran through the valley below. The stream and road looped around a sharp bend directly beneath the ridge on which he and Sakarba'al were standing. They could easily drop down to intercept the girl when she reached a point that was out of sight of the rest of her party. The element of surprise would be on their side so Barakba'al hoped that with the help of the gods they might kill her and get away before the others cleared the bend in the road.

He was not worried about witnesses: knowing the party was made up of children, one old woman, and a single armed man accompanying them. The man might be a problem, but Barakba'al and Sakarba'al outnumbered him. If they had to, they could put the guard down quickly, then deal with the woman and the children. There would be no witnesses left. He quickly explained his plan to Sakarba'al and they hurried down the slope and crossed over the road to hide in the underbrush.

Melita rounded the bend and passed from the sight of the others. She was still thinking about the funeral and the strange behavior of the scribe and the servant girl. Wrapped in thought, she wasn't paying attention to her surroundings until she heard a rustling in the brush beside the road. She looked toward the sound and was shocked and terrified at what she saw. The same two men that had tried to kill her the night of the fire were running toward her. She stood frozen in fear. The sailor with the rotten teeth reached her first, and was on her before she could react. He threw his arms around her and hurled her to the ground, using the weight of his body to pin her down.

She screamed as she hit the ground, but lost her breath as Sakarba'al's weight landed on top of her.

"We meet again little one! Remember me?" He spat the words in her ear, then stood her on her feet, holding her tightly by the upper arms to face his master. He didn't want a kick in the groin this time. Barakba'al stopped in front of them with his sword in his hand. The long blade flashed in the sunlight and her heart hammered in her chest at the thought of what would come next. She knew this time she would die.

A loud roar broke from the throat of the Lukka guard as the big man came around the bend and saw the danger to Melita. He dashed forward with amazing quickness considering his great size. His right arm flew forward as he ran, hurling his javelin at the tall man holding a sword over Melita. The sword was raised, ready to strike a killing blow, but the guard's cry and the sound of sandals pounding toward him from behind, caused Barakba'al to turn and step aside. The javelin missed him, and flew straight into Sakarba'al's throat. Its bronze head missed Melita by barely a palm's width, but the heavy shaft struck the side of her head with great force, knocking her senseless.

Sakarba'al's hands still gripped her upper arms, and the force of the javelin's impact knocked them both backward and to the ground. Melita lay there, unable to move beside Sakarba'al.

The big guard reached Barakba'al a second later, but the mariner leaped aside to avoid the man's rush. At the same time, he swung his sword in an arc that was purely instinctive. More by chance than skill, the blade sliced into the guard's right arm above the elbow. It opened a deep gash that began to bleed profusely. It was a serious wound, but not enough to immediately disable the guard.

The big man was staggered by the blow, but kept his feet, turning quickly to face Barakba'al. He placed himself between the former ship's master and Melita, shielding her with his body, and ready to defend her to the death if necessary. But he knew the shock from his wound and blood loss would weaken him rapidly. If the fight lasted very long, he would lose. His only weapon had been the javelin, and it was out of reach, still embedded in the neck of Sakarba'al's lifeless body.

Barakba'al circled around the guard, trying to gain an opening to strike another blow. The guard countered by turning to keep himself facing the ship's master and blocking him from reaching the girl. Having the only weapon gave Barakba'al a huge advantage, but the guard was a veteran warrior. Despite his wounded arm, his skills far outclassed Barakba'al's. The mariner's experience was the kind one acquired in tavern brawls, or by cutting the throats of unwary victims. He would have been no match for the guard in an even fight.

The two men circle each other, while the other children and the nursemaid came around the bend in the road. Shocked by the scene before them, they halted and kept their distance. All three children were terrified and screaming. The girls were clinging to the nursemaid while their little brother stood frozen in fear. Horrified herself, the nursemaid somehow had the presence of mind to hustle her charges off the road and into the brush. She kept urging them forward until they were well away from the fighting men and could safely regain the road.

From there she called out to Melita, "Run to me little one!" But Melita lay where she had fallen next to Sakarba'al and didn't seem to hear. Her eyes were locked onto the shining blade of Barakba'al's sword. In despair, the nursemaid saw she could do little to help Melita, but could still protect the other children. The best way to do that was to get them back to the city as quickly as possible. Though it broke her heart, she turned them in that direction and urged the children to run.

Barakba'al knew the guard was weakening from his wound, and would not be able to fight him off much longer. But before long the other children and their nursemaid would reach the city and be able to summoned help. Time was short, so he made a feint to his left, in the direction of the guard's wounded right arm. Then as he closed, he pivoted to his right and swung his sword at the guard's left side. The big warrior jumped away to avoid the blow he thought was aimed at his injured right arm, but was too late to avoid the threat to his left side. The sword caught him on his ribs and slid along his leather breastplate, cutting into it and scoring another, shallower cut.

Barakba'al's confidence was growing. He felt he could easily finish the big man quickly, with time to kill the girl and make his getaway before any help could arrive. So, he waded in toward the guard, swinging his sword in rapid strokes that cut the air and forced the big man back. The guard stumbled over the feet of Sakarba'al's corpse and fell backwards. Barakba'al closed in for the kill.

But while he had been battling the guard, Melita had recovered her senses. She remembered the sailor carried a knife and crawled and reached inside his cloak to find it. As the guard fell backward her hand closed on the knife's handle and she pulled it free from the dead man's belt.

The fallen guard's hand landed, palm up, across her chest, and Melita placed the handle of the sailor's knife in his palm. The guard was surprised to feel the weapon in his hand but he reacted instantly. He jerked his arm forward and stabbed at Barakba'al's sword arm as it came forward for the final blow. The razor-sharp blade of the sailor's knife sliced into the flesh of Barakba'al's right wrist, severing muscle, tendons and veins. Barakba'al instantly lost the ability to grip the sword and it fell from his hand. He staggered back, grabbing his wrist as a fiery pain shot up his arm and blood gushed from the wound.

The guard slowly regained his feet, dropped the knife, and reached out to take up the fallen sword. Now Barakba'al was the one facing an armed opponent with only his own sailor's knife for protection. The whole length of his right arm, from his bleeding wrist to his shoulder, throbbed with pain. He was enraged at failing to kill the guard and glared at him. As the Lukka warrior took a halting step toward him, Barakba'al turned and ran off up the slope behind him, disappearing over the crest of the ridge.

The guard took a few steps forward to follow him, but was in no shape to climb the slope. He felt light-headed from the blood he had lost and his knees were weak. He sat down in the road next to Melita and she wrapped her arms around him and began to cry.

"No, no, small one," he said in his halting command of her language, "No make tears. Enemy gone! You very brave. Very smart. Make warrior of you yet! You save us with knife. Safe now."

She hugged his neck tighter until her deep sobs subsided after several moments. In the back of her mind she realized that her actions *had* saved them, and the thought gave her a rush of relief. After the attempt on her life the night of the fire she had felt weak, powerless, and afraid. Now that fear had left her, and as her tears dried, she smiled.

But something was wrong. She felt the guard's shoulders slump, and his body started to tip away from her. She looked up and saw that his eyelids were fluttering and his gaze was unfocused. She released him and gently helped him onto his back. Only then did she notice the blood that was still flowing from his two wounds and pooling on the road beside them. She felt a rush of panic, realizing he could die while she watched. Something must be done at once, but what?

She had never seen a wounded man before and she knew nothing of how to treat such injuries. But she knew that the blood he was losing was not a good thing. She had seen a few people with bandages for one reason or another, and was acquainted with the cloths that women used for their moon days. Maybe that was what she should do for the guard's wounds.

She tore strips from the lower part of her skirt's many layers. He was unconscious now, laying on his back. She used the bloody knife to cut the leather thongs that held his breastplate in place and moved it aside so she could see the source of the blood flow. The wound was less serious than the gash in his upper arm so she went to work there first. She placed his arm across her lap and began winding the improvised bandage around it, until the bleeding appeared to stop. She tied it as tight as she could, then went to work on his side. For this she had to maneuver him into a slumped-over sitting position, which given his size and bulk took some doing. She was barely able to lift his upper body, but once she managed to get him sitting upright it was not too difficult to wind bandages around his torso until she was satisfied that the bleeding there was also staunched.

She eased his barely conscious body back down and rested her head on his shoulder. She tried to think of some prayers or incantations that she could use to invoke the aid of Eshmun or some other god. None came to mind. Anyway, she thought perhaps his foreign gods were the ones she should pray to, but she knew nothing about those gods. Instead she simply reached out in her mind and silently prayed to Ba'alat Gebal, asking the goddess to heal this brave man who had risked his life to save her. She closed her eyes and kept repeating this same heartfelt prayer.

It was late afternoon by the time the nursemaid and other children of Paltiba'al and Tallayba'al reached the city gates and alerted the guards to what had happened. Six guardsmen ran down the cemetery road at once, and soon reached the bend in the road. There, as the sun began to set, they found Melita with her protector lying in the dust; her head still resting on the shoulder of the wounded Lukka guard.

As host and hostess of Yutpan's funeral celebration, Lord Paltiba'al and Lady Tallayba'al were still at the family's tomb as evening approached. Tradition called for them to be the last to leave, and it was normal for celebrations such as this to go on well into the night, or at least as long as the wine and food lasted.

Paltiba'al was known as one of the most gracious hosts in all of Gebal, and only his wife was considered his equal in that regard. They ate lightly, while moving from one group of guests to the next, breaking a small, ceremonial loaf of bread with each group and drinking in honor of the shade of Yutpan. To avoid becoming intoxicated their wine was well mixed. Two-parts-water to one-part-wine, and they restricted their drinking to small sips with each toast.

Their mingling with the guests brought them at last to Adoniba'al the priest and his two acolytes. Paltiba'al was sorely tempted to ignore them and pass by without showing the customary and appropriate courtesy. All three were obviously drunk, with Adoniba'al's red face-paint smeared and his black eye makeup streaked down his cheeks. He had not been far from the table where the wine was being served since the first libations were poured out. The acolytes, young boys really, were sitting at his feet, giddy with drink, and were stuffing their mouths with chunks of cheese, bread and roasted meat. One had thrown up earlier and vomit was streaked down the front of his tunic.

Disgusted at the sight this trio made, Paltiba'al turned to pass them by when his wife stopped him. She took his arm in hers and whispered in his ear.

"Dear husband, I know what your heart wants you to do, but listen to your head instead. It would be very unwise to insult the priests of Ba'al Šāmēm. To do so is an insult to the god himself. Not to mention how the high priest will view such discourtesy when he hears of it. Don't give him another weapon he can use against you."

Paltiba'al's face had grown red again, remembering that Ili-Rapih should have been the one to officiate at the funeral, but had instead sent this imbecilic junior priest and these two useless acolytes. He was certain that was a deliberate slight to Yutpan's shade and to the whole House of Abdhamon. Paltiba'al was not a man to ignore such disrespect, but as he listened to the words of his wife, he checked his wrath and forced a smile to his lips. This was not the time. It was not the place. But the time would soon come to settle the score of this and many other slights.

His wife was right, and he knew her words were wise, so he set his pride aside and determined not to return disrespect for the disrespect directed toward him. Just then, as he was about to extend a formal greeting to Adoniba'al, he was interrupted by a commotion from the cemetery road. Two of the city guards were shouting his name and searching for him in the crowd. They brought word of the attack on his children and all further thought of celebration was driven from his mind.

Paltiba'al and his wife looked into each other's eyes and had the same instantaneous reaction. Paltiba'al signaled to his guards and began running down the path from his family's tomb to the cemetery's entrance. His wife summoned the rest of their servants and started down the path after him as quickly as she could go.

Chapter 43

The Hunters Return

In the city of Gebal

The city of Gebal had been buzzing for two days with the news that Ahinadab and his hunting party were about to return from a successful lion hunt on the White Mountain. When the party was still a day's journey from the city, a messenger was sent ahead to inform the ba'alat Nikkal, and the news spread quickly. The hunting party had been gone for over a month, and no word from them had been heard, so it was natural that all kinds of rumors and speculation had circulated during their absence. But at last a messenger had arrived to announce the party's imminent return. At dawn the next day, almost the entire population turned out to welcome the hunters.

Nikkal was frantic when she first learned that Gamil had been seriously injured. It was all she could do to keep from rushing out to meet the party on the road. But by the time the messenger reached the House of Dan-El it was already late in the afternoon, and she realized that nothing could be gained by panicking. Instead, she quizzed the messenger mercilessly until she had learned all that he could tell her about her son. She wanted to know every detail from the time the hunting party left the city, how he came to be injured, and what his condition was now.

When he had answered all her questions and could say no more, she thanked him and released him to the care of rab-tamkari Hesham, who provided him with a hearty meal and a place to sleep for the night. Nikkal then dismissed her maids and withdrew into her chambers. Alone there, she lit a small brazier of incense and opened the doors to a simple wooden shrine that stood against the eastern wall. Inside it was a small statue of the god El stood. It was made of *èlektron,* the "whitegold" of the Achaeans, that was mined in the mountains of Arzawa.

This naturally-occurring alloy of gold, silver, and copper was highly prized for its pale-yellow color and rarity. Sometimes if the copper content was just right the "white" gold took on more of a green coloration when seen under certain lighting conditions. In twilight, moonlight, or low lamplight, the metal sometimes seemed to emit a dim greenish glow, lending an air of mystery to anything made from it. Due to this glow, the metal was known among the Kena'ani and other neighboring peoples as "green gold," and was believed to be sacred to the gods. The pharaohs of Kemet also believed this, and used green gold to manufacture sacred items of all kinds, and even use it to face the capstones of their pyramids.

The subdued light of the setting sun filtered into Nikkal's chamber through the silken drapery of her western windows and fell upon the shrine. The great lady knelt before the statue of El and waited for her mind to settle, trusting that in a short while the presence of the god would be manifested. The fading rays of the sun illuminated the statue and it began to shine with a weird reddish light that was reflected in her eyes. This was the sign she had waited for, and Nikkal began her prayer to the patron god of the House of Dan-El.

"Hear the cry of my heart, Almighty El, Rider of the Clouds, who is high above all other gods. Praises be to you for the wonders you perform. See how I bow before you in humble thanksgiving for your great kindness in sparing the life of my firstborn son. You have delivered him from the claws of the lion, even from the jaws of the beast, and have returned him to his home!

I thank you also for preserving my husband and those with him from thieves, wild animals, and disease. You have granted them a great victory over the evil one that preyed upon his people as they labored on the White Mountain. All praises be to you, my Lord and my God!

If I may ask further of you, I humbly pray you will bring them all safely within the walls of the city tomorrow, and let no misadventure befall them on this last night of their journey.

Grant your blessing to this house I pray, and stretch out your mighty arms to enfold my son, Gamil, in your all-powerful embrace. Intercede for him with Eshmun I pray, that he might be healed and made whole again. Oh Lord, show us your mercy and restore his strength. For your help I vow that we will dedicate a new shrine to your glory, where we will offer our sacrifices of thanksgiving to you for all you have given us. I have spoken it, and so it shall be done."

Ending her prayer with that, Nikkal felt a sense of peace that she had not known since the hunting party left for the White Mountain. Still kneeling before the shrine, she watched as the last rays of sunlight now painted the image of the god with a reddish glow that sparkled and danced across its surface. She watched in fascination until the reddish light failed completely, and was amazed to see that the statuette continued to shine in the twilight. Then, quite suddenly, it began to glow with that unearthly greenish halo that Nikkal understood to be a sign of El's approval of her requests.

She rose from her knees and left her chambers; leaving the doors to the shrine open and the incense still burning. Its fragrance filled the room and followed her figure as she descended the staircase. She called for the servants and gave them orders to prepare the house for her husband's and son's return. She wanted everything to be in perfect order, and just exactly as it had been when the hunting party left for the White Mountain. Then she summoned He-sham and instructed him to arrange a triumphant ceremonial entry for the hunters in the morning.

Chapter 44

A Hero's Welcome

From the city gates to the House of Dan-El

The next morning, when the gates had been opened for a space of two hours, the hunting party finally reentered the city. A crowd of well-wishers had gathered to greet them, and to admire the great pelt of the lion, which was stretched out on a large frame and held aloft on long poles in the middle of the procession by four of Ahinadab's porters.

Ahinadab was well aware that this was a rare opportunity to make a strong impression on all the people of Gebal, and he made the most of it. He had used the first two hours of the day to ensure that his entire hunting party looked its very best. Overnight their travel-worn clothing was freshly washed and mended. They had all bathed in the river north of the town, and had been anointed with fresh olive oil. Their hair and beards had been curled and oiled, so that their hair gleamed and sparkled in the early morning sun. Their weapons and the bronze plates in their armor had been cleaned and polished.

Ahinadab was resplendent, wearing his full armor, which reflected the brilliant morning sunlight. He wore colored ribbons in his raven-black hair and freshly curled beard. His horse had been rubbed and combed until its hide glowed. Its tail and mane were hung with ribbons matching those of its rider.

He rode skillfully and guided his mount with his knees alone, leaving his hands free. In his right hand, resting on his shoulder, he held his great khopesh. His bow and quiver were slung across his back and his javelin was couched in the crook of his left arm. The effect was awe-inspiring as he led his hunting party through the city gates, past the seats of his fellow shofeṭim and along the street that ran between the three great temples to where it entered the marketplace.

All along the way people were cheering, shouting, and praising the hunters' success. The party passed by the temple gates where groups of priests were singing hymns of praise to the gods and playing on their instruments. The high priests chanted their blessings on the procession as it passed by. Only Ili-Rapih was conspicuously absent. He could not bring himself to impart a blessing on Ahinadab's successful return.

At the marketplace young girls came forth to carpet the pavement with flower petals all along the party's route. Citizens had come from every quarter. The elders and high-born, the merchants, financiers, and tradesmen were there. Among them were shipwrights, ropemakers, sail makers, along with fishermen, ships' masters, and common sailors. Only the slaves who dared not leave their labors, were absent. Everyone else had come out to see the spectacle of the hunting party's return.

It was certainly an expensive spectacle. Weeks before, the ba'alat Nikkal had made arrangements, which were set in motion with great haste after learning of her husband's imminent return. She knew how important this event would be, and that it must properly reflect the power and wealth of the House of Dan-El. After the losses suffered in the fire their resources were only a fraction of what they should have been. But thanks to a timely loan from Lord Paltiba'al she was able to covered the costs.

She had made sizable offerings to the temple priests, to ensure their participation. She had hired musicians to create a festive atmosphere at the marketplace, knowing their tunes would draw a large crowd. She had hired vendors to pass among the people there with bread, wine, and beer, to keep everyone in a good mood while they waited for the procession to begin. Now these preparations were bearing fruit.

The crowd in the marketplace parted before Ahinadab and the hunting party. As their procession passed, people pressed in closely to touch the heroes in hope of gaining some of their virtue. Some, in an excess of excitement were striving to touch the lion's hide. They were pulling on the tail and paws, trying to pluck a few hairs from the pelt as souvenirs. This threatened to drag it down to the pavement, which would have been disastrous. But seeing the danger, Ahinadab urged his party forward as fast as possible and was glad when they finally exited the marketplace on the eastern side, and turned into the residential district where the homes of the high-born stood. They followed the rise of the street, climbing the small promontory on which the House of Dan-El stood. The crowd followed close behind, still cheering with excitement, right up to the very gates of the house itself.

Dressed in her finest, Nikkal had observed the party's progress from the upper level of the gatehouse. As the procession exited the marketplace and approached the gatehouse, she signaled Artros, who led his guards outside to keep order and hold back the crowds. The watchmen on the parapet raised their trumpets and blew a long and lively fanfare. Then Nikkal withdrew through the courtyards to stand before the front door to the house proper, there to await her husband and her son.

The head of the procession halted before a double row of the household guards that lined the path leading from the street to the gatehouse. The guards, all turned out in full battle array and standing at attention, faced each other in pairs. They held their spears at a forward angle to cross those of the men facing them, blocking the entrance. As their master Ahinadab urged his horse forward toward the first pair of guards his hunters blew a loud blast on their hunting horns and a shout went up from Osiris the master of huntsmen.

"Open for the lord Ahinadab and let him pass, for he has returned to his home. Make way for him and all his people!" Hearing this, the guards raised their spears, uncrossing each pair, one after another, front to back, to make a clear path for their lord to pass with his entourage. The hunting party entered the outer courtyard through the open gates to where the long journey finally ended. When the last of the oxcarts was through, the gates were closed and the guards took up positions between the gatehouse and the admiring crowd.

"Welcome home, my lord husband!" Nikkal called out excitedly from the steps in front of the house as Ahinadab rode through to the inner courtyard. He passed his weapons to his bodyguards and, dismounted. A servant took hold of his horse's bridle and he rushed up the steps to sweep her into a passionate embrace and kissed her long and hard upon the lips.

"Where is my son?" Nikkal demanded as soon as their lips parted. The joyful expression she wore as she greeted Ahinadab had melted into one that was blissful and eager for more than just his kisses, but then was quickly replaced with a deeply worried look. Her body had relaxed in his embrace, but now tensed up as she stared into his eyes, looking for signs of reassurance.

"Do not fear, my love!" Ahinadab said, "He is there, in the first cart. The one draped with the striped canopy. My body servants rode with him and attended him all the way home. Go to him."

Nikkal needed no encouragement. Ahinadab released her from his arms and she ran to the cart. There she looked inside to find her son resting on soft bedding, propped upright with his chest heavily bandaged. The servants climbed down to make room for her and stood by in attendance. She took their place in the cart, anxiously looking her son over from head to foot. Then, not trusting her eyes alone, she drew close to his chest and sniffed at his wounds for any hint of the odor that always accompanied corrupted flesh. She took in several deep breaths to be sure, and when she could find no evidence of the rot that often signaled the approach of death, she let her breath out in a long, deep sigh of relief.

"Hello mother." Gamil said in a low voice. His words were more than just a greeting, there was also a question in his tone. Throughout the journey home, he had grown more and more concerned about how she would receive him. "I'm sorry I caused you so much worry. I didn't think..." His words trailed off and she reached for him, scooped him up in her arms, and clutched him tightly to her breast. He felt hot tears falling on his head, and felt her body shake with the release of all her suppressed worries. It was several minutes before she managed to speak. When she could, it was with a voice choked by emotion, and with more tears gleaming in her eyes.

"Praise be to Almighty El for keeping you alive and bringing you back to me!" she said. "Now we must get you inside."

Nikkal waved to a pair of servants who had been standing by with a litter. Gamil was quickly moved onto it and was carried inside the house and up to his chamber. The servants settled him in his bed under the watchful eye of their mistress. When this was accomplished Nikkal swung into action. With the servants help she gently removed the bandages, and examined his wounds. The three long gashes left by the lion's claws were a witness to how close he had come to death. The full realization of this struck her like a blow. She gasped and blinked back more tears, but forced herself to remain calm. Tears were not what her son needed at that moment.

Instead she forced herself to look past his suffering and focus on treating the wounds. This helped her organize her thoughts and pushed her initial reaction to the back of her mind. She studied the wounds closely, taking in more details. She noted they were not as deep as they looked at first, and had not damaged any of his organs. She could see they were not immediately life-threatening. The paleness of his face told her he had lost a lot of blood, but it seemed he was recovering from that. Aside from lingering weakness in his limbs and some light-headedness, she could see he was already beginning to mend.

The real threat now was from corruption that might still enter the wounds if care was not taken to prevent it. It was well known that even the smallest injuries, sometimes no more than mere scratches, could quickly begin to fester. Wounds that were already healing could suddenly become corrupt and take the life of the victim unless the proper remedies were applied and the right offerings were made to Eshmun. If the rephaites chose to cause trouble they could also bring about a sudden and unexpected change for the worse.

"You have done well in caring for my son. I thank you from my heart." Nikkal said to Ahinadab's body servants. They had remained in the room to assist her. She could see that the flesh was already closing up and scabbing over in the shallower places, while some blood still seeped from the deeper areas where the gashes had been stitched together.

She could find only minor signs of corruption, merely some reddening of the flesh at the sides of the gashes. This redness occurred with any break in the skin, and was regarded as a sign of healing.

"Fetch water and soap." Nikkal ordered, "We must wash his wounds thoroughly." One of the servants went for these things, and Nikkal noticed the remains of the poultice on his skin and asked, "What is this?"

The second servant answered, "The mistress of the woodcutters' camp, the woman named Ja-rune, mixed wheat flour with honey to put on the young master's wounds after washing and sewing them shut. She told us we must keep the wounds covered with this mixture and showed us how to spread honey on his bandages each time we changed them. This, she told us, would ward off the corrupting spirits. But the honey was all used up two days ago, so what you see are only remnants of the last application."

"Ja-rune must be very wise to know such a thing. I have heard that Eshmun smiles on the people of the White Mountain and they are very wise in all types of remedies. I am grateful that she was there to save the life of my son.

Go to the cook, and tell her to give you all of the honey she has, along with a large bowl of wheat flour. Bring it here at once." One servant left to find the cook just as the other returned, bearing a large basin, an ewer of water, a large sponge and some soap. Nikkal took these and set to work. She gently and carefully began to clean his wounds, trying not to cause him too much pain, though some was unavoidable.

Gamil sucked in his breath and held it as long as he could, reacting to the pain, while his mother continued to wash his wounds. He concentrated on not crying out or showing any unmanly signs of weakness. But despite his best efforts, he still felt faintness creeping over him and a cold sweat broke out on his forehead when she worked on the worst places. His face was drained of color by the time she finished cleaning his wounds and dressing them with the honey-wheat poultice and fresh bandages. He lay back, exhausted by the ordeal, and his mother let him rest.

Nikkal would have gladly born his pain herself, rather than having him suffer so. She watched him lay there with his eyes closed and his bandaged chest rising and falling peacefully. She had been totally focused on treating his wounds, but now she studied him more closely. She was surprised to notice the subtle changes that had occurred in the brief time since she had last seen him. Was she imagining it, she thought, or had she simply not noticed these things earlier?

She knew that a mother's eyes could easily overlook day-to-day changes in her growing children, picturing them in her mind as if they never changed at all. But now, having been away for more than a month, he seemed taller, and the muscles of his chest and shoulders were larger and more developed. Overall his face had lost much of the softness of a young boy, and he was beginning to look more like an adult.

"He will be a fine-looking man," she thought, *"if he lives. We must do everything possible to make sure he does!"* She made a sign with her right hand to ward off evil. Then with a deep sigh, she left him to sleep and went to her chamber to kneel in prayer before the shrine to El.

Chapter 45
A Hero's Welcome

In the House of Dan-El

Before long, the story of Gamil and the lion spread throughout the city. The moment they were dismissed, the hunters headed for their favorite taverns to trade their accounts for free drinks. Soon it spread to all parts of the city, gaining new embellishments as it went. It grew with every retelling until Gamil's stature was almost that of a demi-god. A day later, highly exaggerated versions were making the rounds in the city and surrounding villages.

High-born visitors and well-wishers began to call upon the House of Dan-El, both to congratulate Ahinadab on the success of the hunt, and to hear the story of his son's exploits firsthand. It was understood that Gamil had achieved something extraordinary and it was expected that his father would acknowledge the boy-hero as his son very soon. All the visitors wanted to see him, but Ahinadab and Nikkal graciously and firmly, deflected all requests. Gamil was still not up to receiving company they said, offering instead an invitation to a celebration to be held in his honor as soon as he was healed enough to bear the excitement.

Ahinadab had the lion's skin displayed outside the gates for the people to marvel over. All could see how great a monster it had been. Two of the household guards stood watch to protect the hide from anyone who tried to pluck the lion's hair or cut off pieces to make into amulets. Relics such as these were thought to impart great spiritual virtue to the wearer. A lion's hide was such a rare object, and this one of such great celebrity, that by the end of the first day there would have been nothing left of it. But the guards kept anyone from touching it, and after a week it still was drawing crowds. Few people in Gebal had not seen it at least once. Even the sailors and visitors from foreign places were drawn to it and marveled at its size. People began to compare Gamil's slaying of this lion with the hero-king Izdubar, legendary slayer of many lions.

Gamil was dimly aware of the extra activity that was going on in the house below while he rested in his chamber. Except for his parents and the household servants, only the priests of Eshmun had seen him. A troop of seven priests, including the high priest, had arrived in the early hours of the morning on the day after the hunting party returned. They were brought to Gamil's bedchamber where they examined his wounds and anointed them with a mixture of oils and herbs that smelled of camphor and other powerful medicines. They gave him a potion with poppy oil to ease his pain and help him to sleep.

They hung seven amulets above his sleeping palette to ward off evil spirits and powerful incantations were chanted to invoke the power of Eshmun on Gamil's behalf. A cloud of fragrant incense filled the room, causing Gamil to sneeze and hug his damaged ribs. Drums were beaten and small hand bells rang to attract the attention of their god and some of the priests began to sway and dance to the rhythm.

This continued for several hours, until the priests were satisfied that their ministrations were complete and their prayers had been heard.

Then they were ushered from the room by He-sham's assistant, Han-nu, who led them down the stairs. He-sham led the high priest into his office for private conversation. There he questioned the priest as to Gamil's health, and prognosis before opening a negotiation of the payment for their services. While this was happening, Han-nu led the other priests to the foyer where they were served wine, cheese and other refreshments.

Wine was also brought into the office, and the high priest and He-sham drank to the health of the young patient. He-sham offered a toast to salute the priests of Eshmun and the high priest answered by invoking the god's blessing on the entire household. After the toasts, it was time to settle on a price. This was the proper and customary way to open a negotiation.

All negotiations involved some haggling as a matter of course, and this was no different. The high priest's opening price was predictably excessive. He-sham knew he would pad the bill with a significant amount above the cost of the ointments, oils, incense and amulets used in the ceremony. Even the charge for the priests' services would be inflated.

Naturally, He-sham countered with a figure that was correspondingly too low. In time-honored fashion, through an exchange of offer and counter-offer the haggling eventually resulted in an agreed price that was much lower than the original figure, but still quite generous.

He-sham, a veteran of hundreds of similar negotiations, knew his business well. Without being obvious, he deliberately over-paid in order to ensure good will between his master's house and the temple. This demonstrated both proper respect for the god and his priests, and underscored the House of Dan-El's position of power and great wealth. A scribe recorded the transaction and made a copy for the temple. Han-nu prepared a purse with the agreed payment and brought it into the office. He-sham handed the purse to the high priest and the two embraced.

With this business concluded, He-sham escorted the high priest and his helpers to the front gate. As they left the house all were smiling. It was a sure sign that Eshmun was smiling too.

Chapter 46
Ili-Rapih the Schemer

In the temple of Ba'al Šāmēm

One person was not pleased to see Ahinadab and the hunting party return in victory. Ili-Rapih, the high priest to both Ba'al Šāmēm and Yam-Nahar, would have preferred that Ahinadab never returned at all. Seeing his adversary succeed in anything always angered him, especially when it interfered with his own schemes. The greeting Ahinadab and his men had received, the parade through the city, and the continuing excitement, made Ili-Rapih's blood boil.

For years Ahinadab and his supporters had managed to frustrate Ili-Rapih's most egregious attempts to control the actions of the council. Just before the hunting trip, Ahinadab persuaded the council to disapprove a special exemption for the temples, freeing them from a new tax levied by the pharaoh, on imports of papyrus, incense, and other commodities the priests used every day. Ili-Rapih wanted the council to pay this tax instead of the temples. This would have saved the temple treasuries hundreds of talents of gold and silver. That was wealth that Ili-Rapih had plans for.

He needed to send rich gifts to the court of Suppiluliuma, the powerful ruler of the Hittite empire, and at the same time, wanted to buy the favor of Akhenaten, pharaoh of Kemet. He was subtly playing these two rulers against each other in a time when the Hittite ruler was expanding his empire southward, encroaching on the lands ruled by the Pharaoh. Akhenaten was less concerned with protecting his northern holdings than his predecessors had been, and it seemed that the Hittites might soon succeed in seizing many of his northern vassal cities, including Gebal. Suppiluliuma had already taken the lands along the coast, south of Ugarit, up to the outskirts of Arwad. Ili-Rapih's brother, Rib-Hadda had been begging Pharaoh to send troops to Gebal to bolster its defenses, but the response was minimal. The high priest saw the need to secretly curry favor with the Hittite ruler in case he became the city's new master.

But no matter how the contest between Hatti and Kemet played out, Ili-Rapih wanted to appear loyal to the winner. That meant he needed the trust of the Pharaoh Akhenaten as well.

Akhenaten was suspicious of all the priests of Kemet's gods, and by extension, the priests in his vassal states. He vigorously suppressed the priests of Amun whom he felt had interfered too much in the affairs of his reign. He decreed that Kemet would only worship his personal deity, the Aten.

So far, this decree did not apply to the vassal cities, but Ili-Rapih wanted to make sure that it never did. He had been secretly sending expensive gifts to the Pharaoh's court for some time, hoping to win Akhenaten's trust and favor. If Kemet retained control of Gebal, he would need pharaoh's approval for his scheme to overthrow his brother and take the throne himself. He was confident that he would succeed in all these things, if not for Ahinadab's interference.

So, on the day the hunting party returned, the high priest sat inside his house, brooding on the many times and different ways his adversary had frustrated him. He vowed to Ba'al Šāmēm that he would find some way to bring down the House of Dan-El into utter ruin. But that could not happen while the multitude in the streets held Ahinadab in such high regard. Not to mention the near worship of the crowds for Ahinadab's son. What was the boy's name? Camel? The boy might provide a way to get at his father, if he lived.

The rumors were that the young "hero" was badly injured and might still die from his wounds. That would be a crushing blow to Ahinadab. Ili-Rapih would patiently wait for the outcome. In the meantime, he plotted and schemed his schemes. When an opportunity to strike at the House of Dan-El presented itself, he would be ready.

Chapter 47

Gamil's Secret

In the House of Dan-El

Whenever Gamil was left alone for more than a few moments his mind started to dwell on the events leading up to his supposed victory over the lion. He was fully aware of the excitement that still permeated the city, fed by the continued displaying of the lion's hide outside the gates of the House of Dan-El and the endless repetition of "the legend."

This "legend" had grown out of proportion to the reality. Many claimed to personally know a member, either of the hunting party or the woodcutters' company, who had witnessed the slaying of the lion. Others claimed they knew Gamil, or were friends of his family. It amazed Gamil to hear such nonsense. Only he knew the real facts. He had been foolish to disobey his father and seek the lion by himself. He had ignored the danger and should have been killed. He couldn't see himself as a hero, and it made him feel guilty that everyone else did.

Even the household servants who had known Gamil from his infancy now looked on him with awe and were excited to be in his presence.

Their gossiping about his ongoing recovery inevitably made its way to both Ili-Rapih and Rib-Haddad. The high priest and his brother both followed the news with great interest.

One servant in the House of Dan-El was Ishba'at. She had been Gamil's nursemaid since he was a baby. She had stopped bathing him when he entered puberty, but had been giving him sponge baths during his recovery. He felt somewhat embarrassed to be so dependent upon her, and was disturbed by this intimate care. Like his parents, she had noticed the changes in him since his return. Childhood was fading and the man he would become was very evident to her. There was a new gleam in her eye as she washed his naked body, and her touch became more of a caress than was required to insure cleanliness.

"Young master," she said in a sultry voice, "the people of the city have started calling you "Gamil, Slayer of Lions" and sometimes even "Gamil the Brave" or "Gamil the Mighty". Many new mothers are naming their male children "Gamil" in hope that their sons will have your courage and strength. You should be very proud." Her eyes were focused on his genitals as she spoke, and her voice took on a low-pitched, husky tone.

Strangely, her touch was causing a stirring in his loins as the sponge neared his genitals. This sensation was embarrassing and he grasped her wrist to stop her from making the kind of contact she seemed intent upon.

Undeterred, she made full eye contact with him and boldly said, "In fact, I would be proud to name my own son Gamil, especially if his namesake was also his father."

Her other hand "accidentally" brushed against his now quite rigid penis, sending an alarming jolt of pleasure to his brain.

"Uh, I think that will be all for now, Ishba'at!" he stammered, his voice sounding thicker than he hoped it would. "I'm well enough to wash myself from now on. Thank you for your care. You may leave me now."

"I am sorry if I have displeased you, young master!" she replied with a note of disappointment in her voice. "You are not a little boy any more, and I thought you might have other, more manly, needs that I could attend to. If you need my help, with *anything*, you need only to call for me. It would be my pleasure to *serve* you."

"Uh, thank you Ishba'at. That is, um, very kind of you. If I think of anything, I will call for you. Go now! I want to be alone."

Ishba'at left the room, swaying her hips provocatively as she crossed to the door. She smiled and winked her eye at Gamil as she pulled his door shut. When she was gone, he let out his breath in a long, low sigh. He hadn't realized until then that his heart was beating fast, and his body seemed charged with an unfamiliar energy. What, he wondered, was this all about? Why had Ishba'at treated him the way she had. If this was what it was like to be an adult, he wasn't sure he was ready for it. He was certain that he wasn't ready for whatever she seemed to have in mind. But something in the back of his brain that he couldn't quite grasp was aroused and exhilarated like nothing he had ever felt before.

He took up the sponge and soap that Ishba'at had left and finished washing himself. The bandages were gone now, and his wounds were scabbed over and healed for the most part. There would forever be those three long scars to remind him of his brush with death, but they didn't seem to hinder his movement any longer. Only his damaged ribs still hurt when he took deep breaths or turned his torso too abruptly in the wrong direction.

He dried off with a large linen towel and dressed in a fresh loincloth, kilt and tunic. His erection was still causing a potentially embarrassing problem. He was barely able to get his loincloth on, and his kilt was standing out from his body in front. He tried to clear his mind from the memory of Ishba'at's provocative words and actions. He focused his thoughts on that day at the slope above the woodcutters' camp and eventually things settled down and his garments assumed their normal and more polite arrangement. He slipped on his sandals and walked out of his chamber for the first time since he had arrived home three weeks earlier.

It was well into summer now, and the upper level of the house was uncomfortably hot. Gamil walked from his chamber to the end of the landing and out onto the back balcony. He climbed the stairway leading up to the roof, where the air was cooler. Light breezes blew in from the sea, carrying a fresh, salty, slightly-fishy aroma.

The sun dazzled his eyes at first, as he walked around the roof to stretch his legs. He reached a spot at the front of the house where he could lean against the low wall that surrounded the roof and looked out toward the front gate.

He saw a small crowd of people gathered there to marvel over the lion's pelt. He had heard that visitors were still coming by to gawk at it, even this long after the hunters' return. He would have thought the whole world had seen it by now, yet here these people were, still amazed by it. He hadn't seen it himself since it was still on the lion, but from his spot on the roof he could just make out the tips of the tail and the back paws that were stretched out and up above the wall.

A man from the crowd looked up and saw him. He pointed excitedly and said something to the others that Gamil couldn't hear. Every eye instantly turned and looked up toward him, and to his surprise, the people below began to cheer and call out his name.

"Gamil, Lion Slayer" they chanted in unison, over and over. "Lion Slayer, Lion Slayer..." the volume rose. They waved at him and jumped and down to get a better look at him. Little children were lifted up onto their parents' shoulders and some of the people tried to climb the wall. The commotion brought six of the household guards rushing out of the barracks to join those guarding the lion's hide. Together they quickly restored order before anyone was injured.

Gamil didn't know what to make of all this. The crowd's enthusiasm was contagious, bringing a smile to his face and causing him to wave back This brought the cheering to new heights. "Blessings be upon you, Gamil, slayer of lions!" a woman with a loud voice exclaimed. Her cry was picked up by the others who began to chant it as well.

Gamil was delighted and embarrassed at the same time. He didn't know what to do, but kept on waving at the adoring crowd. He didn't notice that his mother had slipped up behind him until she put her hand on his shoulder. He was almost as tall as her now, and she was pleased that the crowd was recognizing him in this way. He looked at her and dropped his hand, not sure if she approved. She smiled at him, raising her own hand to wave. Relieved, he renewed his own waving with even greater enthusiasm. Now they were cheering for both the Lion Slayer and his mother.

They kept waving to the crowd until their arms grew tired. Finally, they turned away from the roof's edge and moved to the pavilion. The shouts from the crowd dropped off to an excited murmur as Nikkal and Gamil seated themselves on the pavilion's couches and looked out over the city and the sea beyond.

"Mother," he asked, "What just happened? Why were the people shouting my name and calling me Lion Slayer? I don't understand. Before the hunt I'm don't believe more than a few of them even knew I existed, and now..."

"Gamil, word of your victory over the lion has spread well beyond the walls of the city. Your story is told over and over again every day with your deeds embellished more and more in each telling. I've even heard that a song has been made, setting the tale to music. It is sung in the taverns and down at the docks."

"But why?" he asked.

"Well, most people don't have much to divert their thoughts from the routine activities of daily life. Whenever something new takes place it captures their imagination for a while. It remains the talk of the city until something else gets their attention and the former thing is almost forgotten."

"Then I hope something else will happen soon, so they can forget about me." Gamil said, "I don't want crowds following me around the city! And I really don't want them singing about me!"

Nikkal laughed and said, "Enjoy it while it lasts Gamil. Not everyone gets to be celebrated as you are now. It will add luster to the reputation of our house, and will raise the status of your father in the eyes of the people. Your own status will rise as well, for between you and me, he intends to name you as soon as you are recovered enough to endure the ceremony and banquet. From the look of you now, I will be able to tell him you are almost ready."

"*WHAT*! Mother, is this true? You would tell him that? He will do that?" Gamil could hardly believe it. His fondest wish, to be named the son of Ahinadab, was about to come to pass.

"I am certain of it, Nikkal replied, "He has had the scribes preparing invitations to the ceremony and banquet for weeks now, but has held them until you were ready. When he returns from holding court at the northern gate, I will speak to him and I'm sure he will send out the invitations this very day. Then, in a few days, the hall below us will be filled to the walls with the high-born and finest families of

Gebal. Even the inner and central courtyards will be opened to the lesser citizens so that all may enjoy the festivities."

Gamil was overwhelmed with emotion and wanted to cry for joy, but held his tears. He could not show any unmanly or childish excitement. Especially not now.

"Will he invite my friends and their families? I want them all to be there when he names me."

"I think you can trust your father to see that they are included. But now, if you feel up to it let us go down to the kitchen and find you something to eat. You need to build up your strength. You still are much too pale."

They left the roof and went down the back stairway to the kitchen behind the house proper.

That night Gamil lay sleepless on his pallet, unable to stop thinking about the coming ceremony and the excited crowd at the gates. Had they been cheering for him, or for the hero they took him to be. Only he knew that the lion had found him instead of the other way around. Some hunter he was!

Worst of all, he knew for certain that if he had not stumbled over the tree root at exactly the right moment, and if the point of his javelin had not been at exactly the right angle, he would have died on that mountain. It was not by any strength or skill he possessed, but could only have been an act of Almighty El.

He was troubled deeply by these thoughts and wanted to confess his unworthiness to his father and the world. But this supposed victory over the lion was the thing that made him a son his father could proudly acknowledge. Without it there would be no naming ceremony. Gamil could not risk losing that sacred moment no matter what. So, he kept these thoughts to himself, and continued to struggle with his guilt.

It helped him justify his silence that his father had already invested much of his own status in his son's heroic actions. To contradict that now would make Ahinadab seem foolish, or worse, a liar. Instead of basking in the reflected glory from his son's celebrity, he would be a laughing stock.

No! That could never be allowed to happen. Only Gamil and Almighty El knew the truth, and whatever the cost to his own integrity and self-image, he would keep that secret locked in his heart.

Chapter 48
Plans and Preparations

In Ahinadab's office

"My lord, here are the lists you requested for the ceremony and banquet. I have included a few suggestions for your approval, if they please you." He-sham stood before his lord inside Ahinadab's office, where the shofeṭ was seated at his great ivory-inlaid table. He presented a large papyrus scroll to Ahinadab, bowing as it was taken from him. Ahinadab unrolled the scroll across the table top, glancing at certain items that caught his attention.

"I see you have made the changes I requested. Have the invitations been delivered?"

"They were sent out this morning, my lord. There were so many it will be evening before all are delivered, but we have already received the first of the replies. The response appears to be excellent."

"As it should," Ahinadab said, "It has been some time since one of the great houses held a celebration such as this. I expect it will be remembered for many years."

"Indeed, my lord. Just the rumor of these preparations was enough to set the city buzzing like a hive of bees. The expectation is that you will be naming the young master Gamil as your son and heir, and the banquet will be appropriately magnificent."

He-sham, as the rab-tamkari of the House of Dan-El, was responsible for procuring the tremendous amounts of food stuffs, wine, gifts, and other items that were needed for what his master was planning. He gave orders to the cooks as to what and how everything should be prepared, how the great hall was to be decorated and the courtyards cleaned and set up with trestle tables to accommodate as many of the common people as possible.

He-sham had a keen understanding of this event's importance, both as it marked a major turning point in the life of his lord's son, and how it would impact the reputation and status of the House of Dan-El. Successful events were critical to success in business and in the politics of the city. Major events like the ceremony and banquet being planned would, if carried off well, ensure the continued prosperity of the house for years to come.

"My lord, I know you instructed me to spare no expense, but several items have run higher in cost than is usual. For example, if you will examine the sums for the golden wine chalices you will note that the quantity specified is 100 at a final cost of one-half silver talent. That is double the price we would have paid last year."

"Yes, I see!" Ahinadab's brows shot up and his expression showed great concern. "Why such a large increase in price?"

"It is mostly the aftermath of the fire my lord" He-sham explained. "The losses from the fire were tremendous and affected so many of the great houses and small businesses that our financiers and money-lenders are having trouble meeting the demand for loans. Everyone is straining to rebuild and replace what was lost. Our own outlays for the three new ships you ordered have cost far more than normal. Everything needed to equip them is priced higher than I have seen in all my years of service."

Ahinadab pondered this as he studied the scroll, quickly totaling up the other items that showed grossly inflated costs. Overall expenses for the celebration were running close to three times as much as he had expected, and would probably go higher before it was all said and done. He would gladly spend twice as much for the naming of his first-born son, but the financial realities could not be ignored. He knew the expenses would eventually be recouped many times over in both the good will and future business it would generate, but some savings would have to be made.

"How stands our treasury?" Ahinadab asked. "I don't want it drained to the last scrap of copper."

"My lord, the household treasury has been hard hit since the fire. The lost profits from the ships that were burned and the higher operating costs for the remaining ships have combined to cause a gap in our revenues. Presently we have about one month's reserves above the lowest point I feel comfortable with. When the costs of the ceremony and banquet are paid, we will have exhausted most of our treasure."

"Continue the preparations as planned, but try to find some savings by cutting a few corners. Instead of solid gold chalices have them made of bronze and dipped in gold. The difference should not be noticed. No, wait! Be sure that the guests who will be seated at my table have solid gold chalices, as I intend for them to keep them as mementos of this event, and I can't have it discovered that I scrimped where the elites are concerned.

Beyond that, do as seems wise to you. Keep me informed of your progress and of any additional expenses as they come up. I will meet with lord Paltiba'al and arrange a loan against our profits from the sale of next season's cedar order. That should carry us through."

"As you wish my lord!" He-sham replied. "I will see to it." This should have signaled the end of the meeting, but He-sham hesitated.

"My lord, if I may? There is important news regarding the men who set the fire at the harbor."

"You may speak." Ahinadab said.

"As I reported to you last week, the men who set the fires were identified by the daughter of lord Paltiba'al and one of his household guards. The main culprit was none the less than the former master of the *Cabax*, Barakba'al. Paltiba'al's youngest daughter, Melita, was attacked twice by these same two men. First, on the night of the fire, when she saw them start the blaze and murder one of the city guardsmen. The second time was as she and the other children of the lord Paltiba'al were being escorted home after the funeral of his servant Yutpan.

During the second attack, the household guard escorting them, killed one of the attackers, a sailor from the crew of your ship the *Cabax*, and seriously wounded Barakba'al, who managed to escape. Despite a thorough search, he has not been found, even though he left a bloody trail, leading away from the city and into the wild hill country. The guard who fought him believes his wound was serious. Enough so that he might be dead of it by now."

"Yet you sound as if you doubt his corpse lies rotting in the hills. What have you learned since the last report?" Ahinadab prompted.

"A ship of the Achaean's docked at the southern port last night. Some of the crew visited the taverns along the waterfront, where you have eyes and ears. This morning one of your watchers learned that the

Achaeans, while on the island of Athar, heard a rumor that Barakba'al had been seen heading to the north, on the road to Ugarit. His right arm was said to have been heavily bandaged, and it seemed as if he had lost the hand below that wrist. This would be the same wrist lord Paltiba'al's guard had wounded."

"Hmmm." Ahinadab mused, "This seems thin to me. But if it is true then Barakba'al is well beyond our reach by now. I will send word to our agents in Ugarit, urging them to be vigilant. If he does enter that city, they can inform my cousin, Urtenu. He is an advisor to king Niqmaddu and perhaps can persuade his lord to seize Barakba'al and return him to us for judgment.

But in any case, I will warn my agents to secure all of our investments there. We cannot afford any more losses, and Barakba'al has proven himself to be a thief and a murderer. He has already done great harm to this house in a number of ways. We must assume he will try to do even more if he has an opportunity. Is there anything else?"

"No, my lord. If it pleases you, I shall return to the preparations for the ceremony."

"Very well!" Ahinadab said, handing the scroll back to his rab-tamkari. He-sham bowed low and took three backward steps toward the door before turning and exiting the office.

Chapter 49
The Naming

In the House of Dan-El

The early morning light crept through the window in Gamil's chamber to find him already awake and preparing for the day. This was *the* day, the one he had been waiting for his whole life. Today his father would acknowledge him as his true son and heir. He would no longer be known only as the son of ba'alat Nikkal. From this day forward he would be known to all men as the son of Ahinadab, of the House of Dan-El!

A shiver of excitement came over him as he pondered the meaning of those words. The preceding month had been spent preparing him for this day, and now it was here. He had been told what to expect and what was expected of him. He had been measured and fitted for new garments appropriate for the occasion, and tutored in the proper etiquette for this, his first public appearance as an adult. He had watched in awe as cartload after cartload of food, decorations, new table service, and vessels of gold and silver arrived in what seemed like an unending stream. Just yesterday the last of the banquet materials finally arrived.

His father had purchased nine new slaves to help serve the feast and assist with the food preparations. Every corner of the kitchen was needed and awnings had been set up on both sides of the building for outdoor cooking. Whole pigs were steaming in pits below the awnings, while deer, sheep, and goats were roasting on large spits nearby. The spits would be turned for hours until the venison and mutton were seared to a golden brown, and glistened with melted fat. The aroma had drifted into Gamil's chamber even before the dawn light and made his mouth water.

Several hundred loaves of bread were baked in the great oven of the kitchen, which could hold thirty loaves at a time. When done, they were set on racks to cool, with each loaf adding its own yeasty fragrance to the mix of scents that filled the air.

Ahinadab swore that no person in the entire city would go hungry during the four days of the celebration. Not even slaves. The kitchen gardens were completely stripped of everything edible, and dozens of cabbages were set to boil, along with peas, carrots, leeks, and squash. The cooks would add the flesh of chickens to these vegetables to make a savory porridge. This would be served to the common guests with bread and beer.

The elite citizens would dine on choice cuts of meat, along with wild fowl, peacocks, ducks, doves and partridges. Fresh fish of many kinds were brought up from the southern port, with several kinds of clams, prawns, mollusks, crabs, lobsters, squid and octopus. The fish could be baked or boiled, depending on their species. The clams and mollusks were seethed in a rich garlic sauce. The prawns were fried in olive oil, the lobster and crabs were boiled. A sweetened and spicy sauce of grape vinegar, honey and mustard was served with the squid and octopus, which might be served raw, or boiled depending on the preferences of the guests.

From the island of Alashiya came a shipload of large amphorae holding hundreds of small songbirds, pickled in brine. These would be boiled or roasted and eaten whole. This rare delicacy, known to the Achaeans as "ambelopoulia" was very popular throughout the region. Expensive and hard to come by, its presence on the menu added luster to an already stellar feast.

One hundred large amphorae filled with garum sauce were standing by for everyone's consumption. This pungent fish sauce was a universally popular condiment used to flavor all types of food according to each individual's tastes. No meal was complete without it.

Great quantities of fruit, in every variety, rounded out the feast. Most of these were served fresh, but were also stewed, cooked or otherwise prepared into delicious desserts. The ever-popular raisin-filled honey cakes, and fried fruit pies were in abundance, along with "koupes", the small loaves of cracked wheat bread, stuffed with spiced lamb meat and garnished with peppermint leaves. There were also stuffed grape leaves and other favorites.

Five kinds of wine would be served from decorated amphora by slaves that circulated around the tables. The decorations on the amphora indicated what kind of wine was within, and guests could have their choice by raising their chalices as their favorite wine passed by. In the early hours all the wines would be well watered to avoid anyone becoming drunk before the ceremony. After the ceremony stronger wine would be brought out as the banquet continued.

In all it was designed to be an event that would be the talk of the city for months to come, if not years.

The walls of all the buildings inside the compound were freshly whitewashed until they shone like the snow-topped peaks of the White Mountain itself. The courtyards were swept clean and any broken, or worn paving stones, had been replaced. There was not a speck of mud or dust anywhere in the three courtyards. Garlands of fresh-cut cedar boughs were draped along the eaves of the buildings and wound around the pillars of the altars and galleries. The great bronze doors had been polished and burnished until they shone like the sun itself. The trestle tables were draped with linen cloths and set in rows beneath awnings of striped sailcloth.

In the outer and center courtyards, the foodstuffs for the common people and craftsmen were laid out at dawn, under layers of gauze to keep flies and other insects away. Then, at the eighth hour, a loud trumpet fanfare signaled the opening of the gates, and the waiting crowds were invited to enter. A band of musicians played lively, happy tunes as the seats began to fill and the excited buzz of many conversations could be heard.

The entire population of the city had been invited, except for slaves and servants who would be fed generously at the marketplace. The banquet would last four days, with citizens from each quarter of the city attending on different days.

According to tradition, the king, the high priests, the elders and the elite families were asked to come on the first day, one hour before noon. As these favored guests began to arrive, they were ushered into the inner courtyard where they were offered wine, cheese, and fruit while their feet were washed. They were seated on cushioned stools and cooled with ostrich feather fans by slaves whose job was to make each guest comfortable.

Most of the elite guests chose to mingle with their peers, rather than sit. Once their feet were washed, greetings were exchanged and a certain amount of business was conducted. In short, all this was as it should be, and as expected.

At the exact moment the sun reached its absolute zenith, six trumpeters stood forth on the roof of the house, facing the courtyards below.

They blew a loud, triumphant fanfare, which was repeated three times.

The last notes faded, and every eye was raised to the rooftop. Ahinadab stepped forward to the low wall at its edge, and a hearty cheer greeted him. He was resplendent in a snow-white tunic of pure silk, embroidered with geometric patterns in a multitude of bright colors. He wore the traditional headgear of the elite class, a tall conical miter topped with a ball-like ornament, somewhat similar to the white crown of the Upper Nile worn by the pharaohs of Kemet. In Ahinadab's case this miter was pure white, representing his office as a shofeṭ.

Around his neck he wore a broad, semi-circular collar, fashioned in the style of Kemet, which covered him from his throat to the ends of his collar bones, and down his chest to the end of his sternum. It was composed of elongated, cylindrical, beads made of bright-colored precious and semi-precious stones, in rows of alternating colors backed with thin gold plates. The plates, strung together with gold wire, were shaped to follow the curve of his neckline and fan out from there to fall across his broad pectoral muscles. It looked as if his neck were surrounded by concentric circles of gold and jewels, all of which sparkled and reflected the sun's light in a dazzling display.

A brightly-colored, heavily-embroidered mantle was pinned at his right shoulder and draped to hang in graceful folds down the left side of his body. His waist was bound with a broad belt of copper-, silver-, and gold-threaded fabric, with his mighty khopesh hanging from it. His fingers were covered with jeweled rings, and plain solid gold bands were wound in three twists around his wrists and upper arms.

His hair was oiled, curled, and dyed a dense black to hide the gray strands that had crept into it of late. It fell like a billowing cloud from below his miter to the top of his shoulders. His thick beard was also dyed, tightly curled, and tied with bright ribbons in many colors. He let the crowd show its appreciation for several moments, then held up his arms, palms outward, urging them to quiet down.

"Citizens of Gebal, Children of the Ba'alat Gebal, People of the Almighty El, hear my words. I am Ahinadab, son of Nat'n-El of the House and Lineage of Dan-El. I have invited you here this day to celebrate a sacred tradition of our people. This day I call upon you all to witness the naming of my first-born son and heir."

Cheers and applause burst forth, and it was several moments before the excitement ebbed enough for Ahinadab to continue. When the crowd settled down, he raised his arms, and looking to the heavens he cried, "Let the son of the ba'alat Nikkal, who is called Gamil come forth!"

Gamil trembled as he took a half dozen paces from beside his mother, to stand at his father's side. Upon seeing him, the crowd erupted into a joyful frenzy, and began chanting the name he had been hearing since he arrived back at home.

"Gamil, Slayer of Lions!" the crowd shouted over and over. "Hail Gamil! Hail Gamil!

His dress was less elaborate than his father's, but just as splendid. He wore a new white kilt, embroidered with brightly colored geometric patterns. But this was not like the kilts he had worn as a child and youth. This was the full, knee-length *shenti* of an adult of high rank. It was parted at the two sides leaving his legs bare to the waist. The shenti was elaborately ornamented with a richly adorned lappet in the front, which fell to just below his knees.

Like his father, he wore the mantle of an elite male draped over his left shoulder. But under it he wore only a short, tight-fitting tunic with sleeves that barely covered his shoulders. The tunic front was open to the waist leaving the three long scars from the lion's claws visible to everyone.

Gamil also wore a smaller version of his father's collar, with fewer rows of the beads, but matching the pattern of colors his father wore, further marking him as Ahinadab's son. On his head, instead of a miter, he wore a simple skullcap of black felt, worked with pearls and colored beads in patterns representing the symbols of the major gods and goddesses of Gebal. At the apex of this cap was the figure that represented Almighty El, embroidered with gold and silver thread.

Last but not least, though it could not be seen by those below, Gamil wore just one silver ring on the first finger of his right hand. This was a gift from his father for this occasion with a special significance. A red stone was set into its face, carved to show the likeness of a leaping lion with its body pierced through by a javelin. This symbol of the slain lion would become Gamil's own signet for the rest of his life.

Standing there beside his father Gamil's chest swelled with pride. The people loved him, and he returned their love with a full measure of his own. It occurred to him for the first time in his life, that he had never held any deep feelings for these people before this. They were a part of his world, but beyond his family and a few close friends, he had felt no personal connection to them. That was changed forever now, and he knew himself as a son of Gebal for the first time.

His thoughts were interrupted by his father's loud voice, booming forth for all to heed what Gamil had waited to hear for so long. Ahinadab placed his hands on Gamil's head, and spoke.

"Let all men know that this is my son, in whom I delight! You have known him as Gamil, son of ba'alat Nikkal. But henceforth you shall know him by a new name. A name you, his people, have already proclaimed, and that I give to him this day.

"Behold, *Aleon-Tabah,* the Lion Slayer of Gebal, son of Ahinadab, and heir to the House of Dan-El! I call upon Almighty El to watch over him, be gracious to him, and bless all his issue, now and forever."

The guests roared their approval of this new name and began to chant it loudly. But among the elite guest in the inner courtyard were two who did not share the joy of those around them.

Ili-Rapih, and his son, Aderba'al, deliberately arrived late, making a great show of their tardy entrance through the outer and middle courtyards. They reached their reserved places in the inner courtyard just as the trumpets rang out. The attendants, whose job was to see to the guests' pre-ceremony comfort, were caught in a dilemma. They were told to stop what they were doing when the trumpets sounded. The ceremony was beginning, but a half-dozen obviously important guests had just arrived. The attendants didn't know if they should serve these new arrivals or not. To leave them with the dust of the streets coating their feet would be an unforgivable breach of etiquette, but their orders were clear. One started moving toward Ili-Rapih's party anyway, but was stopped by a signal from He-sham. The rab-tamkari waved all the servants off and they stepped back.

He-sham was keenly aware of the high priest's intense jealousy and contempt for Ahinadab, and expected him to do something to spoil the celebration, if he could. Ili-Rapih's late arrival was supposed to force Ahinadab to delay the start of the ceremony. Certainly, he thought, Ahinadab would not begin until his most important guest had arrived, was properly welcomed, and attended to. That was customary, and after all, this event was nothing more than a routine rite of passage, one that every well-born son experienced at some point. The boy was certainly nothing special in any case. The high priest arrogantly thought this would be an occasion to demonstrate his superior status and reinforce his position in the city's hierarchy. Everything else was of no importance. It galled him that Ahinadab had dared to use this trivial ceremony to publicly embarrass him instead.

As a sign of his immense displeasure, Ili-Rapih did not rise to his feet when Ahinadab began to speak, as would have been proper. His entourage took their cue from him and remained in their seats as well. All the other guests did rise and gave their full attention to the speaker on the rooftop.

Aderba'al was also displeased, but not for the same reasons as his father. He loathed Gamil, and in their childhood interactions he often bullied the younger boy, considering him inferior in every way. He resented being forced to participate in celebrating this worthless child's elevation from boyhood to manhood and into full membership in the high-born society of Gebal. His sense of outrage showed in his scowling features, which unlike his father, he was too artless to hide. He-sham saw this and noted it for future reference.

As the cheers of the crowd continued, the doors of the house proper were opened and the elite guests were ushered through the foyer, directly into the great hall. As their numbers thinned out in the space surrounding Ili-Rapih's party He-sham signaled the attendants to recommence their ministrations. Ili-Rapih's party was quickly surrounded by a whirl of activity. Once Ili-Rapih's feet were washed and perfumed, He-sham approached with his deepest bow and most formal greeting.

"Hail lord Ili-Rapih, high priest and most beloved of the gods, intercessor to mighty Ba'al Šāmēm and majestic Yam-Nahar. My lord and master, the shofeṭ Ahinadab, welcomes you to the House of Dan-El, and is delighted that you could join him on this day of celebration, and the naming of his firstborn son, the young lord Aleon-Tabah. May the blessings of El be upon you and your sacred houses. My lord has commanded me to prepare a place for you and your people at the high table, next to your brother, king Rib-Hadda and his family. Pray take your time and join them at the banquet whenever you are pleased to do so."

He-sham's flattery and flowery words had a slightly mollifying effect on the high priest, who consoled himself with the thought that at least he wouldn't be seated next to his host, making small talk and acting as if he were enjoying the feast. Too bad he had to sit next to his fool of a brother, but perhaps even that could be worked to an advantage.

Throughout the long afternoon and evening of feasting Ili-Rapih brooded as he reclined on an ivory-paneled couch. Once the main courses had been served and cleared away, the best wines were brought forth and many toasts were made in honor of Ahinadab and his son. Ili-Rapih smiled and saluted along with the other guests, but his heart was not in it. His real mood grew darker and darker as the day progressed.

Costly gifts were given as the guest tried to outdo each other in showing their appreciation of Ahinadab and his son. The city's most popular poet entertained the guests with a glorified version of *Gamil The Lion Slayer*. Aleon was deeply embarrassed by this overly dramatic recitation of his exploits, especially with the additional flourishes the poet included. He was relieved when it finally ended.

The poem was followed by several songs about the glorious deeds of Ahinadab's ancestors, beginning with the epic *Legend of Dan-el*, king of the Haranimites, who became the father of the hero Aqhat. After Aqhat was killed, Dan-el went on to father many other sons including Ahinadab's father, Nat'n-El, who had first brought the family to Gebal from Ugarit.

Next came the *Song of Ahinadab*, which told of his friendship with pharaoh Akhenaten who bestowed on him the gift of the famous khopesh. Ahinadab's exploits as a young sailor, a shrewd trader, and wise shofeṭ were highlighted. But the final verses were about his son, the newly named Aleon-Tabah.

Aleon's part of the song was another highly embellished version of his encounter with the lion, in which Aleon had been much cleverer and his actions much braver than in reality. Aleon's undaunted courage, the strength of his arms, and his handsome features were detailed in gushing terms. Aleon had never been the subject of such outrageous flattery before, and blushed to hear it. The contrast of the lyrics and his own knowledge of the actual facts was almost too great for him to bear. He began to squirm in embarrassment as he lounged on his own ivory-paneled couch, wishing the song would end.

When it finally arrived at the climactic killing of the lion and the last notes died away, Ahinadab rose from his couch and called for the guests' attention. He had another gift for his son in honor of the occasion.

As soon as the hunting party returned to Gebal, Ahinadab called for craftsmen from the jewelry district to prepare something rare and very special. Osiris had taken the four claws from the lion's paw that had wounded Gamil and saved them. Ahinadab gave these to the craftsmen with orders for them to fashion a necklace that would be like no other work they had ever made.

The bases of the claws were set into solid gold bezels with loops that allowed them to be hung on a plain golden chain. Each claw was incised with gold filled letters of the Kena'ani script that spelled out the name 'Aleon-Tabah'. Between the claws large, perfectly-matched, blood-red carbuncles were added. These were polished to the shape of perfect spheres and looked like great drops of blood. Mounted in the very center of the necklace and surrounded on both sides by the stones and claws, was a solid gold, miniature replica of the head of the javelin that had killed the beast. The necklace had cost Ahinadab dearly, but as he placed it around the neck of his son, the murmur of approval and awe that rippled through the great hall made it well worth the price.

King Rib-Hadda, already deep in the influence of the evenings wine, chose this moment to rise unsteadily from his couch to offer a toast. Ili-Rapih had been waiting for such a moment and made a sign to one of the priests in his entourage. The priest rose and made as if to steady the king, but in fact, he placed his foot on the hem of Rib-Hadda's mantle. As the tipsy king began to stand a subtle move from the priest's other foot caused Rib-Hadda to stumble and fall forward.

This happened as the king had just begun his toast, "Raise your chalices and wine bowls, one and all..." But his words were cut off as he felt himself falling. The chalice he was holding flew from his hand, spilling its contents over guests and servants alike. With a great crash his heavy body knocked over the table in front of him. Food, utensils, crockery, wine bowls, and chalices were scattered across the floor of the great hall.

His chin hit the floor hard, and he was knocked unconscious. He lay on his large belly amid the broken dishes, smashed foodstuffs, and spilled wine. His royal crown was knocked askew and was hanging down over his eyes.

All the guests were shocked to see the king fall. Was he hurt? Had he been poisoned? Was he dead? No one could tell what had happened. But after a moment, Rib-Hadda began to snore loudly, for he really was profoundly drunk. The concerned whispers quickly changed, first into tittering, and then into open laughter at the comical scene. Thus, what should have been a great moment for Aleon, at the height of the banquet, was overshadowed and the king's stature was greatly diminished in the eyes of the elite families of Gebal.

Ili-Rapih was immensely pleased. Things had worked out better than he had hoped. He quickly forced a look of deep concern to cover his face as he and Ahinadab both moved to assist the king. Ili-Rapih was closer, and was first to reach the king. He locked eyes with Ahinadab for an instant, then they lifted the king back onto his couch. That brief look into Ili-Rapih's eyes told Ahinadab what really happened.

The king's attendants, with help from the royal guards, carried him from the couch and up the stairs to one of the guest chambers, where he would spend the night sleeping off the effects of the wine.

Other attendants quickly righted the overthrown table, cleared away the mess, reset the utensils and replaced the foodstuffs and wine. The banquet continued for the rest of the evening with no further disruption. None of the guests suspected that this was more than just a tipsy king stumbling over his own feet. But the damage to Rib-Hadda's reputation was done, just as Ili-Rapih had intended. For the rest of the evening, and for weeks after, the king's disgraceful behavior was the fuel for disapproving gossip that soon spread throughout the entire city and into the surrounding countryside. Ili-Rapih and his son, with their entourage, left the banquet after the high priest had made a great show of concern for his brother's well-being. Outside the gates of the house he allowed himself a satisfied smile. From his perspective, things had gone well.

Chapter 50

Aleon Goes to Sea

Late fall, 1330 BC, at the northern harbor of Gebal

Two and a half years had passed since the naming ceremony, but the event was still remembered with great approbation. At the time, it was exactly what was needed to lift the spirits of the people of Gebal, coming as it did just three months after the disastrous fire at the port.

It had taken two years for the north harbor to be completely repaired and enlarged, and for the shops and buildings along the waterfront to be rebuilt. But now, the normal flow of commerce had resumed, and the wealth and power of the city was even greater than before the fire.

Much had changed since Aleon last stood on the wharf beside his father's ships, and in that time he had also changed. He had been at sea for most of two entire sailing seasons that had changed him from a boy to a young man, who was now a well-seasoned mariner. He stood on the wharf with his mind thinking back to his earliest days at sea.

Following the naming ceremony, Aleon's father had stepped up his education with a new sense of urgency. Before the lion hunt it had seemed to the boy that his father would forever see him as a child. But since he recovered from his wounds, it was as if father couldn't wait a moment longer to see his firstborn son a fully-grown man. To make up for lost time, everything concerning Aleon was now Ahinadab's highest priority.

Ahinadab's children, including his daughters, had always had tutors and teachers. But two new slaves had been purchased for the express purpose of preparing Aleon for the role he would one day have. One of these slaves was an older man well-versed in the languages, geography, and customs of the lands surrounding Gebal, the other was younger with skills in the arts of mathematics, accounting, finance and trade.

These two, along with Aleon's other teachers, had done a thorough job of preparing the young lord for his future. They found their young pupil quick to grasp whatever subject matter they shared with him, and marveled at his ability to comprehend and retain the knowledge they imparted. His progress was rapid.

He had a gift for languages, and had learned from the scribes how to read and write most of those that were important for everyday commerce.

Ahinadab received daily reports from Aleon's teachers and was well pleased with his son's progress. After nine months of intense study Aleon's father judged it the proper time for the boy's education to enter a new phase. Thus, at the beginning of the next sailing season and near the time of his fourteenth birthday, Aleon was sent to sea.

Six new and larger ships had replaced the three lost by the House of Dan-El in the fire, and one of these bore the name *New Cabax* in remembrance of the vessel it replaced. She was the pride of the

Dan-El fleet and from the day she was launched she had been under the command of master mariner Abirami.

Aleon stood on the wharf the morning his first voyage was to begin, looking up at the *New Cabax* with an overwhelming sense of excitement and awe. He wondered what life aboard such a splendid vessel would be like. He had always envied mariners, and loved watching from the shore as they set forth on voyages to places far away. He had never been to sea, but was thrilled to finally be about to do so. This was the start of a whole new kind of life for him.

All he knew of the Great Sea up until that day was what others had told him, plus whatever he could observe for himself from the beach. He had dreamed of going to sea for almost as long as he was able to remember. His father's frequent tales of his own adventures at sea fueled Aleon's interest in everything to do with ships until it had grown into something of an obsession.

As a young boy, he spent most of his free time down at the harbor watching the ships arrive, unload, reload, and depart. He always tried to imagine where they were going, and what their destinations were like.

Most of the ship masters in his father's fleet knew Aleon well, and paid him the respect due to the son of their lord. They frequently allowed him to come aboard their vessels to satisfy his unquenchable curiosity. He was welcome as long as he stayed out of the way of the crewmen and stevedores. But his intensified study regime over the last nine months had kept him so busy that he hadn't had any spare time to visit the harbor until this day, and now he was about to embark on a whole new stage of his life.

Chapter 51
The *New Cabax*

At the northern harbor

Ahinadab watched with great interest as the *New Cabax* was built in the months following the fire. Master mariner Abirami and the shipwrights had recommended several innovative design improvements. Ahinadab saw merit in most of these, and added a few refinements of his own before enthusiastically including them in the ship's construction. When finished, the *New Cabax* was the finest ship in the Dan-El fleet, and arguably, the finest ship ever launched from Gebal.

She most certainly was the largest, and most advanced cargo vessel that had ever been built in the city's shipyard. From bow to stern she measured sixty cubits in length and twelve cubits at her beam, or nearly one hundred feet by twenty-five feet. She could carry over 900 talents, almost fifty-eight tons, of cargo.

The wood used to construct the *New Cabax* was cut from clear lengths of fine-grained, resinous cedar wood. Cedar was plentiful and easy to obtain in the mountains above Gebal, and it had the added virtue of being resistant to the ravages of sea worms, the scourge of all wooden vessels.

Everything above her waterline was rubbed down regularly with thickened olive oil to protect the wood from the desiccating effects of salt spray and harsh sunlight. This imparted a radiance to the whole hull and created a regal appearance to the *New Cabax* that delighted the eye.

She was rounded and tapered at both ends, after the manner known as *golah* in the Kena'ani language, but called *gauloi*, meaning "rounded" or "tub-shaped," by the Achaeans. These ships were also called "*hippoi*", which was the Achaean word for horses. No doubt the carved horse heads that graced the bows of all Kena'ani trading ships helped inspire this last epithet.

The hull's shape increased cargo space and gave the *New Cabax* superior stability, even when making sharp turns or dealing with high seas. Her bow and stern were lifted high above the waterline to minimize the wetted surface area of the hull. This reduced the effects of drag as she passed through the water, making her easier to row and adding to her speed and maneuverability.

Her principal method of propulsion was provided by two rows of nine oars, one on each side, manned by eighteen crewmen. The oars extended through loops of rope tied through holes in the gunwales. These loops let the oars pivot with each stroke and allowed the oarsmen to row while sitting on the deck, or standing for added power when maximum speed was wanted.

Rowing was demanding work and the oarsmen suffered enough from their exertions without having to sit under the sun's direct rays. Light-weight canvas awnings were hung overhead, above the oarsmen, to protect them from over-exposure.

A single mast was stepped at the center of the hull, with its base resting on the keel and its length passing upward through the main deck. It stood to a height of twenty-five cubits, or about thirty-seven feet, from bottom to top. It supported a single yard made of two overlapping poles bound together at the center by half their length. This composite yard reached beyond each side of the ship about six cubits, or almost nine and a half feet. A great, square sail of heavy linen canvas was attached to the yard with loops of rope. The sail was furled and bound tightly to the yard when not in use. But when winds were blowing from astern, the yard and sail could quickly be loosed and raised by hauling on a set of eight ropes. Once raised, the ropes were secured to the base of the mast to brace the yard and hold it steady.

The sail was managed by means of six other ropes. Four were attached along the bottom edge of the sail and one each attached to the outboard ends of the yard. These lines were manned at all times and skillfully handled by crewmen who hauled on them to take maximum advantage of favorable winds. Even under a full load, with the wind in her sail or propelled by oars, the *New Cabax* was one of the fastest ships of her kind ever built by the shipwrights of Gebal.

The hull was decked over completely, Below the low gunwales with four hatches for loading and unloading cargo. Chest-high removable fences of rope netting, mounted on sturdy posts, ran down the sides of the ship to keep loose objects or crewmen from falling overboard. These were taken down when in port, to allow for loading and unloading.

Similar fencing surrounded the top of a low cabin that took up the aft quarter of the ship. The master mariner commanded the ship from the cabin's roof, while inside were the master's quarters, the small galley, storage space for food, drinking water, weapons, and supplies of all kinds, and special trade goods that were too fragile or valuable to be stored below deck.

Two long, paddle-shaped sweeps were mounted aft of the cabin on either side of the tail riser. They were joined by a crossbar that made it possible for a single sailor to work the sweeps, or if conditions made steering too difficult for one man, a second sailor could help.

The tail riser was an extension of the keel that rose two and-one-half cubits, or about four feet, above the aft cabin and ended in a carved fish's tail. The tail riser was matched by a bow riser of equal height.

The bow riser was topped with the iconic wooden horse's head, which was more than a mere decoration. The horse's head identified the ship as a merchant vessel of Gebal's fleet. Wherever the "horse" ships sailed, the distinctive bow ornament was a sign that they came to trade and carried rare, highly desirable merchandise. Of course, this also made these ships targets for pirates.

Pirates from many lands had to be avoided on every voyage. It took real courage to sail in the merchant fleets, and master mariners needed great skill and knowledge to avoid capture. If they managed to escape the pirates, they also faced the natural hazards of the sea itself. For that they needed the help of Yam-Nahar.

Below the horse head, a small niche was carved into the bow riser of every Kena'ani ship. A small, gold and ivory statue of the god Yam-Nahar, lord of the sea and rivers, stood as an amulet to ward off any seaborne evil: including storms, unfavorable winds, unseen reefs or rocks, and sea monsters. Each day at sunrise fresh offerings of food and incense were laid out before this effigy of Yam-Nahar in a simple ceremony, with hope that he might be pleased and look with favor on the ship and her crew.

But Yam-Nahar could be temperamental. He ruled the sea and the rivers, but was also the god of chaos, and the sea was his favorite playground. No Kena'ani seaman would dare set sail without Yam-Nahar's effigy on board to keep the forces of chaos under control.

The ship itself was the opposite of chaos. The items needed for each voyage: from cordage and caulking, anchors and tackle, tools and utensils, weapons and cargo, were organized and stowed to take up as little space as possible. All of these things had to be arranged carefully to balance the load and maintain the ship's trim.

It was important that the position, quantity, and type of every item was noted by the master mariner and his assistant. Everything had to be located where it could be reached quickly when needed. This could mean the difference between life and death if a sudden storm arose or enemies attacked. There was no time to waste in searching for items that were carelessly stored or awkwardly placed.

The *New Cabax* required a crew of one and twenty souls including the master mariner, his assistant, the eighteen oarsmen, and one sailor to man the steering sweeps. This was considered the luckiest number for any group endeavor, and was exactly right for efficient handling so large a ship. For Aleon's first season at sea he was assigned to serve as the master's assistant, making him the twenty-first member of the crew.

Chapter 52
Aleon's First Voyage

Aboard the New Cabax

Aleon's first voyage was a short run north from Gebal along the coast, stopping first at Arwad to take on a cargo of terebinth resin, a costly ingredient used in making perfume. From Arwad the *New Cabax* cruised to the city of Ugarit where crafted items made in Gebal were unloaded and a cargo of scrap metal for transshipment to the port of Kit'ion, on the island of Alashiya, was taken on. At Kit'ion they picked up sixty "ox hide" ingots of copper to take back to Gebal. Although it was short, this voyage opened the young lord's eyes to a much wider world than he had ever known. His mind was awakened and whirling with the countless details of shipboard life, with the teeming multitudes of living things in the waters they passed through, and with the sheer size and power of the Great Sea itself.

He learned what it meant to be the master's assistant, with all of the duties and tasks involved in that position. He started each day by making an inspection tour of the entire ship, noting in the ship's log the number and location of every item on board. This daily log was a book-like tablet of wood with a hinged top. Its inside was coated with a layer of soft wax which could be written on and erased as needed. Aleon repeated this inspection again at the end of the day, and any change or discrepancy was written down and reported to the master mariner. A formal log of the current voyage was composed each evening from the highlights of the daily log, with any additions the master wanted to have included.

Aleon was responsible for composing this formal log, and learned much from the many remarks master Abirami dictated for the log. He was encouraged to note his own observations as well.

By acting as the ship's scribe, Aleon learned a great deal of the lore of the sea, of ships and how they are sailed, and the all-important arts and mysteries of the international trade that was the very life's blood of Gebal and her sister cities. In all these things, Ahinadab could not have found a better teacher for his son than master mariner Abirami. Abirami, in turn, was delighted that Aleon was as fine a pupil as any he had ever seen.

One of Aleon's first lessons about life at sea came early on the first day out. The *New Cabax* left port at dawn and eased its way north, accompanied by a pod of porpoises that kept pace with the oarsmen's progress. They were leaping and frolicking in the ship's bow waves. Aleon had never seen such a show before, and rushed forward to watch them. A light chop developed that caused the ship's bow to rise and fall slightly, with growing intensity as the morning wore on. Aleon had eaten a hearty breakfast of porridge and goat's milk cheese. That proved to be an unfortunate combination as his stomach began to react to the ship's movement in an unsettling way.

He was watching the porpoises leap and play in the waves below him when he suddenly felt dizzy and nauseated. He began to sweat heavily and his skin felt clammy. His vision began to swim as the ship's rocking reached new heights. He sat down on the deck and closed his eyes, but the nausea continued and grew more intense.

Suddenly he felt his gorge rising and clapped his hands over his mouth as the impulse to vomit seized him.

A pair of calloused hands grabbed his shoulders and turned him around while another hand on his back bent him forward over the gunwale just in time for his stomach's contents to spew forth into the sea. As Aleon retched and heaved the two crewmen who were holding him began to chuckle as his stomach finally emptied and the retching subsided. One of the men spoke reassuringly in his ear.

"Ah! There now young lord. Yam-Nahar has just welcomed you to his watery domain, and he has accepted your first sacrifice to him. Don't worry, you will soon recover and, after a time, this distress of the stomach will cease to bother you. All landsmen are welcomed in this manner when they first go to sea. Make your way aft to the galley and help yourself to some bread and water. But eat slowly and do not take too much. It will ease your stomach and help speed your recovery."

Sheepishly, Aleon thanked the men and rose unsteadily to his feet. Still dizzy, he held onto the rope fence as he made his way aft, walking slowly past the oarsmen and other crew members, occasionally staggering a bit as the ship's deck moved through the choppy water. As he passed, the sailors continued to chuckle good-naturedly at his obvious discomfort, and encouraged him with bits of advice.

"Keep your head up, lord."

"Look to the horizon, lad. It will ease the dizziness."

"If you feel yourself about to heave again, lean over the rail. Yam-Nahar doesn't want his sacrifices smeared all over the deck."

There was more advice of this kind, and Aleon felt his face flush with embarrassment at all this unexpected attention.

"Ah! There now. Your color is improving. You don't look so green around the gills young lord."

This last brought on a gale of open laughter as Aleon finally reached the shelter of the aft cabin and went into the galley. A large basket was hanging there, filled with small, hard loaves about the size of his palm. He took two and dipped a bowl of water from an amphora that stood nearby. He had to sit down on the deck again as his dizziness continued, and he took a sip of the water to wash the foul taste from his mouth. He wanted to spit the water out, but didn't want to make a mess, so he swallowed instead.

That was a big mistake! As the water hit his stomach it began to churn again, and because there was no time to get to the rail, he grabbed a nearby bucket and heaved into it. This time his empty stomach produced nothing but water and bile, having emptied itself earlier. Aleon lay flat on the deck, wishing he could die. Instead he found that laying there helped ease his dizziness and after a few moments it was mostly gone.

He risked a nibble from one of the loaves and chewed it slowly. It was hard, dry, and thankfully almost tasteless. He swallowed and braced himself for another bout of retching, but none came this time. He ate a little more of the bread, chewing it slowly and thoroughly as before. It felt good in his stomach, and there was no new nausea.

Chapter 53
Lessons in Seamanship

At sea aboard the New Cabax

After finishing the rest of the loaf and washing it down with more water Aleon felt good enough to sit up, and then stand. He put the second loaf back in the basket, remembering the warning not to eat too much and went back out onto the deck. The wind had changed direction and was now blowing from astern. The choppiness of the sea had eased and the sail had been raised. The oars were shipped and the *New Cabax* was now flying over the following waves smoothly and at a steady clip. Though he didn't know it then, the ship had just picked up the prevailing current that flowed north along the eastern coast of the Great Sea, between Gebal and Alashiya, passing Arwad and continuing all the way to Ugarit.

Aleon looked up at the great sail for the first time, noticing that it bore three wide vertical stripes of purple canvas, separated by two equally wide white stripes. In front of these stripes, in the very center of the sail, was the silhouette of a horse rearing up on its hind legs, shown in profile. The image was embroidered in black and gold thread. Aleon recognized it immediately as the signet of the House of Dan-El; just as he had seen it many times on objects and documents sealed by his father to mark them with his authority and identity. Aleon had never seen it depicted on anything this large before, and realized that it must be easy to recognize from a great distance; declaring for all the world that this ship belonged to the Dan-El fleet.

As the sail flexed and waved with the wind, the great horse almost seemed to dance above his head, and Aleon felt his heart swell with pride.

Abirami was standing atop the aft cabin and saw his young assistant admiring the sail. He called for Aleon to join him. A short ladder with rope hand grips gave him access to the aft cabin's roof and he stepped over to where Abirami stood with his hands braced on a waist-high stretch of rope netting that surrounded the aft cabin top. There was a short bench next to Abirami and he signaled Aleon to be seated.

"I am glad to see you are feeling better now, young lord. Do you think you can tolerate a few lessons in seamanship?"

Aleon nodded enthusiastically. "Most certainly master, I want to learn everything you can teach, as fast as I can."

"Good! There is much to teach, and I have heard that you are a quick learner. Let's begin with the way the ship has been handled since we left port. Did you observe how she was set when tied up at the wharf?"

"Yes, master. Like all ships we were tied up with the bow pointing away from the shore and toward the mouth of the harbor, which is why that side of the ship is called the port side."

"Very good. And do you know why we do that?"

"I think it must be to allow you to leave your berth quickly and exit the harbor with the least amount of maneuvering in confined spaces."

"Excellent. You are correct. Now, what did you notice as the oarsmen began to row?"

"Once we cast off from the wharf, the men on the port side used their oars to push us out far enough for them to let their oars down into the water. Then the men on both sides began to row."

"That's right. And did they row haphazardly, or like a team of horses, with each man matching the stroke of those on his side?"

"Ah! I see what you mean. They were indeed stroking together and in time with those on the other, that is, the starboard side of the ship. One of the oarsmen began to sing and the others all matched their rowing to the rhythm of his song."

"Good. And how did they maneuver and turn the ship to get her out through the entrance to the harbor?"

"I'm not sure...No. Wait! I saw that the men on one side sometimes held their oars out of the water, while those opposite them stroked. That turned the ship's bow to the side where the oarsmen weren't rowing. Then when the bow was going in the right direction both sides resumed stroking together with all their oars, moving the ship forward in a straight line, with the steering man adjusting the course as needed."

"Wonderful! I see you were paying attention! That is important, and now that we are under sail, what do you see the oarsmen doing?"

"Some are manning the four ropes that are attached to the yard and the two lines attached to the yard-ends; several others are oiling the deck and hull, while the rest of the crew are below deck or in the cabin."

"Excellent! We will make a first-rate sailor out of you before you know it. And without the oars to maneuver her what keeps the ship on a steady course?"

Aleon pointed to the stern, where a sailor stood manning the sweeps and making slight adjustments to prevent the waves and current from working to move the ship away from her intended course. "There!" he said, "The sailor manning the sweeps must know where we need to go, and he corrects the ship's heading as required. But, master, how does he know where he is on the sea, and how does he find his way?"

"That is the art and mystery of navigation that all seamen must learn or they are limited to forever stay within sight of land. We Kena'ani have discovered many secrets not known to other peoples. This allows us to sail wherever we wish across the open sea. You must learn these secrets.

To begin, I will have you study my charts so that you will know what currents and prevailing winds we may use to our advantage. My charts also show where there are shallows, rocks, reefs and other dangers we must avoid at all costs. Later tonight I will show you how we find our way by following the stars."

"Is that one of your charts in your hand, master?"

"It is. Here, let me show you how I use it to plot a course." Abirami spread the chart out across the bench beside his assistant, who sat on the deck to make room.

The chart was a single, rectangular roll of soft, tanned goat's hide, with the hair of the animal on the outside. The inside had been scraped to produce a smooth, clean, regular surface. Aleon saw a long, irregular, inked line that ran all around the sides of the chart with many straight lines that crisscrossed each other inside the area defined by the outer line. He was completely puzzled, and his mind buzzed with a thousand questions.

"I see from your face, young lord, that you have never seen a mariner's chart before." Abirami smiled. "I can always find our exact position on the sea with this chart.

"How so, master? Can you show me where we are right now?"

"Of course. Let me teach you how to read the chart. See this line that surrounds the others? That line represents the edges of the Great Sea, with all of its coasts and islands. Outside that line is the land."

"So, the straight lines inside that space are the surface of the water?"

"Exactly so! I see that you are starting to understand."

"Then what are the straight lines for?"

"Those lines represent the courses we sail from one point to another when we are out of sight of the coasts. See this one here? Notice the word written where it starts."

"Oh!" Aleon exclaimed with excitement. "It says 'Gebal'! So that is where our home is!"

"Indeed." Abirami was impressed with how quickly Aleon had grasped the information he was receiving. "Following that straight line from Gebal to where it ends, what is the word you see?"

"It says, 'Kit'ion'. So that must be on the island of Alashiya!"

"That is right! Kit'ion is one of the ports that we will visit on this voyage. But first we will follow the coast north to Arwad and then Ugarit. When we leave Kit'ion we will follow the course across the open sea to Gebal. Here is where we are right now." Abirami pointed to a spot on the chart.

Aleon traced the route with his finger as Abirami named these ports, and was amazed.

"The gods be praised! What magic has made this possible?"

"For more than a thousand years the mariners of Gebal and other Kena'ani cities of the coast have made notes and compiled the records of their voyages to make this chart possible. It is this knowledge from our ancestors that is one of the real treasures of our people.

Our sea charts are never shared with foreigners, and must be kept secret at all costs. If we are captured by enemies, I will toss all my charts overboard. See the lead weights at the corners? They will make sure the chart sinks into the sea to keep it from the hands of our enemies.

The charts show important landmarks along the coasts and the distances between them are noted. See these numbers. They indicate the normal sailing times from point to point. That is knowledge based on the records of many voyages by different ships. The top number is the best speed, and the bottom number is the slowest. That is how I know where we are when we sail within sight of land"

"And these lines that don't start at the land, but seem to all come from spots in the sea. What are they? They look like rays coming from the sun."

"Those mark places in the sea where the dominant winds and currents are constant, and you are right. They do radiate out to cross other lines at equal spaces all around the center points."

"What purpose do they serve?"

"As I say, they note the places on the sea where the currents and winds are known to flow and blow in constant directions. They are stable, and unchanging for the most part, so they can be relied on to help us navigate across the open sea. See the small arrows that point in different directions around the centers of the rays? The thinner ones are winds, the thicker ones are currents.

Let us say that we sail to this point here. We know the sun rises in the east and sets in the west. By observing the sun's position as it crosses the sky, we can know where north and south are. And if we turn the chart so that north on the chart is pointed toward the north, we can see which line will lead to the place we want to reach. There is more to it than that, like observing which quarter the wind is in as the ship is pointed northward, but this has been enough of a lesson for now."

"I can see I have much to learn." Aleon said.

With that Abirami rolled up his chart and took it to his cabin. It was nearing the noon hour and time for the crew to eat lunch.

In the days and nights that followed, young Aleon was taught almost all of the basic things that a sailor needed to know about how ships were manned, handled, maintained and navigated. He also learned to identify the stars and constellations of the night sky, and how they circled around the great star the Achaeans called *Astéri ton Foínikon*, the "Star of the Phoenicians," which was also called the North Star.

Abirami was amazed at how quickly the boy learned and how, once he was shown or told something, he didn't need to be reminded of it. His ability to observe and absorb the essential elements of sailing and shipboard life was keen, and he picked up many things on his own that Abirami hadn't shared. So apt a pupil did Aleon prove himself to be, that by the time the *New Cabax* reached its first stop at the Port of Arwad, he was quite at home aboard the ship and his initial seasickness had left him completely.

Chapter 54

Arwad

Aleon's first port-of call

As the *New Cabax* docked in Arwad, the men hastened to tie the ship up and hustled to make the hold ready to unload and receive cargo. Aleon was fascinated by their every move, and saw that the men worked as a well-practiced team; each member knowing exactly what his job was and doing it with a minimum of wasted effort. The rope fence along the port side of the deck was taken down to clear a path for moving the cargo, and two boarding planks were set in place from the port side of the ship to the wharf below, one fore and one aft.

Once this was done a gang of stevedores from the port came aboard the ship under the watchful eyes of master Abirami and their overseer, Ashtah the Bald. Ashtah conferred with Abirami who presented his papyrus copy of the ship's manifest with notes as to what cargo was to be off-loaded and taken to the warehouse belonging to the House of Dan-El. A second list of what was to be brought from the warehouse and stowed aboard the *New Cabax* was given to Abirami who examined it carefully. When he had done so he used his signet seal to mark the list, signing it in effect, and handed it to his young assistant beside him.

"Aleon, go below and use this manifest to check that all the cargo brought aboard is properly stowed and accounted for. Don't let anything that isn't on the manifest come aboard. Send it back up to the dock. For each item that is listed make a mark beside its name as it is stowed. Be careful to see that each item is stowed properly so the cargo won't shift while we are under way. The remaining cargo and the incoming items should all be divided up and repacked to maintain the ship's trim.

Then, when everything listed is aboard, use your own signet seal to sign the manifest below where you see mine. You will find a block of dry ink inside the scribe's bench next to the mast-step. If you lick your signet and roll it across the block it will pick up enough ink to make good marks. Return the manifest to me when all this is done."

Aleon did as instructed, giving everything his fullest attention. He knew a ship's manifest was the most important document aboard any merchant vessel. It was the official record transferring responsibility for each piece of cargo from the port authorities to the ship's master, and from him to the authorities at the port where he delivered it. The manifest was the basis for assessing taxes and port fees and would be used to account for all cargo delivered to the owners. That such an important task was entrusted to a novice like him was a sign to Aleon of Abirami's confidence in him, and it made his heart swell with pride.

Once the cargo had all been loaded and stowed, Aleon looked over the manifest to be sure everything was marked properly. This was the first time he had ever used a signet seal, and in the rush of activity, with his eyes and his mind focused on his work, Aleon had not looked at the marks the small carved-onyx cylinder seal had left.

His father had given the seal to him, just before he boarded the *New Cabax*. He hadn't looked closely at it then, noticing only that it bore the emblem of the House of Dan-El, which was the image of the rearing horse. He had not seen the other side until now. It showed his own emblem, the image of a leaping lion with a javelin pierced through its chest. His father had made an offering of incense as he looked to the sky and prayed for the gods to protect his son and all those traveling with him. Aleon had knelt before him and felt his father's hands on his head. Ahinadab blessed his son and placed the seal's gold chain around his neck, raised him up, embraced him, and kissed him on both cheeks. He had a lump in his throat as he watched his son board the ship with all the confidence of youth, and a wave of farewell.

Aleon studied the marks the seal left on the manifest. He noticed details he had missed before. On either side of the lion, the craftsman had carved the initials for his name; an *ʾāelph*, the Kena'ani letter A, and a *tāw* or T, for "Aleon-Tabah." This was the same image as the one on the signet ring his father had given him at his naming.

When the seal was rolled over the papyrus manifest, the two figures combined so that it looked as if the lion had been about to attack the horse, but was stopped in mid-leap by the javelin. The seal was small. Just the length of a man's thumb from the tip to the first joint, and no bigger in cross-section than the breadth of a cherry pit. He would not have believed that so much detail would fit so small a thing. But such was the skill of the workmen of Gebal who carved hundreds of such cylinder seals each day, that they could depict almost anything on such small surfaces.

Aleon had never used a seal before, and he had been very careful of the placement and legibility of his marks. All but the first were sharp, clear, and arranged in neat rows, properly aligned with the names and quantity of the items that came on board. His first mark had smudged slightly because his hand shook a bit with excitement. But he quickly settled to his task and every other mark was properly done.

He mastered the trick of licking the seal to wet it, and rolling it over the ink block before setting it in position on the manifest. A quick movement of his hand rolled the seal against the surface of the papyrus to create the mark. He improved with practice and his later marks carried just the right amount of ink. Not too much and not too little, so that all the details of the seal's impression were crisp and perfectly legible.

Looking closely at the later marks Aleon noticed another detail that he hadn't seen before. The image of the horse had three vertical stripes across its chest. His hand went to his own chest and felt the heavy scars the lion's claws had left there. He smiled in amazement at his father's cleverness in using the horse to symbolize both the House of Dan-El, and Aleon himself, a true son of that great house.

He carried the manifest up on deck and presented it to Abirami, who took it from his hand and looked it over carefully.

"Well done! You have the hand of a scribe, Aleon."

As Abirami said this, several nearby crewmen chuckled. They could see the ink stains on Aleon's fingers, an occupational hazard and trademark of every scribe, and more.

"Everything is properly stowed away I trust. I'll check it myself once we're away."

"That is correct, master," Aleon replied, as the men who had been chuckling now broke into open laughter.

Aleon looked at the men, then at Abirami and said, "Is something wrong? Have I made some mistake?"

There was even more laughter at that, and Abirami was smiling broadly. He chuckled and said, "They are amused by your blackened lips and tongue!"

With a shock, Aleon realized what he must look like after repeatedly licking the seal. He felt a bit foolish and his cheeks colored with embarrassment. But he could see the humor in the situation. He had been the victim of yet another good-natured joke: another part of his initiation to life at sea, perpetrated this time by Abirami. He began to laugh at himself, and soon everyone on deck was laughing *with* him, instead of *at* him. Abirami handed him a wetted cloth to wipe his mouth and hand with.

"Next time, use one of the small wetted sponges from the bucket below the scribe's bench." Abirami said, still chuckling.

As the voyage continued, Aleon learned many more new and wondrous things about the sea, about life aboard a ship and what the people and places they visited were like. But most importantly, he learned how to get along with his rough and rowdy shipmates while getting things done.

Chapter 55

Ugarit

In the harbor district of the city of Ugarit

Ugarit was a great port city, but unlike the Kena'ani cities to the south, it was part of the Hittite empire. The Hittite ruler, Suppiluliuma was a warrior king who maintained a huge army and was always pushing to extend the boundaries of his empire into other lands. By the time of Aleon's birth, his armies had conquered the lands to the north of Gebal and were practically at the gates of Arwad. The pharaohs had established a large garrison at Arwad as a signal to the Hittites that the city and lands south of it were under the protection of Kemet.

Although it was under the rule of the Hittites, Ugarit was allowed much of the same kind of autonomy that Gebal and her sister cities enjoyed under Kemet's rule, and for the same reason. The trade from these cities brought too much wealth to their masters to be jeopardized by harsh and repressive rule.

At Ugarit the *New Cabax* put in to unload and take on cargo, and when that work was finished the crew was released to go ashore for the rest of the day. Several of the crewmen invited Aleon to join them for a trip to their favorite tavern and to see the sights of the city.

The chief of the starboard oarsmen was a big sailor named Anuba'al. He led the group along the waterfront and into the streets of the harbor district. Aleon saw many familiar sights along the way, with workmen and women engaged in the same types of activities that were common in Gebal. Nearest the harbor there were rope-makers, sail-makers and vendors of just about anything needed to equip and maintain ships. The waterfront was also home to the taverns and brothels that were an important part of any port.

Everything seemed more crowded and dirtier than the streets of Gebal, and Aleon judged that this might be because it was a much larger city than his home. He guessed there must be four or five times as many people living there. It was also much noisier, with everyone on the streets seeming to shout their words instead of just speaking. Aleon heard many different languages, some of which he had been taught by his tutors, and some that were completely foreign to him.

He was amazed at the variety of costumes and modes of dress of the people they saw. There were groups of merchants from Ur, Karduniaš, and Mari, wearing their traditional knee-length, short-sleeved robes tied with wide belts of bright cloth. They sported long, curled beards and hair. Some with fringes of gold thread on their sleeves and the hem of their robes. Some had many tiny amulets of silver and electrum woven into their hair and beards, often with heavy gold or silver chains around their necks. All wore heavy gold rings and armbands inscribed with images of their gods.

There were many Hittites dressed in ankle-length, short-sleeved robes, some girdled around their bellies with wide sashes of colorful cloth, some with capes draped over their shoulders that hung down their backs almost to the ground. Most wore hats of some kind or another; either tall brimless, towering conical miters or close-fitting, heavily embroidered skullcaps with long, thin ribbons hanging behind. Their hair in every case was braided into three long, rope-like tresses and their beards were short, compared to those worn by other men, but all were braided and curled. Aleon had never seen a Hittite before, but learned that this mode of dress was almost a uniform for them.

There were at least a dozen other nations represented, each with its own types of garments, hairstyles and headgear. Some were very dark-skinned, some a rich brown color, and a very few were almost white-skinned. Everywhere he looked, Aleon saw something new to him and he feasted his eyes on the rich cavalcade of humanity swirling around him as he walked.

The areas nearest to the harbor had the familiar scent of the sea and reminded him of home, but further inland the smells were different. He could smell unfamiliar spices, and the aromas of strange cooking coming from vendors' carts, or from small shops that catered to hungry passersby. In one alleyway within a poorly maintained part of the harbor district, his nose was assaulted by the stench of rotting garbage and human waste. A dead horse had been dragged off the main street and was left there to rot. Flies covered it thickly and large harbor rats scurried over the corpse, feasting on its corrupt flesh. Aleon was shocked. Such a thing was never seen, nor smelled, in Gebal. Only the tanneries at the south side of the southern harbor smelled anything like this. Those were situated where the reek from their vats of tanning hides were downwind from the city.

But the worst was yet to come. The group turned down one street where a stench like no other assaulted their noses. They had come to the slave market, where captive peoples from every corner of the world had been brought for sale. There were large pens, which must have held a thousand of these poor wretches all crowded together. These would be sold as unskilled laborers of the sort that could be used for countless purposes. The pens were exposed to the elements, be it bright sun or chilling rain. The captives stood or sat in mud and their own waste with little or no clothing on their bodies.

Nearby were other pens, where fewer slaves were held in better conditions. These appeared to be individuals with special skills. Most were dressed in fairly good clothing, and their pens were clean, and covered over with sailcloth to provide a minimum of shelter. Some of these were perhaps learned men who might be purchased to serve as tutors for the children of wealthier citizens, or to work in a skilled trade. They would command higher prices than the unskilled. Their worth would be determined by the highest bidders more than by their skills and knowledge.

He thought of his own tutors, and wondered how they had come to be enslaved. Were they captured in battle, or perhaps unable to pay their debts? Or had they sold themselves into slavery for unknown, desperate reasons? Aleon could not imagine what it must be like to be that desperate.

A lively crowd was pressing in on a large platform where an auctioneer was offering a naked woman for sale. It seemed clear to Aleon what her fate was to be, as the men in the crowd shouted for her to turn around, or bend down with her behind thrust out. The auctioneer held her by a heavy chain around her neck, turning her this way and that to display her body. Then, as he ran his free hand over her breasts in a suggestive manner, he called for bidding to begin.

Aleon and his shipmates moved on, eager to reach their goal. He noticed that there was a hazy quality to the air over the city. There seemed to be cooking fires and piles of burning trash everywhere. In some places the smoke hung in low, fog-like patches or could be seen rising above the roof tops, to form a lid-like layer in the sky above the city. The farther from the harbor they went, the harder it was to breathe and Aleon thought of the clean, fresh breezes that washed the air in Gebal. He decided he wouldn't want to live in a place like Ugarit, where even the air was filthy.

Aleon followed his shipmates and soon they had entered the tavern district. Wheezing slightly, with his eyes burning from all the smoke, they stopped at a three-storied building with a bright red door in front. A sign bearing a painted image of a blue dolphin hung above the door.

It took a few minutes before his eyes adjusted to the low light inside the tavern. When he could see clearly, Aleon noticed that the entire ground floor was one large room with two doors at the far end. One door seemed to lead to a back room and kitchen. Servants were bustling in and out with dishes of food and ewers of wine or beer. The other door appeared to open to an alley behind the building.

There was a staircase to one side of the room that led to the second floor, with a long landing that ended in an open doorway. He saw several men lined up along that landing, who seemed to be waiting for something he couldn't make out.

His eye was drawn to the activity on the ground floor. Patrons seated on low benches, facing each other across trestle tables at one side of the room. On the other side, groups of two or three customers sat cross-legged, on plush cushions, around even lower tables. Some were dining on cooked fish, goat, lamb or other flesh, garnished with roasted grains and vegetables. Others weren't eating, preferring to drink wine or beer. Most dipped pottery cups into kraters of resin-infused wine from Gebal, or filled their cups with Assyrian barley beer. A few were enjoying fermented honey mead imported from Sumer. There was laughter and loud jesting, and from the corner nearest the kitchen a small group of musicians played tunes on bovine lyres, horizontal forearm harps, reed pipes and drums.

Anuba'al led the group to one of the low tables and they fanned out on the cushions surrounding it. As they sat, the tavern keeper approached to take their order. Anuba'al spoke for them all, ordering three ewers of barley beer.

"Bring your strongest beer. Our wealthy shipmate will pay. His father owns our ship!" Anuba'al shouted loud enough for the entire room to hear above the noise. The tavern keeper's eyes grew wide and he smiled and bowed deeply.

"Shall I bring bread and meat as well young master?" he directed this question to Aleon.

"Bring us an entire roasted lamb with leeks and vegetables. And bring your freshest bread for the table as well!" Aleon answered. "Oh, and I don't think three ewers of beer is enough. Bring us a krater and keep it full." This brought on a roar of approval from his shipmates. Even as short as this voyage had been, all were ready for a change from the ship's fare of dried fish, porridge and hardened loaves of bread. A chance to eat fresh-baked bread was not to be passed up, not to mention the chance to drink themselves silly with beer.

"It will be a feast to remember, young master!" Anuba'al exclaimed, and the tavern keeper clapped his hands loudly, pointing to the table, to signal his servants to begin making the food and drink. Beer was brought first, poured from full ewers into a large krater set in the center of the table. Individual drinking bowls were distributed to the sailors who began immediately to dip them into the krater's liquid refreshment.

Large loaves of bread were brought and passed from hand to hand around the table with each man breaking off large chunks from the loaves. Laughter and the familiar, salty talk of sailors who were shipmates, as well as friends, rose and became more boisterous as the bread and beer were consumed. Serving women passed near the men to refresh the krater or pass more loaves, and the men made free with their hands to fondle a plump backside or grope an exposed breast. For the most part, the girls didn't seem to mind, and in fact several seemed to encourage this behavior. Up to a point.

The mood around the table grew louder and merrier, until finally the roast lamb, complete with its head still attached, was brought to the table on a great platter, garnished with fruits and vegetables.

The crewmen took turns using their knives to cut off portions of the roasted flesh, eating with gusto as steaming grease dripped from their hands and ran down their chins. Because he was their host, Aleon was offered the prize portions of the lamb, beginning with its eyeballs and brain. Everyone relaxed and became more and more informal with their young master as their feasting and drinking continued.

For Aleon, it felt as if he was now fully accepted as a member of the crew. At first, the men had merely tolerated him, because he was the son of their lord. His presence aboard the ship was seen as more of a nuisance than an asset, although none would have openly said so. But now, here in this place, he was accepted.

The feasting and drinking continued until the lamb was consumed and only crusts and crumbs were left of the bread. The krater had been filled and emptied three times, and most of the men were drunk. Anuba'al and Aleon seemed to be the only two who were still in full possession of their senses. Anuba'al had consumed his share of beer, but seemed to have an almost god-like ability to remain sober. Aleon was used to drinking well-watered wine at home, and found this first taste of a local beer to be bitter and not to his liking. He had downed only a few bowls, and although feeling a pleasant numbing of his senses, was far from intoxication.

Sitting next to his lord's son, Anuba'al put his arm around Aleon's shoulder and shook him good-naturedly.

"Master Lion-Slayer, though I had my doubts, you have shown yourself to be a proper sailor and a worthy companion on this voyage. Now it is time that we, your shipmates, do our duty to introduce you to the customs of our profession. Each time one of us enters a new port for the first time, he must pay his respects and make a sacrifice to the goddess Ishtar, the goddess of love and fertility, lest she withhold her blessing and cause our voyage to be unprofitable."

"A sacrifice? How does one make a sacrifice to Ishtar?" Aleon asked innocently.

"Why, by entering a different sort of port, of course!" The crewmen at the table laughed uproariously at their leader's jest. "Come men, let us take him before the goddess."

With that said, Anuba'al and two crewmen who were not overly drunk, lifted Aleon to their shoulders and carried him up the staircase to the landing above. At the far end of the landing, through an open doorway, there was a curtained alcove that housed a shrine to Ishtar. Through the open curtains Aleon could see oil lamps illuminating a small figurine of the naked female goddess that stood on a waist-high pedestal.

The goddess' likeness was that of a beautiful, naked woman; carved from solid ivory. Her only adornments were a gold collar, gold armbands and large gold earrings. Her eyes were inset with deep red gemstones that matched another even larger one in her navel. Her head was crowned with the golden crescent moon that signified her deity, with its curves resting in her hair and its pointed ends stretching upward like two horns of power.

Four smiling young women stood before the shrine as the sailors set their burden on his feet. A bit tipsy, Aleon steadied himself as the girls slowly drew very near, encircling him and caressing his face, chest and arms. He felt his face reddened from this unexpected and unfamiliar attention from the opposite sex. Then his eyes grew wide and his heart began to pound as he felt hands groping beneath his tunic and kilt to fondle his buttocks and private parts.

He was shocked and suddenly shy, not knowing what to make of all this. He tried to back away, but the men standing behind him blocked any exit he might have made.

"Steady lad!" Anuba'al said encouragingly. "These women are here to accept your sacrifice to the goddess. I see you are new to this custom, but do not worry. They will show you what to do."

The men laughed loudly at this and offered ribald comments and other encouragement for Aleon's benefit and their own amusement. He was pulled forward beyond the curtains and down onto soft cushions that lay on the floor below the pedestal. One of the girls closed the curtains on the crewmen who lingered on the landing outside to catch whatever sights or sounds might issue from within. They jested and laughed among themselves, each man remembering and sharing exaggerated stories of his own first sacrifice, and each in turn trying to out-boast the others. In this way they passed the time until, bored with it all, they drifted back downstairs and returned to their table for more beer. Some drifted off to other nearby establishments to make their own sacrifices to the goddess.

The afternoon had worn on into evening until Aleon finally staggered from the shrine. It was time to return to the ship. They started for the door, where the tavern keeper met them with a papyrus bill in his hand. On a table near the door was a small brass-bound chest and a scribe deposited the tavern's proceeds. Aleon took the bill from the tavern keeper and read it carefully. He was amazed at the sum of all he and his shipmates had consumed in the course of the afternoon and evening, but was happy to pay for the food, drink and his several sacrifices to the goddess.

He took a reed pen from the scribe and added a small amount over and above the total as a sign of his satisfaction with what they had received. This was a custom his father had taught him, as a way of making sure that he would be welcome if he ever came back to the

Inn of the Blue Dolphin. Below the new total he added a note that said, "Pay the amount above to the bearer." He rolled his signet across the ink block on the scribes table and press his seal onto the bill before handing it back to the tavern keeper. It would be presented for payment at the local warehouse of the House of Dan-El, where his signet would be recognized. Then, with a smile on his lips, he and the others left the tavern. Those who could still walk helped the others back to the *New Cabax* to sleep off the effects of the feast. The next day, despite their heavy drinking of the night before, every man was up at dawn and at his oar, ready to depart on the morning tide.

Chapter 56

Kit'ion

The passage to the island of Alashiya

The remainder of the voyage was much the same. The sea was kind to them as they crossed from Ugarit to the island of Alashiya and reached their next port of call, the harbor at Kit'ion, on the island's northeast coast.

Two hours after leaving Ugarit they reached a point where, for the first time in the voyage, the *New Cabax* was completely out of sight of the land. This presented an opportunity for Aleon to practice what he had learned about open water navigation.

Before going to sea, Aleon had read descriptions of sea voyages in his father's library, so he had some knowledge of his people's navigation methods. With Abirami's help he had learned the broader principals that were essential to navigating beyond sight of land. But in practice he quickly found there was much more to it than charts and writings could impart. Without experience, these things were only theoretical knowledge.

Fortunately, master Abirami, one of the finest navigators in the

Dan-El fleet, was there to teach him. Abirami taught Aleon the way currents and prevailing winds were used to speed passage from one place to another. These elements had defined the established trade routes used by the Kena'ani fleets for centuries.

Nearing the island of Alashiya, where the water became shallow, Abirami had his student practice using the sounding weight, a bell-shaped tool carved from stone. The bottom of the weight had a large hole that was filled with tallow. A long thin rope, with knots tied at equal distances along its length, was attached to the weight so it could be lowered over the side of the ship until it touched bottom. By counting the number of knots that it took to reach bottom they could tell how deep the water was. The tallow would pick up traces of whatever was on the bottom of the sea. By taking these measurements, called soundings, it was possible to tell how much water was below the ship as it progressed. This allowed the ship to change course and avoid running aground on dangerous shoals or reefs.

Abirami also taught Aleon to take sightings of the sun's position, using a tool called a cross staff to determine the angle between the ship, the sun, and the horizon. One end of the cross piece was placed on the horizon, and the other end was aligned with the sun. The staff was elevated to the sun's height above the horizon, to create a measurable angle at the ship's end. Once this angle was known the ship's position and heading could be determined using the master's charts. Where the ship was at any given moment was critical to determining what course was needed to reach a destination. Twice each day, the cross staff was used, and course correction were made.

Aleon was amazed at how this simple device could be so useful. Abirami told him that it was a tool first used by the astronomers of Karduniaš to observe and record the positions of the stars at different seasons, but it was the mariners of Gebal that learned to use the cross staff for navigation. On Aleon's next voyage Abirami showed his pupil how to use the cross staff to set a course at night by observing the brightest star in the constellation called Draco instead of the sun. This star was known to the Achaeans as "the Phoenician Star." It was the one most constantly fixed in one location in the night sky. All the other stars revolved around it as the hours of the night passed. By measuring the angles between it and other well-known stars in other constellations a navigator could determine his ship's position on the sea. The ship's heading could be determined by sighting the position of late-rising stars as they crossed the horizon, and any necessary course corrections could then be made.

The passage between Ugarit and Kit'ion only took half a day, even with the wind against them. They reached the port before noon and docked at an available berth along the quay. They quickly unloaded some of their cargo and took on a consignment of copper "ox-hide" ingots, so called because they were shaped like a flattened ox hide that was stretched out with "legs" at the four corners. Each ingot was just about the perfect weight for a single stevedore to carry. Once on board, the way they were shaped made them easy to stack in compact layers that would not shift during transit. These copper ingots were to be transported back to Gebal, where they would be melted down and mixed with tin to make bronze, the metal from which many useful and durable things were made.

While cargo was being unloaded and reloaded, the crew took shore leave. Abirami permitted Aleon to join them, to see the local temple of Ashtoreth in the city. But he cautioned all the crew not to linger at the taverns, as the stop at Kit'ion would be brief, and he planned to depart on the evening tide. Aleon and several crewmen went directly to the temple and marveled at its great beauty. Of course, they all made the appropriate sacrifices to the goddess while there.

From Kit'ion the *New Cabax* sailed directly back to her home port, bringing Aleon's first voyage to its conclusion. That summer he sailed aboard the *New Cabax* on three more voyages, each one longer than the last, and visited nine different ports in all.

Standing on the dock at the end of his first season at sea, he came to the realization that "home" had taken on a new meaning for him. Home was no longer simply the House of Dan-El, which had always sheltered him as a child. Home was not merely the city of Gebal anymore. Home, he now realized, was the Great Sea, with Gebal being just one of many places he might be at any given time. Though it would always be the center of his world, the city's walls could no longer contain him.

He was unaware of it, but Aleon had literally left behind a part of himself in two of the ports of call the *New Cabax* visited. His seed had taken root in the wombs of two of the women he had left his "sacrifices" with. One in Ugarit and one in Kit'ion. There would be others as well, on other voyages. Over the course of the rest of his life, he would give life to twenty sons, and his descendants would spread far and wide throughout the entire world. Something about him, perhaps some gift of the gods, made his seed especially potent. If he had known any of this at, he would have been amazed. But as it was, he had never given any thought to having children. He had assumed that they would come along in time, after he married that awful girl, Melita.

That is, *if* he married her. There must be some way to avoid that. If they ever had offspring, he hoped they would be more like him and not so much like their mother. Not that she wasn't good looking, but her attitude toward him was awful. The way she humiliated him was unbearable. He fervently hoped something would happen to keep him from being yoked to her for the rest of his life.

On the other hand, their arranged marriage might not work out too badly. Uniting their two families' fortunes would certainly strengthen both houses. He might be able to bear it if he could spend most of his time at sea. That would be a blessing from the gods.

The thought gave him hope.

Chapter 57

Homecoming

Late Fall, 1339 BC at the northern harbor of Gebal

In the month of 'Tana'im, or October, on the fourteenth day, the *New Cabax* was sighted from the watchtower above the north harbor of Gebal. She was returning from her final voyage of the year, at the end of Aleon's second season at sea. The House of Dan-El was informed, and the news of the ship's arrival created great excitement in the entire household. There had been no word from the ship for over a month, and she was overdue. Aleon's family, their servants, and slaves had been anxiously hoping for her safe return for more than a week.

The ba'alat Nikkal breathed a sigh of relief and felt a deep sense of gratitude to Almighty El. She offered a brief prayer of thanks to the patron god of the house, for protecting, blessing, and returning her eldest son to his home. She had prayed for his welfare daily since he first went to sea, concerned that some evil might befall him or the ship. Life at sea was hard, with dangers known and unknown. But with relief, she quickly turned to the task of making everything ready for his homecoming.

Aleon had only been free to visit his family twice during the year, in between voyages while the *New Cabax* was in port at Gebal. Both times he had only spent a single night at home before he had to leave again. But this time the ship would remain in port until the following spring.

The weather was changing and serious storms could arise at any time. Throughout the fall and winter months no sane master mariner would risk his ship unless it was a dire emergency. So now, after two full seasons at sea, Aleon's return was a cause for special celebration.

It was customary for high-born young men from the major trading houses to sail on at least three sailing seasons, to learn basic seamanship and become acquainted with all the Kena'ani colonies, trading posts and ports of call around the Great Sea. But because Aleon was such a quick study, and had such an excellent teacher in master mariner Abirami's, he learned more in two seasons than most novice mariners might learn in three. Aleon was now ready for the next phase of his education.

In a year he would begin making long journeys overland, following the great caravan routes to visit those markets where the House of Dan-El kept its agents and warehouses. Until then, he would be immersed in studying the customs, cultures, and languages of the lands and cities he would be visiting. He would learn the techniques and strategies merchant/traders used to succeed in long distance commerce. It would be a busy year for Aleon. But for now, none of this mattered. It was time to celebrate. He was home.

His homecoming celebration would be a small gathering of family and close friends. Invitations were sent to some of Nikkal's kin, two of Ahinadab's business partners, master mariner Abirami, and Lord Paltiba'al. These guests would be accompanied by their wives and some other family members, so the gathering would number about thirty-five to forty persons.

The hall was set up for entertaining, and food preparations were started in the kitchen. All this was taking place while Aleon was still working aboard the ship, checking the manifest as cargo was unloaded from the *New Cabax*. Since it was the end of the sailing season, there was no new cargo to be loaded, but other work had to be done to prepare the ship for winter. Abirami was visited by Gebal's master shipwright, who came to make arrangements for that work to begin the next day.

A few hours after they docked, Aleon marked the last item on the manifest with his signet seal. When the ink was dry, he rolled the papyrus up and took it on deck to find Abirami. The master mariner stood atop the cabin in discussion with the master shipwright. They were making plans for needed repairs and some refitting to be done over the winter months. Aleon stood by, listening attentively to learn what he could.

The shipwright had overseen the construction of the *New Cabax* and was intimately aware of her strengths and weak points. He had inspected the hull, mast and running gear while the ship was being unloaded and was making recommendations to Abirami. Abirami called his attention to some additional concerns that also needed attention. When they finished their plans, the shipwright bowed and took his leave, and Abirami turned to his assistant.

"Is the manifest complete?"

"Yes master. All is accounted for and marked. The warehouse manager has countersigned and everything is now in his care."

"Very good! The crew is free to take shore leave as soon as your father's guardsmen arrive to secure the ship. I would expect that you are eagerly awaited at the House of Dan-El. I have been invited to a small celebration there this evening, so I must go home and help my wife prepare for that. But first, go with me to the customs house.

I want you to see how the fees and taxes are assessed and paid. You should know these things."

"Of course, master." Aleon said. "Will we see the king, do you think? I haven't seen him since my naming ceremony."

"He may wish to greet you and welcome you back to the city, but I hear there are changes in the wind. Rib-Hadda may soon be king no longer. When we made port at Pharos Island in Kemet, I heard a rumor that the pharaoh is displeased with the torrent of messages Rib-Hadda has been sending, begging for pharaoh to send troops to protect him from his enemies and generally exhibiting cowardly behavior that verges on incompetence.

The grand vizier and others of the pharaoh's court have tried to keep most of these messages from reaching the pharaoh's eyes, but enough had to be presented to him that the Akhenaten finally had enough and sent a reply to our king instructing him to cease his constant whining. It only needs now for pharaoh's governor to hint to the council that he should be removed and it will be done. I share this so you can be careful of what you say to him. I hear he has been quite upset and is suspicious of everyone."

"I see." Aleon replied. "Have you heard anything about whomever the council might choose to replace him?"

"Nothing certain. But It has long been thought that your father might fill that office in time. Also, the king's own brother, the high priest Ili-Rapih, is known for his ambition. He covets the throne and might use his influence to persuade the council to make him king in his brother's place. But it is my guess that the council would not want to combine the great power the high priest already has with the powers of the king. That seems a quick path to tyranny."

"You seem to be well informed, despite being so long at sea.

Abirami laughed. "Yes, I find it wise to keep myself current about what goes on at home while I am away. It is vital to my personal well-being, and that of my family. I have a small, but effective group of 'friends' in key places that share many things with me. You will find this to be true of your father also. And I recommend that as you get older you also should develop your own trusted circle of informants."

That was an entirely new line of thinking for Aleon. He had never considered that Ahinadab might have enemies he needed to watch so closely. Then too, the idea that his father might become king one day was shocking. What would that mean for Aleon's own future? It was a lot to think about, as the mariner and his assistant neared the palace precinct and arrived at the custom house.

The palace complex was much more than merely the house of the king. It was the seat of the city's government and the council of elders held their meetings in a hall within the palace. The customs house was situated on the palace grounds and consisted of a few offices and a large warehouse. There each arriving ship's manifest was reviewed, its cargo assessed for taxes, and docking fees were collected. This most often meant that a portion of the cargo was turned over to cover those costs, unless the owners had enough gold or silver to pay the total. All surrendered goods were kept in the customs house until sold or otherwise disposed of, usually by auction.

The same was true for goods that arrived overland. Gebal was ideally situated as a crossroads for trade of all kinds. The merchants who came with the great caravans from the south, the north or the east all paid to bring their goods into the city.

Abirami and Aleon entered the customs house and were immersed in a milling crowd of buyers and sellers, merchants and agents of the great houses, with the same mix of peoples and cultures that Aleon had seen in Ugarit. The master mariner led the way through the noisy crowd to the office of the chief customs officer where a scribe offered them seats in an anteroom until it was their turn to be seen. Their feet were washed by a slave and another brought them wine and bread with olive oil.

As they waited, Abirami asked, "What stands out in your eyes as you view this crowd?"

"I had no idea that so much could go on in this place. In my mind, I only imagined that this is where the king's revenues were collected, but here I see people exchanging one kind of goods for another, and others purchasing cargo brought up from the harbor. It is more like a big marketplace than just a government house. I wonder what it is like when there is an auction. Where do they hold those?"

"Your observations are very good, Aleon. About once each month, on days that the high priests and priestesses of the temples determine to be the most auspicious, auctions are held here in the customs house. Many of the people you see today came to examine some of the goods that they might want to bid on.

Look there. Do you see those three men on our left? The ones with the dark skins, wearing the long robes with the brightly colored turbans on their heads? They are from a land that lies beyond the eastern edge of Karduniaš in the empire of the Assyrians. Those men have brought rare spices from across the outer sea; passing through the Gulf of Elam and up the river Euphrates, through the land of the Chaldeans to the city of Karduniaš. From there they joined a caravan, to travel overland by way of the Emari in the Kingdom of Isuwa and on through the southern lands of the Hittites until they reached Gebal. It is an amazing distance that takes more than a year to travel one way. They will sell their spices for a staggering price and return to their homeland with many of the goods we bring here from all of the western and southern lands."

"Now that my seafaring education is complete, my father will send me to the eastern lands over the next few years. It will further my knowledge of how his business is handled in those places. But I must confess, the idea of traveling overland through such dangerous country does not excite me as much as the thought of going to sea does. I would love to see these foreign places, but not as much as I would love to return to the Great Sea. I have loved my time voyaging with you Master Abirami, and I truly thank you for all you have done to teach me the ways of a mariner. I shall always be grateful for that."

"It has been my pleasure and a privilege to serve the House of Dan-El and you in this way." Abirami said. "But do not think that your education in seamanship is complete. The sea teaches each of us who travel on Yam-Nahar's waves new lessons with each voyage. Never stop learning from those lessons."

The scribe summoned them to go before the Chief Customs Officer. The manifest was reviewed, found to be in order, and assessed. Abirami signed the pledge for payment. He then left Aleon to finish the last details and went home to his wife. The customs officer would send the pledge to Ahinadab's warehouse where his agent would have the assessed portion of cargo transferred to the Customs House.

This business concluded, Aleon was himself about to leave and head for home, when he was stopped by the Chief Customs Officer.

"Before you go young Aleon, the king would like to speak with you. Please follow me over to the royal offices."

Chapter 58

A Private Audience

In the palace of king Rib-Hadda

A bit apprehensive, Aleon did as he was bidden, and a few moments later he was ushered into the king's private audience chamber. Aleon was reminded of his father's office in the great hall of the House of Dan-El. To reach this chamber he had passed through the grand entrance to the royal palace, with its intricately carved and jewel-encrusted doors, not unlike those of Ahinadab's dwelling. The doors led into a large foyer and beyond that lay a great hall for banquets and formal audiences. On both sides were hallways and doors leading to other parts of the palace and other entirely separate wings of rooms for guests and important visitors who often stayed for days while waiting for an audience with the king.

A large curtain of purple covered the wall behind the royal throne near the end of the room. This curtain was richly embroidered with gold and silver thread depicting images of the many gods revered by the people of Gebal, all engaged in heroic scenes from the legends that celebrated their deeds. As the chief customs officer led Aleon up to this curtain, it was parted by two guards to reveal a hidden door that opened into a long hallway. At the end of the hallway stood another pair of guards, protecting a wide door. As the customs officer reached the guards, Aleon thought he heard the man whisper something that caused the guards to came to attention and opened the door for him. Aleon followed him into the king's private audience chamber and stopped three paces behind the customs officer who stood in front of the king's throne; both bowed and touched their foreheads three times to the floor.

The chief officer rose and said, "Oh king, may you live forever. May the favor of the gods be upon you always, and may you be blessed beyond all measure. Here, as you commanded, I present the young lord, Aleon-Tabah of the House and lineage of Dan-El, son of Ahinadab, shofeṭ of the northern gate." Having made this introduction, the officer stepped to the side and backed slowly away, allowing Aleon room to rise and step forward.

"Ah, and here he is, our own lion-slayer!" king Rib-Hadda said. "I had news this morning that the *New Cabax* had made port, and that you were aboard. I am pleased to see how you have grown since I last saw you at your naming ceremony. You seem much more a man now, and no longer a young boy. Tell me of your experiences on this latest voyage. *How* old did you say you are?"

Aleon's tutors had taught him well. He knew how to present himself in front of other members of high-born society. How, and to whom he must bow. How to address his social superiors. When to speak or be silent. He was less nervous than he would otherwise have been, but was keenly aware of the importance of making a good impression on the king. Whatever he did or said would not just affect him, but for good or bad, would reflect on his house and family. This made him more than a little apprehensive. He began to speak in a very formal and careful way as he answered the king.

"My king, may you live forever. I fall at your feet seven times. May it please the king to know that his servant will be seventeen years of age at his next birthday, and has traveled the Great Sea throughout two entire sailing seasons now past, and has seen many things and learned much to make his humble self a good, honest and productive son of your city."

"Yes, yes, yes!" the king interrupted. "I have seen your manifest, and the many notes you made regarding your observations. You are, as I expected, a most astute young man. Skip the formalities. Speak to me as you would to your father."

"Very well my king. If it so pleases you. This last voyage proceeded from Gebal to the island of Kaptara and arrived at the port of Zakros. There we unloaded a cargo of wine and wheat, with many items crafted in Gebal."

"Your notes from the manifest give this in detail. Please tell me of things that you did not write down. I want to know what news you heard while there? What are the conditions on the island? How safe is the port? Who do we have there that I can still trust with our trade?"

Taken aback, Aleon thought for a moment. He had spent little time ashore at Zakros, and wasn't sure how he might answer these questions. He thought back to what he had learned from his tutors about the island and its centuries-long history and association with the Kena'ani people of the coastal cities.

"The port seemed busy enough, and I saw no signs of any danger. The customs house is overseen by an Achaean officer, who I had the feeling was not just open to bribes, but was actually soliciting them. I can't really speak of conditions in the inland cities, but the locals seemed peaceful and not suffering any under their Achaean masters. They speak our language well, and are certainly friendly toward us. Not just because of the goods we brought, but because they are still a kindred people.

More than two hundred years ago, when our ancestors abandoned Kaptara to escape the Achaean invasion, a remnant of our people remained, along with much of our shared culture and heritage. Beyond that, I don't know that I was in a position to judge who might be trustworthy there. The agent of the House of Dan-El seemed reliable enough. I'm sure my father would have removed him if he wasn't."

"Were there no pirate vessels in the harbor?" the king asked. "What of the Achaean soldiers? Did they patrol the streets and keep watch on the warehouses? Achaeans have been robbing us blind for longer than my lifetime."

"I did see one ship in the harbor that looked, or felt, like it might be a pirate vessel. And some of the customers in the tavern we visited seemed overly interested in our ship and what cargo we carried. There were a few soldiers also among the customers, but they mostly ignored us. Our crewmen were very careful with what they said and kept their voices low, not wanting to be overheard by anyone who might have evil in mind. We left the port while it was still dark, rowing as quietly as possible, against the tide, so as to avoid any problems."

"Good! Very Good," the king said, "I see you have a keen eye for what goes on around you. I was sure you would provide me with some solid information. From Zakros your next destination was the Island of Pharos in the delta of the great river Nile. I had Abirami carry a message to the pharaoh for me. Do you know if it was delivered?"

"We did not go ashore at Pharos, but because I had never been there, I was allowed to look around at the docks. I did see Master Abirami hand your letter to Aperel, the *Tjati*, or Vizier, of Kemet's Northern Province."

"And what did the Tjati say? How did he receive my letter?"

"He smiled at first, as Abirami first presented him with a gift sent by my father. It was an elegant sword of the finest bronze, with ornaments of gold worked into the hilt and inlaid into the length of the blade. Then when he learned that the letter was from you, my king, he frowned and sighed deeply. I heard him say, 'Another letter? Gods spare us!"

At that the king's face grew dark, and he struggled to control his emotions. "How dare he?" he said through barely parted lips. "Wait until my letter reaches the pharaoh. He will not dismiss it so carelessly, as if I were a nobody! This letter has important news about the rebellious peoples of Ammiya who killed their lord, the one our pharaoh had chosen and set over them. When he hears this news, I know he will finally send me the soldiers and archers I have requested."

Suddenly the king stopped speaking; realizing that perhaps he had been speaking his thoughts out loud and might have said too much in the presence of this young man of unproven loyalty.

"Ah, well! It is of no matter. Thank you for your news, young Aleon-Tabah. Please greet you parents for me and give them my regards when you reach the House of Dan-El. You may go now."

Aleon bowed three times and began to back to the doorway when he was stopped by the king's voice.

"And do remember to keep your eyes sharp and your ears open whenever you journey from Gebal. I will see you again Aleon!"

Wonderful! Aleon thought to himself. *Now I am expected to be one of his spies!*

Chapter 59

A Celebration

At the House of Dan-El

Home, finally. After four months at sea, it was good to see the gates of the House of Dan-El. He had walked from the Customs House and it was late afternoon as he approached his home. While he was still more than a score of paces from the gatehouse a trumpet sounded from the parapet and the great bronzed and gilded gates were opened and six of the household guards came forth and marched quickly toward him. They formed up into a ceremonial honor guard to escort their young lord the rest of the way home.

Aleon's eyes took in everything as he passed through the outer and central courtyards, and through the inner courtyard to the steps of the house itself. He missed nothing; noticing dozens of small changes that had taken place in his absence. A section of new roof tiles over the barracks; new doors on the stalls in the stable. Was that a new horse, the white one with the black star mark on its forehead?

He paused to take a better look at this new horse, and a large hound came out of the stable and stood staring at Aleon. Aleon recognized him at once.

"Khe-ahn!" he cried. "Do you remember me?" Khe-ahn, the hunting hound that had saved Aleon from the thieves, cocked his head at the sound of his name and began wagging his tail. "Wuff!" the dog replied. He dipped his forequarters playfully, then bounded over to Aleon and jumped up to lick his face.

"Hah! You do remember me! It is good to see you too old friend. Thank you for such a wet welcome." The dog continued to frisk about and jump up to lick at Aleon's face again.

"Come with me to see my parents." Aleon moved on to the inner courtyard with Khe-ahn at his heels.

He saw the familiar faces of the two dozen or so servants who lined up inside the inner court. They cheered and waved greetings to welcome Aleon, who had always been a favorite among those who served him and his family. His hero status had only increased their admiration and affection for him.

Aleon reached down to pat Khe-ahn on the head and told him to "stay". Khe-ahn looked at Aleon, then looked at the servants all around, and finally looked up at Ahinadab and the rest of Aleon's family at the top of the steps. He was very alert, with his ears standing straight up, but he relaxed and took a sphinx-like pose at Aleon's feet.

Aleon looked up at his father, mother and siblings gathered on the landing and filled his eyes with the sight of them. One of the servants broke into song, singing in his clear baritone an ancient hymn of thanksgiving to El for the safe return of a mariner. The other servants joined at the first chorus and their practiced voices blended perfectly. The ancient words rose around him and Aleon felt a lump in his throat. It was a familiar tune, one of Aleon's childhood favorites that was always sung on his father's return from the sea.

He climbed the steps and was gathered into the arms of his father, who greeted him with a kiss on each cheek and a hearty hug. It was not certain which one was more surprised to see that Aleon and Ahinadab now stood eye-to-eye.

Ahinadab stepped back a half pace, held his son at arm's length, and said, "Let me look at you my son. I see your beard is coming in nicely, and there is new muscle and new strength in you from the hard work of a sailor. This pleases me greatly, and I am very proud of you. Welcome home!"

"Thank you, father!" Aleon replied. "I have missed you more than any words could tell, and the rest of our family also."

His father released him and he turned toward his mother. She stepped up and embraced him as his father had done, but had to stand on her toes to kiss his cheeks, which caused them both to chuckle. "Welcome home my son. You are not my little boy, my little Gamil, anymore. I miss that rascal. But like your father, I rejoice to see the man you have become. We are both proud of you."

She stared into his eyes and seemed to read all the hardship and adventure that he had come through since he first went to sea. Confidence radiated from his face in place of the awkward shyness that characterized his younger days. She was very pleased.

Nikkal released him, and his brothers and sisters crowded around to smother him with their own hugs and welcoming words. His youngest brother, Dan-el, who was five summers in age now, looked up with joy and boldly asked, "Did you bring us gifts from your travels?"

His parents joined Aleon's laughter at that. "Why, yes. I think I may have something for you all! But you'll have to wait until I can have it fetched from the ship. It was too much to carry by myself."

Dan-el's eyes grew wide and a huge smile lit up his face. Everyone was smiling too, especially the younger ones.

Little Domina, his four-year-old sister, broke the mood slightly by declaring, "Gami," her name for Aleon, "you stink!"

This brought peals of laughter from everyone, and Aleon had to admit that he really did stink. There was no fresh water to spare for washing on a voyage, and the crew had to bathe as best they could in the sea. This didn't happen as often as they would have liked, and by the time they reached a port where bathhouses were available, the men were pretty ripe. Aleon had not had time to attend to his personal hygiene since the *New Cabax* docked. His trip to the customs house and the audience with the king had prevented that. He smelled like a sailor; a combination of fish, dried sweat, dirty clothes and the garum sauce that was the seasoning that flavored their diet of dried fish, hardened bread and the odd fresh catch from the sea. It all made up a fine stink, indeed.

"Let's not stand around here!" Ahinadab said. "Come inside Aleon, where you may refresh yourself. This evening we have invited some family and guests to join us in welcoming you home. You need time to prepare."

Aleon led the way into the house proper, and started to go up to his old chamber. However, at the top of the landing he was met by his father's body servants who led him instead into his father's chambers where he was soon immersed in the private bath that had been prepared for him. Freshly bathed and anointed with fragrant oils, his hair was curled. His beard, still too short to curl, was neatly combed.

He stood with his naked, sun-bronzed body glistening from the oil while the body servants dressed him in new clothing that his parents had provided. A few quick alterations had to be made to accommodate his unexpected growth, but these were easily accomplished.

Aleon could hear the sounds of guests arriving and the aroma of cooked food rose up to tease his sense of smell.

"*I am home!*" he thought, and with that he felt totally relaxed, perfectly content, and ready to rejoin his family and meet the guests.

In the great hall the family had been joined by Aleon's aunt, uncle, and other members of his parents' extended families and special friends. Aleon saw that for this occasion everyone was seated on cushions at low tables rather than reclining on couches as was proper for more formal gatherings. This seating gave the evening a casual, charming atmosphere.

Abirami was there with his wife and children. Two of Ahinadab's associate shofeṭim had come with their wives. Lord Paltiba'al, Tallayba'al, and their children sat to the right of Ahinadab and Nikkal at the head table. Everyone was dressed in their finest clothing. The whole company glittered with jewels, gold and silver, all of it reflecting brilliantly in the light of a hundred lamps.

Aleon paused at the top of the staircase and swept his eyes over the scene below. Conversations stopped and everyone stood when he appeared. There was applause and a low buzz of excitement as Aleon began his descent. When he was halfway down, he stopped abruptly as his gaze fell on a strangely familiar figure that he almost didn't recognize at first. His breath caught in his throat and his pulse quickened as he realized who he was looking at.

Chapter 60
Melita

At the House of Dan-El

Melita sat beside her father with an empty seat between her and Ahinadab. The empty seat was surely meant for Aleon as it was at the immediate right of his father. It was the place of highest honor.

Melita stood, resplendent in a silken skirt of many colors that fell in layers from her waist to her ankles. Her hair was done up in elaborate curls that crowned her head and formed a dark, glossy, black cloud over her head, spangled with gold and silver beads, with pearls that sparkled like stars in the night sky. It framed her face perfectly, and was pinned back behind her ears. Such delicate ears, he thought, which rested like two small seashells on the sides of her face.

And what a face it was! Her face was tinted with white powder that lightened her whole continence, and her cheeks were brushed with a rosy blush in a way that accentuated her cheekbones and focused attention on her eyes. Her eyes were lined with kohl after the fashion of the ladies in the court of the Pharaoh, with a delicate shade of azure gracing her eyelids and the hollows below her eyebrows.

But more than anything, it was her eyes that had arrested Aleon's gaze. They were focused on him and stared back into his, with an intensity that almost stopped his heart. They were like two ebony orbs that could have belonged to a goddess.

After a brief second, he remembered that there were others in the room, and they were all standing in honor of his arrival. He took a halting step, and had to look down to make sure of his footing. As his eyes left hers, the spell she had cast was lifted briefly. When he raised his eyes to her figure again, he noticed something else. She had breasts! Always in the past she had been flat-chested, with little above the waist that was different than any boy of the same age. But she must be sixteen summers old now and all that had changed.

The top of her silken gown was cut in Kaptaran style. It fully covered her sides, back, and shoulders, with short sleeves that fell to her elbows. But the front was left wide open. A bright red bodice was cut to scoop low in front, coming just under her bare breasts, and a wide purple sash was wrapped around her middle above her slender hips.

Her entire chest, breasts and neck were coated with the same white powder that made up her face and her nipples were painted a bright red. This was the style, borrowed from the ladies of the Island of Kaptara centuries earlier, and had long been popular among the high-born women of Gebal. Aleon was familiar with the style, but he had never seen it worn by Melita. As he remembered she tended to dress in a plainer fashion, with a preference for almost masculine tunics that hid her flat chest completely. Seeing her now, dressed this way, was a revelation to Aleon.

He was unable to take his eyes away from her. The guests were all hailing him and calling out greetings, but he didn't really hear them. He nearly tripped as he rounded the end of the head table to take his seat at his father's right hand and next to Melita.

Aleon sat and the entire company followed suit. As Melita took her place, her hand accidentally brushed Aleon's arm. Her touch was a light as a feather but it sent a shock through him. He felt a warmth and a tingling sensation in his loins. He was glad he was already seated as the beginnings of an erection stirred in his kilt and would have been embarrassing if she, or anyone else, had noticed. The table hid his condition from view and the many questions and comments directed at him provided badly needed distraction. His father rose to address the room and Aleon forced himself to concentrate on what he said. The erection faded, and he shifted in his seat as things settled down.

"Dear friends and family," Ahinadab began, "We are honored by your presence here tonight, to help us welcome our firstborn son to his home. Aleon-Tabah, the Lion-Slayer has just returned from his second season on the Great Sea. We give thanks to Almighty El for protecting him and returning him safely to us. We thank master mariner Abirami for his excellence in guiding our ship, the *New Cabax*, through this and many other sailing seasons, and thank him twice over, for imparting some of his great knowledge and wisdom to our son. May the blessing of El be upon the house of Abirami forever.

The room resounded with applause as Abirami nodded his head in acknowledgment of the compliment and Ahinadab waited a moment before speaking again.

"Now I ask my son, Aleon-Tabah, the Lion-Slayer and an accomplished mariner, to tell us something of his travels and experiences."

Aleon rose and his father returned to his seat. The room quieted, and he began to share some highlights of his voyages, of the lands he had seen, and the people he had encountered. He spoke of his love of the sea. A love which he had felt from the moment he first set out. He spoke with wonder about the many marvelous creatures that dwelt in its depths: the great whales, porpoises, seals, squid, and too many others to count. As he continued it was as if he were experiencing everything all over again.

His words, born of his passion, had a magical quality that captivated everyone. Each guest felt as if they saw all these things through his eyes, and all shared in his delight.

For Melita to see him this way was unexpected. She had dreaded this evening. Her parents insisted that she be there with them, to honor the mighty hero. She expected him to be quite full of himself after all the attention he had received since killing the lion.

But something about him seemed different the moment she first saw him descending the stairs. He had lost the hesitant step of his childhood, and now walked to the table with a confident stride.

When he began to speak, it was not with the uncertain, shyness of a boy. His was the voice of one who truly was a hero. One whose words conjured images in her mind of all the things he had seen and done. This was not what she expected.

She had no idea he was even capable of such deep and moving thoughts and ideas. The more he spoke, the more deeply she fell under the spell of his words. She felt her mind and heart opening up to the same love of the sea that he was expressing.

Without realizing it, her hand reached across to where his hung at his side and she grasped it. He was so caught up in his narrative that he barely noticed, but he grasped her hand in return and gave it a slight squeeze.

Now it was her turn to feel a shock, and a churning warmth began to grow in her innermost depths, and she felt an unfamiliar moisture between her legs. She shivered as her nipples expanded and became erect.

She blushed and was grateful for the white powder that hid her reddened cheeks from the others in the room. Her heart was beating too fast, and she suddenly felt dizzy. Taking a deep breath, Melita shyly took her hand away from his. Feeling its absence, he looked into her eyes but continued to speak. With a puzzled expression he realized, for the first time, what their hands had been doing. She saw confusion in his eyes and had to look away.

Recovering his thoughts, Aleon finished speaking and sat down. There was a hushed silence for a few moments before the whole room began to applaud him, with a chorus of "Congratulations!", "An epic tale!", "Heroic!" and many similar words of appreciation.

Ahinadab rose again and raised his chalice and offered a toast. "To Aleon-Tabah, the slayer of lions and mariner of the Great Sea!"

Every guest drained their cups as ba'alat Nikkal rose and signaled for the servers to bring in the food and more wine. Dinner was served and followed by many more toasts in praise of Aleon, with blessings of the gods invoked by some. At length the evening ended and the guests departed, with a few who had enjoyed too much wine staying the night.

Chapter 61
A Restless Night

In the House of Dan-El

Aleon lay awake in his bed for a long time. He couldn't get his mind off of Melita, and how changed she was. The fragrance of her perfume lingered on his hand and was more intoxicating to him than the wine he drank that evening. He wanted to see her again. His last thoughts before he drifted off to sleep were of their betrothal, which no longer seemed to be such a bad idea. Was this the same girl who had mocked him and poured sand in his face?

Morning came and Aleon awoke before sunrise. It was strange not to hear the creaking of the ship's timbers and other sounds of the sea, or the voices of the crewmen as they worked. His head ached and his stomach felt queasy. The inside of his mouth was coated and tasted of sour wine.

At first, he wasn't sure where he was, but sitting up on his sleeping pallet he recognized the familiar shapes of the furnishings in his darkened bedchamber.

Home. He was home.

Slowly his memory of the night before, with its feasting and drinking returned, and he smiled. His mind was instantly focused on his memory of Melita! He marveled at what different thoughts her name brought to mind now.

He stood and put his hand out to steady himself. It felt as if the floor beneath him was rolling like the deck of the *New Cabax*, but it was just a feeling. Men who spent a long time at sea experienced this sensation, and it was not new to Aleon. After he had moved around a bit it would pass and his "sea-legs" would soon be replaced by "land-legs."

A brazier of charcoal stood next to his open window where its smoke would not cloud the room and its fumes would not smother him. It provided a pleasant warmth through the night, but had almost died out. He prodded the ashes with a bronze rod until he found a few remaining embers and gave them a stir. He picked up one small coal with a pair of bronze tongs and used it to light the three wicks of the large oil lamp that hung by chains from the ceiling. As it flickered to life the darkness was driven away.

He was thirsty and took a long drink from the ewer of watered wine that stood on a tripod near his bedside. That helped to clear his head and rinsed the sour taste from his mouth. It also reduced the pounding in his temples. Drinking too much always gave him roaring headaches, which was the main reason he didn't like to over-indulge. The strong spirits that lived in wine and beer were needed to drive away the evil spirits that dwelt in all but the purest water. Their malicious actions forced everyone to drink either wine mixed with water, or beer, even from an early age. On board the *New Cabax* this had been especially important as days might go by before the ship reached a source of fresh water to replenish their supply.

His stomach churned as the liquid hit it, reminding him of how different the rich food of last evening was from the simple fare he had been living on at sea. Being home would take some getting used to. Perhaps it would help if he went down to the kitchen and found something simple to eat.

He moved to his chamber pot to relieve his bladder, then dressed in the cleaned and pressed clothes the servants had laid out for him. It felt strange to be so pampered again, unlike his shipboard circumstances. He left his room, passed down the landing and exited through the rear door that faced the kitchen garden.

He paused for a moment on the second-floor landing to look up at the darkened sky. Aleon saw stars that had become familiar friends, stars that guided sailors safely from place to place. He thought of all the knowledge of their movements that he had gained. By their positions he could tell that dawn was a little more than an hour away.

How many times had he looked at these same stars as a child without being able to read their messages? What a magnificent gift Almighty El had given men when he created these celestial lights and spun their paths across the heavens. He wondered how men like master Abirami had learned such secrets. Then the moment passed and he went down and walked the short distance to the kitchen building.

Heat and the aroma of baking bread washed over him when he entered the kitchen. He was in the oven room, where Yasha, the head cook, looked up from her work and greeted him. Yasha had served the House of Dan-El since before Aleon was born. The kitchen was her domain, and she was in command of a half dozen slaves and twice that many table servers.

"Welcome, my lord Aleon." she said, "May the blessings of our Lady of the Well be with you. And what brings you to my kitchen so early, as if I didn't know?"

"Greetings to you dear Yasha! I'm afraid I ate and drank too much of your marvelous food last night and my stomach needs a remedy. What have you got that can soothe it?"

"I thought you might need such a tonic. I made up just the thing from freshly plucked mint leaves and other herbs this morning. Drink this potion, and eat one of these honey cakes. But just one, mind you! You must not take too much."

Yasha set a cup of the steaming, tea-like potion and a small plate of fresh-baked honey cakes in front of Aleon as he sat at a side table. She raised her hands above her shoulders, with her palms up and her eyes closed. She said a short prayer to the god Eshmun to invoke his healing power on Aleon's behalf. Then, without further ado, she bustled off to supervise her workers in a separate room, away from the ovens. Some were mixing more dough while others kneaded it and formed it into the more than fifty loaves that would be consumed by the household during the day. Long shelves were already filled with rows of rising loaves that would soon be ready for the ovens.

In another adjacent room a large basket of freshly picked vegetables stood next to a tub of water. One slave washed them before passing them to another who cleaned, chopped, and grated them. The prepared vegetables were either placed in separate pots for cooking, or dropped into a big cauldron along with bits of chopped goat, lamb or other meat. A huge fireplace at the end of this room already held a pair of the big cauldrons on hooks over the fire. The aroma of stewed meat, vegetables, and fragrant spices filled the air and drifted to where Aleon was sitting. It made his mouth water, and reminded him again of all the things he had missed while at sea.

Aleon was always amazed at the amount of food that was needed each day to feed the family and all the household's servants, slaves, and guardsmen that kept the House of Dan-El functioning smoothly. Yasha had come to the House of Dan-El as a slave many years ago, and had taken the ring as a young woman. She dedicated her life to the care of the family, and she was beloved by everyone in the household. She was totally loyal and committed fully to her responsibilities. She had never married or had a family herself, so it was natural that she dotted on Aleon and his siblings as if they were her own children.

Aleon's affection for her had always been great, and throughout his childhood she had enjoyed spoiling him. It is fair to say that he was her favorite. He finished Yasha's potion and the one honey cake that she had set as his limit, and his stomach did feel much better for it. He rose to leave and she bustled back over to him. They hugged each other affectionately.

"Thank you Yasha! You are always kind to me. I have missed you more than words can tell."

"It is my pleasure to have you home again master Aleon. You are all grown up now, and I have too few chances to care for you like this. I confess that I have also missed catching you trying to sneak into my kitchen to steal a few treats."

"Ah, yes! But you always did catch me." he replied with a laugh, "I promise to visit you here again soon. But now I need to let you get on with your work and not distract you any further. May Almighty El look with favor on you, Yasha, and may you have his blessings just as you always have mine." They hugged each other once more and Aleon left the kitchen.

Outside the sky was beginning to show signs of light in the east and a cock was crowing as he walked along the pathway through the garden and out to the courtyards in front of the house.

He considered taking a horse to ride out and see what had changed in the city since he last saw it. He also wanted to visit his shipmates who stood the night watch aboard the *New Cabax*. Since the great fire no ship was left unguarded at any time, even in her home port.

The grooms were not up and about, so he decided not to take a horse and walked to the gatehouse, where the guards on duty jumped to attention and saluted him.

"Hail, lord Aleon!" the senior guard said from atop the parapet. "Do you wish to leave the house?"

"Yes!" he replied. "I want to see what is new in the city and fancy a walk this morning. I will also call upon my shipmates and see to affairs aboard the *New Cabax*."

"Will you require an escort."

"No, but please inform my father and mother of where I am going. Let them know I will return in time for the evening meal."

"It shall be as you command, lord Aleon."

Two guards left the parapet to open the gates. They saluted again as Aleon passed through, then closed and secured the gates behind him.

Aleon wandered the city streets, finding little had changed, but noticing certain things that were new. A new sign hung above the door to a tailor's shop, indicating that it had a new owner. The herbalist's shop had been recently whitewashed, and a large glazed window had been installed. The artisans of Gebal had recently discovered the secret of making glass in sheets large enough for windows. It was a closely held secret and a new source of wealth for the city. This architectural innovation was becoming popular in the Kena'ani cities of the coast and was beginning to spread to other lands around the Great Sea. But even in Gebal, only the richest citizens could afford glazed windows, so here it was evidence that the herbalist must be prospering. It was strange to see how the lamp light inside the shop spilled out through the glass to paint a pattern of bright rectangles on the street.

Dawn finally arrived and the city was coming to life at the start of a new day. Aleon walked down the grand staircase and through the harbor district, to finally arrive at the wharf where the *New Cabax* was berthed. He wanted to see how the shipwrights were doing on the repairs, and was also interested in the crewmen's progress in readying the ship for the winter layover. Master Abirami hailed him from the deck and invited him to come aboard.

"Greetings, Aleon! Have you come to assist us, or did your father send you to check on his investment?"

"Neither," he replied, "Although I would be glad to assist as you see fit, if I may be of service."

"Hmmm. So, you haven't missed your shipmates at all then?" Abirami said with a wink. "I can read your mind Aleon. Your heart is that of a true seaman. The wind and the waves will always beckon you, urging you to return to them and forget the uncaring land. It is hard for men like us to be away from the sea for very long.

I also know you share the bond that exists between myself and the rest of the crew. We are more like family than friends and coworkers. I trust you know your feelings are returned in equal measure by every one of your shipmates, and by me. The *New Cabax* will always be a home for you, and I would be proud to have you sail with me again, anytime."

Aleon smiled at this and said, "You have judged me correctly master Abirami. Only a man of great wisdom could see into my heart so clearly. How can I help?"

"First you could stow the flattery, if that's possible, and take a turn around the ship to see how the repairs and our other preparations are progressing. Make note of anything that needs adjustment, or of anything that has been overlooked. Write it in the log, and bring it to my attention when you are finished."

Aleon did as he was bidden, but found little that needed to be noted. Everything was proceeding in good order, so he mostly just stayed out of the way and watched as the shipwrights and crewmen continued working.

Maintaining a ship and preparing it for winter were important processes that always amazed Aleon. When finished, the ship would be closed up tightly, with the cabin secured and boarded up, the mast, yards, sail and deck fencing all stowed below for the winter. Nothing would be left loose anywhere above deck.

To get the mast into the hold the crew had to remove the deck planking to make an opening big enough to accommodate its full length. Then the sails, yard, all cordage and even the great stone anchors, were secured below. After that, the shipwrights would lay down new decking to completely cover even the hatchways. Then the ship would be rowed from its berth to the open beach, where it would be hauled up and out of the water at high tide by stevedores with teams of oxen so that her bottom could be scraped clean of barnacles and weeds. Finally, a fresh coating of tar would be applied to every surface that would rest below the waterline, and everything else would be coated with a heavy layer of thickened olive oil. Then the ship would remain on the beach until spring.

Aleon reported back to Abirami and handed him the ship's log with his few notes. He gave a brief summary of his findings, but as he was speaking his eye was drawn to a figure walking passed the quay and out along the beach. The figure wore a man's cloak, but even in the distance he could see it was a young woman who's long, unbound hair was lifted and tossed about by the wind.

Chapter 62

A Disturbing Dream

At the House of Abdhamon

Melita also had trouble falling asleep. She kept thinking about Aleon's hand as she held it. It was roughened from hard work. But the way he had gently squeezed her fingers had felt like a caress. One that triggered a response in her that she didn't know was possible. She marveled at the changes in him. He was not the boy she remembered as a weakling. No worry any more that she would have to look down on him. He now stood a head taller than she did. At seventeen summers he had probably reached most of his height, but he might grow even taller. That thought pleased her.

His shoulders were broad, and seriously muscled from the hard work of pulling an oar and other tasks. She knew she would never again defeat him in a wrestling match. Strangely, the very thought of losing to him, of being overpowered by him, seemed like something she might actually enjoy. Where had these strange thoughts come from?

Did she imagine it, or had his face lost its look of innocent childishness to take on the appearance of a man with more than a little experience of life. The beard was part of it, but beyond that there was now some mystery about him. It made her want to know this new Aleon better. Then there was the strange and magical way he spoke of the sea. Could any woman rival a passion like that?

All these thoughts were new to her, and very confusing. Before tonight she had always thought of her own needs and wants first. Her need to control the course of her life was paramount. But now the future seemed to be filled with all sorts of mysterious possibilities.

Her final thoughts as she fell asleep were of their betrothal, an idea she now felt even better about than before, but for different reasons. Marriage to Aleon seemed more than merely a way to achieve her dreams. She now saw him as a man who could provide for, and protect, a wife and family. But was he a man who could love and cherish her? Was he a man who could be her equal in all things, and who would treat her as his equal?

The dawning sun was about to shine its first light on the city when Melita's dreams awoke her. She had dreamed she was looking down on ships at sea, with smaller vessels attacking a large merchant ship. Men were shouting and fighting hand-to-hand with spears and swords while arrows rained down on them.

Then all the smaller ships suddenly changed into great waves that collided with each other in a chaotic boil, and washed across the large vessel's deck. Clouds rolled in and a great storm began to rage.

She suddenly found herself standing on the deck of the big merchant ship, crying out in her sleep as the rain of arrows turned into hailstones that struck her and bounced where they landed. The wind and waves tossed the ship about as if it were nothing. The hailstones on the deck coalesced into an army of small ice warriors who ran toward her and began to climb up her skirt with frozen knives and swords. Their weight began to drag her down and fear washed over her. She was overcome by panic and ran to the side of the ship, knowing her only hope was to leap over the side and into the chaos below.

The icy warriors were washed away as she sank beneath the waves. Then, just as she felt herself drowning, a sea god rose from the depths. He reached out to lift her in his mighty arms and carried her to the surface. Her head broke the surface and she gasped life-saving air into her lungs. The god raised his right arm and the storm disappeared, the waves ceased their pounding, and the sea became smooth and calm. She looked at her rescuer, but could not see his face. It was as if his head was wreathed in a misty cloud. Only his eyes had any form. Strangely, she knew she had seen those eyes before, and with a shock of recognition she awoke.

Melita leaped from her bed with a cold sweat sending chills down her whole body. The room was still dark, and the house quiet. She stood, shivering, as close to the dying embers in her room's brazier as she could. With gooseflesh all over. she wrapped her arms around herself. She could feel her heart pounding with the same fear that gripped her in the dream. Slowly, she grew calmer, and found one of her old tunics to dressed herself.

Sharia, her old nursemaid, now handmaid, was snoring in her small side chamber , and Melita was careful not to wake her. Sharia would have fussed over her clothing and hair, and would have wanted to bathe her, and apply her makeup before allowing Melita to leave her chamber. Tallayba'al had given strict orders in that regard. Melita desperately wanted to avoid all of that this morning. She needed to be alone to think. The dream was still sharp and vivid in her mind.

She carried her cloak and sandals and stepped lightly away, leaving her chamber to go downstairs with as little noise as possible. No one was up and about as yet, but she knew they would be soon. She was still so disturbed by the dream that anyone who saw her would know something was wrong. She did not want to be questioned, especially by her mother, who would try to read Melita's thoughts and probe for the answers. Answers that Melita did not have.

She needed time to sort those out. To try and understand the strange dream. Her conscious mind struggled to remember the details, but her memory of the god's eyes staring into hers was blocking all other thoughts. Where had she seen them before? Then it came to her. Those were the same eyes that had gazed at her from the stairs above the great hall in the House of Dan-El. They were Aleon's eyes!

The House of Abdhamon, lacked nothing in the way of luxury or comfort. It followed a similar plan to the House of Dan-El but was slightly larger. The central hall was slightly smaller, but there was more space given to the servants' quarters, storage spaces, and there were four more rooms upstairs.

Paltiba'al did most of his business in the harbor district, and did not require the large, impressive gateway of Ahinadab's dwelling. His home had a simple double-gated entry instead, with a small guard house. Instead of a series of courtyards, there was a large and beautiful garden, through which Melita now passed as she left the house. She walked thoughtfully through the garden with the smell of night blooming flowers floating on the air. She could hear crickets chirping and an owl hooted in the distance. Farther off she heard a rooster crow in anticipation of the dawn.

Only one guard stood watch at the gate, and as he saw Melita approach he smiled. Her protector from the day of Yutpan's funeral had recovered from his wounds, but was no longer fit for the more demanding duties of a soldier, and his disability would have gotten him dismissed by most other households. But out of gratitude for saving their daughter, Paltiba'al and Tallayba'al kept him on, letting him serve in the lesser capacity of a gate warden. Guarding the gate overnight was all they required of him. If danger arose. he would summon the sleeping household guards by sounding a trumpet.

"Good morning, Grath," Melita said cheerfully, calling the big Lukka guard by name. "How is your arm today?"

"Hail, *Lehyuna*," he replied, using his pet name for her, which in his native language meant *She who saves*. "Arm is very strong today. No pain. No hurt," he said with his limited command of the Kena'ani language.

She knew this was not true, for his right arm, the arm that had saved her life, had not healed well, and was practically useless. It must be causing him great pain each day.

"Please open the gate for me. I wish to take a walk outside."

"I call guards for you." he said, knowing that since the attack she was not supposed to leave the house without an escort.

"No. That is not necessary. I won't be going far, and won't be gone long. I just need to be alone for a while."

"You command. I obey." Grath smiled again and raised the bar, stepping aside to let the gate swing open. Melita passed through and turned left to walk downhill from the House of Abdhamon.

She was deep in her thoughts, still mystified by her dream, and passed through streets so familiar she didn't have to pay much attention to where she was going. She really hadn't meant to go very far, but her feet seemed to have a mind of their own. While her thoughts were focused on her dream, they carried her to the harbor district and out onto the beach below the great quay.

Feeling the rough sand underfoot helped to clear the fog of her thoughts. The sky was brighter now, but the shadow of the White Mountain still lay over the city. In the growing light her eye fell on her rocky retreat near the end of the jetty. It seemed to be inviting her to come and sit a while where she could think in privacy.

Like all the Kena'ani people, she knew that dreams were how the gods spoke to mortals. What messages did this dream hold, and which god had sent it to her? Had the same god been guiding her steps to this place?

The wind stirred her hair as she began walking, purposefully now, toward the end of the jetty. The tide was out and she only had to wade through ankle-deep water to reach her favorite spot.

The wind was becoming brisk and blowing steadily in from the sea. There was a bite to it and a chill that spoke of the coming fall. She wrapped her cloak around herself and sat in the hollow of the rock where it provided the most shelter. She stared out to sea as small waves lapped at the base of the rock and hid the sound of approaching footsteps.

Her mind was still was focused on the way Aleon's eyes had stared into hers when the sound of his voice suddenly startled her.

Chapter 63
A Bond of Love

On Melita's rock by the shore

"Hello Melita, daughter of Paltiba'al." Aleon said. "It is a chilly day for a swim, if that is what you are planning."

Melita caught her breath and almost jumped to her feet. She turned to face him, and didn't know how to respond.

"I...ah...I..." She stammered, at a loss for words.

"My apologies if I startled you. I didn't mean to intrude." Aleon said. He could see that his unexpected appearance had upset her. "I pray you can forgive me for following you here, but I saw you on the beach, and, well, I wanted to see you again. After last night I mean. I have been away so long, and you have changed so much..." His words trailed off as he stared into her eyes and his thoughts failed him.

"You are forgiven, lord Aleon-Tabah," she managed to say. "I came here to be alone, but you may join me if you like."

She was amazed to hear herself say those words. What was going on. Did she really want him to stay? She wished he would look away, but she couldn't take her eyes off of his. In them she saw again that mystery, which she first noticed as he spoke of his travels the night before.

"Please! Call me Aleon, and I hope I may call you Melita. There is no need for us to be formal here. I wish we could have had the chance to speak privately last night, and hope we can do so now. If it would please you, that is."

Melita was silent. She did want to talk with him, to ask if he would share more about his travels, and especially his love of the sea. But she didn't know how to start.

Taking her silence as a way of rejecting his suggestion, Aleon was crestfallen. "Well at least I tried." he muttered with a deep sigh as he turned to leave.

"Wait! Don't go. Please sit. I will talk with you. I have wanted that too."

Was that true? She had said it, but it hadn't really crossed her mind until the words passed her lips. Or had it? She pondered this as he turned back and sat beside her. The wind was stronger now, and the sheltered space was small, so he had to sit close to her.

She could feel his warmth and welcomed it, suddenly realizing how inadequate her old tunic was for the weather. That, and a sudden shyness caused her to shiver and pull her cloak even more tightly around her body. She turned her face away, embarrassed about her lack of makeup and her uncombed hair. What would he think of her, dressed like this? In his eyes, was she still the one who had tormented him all those years? Was he still indifferent to her? Oh, gods! She hoped that wasn't true. She didn't want him to be indifferent!

His nearness was causing the same sensations in her body that so disturbed her at dinner the evening before.

"I enjoyed your talk last night," she began. "You have a gift with words. I didn't know that about you."

"What parts interested you the most?" he asked, taking her lead.

"Oh! All of it I suppose. You spoke of the places you've been, places that I have never seen. That and the people there. We see some of them here too, but I never really paid them much attention. Your descriptions made them come to life in my mind in ways they never had before. But most of all, I loved the way you spoke of the sea and all of its creatures. I wish I could have seen these things."

"*...with you!*" she thought, but did not say.

"It is kind of you to say that." Aleon responded. "I was afraid I was boring everyone."

"*...and I would never want to bore YOU.*" he thought, but did not say.

They fell back into silence for a few moments, watching the waves that were growing closer as the tide rose. In a little while they would have to leave the rock, or swim back to the beach.

"There is another thing that has been on my mind." Aleon said, breaking the silence. "As we both know, our parents decided long ago that we would marry one day. That idea has always troubled me."

"Is that because it wasn't your choice?" she asked, "Or was it because of me? I know how badly I have treated you in the past."

"Honestly," he said, "it was both. As long as our marriage was off in the future, I could ignore it, but now that time seems to be sooner and not later."

There! It was out in the open. Aleon did not want her for his wife! She felt rejected, and was crushed. How odd that she should feel that way. She had always despised the idea of marrying him, and only warmed toward it when she thought of the advantages it offered her. But after seeing how he had changed, the thought that he did not want to marry her was shattering.

He saw the hurt in her eyes before she could look away. It stabbed at his heart. He suddenly could not stand the idea that his words had hurt her. What caused that?

"I mean," he blurted, "that is how I used to feel. But now, after last night, I feel very different about it. I think we could be a good match. That is...if you could stand to be married to Gamil-the-Camel."

Melita burst out laughing at his use of that old, derogatory nickname, which she had plagued him with for so long. It seemed as if the clouds had lifted and the sun was shining. The hurt she felt vanished in an instant, and she felt as if he had pulled her back from the edge of a great cliff just as she was about to fall. She was relieved and her heart swelled in her breast with an inexplicable sense of joy. What was this? Where did he get the power to work such a miraculous change with only his words?

Aleon didn't understand her laughter. Why did he have to remind her of those years of insults? He had wanted to lighten the mood, but she had laughed at him, just like in the past. But it didn't feel the same.

She stopped laughing and caught her breath. "Oh, I imagine I could learn to live with it," she said, "but only if you could stand to marry Bitter-Sweet Melita".

Now it was Aleon who laughed, and she joined him in it. When they both regained their composure, she spoke again.

"I must confess, I have had the same feelings about marrying you. For years, I have been angry with our parents for planning our future without regard for our feelings, and I made you the target of my anger. I treated you horribly, Aleon, which I will regret for the rest of our lives. If you will have me, that is."

Aleon's heart leaped at hearing this. She had taken the thing he most dreaded in life and made it a thing of joy. He was overcome with relief. To him, in that moment she seemed to be the most desirable woman in the world.

She saw the happiness shining in his eyes and reached out her hand to him. When their fingers touched, they both felt again the same sensation that had happened to them the night before, and their bodies began to react in the same ways. He drew her close and felt her tremble as he lifted her chin and kissed her on the mouth. That first kiss lasted for a long time, until the rising water finally reached their feet and broke the spell.

Still holding hands, they laughed and rose up, stepping carefully as they were about to leave the rock, they saw that the water was now waist deep. Without asking her permission, Aleon scooped Melita up in his arms and gently carried her until they reached the sands of the beach.

In his strong arms, Melita remembered her dream of the sea god, rescuing her and lifting her to the surface of the water. Was this what the dream meant? She felt completely safe as he carried her. Leaning her head against his shoulder and neck, she wanted to stay in his arms forever. She was happy.

Aleon discovered how strangely soft and warm she felt in his arms. Whenever they had close contact as children, she had been all sinew, muscle and bony angles. But now she was soft curves and pliant limbs as she rested in his arms. Her arms were gently wrapped around his neck and felt wonderful there. He splashed through the water and reached the shore, but didn't want to put her down.

It was full daylight now and though it seemed like only a few moments had passed, it was more than an hour since Aleon had come to her rock. He reluctantly set her on her feet, but she kept her arms around his neck, clinging tightly to him. His arms went around her waist and pulled her close. They embraced with a firmness that molded their bodies together. They could feel each other's hearts beating, and the hardness of desire rising between his legs.

She gently pulled back and he had to let her go. It seemed strangely unnatural to be apart now, and both wished they could have held on to each other longer. But dawn was turning into day.

"I must get back home!" Melita exclaimed. "I certainly will have been missed by now and poor Grath will have had to face my parents' anger for letting me go out unattended. I should have been there to defend him!"

"I'll escort you home." Aleon offered. "Your parents will be relieved when they see you are not alone, and that you are with me. Especially if we tell them we have been making plans for our life together!"

Melita's face lit up with a smile and they walked on, hand-in-hand. Her mind was whirling with those plans for the future.

I think I love him. She thought.

So, this is what being in love feels like. He thought.

Chapter 64

Red Moon

Late Winter, 1338 BC in the House of Abdhamon

In the month of *Pagrum*, the Kena'ani name for February, four months after Aleon returned, and on the fifth day of the month it finally happened. That thing that normally is a part of life to all women in their child-bearing years. Melita's first red moon had risen.

All the day before she had felt poorly. She was bloated and suffered severe pains in her belly, and felt feverish. She was irritable, and didn't want to see anyone, let alone speak to anyone, and kept to her chamber all day. Those who did see her and had to speak with her, like Sharia, her Nubian handmaid, quickly learned to limit their conversations and gave her a wide berth when at all possible. The women understood.

When she hadn't appeared for the morning meal, her mother went up to check on her. She recognized the problem at once and sent Sharia to the kitchen for certain herbs and medicines that were kept on hand. The rest of the body servants she set to work. From the kitchen they brought situlas of heated water for a hot bath. When the medicines arrived Tallayba'al mixed a carefully measured portion with water and said to Melita, "Drink all of this. It will make you feel better."

After drinking the potion, and making a sour face at its bitter taste, Melita expected to feel at least some degree of immediate relief. But when that didn't happen, she offered her mother a look composed of impatience and disappointment. Tallayba'al took her hand and massaged it gently.

"Give it time, my little one. I have placed a healing spell on that potion, which never fails, but it doesn't always work as rapidly as we would want."

Melita was familiar with her mother's healing magic. She had been the beneficiary of it many times throughout her childhood. Mother seemed to have spells and potions to cure everything from skinned knees to broken bones; from minor aches to raging fevers. But this malady did not seem like anything Melita had ever experienced before. Of course, she knew what her symptoms meant. She was at the beginning of her moon days.

Her mother and older sisters had taught her what to expect. It was a natural part of growing up and meant that it was the gods' way of preparing her ripening womb to bear children in time. It was normal for girls in Gebal to have their first red moon as early as their ninth year. But Melita was sixteen now, and had been worried that something might be wrong with her body. It had happened for her friends, but not for her. Her mother explained that girls who were more athletic, like Melita, did not see their first red moon as early as others.

"My own first red moon came in my fifteenth summer." she explained. "Indeed, most of the women in our family have been late to begin, though none have ever been as active as you, so there is nothing to worry about."

The potion and the spell, but mostly her mother's reassuring words, had their effect, and Melita did feel much better. But she had mixed emotions about the impact this change would have on her life. While she was relieved that it was finally happening, she felt angry that only women had to suffer in this way when men did not.

"Mother," she asked, "Why would the gods make women to suffer like this?"

Her mother thought for a moment and then said, "It is a mystery that we do not have an answer for. But there are legends.

The priests tell us that the red moon is a curse that was placed on Nikkal-and-Ib, the first woman, by the goddess, Anath, as punishment or revenge. Anath desired Yarihk, god of the moon, and wanted to mate with him. But Yarihk's heart was elsewhere. His eye had fallen on Nikkal-and-Ib, the great lady of first-fruits, whom he had seen as she bathed naked in his moonlight, and he desired her greatly. In his bodily form he descended from the night sky and embraced her until morning. Anath was furious, and threw a cup of wine, mixed with blood in the face of Yarihk, and pronounced her curse on Nikkal-and-Ib, saying to Yarihk, "Just as this bloody wine pours over your face, so will my anger be poured out upon the woman for whom you lust." The anger of Anath caused Nikkal-and-Ib to suffer her first red moon, and, as she was the mother of all women, her curse now falls on all of us to this day."

"But it wasn't Nikkal-and-Ib who was at fault!" Melita shouted. "Yarihk came to her, she didn't go to him!"

"Perhaps you are right, but to Anath, it looked as if she was seducing him by bathing in his moonlight. Yarihk was saddened because of Anath's curse, and he ask El to help the woman. El had mercy and used his power to turn the curse into a blessing by making it the way all women conceive and bear children. In any case, this is how the legend goes. How else can we explain the red moon that we all experience?"

"I still think it is very unfair!" Melita muttered. "And it doesn't feel like a blessing!"

"Finish your bath, my love. Sharia will dress you and you will feel better. Then if you feel well enough, you should come down and eat something from the kitchen. Or I can have food brought up to you if you'd rather keep to yourself for the day."

"I will stay here. I don't want anything to eat. I just want to be alone."

"Very well. But if you feel differently and are hungry later, send Sharia to the kitchen. You must eat something."

Chapter 65

A Sacrifice to Ashtoreth

Mid-Summer, 1338 BC the festival of Adon

Each year in the month of *Kiraru*, or July, the festival of Adon was celebrated by the women of Gebal, as it had been for longer than anyone could remember. It was a festival that commemorated the death and return to life of the god, Adon, who was killed by a wild boar and brought back to life by his lover, the goddess Ashtoreth.

The festival began on the first day that the dog star, Sirius, could be seen rising above the eastern horizon. It was visible for a few moments before the light of the rising sun obscured it, and was observed by priests who stood watch for that moment on the rooftop of the temple of Ashtoreth. Trumpets signaled the beginning of the festival, which was anticipated with joy by women throughout the city.

In the last hours before dawn, all women except for young girls, the very old, the infirm, or slaves, dressed themselves in sackcloth and marked their foreheads with ashes to mourn the dead god. They filled the streets of the city at daybreak and paraded solemnly from their homes to the temple of Ashtoreth. Along the way some would pluck out strands of their hair, and some would tear their clothing with much weeping and profound sorrow. They circled the temple three times before noon, then dispersed to their homes where they maintained a fast until nightfall.

Darkness descended, the dog star blazed in the eastern sky, and the mood turned from mourning to celebration, rejoicing in the resurrected god's return from the dead. The women would gather in groups on the rooftops of their homes and sing hymns of praise to Adon, extoling his great beauty and love for all women. Adon was known as much for his sexual prowess as he was for his surpassing beauty, and for having uncountable numbers of satisfied lovers. His potency was considered critical to the fruitfulness of the summer crops, and his reappearance was a sure sign of a successful harvest in the coming fall.

Ashtoreth, the goddess of love, who was famed for her great beauty, was his favorite. He chose to spend most of his days with her when he was not roaming the forests in search of game. He was a mighty hunter, and in the annual cycle of the seasons when summer turned to fall, he would be killed by a wild boar. His blood would flow into the river that was named after him, causing the water to run red. Vegetation would begin to wither, leaves turned to fall colors then fell from the trees, and the daylight hours shortened. Cold weather came and lasted throughout the winter months as all of nature mourned the passing of Adon.

But with the coming of spring, the earth was reborn in response to his resurrection, and at nightfall the first day of the festival the women's celebrating included much drinking of strong wine, feasting and dancing, with the songs they sang becoming increasingly bawdy. This continued long after midnight, until many of the celebrants at last fell into an exhausted stupor.

On the second day of the festival the women woke late, taking time to recover from the prior night's revelry and prepare for that evening's events. That night all women of childbearing age who had never made a sacrifice to Ashtoreth were required to offer themselves as sacred prostitutes for this one night only. This applied to all classes and ages of women, but young girls were the most common participants. The majority of the female population had previously made their required sacrifices, and continued their celebrating all day long.

But those whose daughters or younger sisters would make their sacrifices that evening had to spend the day preparing their participants for the night's events. The participants were dressed in their most provocative apparel, with their hair and makeup done as if for a wedding. They would report to the temple of Ashtoreth in the afternoon and would be individually stationed in temporary pavilions on the temple grounds. There the priests provided them with food and wine, and saw to their every need. In the late afternoon a crowd of men gathered before the temple gates waiting for the trumpets that signaled the beginning of the sacrifice. Most single men in the city, except the old, the infirm, or slaves, took part in the sacrifices, including foreigners. It was not uncommon for men from far away to visit the city during the festival of Adon for the express purpose of participating in the sacrifices.

When the gates opened the men pushed and shoved to enter, each one seeking to be the first to place his piece of silver or gold in the hand of the woman who most appealed to his eye. The women were not permitted to refuse any man who offered them payment, and had to give themselves to the first man to approach them, so long as he was not a family member. This once-in-a-lifetime sacrifice to the goddess was believed to be essential to the fertility of the land.

The men, as representatives of Adon, were expected to treat the women gently, with respect, and to present themselves bathed and anointed, with beards and hair braided and curled, and dressed in their finest clothes. But once the gates opened and the men crowded in, there was no way the priests or temple guards could turn anyone away, well-groomed or not.

Melita had always been too young to participate in the celebration or the sacrifice. She was forbidden to attend any of it until after she had experienced her first red moon. The day she finished her purification rites for the first time she realized what this meant. The thought hit her with a cold shock that almost made her heart stop. When the festival came this year, she would be required to make her own *virgin* sacrifice.

She knew there was only one way to avoid this highly important duty. A woman who refused the sacrifice could surrender herself to the temple priests on the first day of the festival. She would be taken to the marketplace and there, witnessed by the gods and all the people, her hair was cut off down to the scalp using sheep shears, and a bronze razor was used to remove the remaining stubble. As a final humiliation, her entire head would be painted red. All who witnessed her shaming hurled insults and heaped curses on her for refusing the sacrifice.

She was required to keep her head shaved for three years. During that time, she could not marry, or take part in anyone else's wedding, nor could she have intercourse with any man. She could not appear publicly during any festival or holy day. For those three years she would be ostracized by the entire citizenry, except for her family. Needless to say, it was very rare for a woman to choose this alternative to the sacrifice.

Chapter 66
A Desperate Plan

At the House of Abdhamon

Melita was tormented by the feeling that she was caught in a trap, with no good way out. Wild thoughts raced through her mind as she tried to come to grips with the horror and revulsion she felt. As a virgin her sacrifice would be doubly sacred to the goddess, and postponing it would be doubly shameful. What could she do?

She thought of asking her mother for help, or her father. But they would think she was just being foolish. Her older sisters had both made their sacrifices and there was never any shame attached to them for doing so. In fact, they had been treated like princesses afterwards, and parties were thrown for them to mark their entry into womanhood. Even her friends, Shema and Zephratha had both done the same after their first red moon. They would be no help. Where could she turn?

She thought of the one person whom she believed she could trust. Aleon! He would understand and help her make up her mind. But would he think less of her because she was afraid, or because she could even think of shirking her duty to the goddess? There was only one way to find out.

The next day Aleon presented himself at the gate to the house of Abdhamon. He was there to call upon his future bride. He had been a regular visitor to the house since the day they had first kissed, and her parents and family were delighted at the young couple's obvious affection. Both the houses were beginning to plan for their children's wedding, which could not take place until Melita's two older sisters were both married. The eldest had been wed to a wealthy merchant from *Zidon*, or Sidon, and the second sister was to marry in the fall that year. This meant that Aleon and Melita's wedding was to happen on the first auspicious day in the spring of the year after.

Until then, the couple was frequently together, but always in circumstances that maintained their respectability. No physical intimacy was allowed, beyond the holding of hands, and perhaps a light kissing of the cheeks in greeting or on parting ways. But the couple was encouraged to make plans for their life together, and many preparations for their wedding day were already under way.

Aleon was greeted and invited into the house. He was led to the hall where servants washed his feet and offered him wine, fruit and cheeses. Melita joined him shortly, and after an embrace and exchange of kisses, she whispered in his ear, saying, "I must speak with you privately, my love. I told my mother that you would escort me to the market today, so we may choose some household furnishings we will need after our wedding."

Aleon sensed her agitation, and wondered at the cause. But he was wise enough to play along with her strategy, waiting until they were alone to learn what was troubling her. He was concerned that she might be having second thoughts about their marriage. But whatever it was, she kept it hidden behind a bright smile and cheery demeanor.

Melita's mother joined them, and after an exchange of pleasantries, she sat a little bit apart from where the two sat together on a couch and talked nonchalantly about the kinds of items they would shop for. Melita fancied a certain rug that was imported from Kemet, and Aleon wanted to show her a pair of sleeping couches. They would occupy one of the larger guest rooms in the House of Dan-El rather than Aleon's smaller chamber. Tallayba'al offered some suggestions that would be useful in making their room more comfortable. They thanked her and took their leave; exiting the house and walking hand-in-hand toward the marketplace. They did not notice the figure that followed them through the crowded streets.

All the way to the marketplace Aleon wanted to ask Melita what was so urgent. He could see how agitated she was, but there was no good chance to ask her what was wrong. Mingling with the host of people in the crowded market square, Aleon stopped and looked curiously at Melita. She swung her head around and saw how crowded it was where they stood and said, "Not here! Come with me to the alley behind the fruit seller's stall."

The fruit seller's stall was a large, open-air pavilion, covered on three sides with tent cloth and a peaked roof supported by tall poles. Beneath this pavilion were baskets filled with every kind of fresh fruit from the local area, and dried fruits of exotic varieties that were imported from lands across the Great Sea, or brought to Gebal from the dark lands south of Kemet. Behind this pavilion there was an empty, open space where trash and spoilage were placed until everything could be removed at the end of the day. There was just enough room for the small cart that was parked there. It was already half full of trash.

The day reached the noon hour, as Melita led Aleon into the fruit seller's stall. They wandered through the interior, as if they were shoppers. Passing a half-dozen customers, and the fruit seller himself, they reached the last row of baskets in the back. She waited until no one was looking their way and lifted the canvas back of the stall and stooped to pass under it. Aleon followed her to the space behind the pavilion.

He gripped her upper arms and spun her around to face him. "Melita, my love, tell me! What is all this about? What is upsetting you?"

Looking deeply into his eyes, Melita broke into tears and could not speak at first. She wasn't sure how Aleon would react to her fear of the coming sacrifice. She had formed a plan in her mind, but she needed him to help her succeed. If it went well, everything would be alright. But if he refused to play his part, it might ruin their future.

She mastered her tears and took a deep breath and let it out slowly to calm her nerves. Then, with her heart pounding she began to tell him everything.

Chapter 67

Overheard

At the marketplace in Gebal

The figure that followed them to the marketplace stayed back a safe distance and they did not know he watched as they ducked into the fruit seller's stall. From outside the entrance he saw them make their way to the back and disappear under the canvas.

Like them, he browsed his way through the stall and stood near the spot where they had exited. He could hear Aleon's voice, and Melita's sobs through the fabric. A crafty smile came over his features as he listened and overheard every word. Their conversation ended, but before they came back inside, he quickly slipped out through the entrance and hurried away from the marketplace.

This man who had been stalking Aleon and Melita and had overheard their conversation was Radmanu, the close friend and childhood crony of Aderba'al, son of Ili-Rapih the high priest of Ba'al Šāmēm and Yam-Nahar. He quickly made his way to the temple of Ashtoreth, where he passed by the gateway and crossed the courtyard to find his friend.

Although Aderba'al was now a novice priest of Ba'al Šāmēm, he came often to the temple of Ashtoreth, where, in deference to his father's high status, the priests of Ashtoreth allowed him to make free use of the sacred prostitutes without paying for their services. Radmanu knew he could find his friend there almost every day at this same time.

"Greetings Aderba'al!" Radmanu cried as he drew near. "I have some most interesting news of such good fortune that you will not believe your ears!"

"Greetings Radmanu. May the blessings of Ba'al Šāmēm be upon you. Tell me then, what news could be so wonderful that you stop me as I am about to visit one my favorite whores? It had better be something good!"

"Oh, it is very good, for certain!" came the reply. "Can we speak privately? This should only be for your ears!"

Aderba'al raised his eyebrows and looked sharply at Radmanu. "Very well. Cross over through the garden of the sacred prostitutes with me. We can use the abandoned shrine on the far side of the temple grounds."

Radmanu followed Aderba'al to the shrine, humming a happy tune as they walked. They entered the shrine, and Aderba'al said, "Now then, out with it! Be quick, for I have urgent business that needs my attention!" He winked his eye as he said this.

"I have just come from the marketplace, where I happened to see our old friends, Melita, daughter of Tallayba'al and Paltiba'al of the House of Abdhamon, together with Gamil, the so-called Lion Slayer, as they hid themselves behind a fruit seller's stall. I was able to overhear their conversation, which they obviously wanted to keep only to themselves."

"Hmmm!" Aderba'al said. "And what did those two have to say that fascinated you so?"

"Well, as you know they are betrothed and will marry next year if all goes well for them. Because that is such a long time to wait, I first thought they were sneaking off to a place where they could be alone to sample the pleasures of the flesh before their wedding day, but that was not the case."

"So, nothing happened? You bore me Radmanu! I'm not interested in mere gossip. Tell me what you are so excited about and be quick about it!

"It is not what they did, or rather, didn't do. It is what I heard them *planning* to do!"

"Explain!" Aderba'al demanded, showing a keener interest now.

"As you know, Melita is sixteen summers old now, and still a virgin, if that is to be believed, though I have my doubts. She is much too beautiful and desirable to still be untouched. I can't imagine if I were her betrothed how I could keep my hands off of her..."

"Yes! Yes! Get to the point!"

"Well, she has just had her first red moon, and is terrified that she must make her sacrifice to Ashtoreth during the festival of Adon,"

"Terrified, eh?" Aderba'al's attention was now fully engaged. "I would love to have seen her in such a state! The Melita I remember was never afraid of anything. Go on then. What else did they say?"

"She was in fear of what Gamil, I mean Aleon, would think of her if another man took her maidenhead before they were wed. And she was also afraid of what he might think of her if she refused the sacrifice and her head was shorn instead.

The shame would fall on both of them, and their families! She did not know what to do.”

“Now we are getting somewhere!” Aderba’al said with a smirk on his face. “Was there more?”

“Oh, yes! And this part you will love! Radmanu replied. “It seemed to me that Aleon was shocked at first, but after a moment he thought of a third way to deal with Melita’s problem. A way to satisfy the requirements of the sacrifice and still remain faithful only to him.”

“You mean,” Aderba’al interrupted, “he plans to be the man who takes her virgin sacrifice himself? That is most clever of him! I wouldn’t have given him credit for being able to devise such a perfect solution. What did she say to this?”

“She was delighted, to say the least! I heard her say she was surprised that she hadn’t thought of this herself. After that I could tell they were kissing, and from the sighs and soft moaning that went on, I could tell that more than kissing was going on. My cock was twitching from the mere thought of it. But unfortunately, they broke it off before things went too far.”

“Was anything else said after that?”

“Not that I heard. The tent wall began to shake, and I could tell they were going to sneak back into the pavilion the same way they had left. Before they reentered, I slipped out of the pavilion and rushed here to share this news with you.”

“And you were right to do so, my friend!” Aderba’al said. But as he spoke his mind was already churning with how he might use this information. His hatred for Melita had festered for years, ever since the humiliation she had heaped upon him the day at the beach when she had broken his nose with that well-thrown rock. It had healed badly, marring what to his mind had been his handsome profile. Each time he saw his reflection, he remembered that day, and his anger over it would never end. He craved revenge. He wanted to hurt and humiliate her for what she had done to him.

His hatred for her was almost matched by his jealousy of Aleon. As Gamil he was of no account compared to the accomplishments Aderba'al, the son of the high priest, could boast about. But that changed after the lion hunt and Aleon's victorious return to the city. The people loved him for that, and his killing of the beast was still celebrated by the story-tellers and singers everywhere. Even beyond the city he was known as a hero whose exaggerated deeds were legendary now. Aleon fed this adulation by wearing that stupid necklace with the lion's claws around his neck. Everywhere he went, people recognized what it signified and would bow to him as he passed by, almost as if he were a god!

Adding to this, the humiliation Aderba'al and his father had suffered at Aleon's naming ceremony still rankled. Aleon's father had made them a laughing stock by snubbing them and starting the ceremony before they had been properly honored. Such disrespect was completely unacceptable and must be answered. But the books were still open and the account had not been settled as yet. Aderba'al sensed that now the time might be ripe.

Here was his chance to strike at both Melita and Aleon at the same time. But how? Filled with this new information, his mind churned and spun until, in time, a bold idea came to him.

Chapter 68
Preparations

The second day of the festival of Adon

The day Melita dreaded finally arrived. The city suffered for two days under a blanket of hot, humid air, unrelieved by the cool breezes that normally came from the Great Sea. But Melita was cold. Her face was drained of all color and her nerves were frayed from weeks of anxiety over the inescapable sacrifice she had to make.

Her mother had come to her bed chamber early, with a half dozen body servants, to begin the process of preparing her for the evening's ceremony. Melita was in such a state that she was almost paralyzed. Her mother did all she could to comfort and support her daughter, but Melita was inconsolable.

One moment she was overcome with terror, and in the next she rallied and seemed determined to get through the experience with her head held high. Then her mood would change again and she would lash out in anger at anyone near her, outraged that this sacrifice was demanded of her.

Surrendering her virginity was a moment that could only come once in a lifetime. She believed with all her heart this should be something that she, and only she, had complete control over. It was something that no other person should have even the slightest influence on. Except for Aleon.

As the day approached her love for him had grown stronger and her determination that he would be the first, and only one, to make love to her intensified. But for that to happen, their plan for this evening had to work perfectly, and she knew that things could easily go wrong.

But with all her hopes fixed on Aleon and their plan, she managed to calm herself enough to go forward. The servant girls bathed her gently, then wrapped her in a soft blanket of brushed linen.

Two girls combed out her hair to dry and untangled it, while two others shaped and painted her fingernails. After that they painted intricate designs on her hands with henna. As a last touch, tiny gems were glued onto her nails to add sparkle. As this work was going on, the last two girls worked on her feet. They rubbed them with perfumed oil and aloe, then trimmed her toenails before painting them and adding the tiny gemstones.

When their work was finished, Melita turned onto her stomach so Sharia could massage her with fragrant oils. This was to help her relax and calm her jangled nerves. While Sharia's hands worked this magic, the other girls anointed her hair to make it glisten, and began dressing her tresses with heated bronze rods to curl and shape then into a crown of gleaming black coils. These were done up on top of her head and held in place with gold hair pins and small combs. A net of fine silken threads, adorned with close to 100 tiny white pearls, was spread over her hair. It would help hold her curls in place and complete the look. The effect was stunning.

Next came her makeup. For this most important step, Melita's mother had hired ba'alat Beshal, a woman of Kemet who was the best and most expensive beautician in the city. Beshal arrived at the ninth hour with two of her servants and a full kit of makeup and perfumes. They had waited patiently while the other preparations were completed, and now went into action.

First, Melita's pubic area was completely shaved in honor of the goddess, and massaged with a perfumed ointment. Next, white powder was applied to the front of her upper body, as far as her waist, with special attention paid to her breasts, neck, chin and face. Even her ears were covered with it. Purple eye makeup was smoothed onto her eyelids and into the hollows below her brows. Black kohl was brushed onto her eyelids at the edges of her lashes in a variation of the Kemet style that was the latest fashion. Finally, her lips and nipples were painted a very vivid red.

Beshal stood back and admired her work. "Beautiful!" she said, as much to herself as to Melita and her mother. "Simply beautiful! I think this is some of my best work ever!"

To her mother, Beshal said, "I am certain that your daughter will be the most beautiful young virgin to ever make her sacrifice to Ashtoreth. She will be the envy of every other woman in the city." The beautician held out her hand, palm up in a casual gesture that was perfectly understood by Tallayba'al, who snapped her fingers. A servant came forward with a leather pouch of gemstones, the beautician's preferred form of payment. It was a heavy pouch, worth far more than lord Paltiba'al would have approved, if he had known about it. Tallayba'al had wisely kept her husband ignorant of this arrangement. Beshal smiled as she weighed the pouch in her hand, bowed politely to her patron to signify her satisfaction. She watched as her servants carefully packed up the makeup kit. All three women bowed again. Then, escorted by Sharia, they left the house.

Tallayba'al's body servants then dressed Melita, who had been naked while all the preparations were done. Now she was growing impatient as the final steps in the process dragged on. Her mother was unusually fussy about what her daughter would wear. The servants brought first one, then another, and another outfit for her approval. Each seemed to be too bright, too loose, too dark, or whatever. Finally, Melita had taken all she could stand.

"For the sake of all the gods, mother! Please just make a choice! Or better yet, let me decide for myself."

Tallayba'al blinked her eyes at this unexpected outburst. "Oh!" she said, "I see that I am making this harder than it needs to be. Forgive me dear!"

Then to her servants she said, "Very well then! Let us have the blue silk tunic with the gold thread and the white gossamer veil. I want the gold and silver slippers for her feet, and the purple bodice with a yellow silk sash."

These garments were brought forth and Melita was soon dressed accordingly. As she stood in the center of the room, her mother looked her over from head to toe, admiringly! She gave a deep sigh and spoke.

"You look perfect my dear! No other woman in the city is as beautiful as you are this day! I am so proud of you." She began to cry softly.

"Mother." Melita said, "I know I can be difficult at times. Well, most of the time, maybe. But I do love you so much it makes my heart feel like bursting in moments like this. Thank you for all your love, and care, and all the things you have taught me. From now on I will try hard to be the kind of daughter you have always wanted."

"Nonsense!" Tallayba'al wiped her eyes to stop her tears. "You should be the woman you want to be, and should have all your hopes and dreams fulfilled. That is the kind of daughter I truly want. If I have been hard on you in the past, it is because I know how determined you are. Yes, and difficult sometimes. But I wouldn't change a thing about you if I could."

"I know you want me to take over your business one day."

"True, but I know that is not your heart's desire. It is just that you are the best suited of my daughters to follow after me. I know you would handle the business more easily and successfully than either of your sisters can. I do want to pass it on to you in time. But only if you want it."

"I really don't know mother! You built that business with your heart. It is a great success and you've made it a source of real wealth for the House of Abdhamon. But I could never love it the way you do.

So much depends on what my life will be like when I marry Aleon. What he and I will want then is unknown right now. We shall have to wait and see what the gods have designed for me. Perhaps I'll feel differently when the time comes. For now, if it pleases you, I'd like to keep following in your footsteps to learn whatever I can about the business. I promise to be a better student."

"That would please me! And I'm pleased to see how wise and grown up you are! Let these thoughts rest with that. We should go down and have our noon meal a bit early, since we haven't eaten anything yet."

With that said, the Lady Tallayba'al led the way down the staircase to the hall below.

Chapter 69

Melita's Sacrifice

At the temple of Ashtoreth

The morning passed too quickly for Melita's liking. It was shortly past noon when she had to appear with the other women at the temple of Ashtoreth. There were offerings to be made and prayers to be prayed. The priests had to study the auguries to be sure the sacrifices, on which so much depended, could be made that evening.

When all was done, the priests blessed the women, invoking the goddess to bestow her virtue on them for this night when they would stand in her stead. Their sacrifices would restore Adon's life and reawaken the earth to fruitfulness and the land to prosperity.

An hour before sunset the women were allowed to enter their individual pavilions on the temple grounds. They settled in on comfortable couches and were served wine with various types of food by the temple acolytes. The sun sank low and twilight grew. Special red lamps were lit to illuminate the pavilions. In the growing darkness they cast a bright ruby glow over the temple grounds. The glow reflected off the temple walls and was seen by the crowd of men gathered at the gates. They began to stir in eager anticipation.

Aleon had been one of the first to arrive at the temple and stood as close to the gates as he could. He was joined by hundreds of excited men, all dressed in their finery. The mood of anticipation was contagious, and Aleon found himself looking forward to discovering Melita's most intimate charms.

According to his plan, she would wait for him in a small abandoned shrine on the east side of the temple grounds. He had been told about it and knew it was no longer an active shrine, but was now used as a storage place for tools and other items needed to maintain the temple gardens. It was a permanent structure, unlike the temporary pavilions that were erected to house the women this night. Aleon would have had a hard time locating her in one of those, but no one would expect her to hide inside the shrine until he came for her. Only Aleon would know to look for a woman there, while so many were conveniently available in the pavilions. Or so they thought.

Inside the temple grounds, Melita had taken her place in a pavilion close to the old shrine. The acolytes served her wine and food and left to tend to others. While they were all occupied elsewhere, she slipped out unobserved and made her way to the small shrine. Her mind was filled with thoughts of what would happen when Aleon came to her.

She was both excited and apprehensive about the sacrificial act itself, but her love for Aleon overcame her trepidation. She was sure that what they were about to do would be an expression of their love, and it would be as pure as it was pleasurable. Her obligation would be fulfilled in a way that would certainly be most pleasing to the goddess of love.

With that thought in mind she moved some tools and other items to clear a space in a back corner. Then she dragged sacks of grass seed to the corner and used them to make a small couch of sorts. When that was done, she straightened her garments and sat to wait for Aleon.

Neither she nor Aleon knew their plan had been overheard in the marketplace. Nor that Radmanu had shared the information with Aderba'al. They had no idea that his hatred of them was so intense that he devised his own plan to destroy their happiness.

A key part of his plan had already started. Aderba'al entered the temple early in the morning, on the pretense of helping with the preparations. He was well known to the priests and acolytes of Ashtoreth, and as the son of the high priest of Ba'al Šāmēm and Yam-Nahar, he was always treated with deference. His offer to help with the preparations was gratefully accepted, and he went to work with the temple priests setting up the pavilions and all the furnishings. After dark, he hid in the shadows near the old shrine and saw when Melita enter it. A wicked smile crossed his face as he stood there. His trap was set, and he only needed to wait for the trumpets to announce the opening of the temple gates before it was sprung.

Chapter 70
The Trap is Sprung

Inside the temple grounds

Outside the temple gates, Aderba'al's friends, Radmanu and Sudru, inched their way through the crowd to get close to Aleon. Their part of the plan was to intercept him inside the gates, knock him down, and delay him long enough to give Aderba'al time to get his revenge on Melita. Aleon had noticed these two in the crowd. He knew them as the childhood friends of Aderba'al, but didn't suspect anything.

The crowd of men outside the gates was growing more and more impatient as they waited for the trumpets signal. There was a lot of jostling and jockeying for positions close to the front, and Aleon was kept busy maintaining his spot.

At last, the dog star made its brief appearance just as the sunlight faded enough for it to be seen, the priests on the temple rooftop raised their trumpets and gave the signal to open the gates. The temple guards lifted the bar, the gates swung back and the crowd of men surged forward with those nearest the front moving quickly to avoid being crushed in the stampede.

Aleon managed to get through the entrance and stepped to the side, passing the guards who were struggling to keep order. He had taken a half dozen steps further in the direction of the old shrine and was passing through an unlighted spot, when he was struck on the head from behind. Radmanu had hidden a small, heavy club in his cloak. He ran to catch up to Aleon and used it to stun him, while Sudru tripped him. Their combined assault brought Aleon to the ground, and before he could react, Radmanu was on him, pinning him face-down on the grass. The trap was sprung.

The moment he heard the trumpets, Aderba'al made his move. It was time for the second part of his plan to happen. He left his hiding place and quickly went to the door of the small shrine.

The door was slightly ajar showing complete darkness within. Melita heard the hinges squeak a little as he pulled it open far enough to squeeze his big belly through. The red light outside had preserved his night vision enough that he could begin to make out her form. She was sitting on a pile of seed sacks in the back corner of the building. In the darkness she could not make out who had just entered, but of course it must be Aleon. Or so she thought.

"Aleon! My love, you're here so soon!" She said, " I thought I would have to wait longer."

"Well, I have been eager to meet you here, Melita, my pet!" Aderba'al said, his voice dripping with irony.

Melita's heart froze as she heard these words, immediately recognizing his voice. "What are you doing here, pig-face!" She spat at him.

"Why I've come to help you make your virgin sacrifice, my sweet one! Isn't that why you're here?"

"My sacrifice is not for you Aderba'al! You can forget about that. Leave this place at once!"

"Now! Don't be like that. You know you can't refuse any man who brings you his offering! Two copper rings ought to be enough for *your* maidenhead." As he said this Aderba'al moved closer to Melita, and clinked the two copper rings in his hand to emphasize his point. Melita had stood up as soon as she realized he wasn't Aleon and backed off to the side as he moved forward.

"Your payment is unacceptable to me, and to the goddess as well!" She shouted at him. "You cannot buy my sacrifice with any amount of gold or silver, and certainly not with mere copper. Get it through your head that I am not for you. Not *Ever*! Leave *now*!"

"Unacceptable, am I?" Aderba'al shouted back, "Get this through *your own* head, Melita! I'm going to have you one way or another, and you can't stop me!"

This was getting completely out of hand, and Melita began to feel real fear. Until now she was mostly just insulted and angry, but not any longer. She was effectively trapped in the little shrine, with the only exit blocked by Aderba'al's bulky body. She grabbed a mattock from a stack of tools beside her and raised it threateningly. She remembered Aderba'al as a bully in their younger days, who always backed down when confronted. But that was in the past. Now he was quite a bit bigger than her, and years of soft living had given him a serious weight advantage. "*Where are you Aleon?*" her mind cried.

Aderba'al hesitated when he saw the mattock in her hand, but wasn't worried about such an unwieldy weapon. He could see from the way she held it that he could brush it aside easily. There really wasn't anyway for her to stop him. He waited a few seconds, then suddenly lunged at her.

Melita was quick to respond, and swung the mattock with all her strength. But in such close quarters she aimed for his head, but missed. It struck Aderba'al on the shoulder instead and glanced harmlessly off to the side. It bruised him slightly, but that was all it accomplished.

His momentum carried him past her clumsy weapon and he grabbed her by the throat with one hand as his other hand tore at her clothing. The silk fabric was strong, but loose and low-cut to leave her breasts exposed anyway. The torn bodice fell away and her gown slipped from her shoulders, passed her hips and ended on the floor. He pushed her up against the wall and pinned her there with his bulk. She flailed at him with her arms, striking him as hard as she could, but it did no good.

Melita could feel his stiffened member poking at her stomach and knew she would have to do something soon. She scratched at his face and managed to rake four bloody furrows in the flesh of his right cheek, narrowly missing his eye. All it did was infuriate him, and his grasp on her throat stayed firm as he squeezed even harder. She couldn't breathe, let alone cry out for help. Spots appeared before her eyes and she knew she was about to pass out. If that happened, Melita knew she could not stop him from raping her.

With almost her last thoughts she wondered what had happened to Aleon? Where was he?

Chapter 71
The Trap

Inside the temple grounds

Face-down in the grass that formed the lawn of the temple grounds, Aleon recovered from the blow to his head, and found that he was neatly pinned to the ground by Radmanu's heavy bulk. Even so, his situation was not as hopeless as it seemed. Radmanu and Sudru were city dwellers, and were barely older than Aleon himself, with no great experience in fighting or wrestling beyond childhood scuffles. Aleon had spent the last two years in the company of seasoned sailors, who taught him a few tricks to help him protect himself.

In this situation he knew that the only way to get out from under his assailant was to do the unexpected. Radmanu's mouth was close to Aleon's ear, and he was muttering curses into it, laughing and taunting Aleon. Aleon's hands were free. A mistake on Radmanu's part. They were strong arms, made so by months at sea on the oars of the *New Cabax*. He pushed his upper body off of the ground far enough so that he could swing his head, first down, and then suddenly upward. He head-butted Radmanu squarely on the nose, stunning him and causing him a stabbing, shattering pain from his broken nose. Blood was gushing from both nostrils.

Radmanu's response was automatic. He raised his body up so he could grab his bleeding, damaged face with both hands. Aleon twisted below him and reached up to stab his fingers into Radmanu's eyes. This was more than Radmanu could take. He fell backwards and rolled completely off of Aleon, who pushed himself up and onto his feet, turning quickly to face Sudru, who was coming at him with Radmanu's cudgel raised to strike. But before he reached his target, Aleon kicked him forcefully in the crotch. Sudru staggered, then fell to the side where he lay on the ground, clutching his groin.

Aleon looked around, but there were no other assailants. Radmanu had risen, saw the fate of his partner, and like the coward he really was, ran away with both hands clasped to his face as blood continued to stream from his broken nose.

Aleon bent down over the prostrate Sudru, and grabbed him by the neck. "I know you Sudru." He said. You are a friend of Aderba'al. Where is he, and what is this all about?"

Sudru cringed and shied away, still holding his crotch and whimpered, "We were just supposed to delay you. To buy him enough time..."

"Time?" Aleon barked." Time to do what? Where is he?" But as he said this, Aleon guessed why Aderba'al wanted to delay him. If he was right, Melita was in serious danger. He sprang up and left Sudru's cowering figure on the grass. He ran toward the small shrine as fast as he could, dodging between the pavilions as he went, barely aware of the sounds of lovemaking that were starting to fill the night air.

When he drew near, he heard a different kind of sounds from within the shrine, sounds of a violent struggle. There was loud but indecipherable shouting, muffled by the thick stone walls. This told him that Aderba'al had reached Melita first, and his heart nearly stopped at the thought of what he might have already done to her.

But his fears turned to rage as he reached the door and rushed inside. The dim red light from the open door cast a weak illumination on the interior, and he saw Melita, naked and pinned against the far wall, with Aderba'al grasping her throat with one hand while he fumbled with his garments, trying to free his member from within. Melita had ceased to struggle, and was slumped in near unconsciousness; barely able to stand.

Aleon flew through the door and his left hand grabbed a fistful of Aderba'al's oily hair. He pulled the priest's head back and down as he brought his knee up into Aderba'al's back with a punishing force. Almost at the same time, Aleon's other hand caught Aderba'al's right wrist and tore his hand free of Melita's throat. He twisted it up and behind the priest's back, with a rage so great that he kept on twisting until he pushed Aderba'al's arm past the point of its natural limit. He heard tendons snap.

Aderba'al screamed and Aleon released him to fall to the floor. The intense pain that seemed to fill his entire body was all Aderba'al knew. His damaged arm sent bolts of fiery agony from his right shoulder to the tips of his fingers. He lay on the floor writhing in so much agony that Aleon almost felt sorry for him. Almost, but not quite. Instead he felt elation, and wished he could do even more damage to the swine. He settled for a solid kick to Aderba'al's well-padded side, followed by another.

Aderba'al knew he couldn't take any more punishment of this sort, and his survival instincts propelled him up, onto his feet and out through the door. He vanished into the red light and the maze of pavilions in the temple courtyard, with his right arm dangling limp and useless at his side.

Aleon heard a harsh coughing from behind him, and realized that Melita needed help. She had been choked severely and was struggling to breathe. He picked her up from the floor and carried her to the makeshift couch that she had made for their bed. He laid her down gently and she slowly began to regain her breath and strength. Aleon looked her over, fearing to find other injuries, and was relieved to see that she hadn't been badly hurt and was not in any real danger.

It was the first time he had seen her naked since they were both little children swimming in the sea. She had grown into a truly beautiful woman, and he was stunned to see her perfect unclad form. Much of the white powder and makeup had become a smeared mess in the struggle with Aderba'al, but even so, he had to appreciate all the care and attention that had gone into preparing her for this all-important night. He thought of her love for him, and his heart swelled with a love that matched hers.

It was not the only thing that was swelling as he gazed at her naked body. He could not take his eyes away, and was drawn to her like never before.

All of his previous experiences with women in different ports of call were born out of lust, with no more thought of anything but his own pleasure. What he felt at this moment, for this woman who would soon be his wife, was a need that had no lust in it. It was a pure desire to merge with her, and become a part of her, or for her to become a part of him, or both things at once. He wanted her, and needed her. All of her. Now, and forever.

Melita's breathing was becoming more normal. She was coming to her senses and realized where she was and who was with her. Aleon! He had saved her! Relief and joy filled her heart. He had been holding her hand since he laid her on the rude couch, but now she shook it free and reached out to him with both arms.

As he sank into her warm and urgent embrace she felt as if she never wanted to be anywhere else but in his arms. That was exactly where Aleon most wanted her to be.

She could feel his heart pounding with excitement, could feel his breath, soft and warm upon her neck, and wanted him to be even closer. In that moment she realized there was only one way that could happen.

Strange that she had never thought or felt this way before. But now she would never again think the act of making love was anything less that this desire to bond with him, to merge their hearts, their minds, spirits and bodies into one new creature.

"Aleon." She said his name softly, and with a love that was so strong it almost hurt.

He heard her voice, still raspy from the grip of Aderba'al's fingers, and thought it was the most wonderful sound he had ever heard. As she spoke his name, he heard all the love, all the joy, all the promise, and all the same desire that he felt toward her. "Melita, my love," he said, with his voice echoing these feelings to her.

"We must fulfill the sacrifice." She said with an urgency that proved that her ardor was equal to his own, but he felt a caution, a concern for her wellbeing.

"Are you sure, after what just happened?" he asked. This was not what we planned."

"I am sure. Do not doubt it and have no fear for me. I am tougher than you might think. Please, take my sacrifice now!"

"With joy, my love! With great joy!"

The moon had risen and would soon set by the time Melita and

Aleon emerged from the little shrine. She was wrapped in Aleon's cloak over the torn remnants of her silken gown. Few of the other participants in the sacrifice were left in the pavilions, and only a handful of priests still lingered in the gardens.

Most women, once they had coupled with the first man to visit them, took his payment and surrendered it to the priests who blessed them both. The women then quickly left. Escorted by one or more of the temple guardsmen to their homes. Most, however, were met at the gate by their family members or personal guards for the trip home. It was not a night for any woman to be out on the streets alone, especially those who had just been a part of the sacrifice to the goddess of love. It was a night ruled by masculine lust, and drunken men were everywhere. The usual norms of behavior between the sexes were too easily disregarded after all of the sexual activity, and the amount of beer and wine that was consumed by those who celebrated. The festival loosened everyone's inhibitions.

Some men who saw a woman walking down a dark street after coming from the sacrifices at the temple might decide she hadn't sacrificed enough as yet. The city guards were alert during festivals, and even more so on this night dedicated to the goddess of love. Attacks on young women, though rare, were not unheard of.

As usually happened, more men came to participate in the night's events than could be served by just the women who had come to make their once-in-a-lifetime sacrifice. The overflow crowd was served by the cadre of permanent sacred prostitutes. In this way, no man ever left the temple grounds unsatisfied on this night dedicated to Ashtoreth, and the temple coffers were kept full.

Of course, the purpose of all this activity kept the goddess happy, and the land prospered under her blessing.

Aleon escorted Melita to one of the few priests still on duty, where she presented her payment of two solid gold rings, rather than the stingy copper rings that Aderba'al had intended to leave with her as a sign of her humiliation. He had wanted the priest of Ashtoreth to know she wasn't worth any more than that. But Aleon's payment in gold showed the exact opposite. But beyond that, she was priceless in his eyes.

She also presented the priest with a linen cloth that had caught the few drops of the blood from her maidenhead, proving that hers was indeed a *virgin* sacrifice, and therefore it was especially sacred to the goddess.

The priest's eyes sparkled at the generosity of this young man's payment, and thanked him. He recognized Aleon, of course, and bowed respectfully to him before pronouncing the blessing of the goddess upon both Melita and her handsome escort. He smiled as they left the temple grounds.

At the gates Aleon waved the waiting guards off. He wanted to escort Melita to her home himself, but two of her parents' household guards had been sent to meet them. So, with her duty to the goddess fulfilled, and with Aleon at her side, Melita, led her party of escorts homeward. Her head was held high, her heart overflowed with love, and her mind marveled that she could have ever been so afraid of this night.

Chapter 72
Shock and Revelation

At the House of Abdhamon

Aleon and Melita reached the safety of her father's house without further incident. They were met by her parents who had anxiously awaited her return from the temple, worried by the lateness of the hour. They were shocked when they saw the condition their daughter was in. Her carefully styled hair and makeup were a mess, and when Aleon helped her remove his cloak they were horrified to see the state of her clothing. Clearly, something bad had happened. But both Aleon and Melita were smiling, and sharing adoring looks with each other.

Tallayba'al immediately wrapped her arms around Melita and ordered the nearby body servants to escort her daughter to her chamber. The ritual bath that was customary after a woman's sacrifice, had been prepared for her, had grown cold, and was now replenished with fresh hot water. As Tallayba'al led Melita from the room her eyes shot hard, questioning looks at Aleon.

Paltiba'al was livid, and confronted Aleon as soon as the women were gone. "What happened to my daughter?" he demanded; his face red with barely suppressed anger. Clearly, he suspected that Aleon had played some shameful part in the night's events.

"Why has she returned so late, and in such condition? And why are you here with her? Explain these things to me at once! If you have done anything to harm her, I promise you will be held to account!"

Aleon dropped to one knee before his future father-in-law, crossed his arms in front of his chest, and bowed his head. In this posture of reverence and submission he began to speak.

"My Lord Paltiba'al, do not let your anger burn against me. I will answer all your questions fully, in detail, and in truth."

With that said, Aleon went on to explain the plan that he and Melita had agreed to. "Remember the covenant that you and my father made long ago, for your noble daughter and I to wed one day. But we were young and did not love each other as we do now. Our wise parents knew that this would change as we grew older, and so it has, as you all have seen. I would give my life before I let anything happen to Melita, and I know she would do the same for me.

I could not bear for her maiden sacrifice to Ashtoreth be with any man but me, her betrothed. And I made a plan to ensure that only I would lay with her this evening. No man had touched her until this night when I was her Adon and she was my Ashtaroth."

Aleon began to explain the details of their plan, taking the full responsibility on his own shoulders, omitting Melita's compelling anxiety. But Paltiba'al stopped him.

"Your father must be with us to hear all of this." He prepared a short message for Ahinadab, saying "Come at once. It concerns your son!" He handed it to one of his guards with orders to take it, in all haste, to the lord of the House of Dan-El. Paltiba'al servants brought wine and a light meal of bread and cheese to his office. Aleon followed him there to wait for Ahinadab's arrival.

After a moment, Paltiba'al noticed blood on the back of Aleon's head from its collision with Radmanu's nose. Then he saw the welt on the side of his head where Radmanu's club landed. He wondered about these injuries, but held his questions until Ahinadab could join them.

Despite the lateness of the hour, Ahinadab arrived with his two bodyguards and Paltiba'al's messenger. He was quickly made aware of what had transpired, and what Aleon had shared so far.

"Aleon has more to tell us, but I wanted him to wait until we could both hear him out. Here, in my inner office, we can speak privately." The guards were dismissed to wait in the courtyard.

"Before you continue Aleon, I want you to know that I have guessed that your plans did not remain a secret, and you were spied upon by someone who wanted to spoil this night. I have my suspicions as to the name of this someone, and if I am correct it would be dangerous for that name to be known our houses. I urge you, Aleon, to tell us, and only us, what happened."

Aleon stood before the two lords and shared everything that had happened that evening. He reported the attack that delayed him and almost kept him from reaching Melita's hiding place in time. He shared his outrage at what he found at the old shrine, and how he prevented Aderba'al from raping her, and that he and Melita completed her virgin sacrifice, then paid the priest before leaving the temple.

When he was finished, Paltiba'al called Ahinadab's attention to the blood and the welt on Aleon's head. Ahinadab had already noticed it. Both men agreed it was evidence that confirmed Aleon's story.

"We should see to your injury. It doesn't seem serious, but I will summon a priest from the temple of Eshmun to attend you in the morning. What became of Aderba'al after you defeated him?" Ahinadab asked.

"His arm was badly injured, and he ran off as fast as he was able. I don't know where he went."

"I would guess he is hiding in some inner chamber of the temple, licking his wounds until he can slink home to his father's house." Paltiba'al said.

"You're probably right. After his father hears of it, we can anticipate some retaliation from the high priest. He will consider this an insult to his own dignity, even more than to his son's, and even if no one outside these walls hears of it." Ahinadab rejoined.

"Yes, Ili-Rapih is always seeking to increase his own power. But his son's assault on my daughter gives us something that he knows we can use against him. He will expect us to quickly expose his son's crime, and will want to move against us in some way before that can happen."

Aleon said, "Aderba'al wanted to humiliate Melita as much as he wanted to hurt her physically. Instead I have harmed and humiliated him." I had hoped that would be the end of this, but I see his father is the greater threat."

The room grew quiet while all this sank in.

Ahinadab was the first to break the silence. "Lord Paltiba'al and I have recently been discussing the timing of your marriage. Now that Melita has had her first red moon, and has made her sacrifice to Ashtoreth, there is nothing to hinder it. By custom, her two older sisters must marry first. But Arshut, the oldest, was married last year, and Izabel is to be wed later this month."

Paltiba'al picked up that thought, "For your wedding to Melita, the high priestess of Ba'alat Gebal determined the most auspicious date after Isabel's wedding would not come until the harvest festival. But after tonight, I think it best to have your wedding sooner. The joining of our two houses will strengthen all of us, and the House of Dan-El is better suited for protection than we are here. It is smaller, but was built like a fortress, and the household guards are more numerous and better fighters than mine. I would not admit that outside this room, but it is true. You will both be safer living there.

"I agree." Ahinadab said, "We do not know what Ili-Rapih might try, but we should prepare for him to attack us, in whatever form he chooses."

"So be it." Paltiba'al declared. "The high priestess will be consulted for an earlier date, and we will begin the wedding preparations at once. But first, you and I must share what we know with your son."

Not knowing what to expect from his father and Paltiba'al, Aleon gave them his fullest attention. He held his peace and waited.

Ahinadab spoke first. "Aleon, by the customs of our people, fathers have the power to arrange the marriages of their children and so it was a wise and proper covenant that your mother and I entered into with Melita's parents on your behalf. That covenant can only be set aside in case of the death of you or Melita, or if she fails to bear you sons.

But you have shown yourself to be wise beyond your years and I deem it proper to consult your wishes regarding your marriage before we move forward. Lord Paltiba'al has agreed to consider your thoughts as well, and he will consult his daughter regarding her wishes. If either of you choose to void the covenant, we will honor your desires."

Paltiba'al added, "Although the marriage was arranged when you and Melita were infants it is always best if the groom and his bride both agree to what was arranged for them. I do not wish to force you or my daughter to enter into a marriage that either of you would find unacceptable. I know your father wants the same for you both."

"Lord Paltiba'al has said it well. We also want you both to know the reasons why we arranged your marriage. You are surely aware of the many advantages both houses stand to gain if our interests are joined by this marriage. They are advantages that would extend beyond us, and beyond you and Melita, to your children's children.

The wealth of the House of Dan-El, its fleet of ships, extensive trading routes, and connections to a multitude of customers in many lands, is massive. The financial resources of Abdhamon, which includes the investments of many elite families in the city, is greater than some kingdoms. Combined, our houses will have tremendous power to influence the actions of the council of elders, and enable us to drive forward many good things for our people while restraining what is harmful."

Paltiba'al added, "My only son, Bōdashtart, does not wish to carry on my business after me. He has many fine talents, but lacks a mind for finance. He has chosen to dedicate himself to the priesthood of the god Adon. Therefore, your father and I have agreed that you, Aleon, will inherit the control and enormous responsibility of all the wealth of both houses. You will become a member of the council of elders, and possibly a shofeṭ as your father is."

Ahinadab added, "What may come in time cannot be foreseen. But both houses have many enemies. There are those among the elders and elite families who envy what we have, or who differ with us in the council, especially the high priest, Ili-Rapih. The events of this evening were not simply meant to harm you or Melita. We see them as part of Ili-Rapih's plot to weaken us and to clear the way for his rise to the kingship. He has been scheming for years to replace his brother on the throne, by any means necessary. We suspect he was behind the attempts to have the king killed.

For several years he has worked against our interests in an effort to weaken us and diminish our support for Rib-Hadda. He connived with master mariner Barakba'al, paying him to steal from the cargos under his care, which damaged the reputation of our house and caused us to lose business and goods."

Paltiba'al said, "My sources have confirmed that Barakba'al was paid by the high priest to set fire to the *Cabax*, though the destruction of the entire harbor was not expected. That was an outcome that hurt Ili-Rapih's own ships as much as it did your father's. A rare blunder on his part.

Needless to say, we must expect the high priest to continue to work against us. Tonight's assault was another blunder, committed this time by his son. I doubt that Ili-Rapih would have been so careless as to come against us directly. He prefers to work through others and keep at a distance. He may not have known what Aderba'al was planning. He will be livid with his son for this."

Ahinadab said, "I expect it will be some time before the high priest makes any further moves against us. He will be off balance, wondering when we will use tonight's events against him. If we keep him guessing, there is time for your wedding and for us to prepare against his future moves."

Paltiba'al summed everything up, "Knowing all these things, are you willing to freely enter into this marriage?"

Aleon thought hard. He hadn't realized that so much more than just his love of his bride-to-be was involved. He felt as if his father and lord Paltiba'al had lifted a curtain and allowed him to peek inside their world, and into his future. He was at a crossroad and wasn't sure he wanted all that his father and lord Paltiba'al desired. He was tempted to say he would rather become a master mariner and command a great ship of his own. But in the end, his love for Melita won out, and he answered.

"My lords, my fathers both, my answer is yes. With your permission, I will marry Melita, the love of my life. And I will do all I can to bring honor to both your houses."

Both fathers smiled and clapped him on the back. Paltiba'al called for a servant to bring more wine. "We will drink to your wedding, and to your future!"

Chapter 73
The Wedding Contract

In the city of Gebal

According to the high priestess of Ba'alat Gebal the next auspicious time for the wedding of Aleon and Melita fell on the twelfth day of the month of *Sah*, or August, although she urged Paltiba'al to plan the wedding for the preferred date of the nineteenth day of *Tishrei*, or September, which was the first day of the harvest festival. She warned him that moving the wedding to the earlier date could incur the wrath of Ashtoreth, goddess of fertility, and could bring trouble for Melita in childbearing.

But Paltiba'al, as the father of the bride, began to plan for the event to occur on the seventh day of *Sah*, and made sacrifices to Ba'al Šāmēm and offerings to all of the temples to ward off any ill effects.

There were many myths and superstitions attached to such socially and personally important events as weddings. For the wedding of Paltiba'al's daughter to the son of Ahinadab, everything had to be perfect. For the city, it would be the most important event of the year, with much at stake for the social status of the new couple as well as their families. All things had to be done in the proper order to avoid catastrophe, which could take many forms and come in unexpected ways.

Responsibility for all of the wedding preparations rested on the father of the bride-to-be. Ahinadab, as father of the groom, provided Paltiba'al with every assistance. Their cooperative efforts began with the formal signing of the marriage contract, regarded as the official declaration of the betrothal that had been agreed on many years earlier. The terms of the marriage contract were set down in written form, detailing exactly what each party brought into the marriage and what duties and responsibilities were expected of each.

The bride price, symbolizing the "purchasing" of the bride from her family, was paid by the groom's father when the contract was signed. At the same time the father of the bride paid the dowry to the groom, symbolizing the value of the precious daughter he was "selling". Both were of equal value, so that this exchange was really a transfer of funds from Ahinadab to his son and of Paltiba'al to his daughter. The combined funds were to be held by Paltiba'al in trust for the couple to use when they established their own household.

At least a dozen copies of the marriage contract were made. The high priests and priestesses of the temples each received a copy and the rest were posted prominently at the Well of Gebal, at the market place, and at the four gates of the city. For such an important wedding, copies were also presented to the king, and the council of elders. In this way the entire city was given notice and a sense of anticipation began to mount among the citizens. Soon the entire city was abuzz with talk of the wedding. From the elite families to the low-born, and even among the slaves, the topic was widely discussed. Every implication, ritual and even the sacred symbols associated with marriage in Gebal were discussed, debated and revisited from day-to-day. The excitement continued to build in the days that followed.

A series of elaborate wedding events followed the signing of the contract. The first was the prewedding ceremony, Followed by the wedding feast, the wedding ceremony itself, and the post-wedding celebration. For Aleon and Melita, marriage marked their entry into full adulthood. Among elite families, it was also the first step in establishing a young couple's status among the people of the city.

On the thirtieth day of *Kiraru*, a week before the wedding and nine days after the festival of Adon, two elaborate processions came forth from the houses of Dan-El and Abdhamon, each led by their respective lords. Drummers drummed and lyres were strummed as the twin processions advanced toward the marketplace.

At the center of the market, Ahinadab and Paltiba'al met on a raised platform dressed in their finest robes, with their curled hair, their beards decked with bright ribbons and gold ornaments. The stood there together while their entourages fanned out around them. Everything came to a full stop, trumpets were raised, and a long fanfare was sounded to command attention and hush the crowd. The two men embraced each other and exchanged the customary kisses on both cheeks.

"Hail lord Paltiba'al. May the gods smile upon you this day, and may Almighty El bless this meeting of our houses!" Ahinadab exclaimed in his loudest and most formal voice. He was heard by all the members of the two parties and by the great crowd of the townspeople that gravitated to the event from all over the marketplace.

Paltiba'al responded in the same manner, "Hail to you, lord Ahinadab! May the gods always be with you, and bless your house and all who dwell in it."

On He-sham's signal, Ahinadab's servants began to parade in a circle around the platform. The household guards of both men kept watch on the crowd, while servants carried chests of gold and silver, ingots of copper, amphora filled with fine wine, bolts of colorful silk and linen cloth, and all manner of other riches that constituted the agreed-on bride price.

The quiet that prevailed since the trumpets sounded was replaced with a murmur of appreciation as each item was set before Paltiba'al, where it was examined closely by Itthobaal, rab-tamkari of the House of Abdhamon, who checked it against a copy of the marriage contract. A half hour later the full accounting of the bride price was complete.

The trumpets sounded again and the servants of Paltiba'al began their own circular parade around the platform in the same manner as before. Half an hour later, He-sham finished checking the dowry against the list, and a final trumpet fanfare signaled the completion of this important event.

The crowded market place erupted in cheering and applause. The people of Gebal showed their hearty approval of the way the accounts were settled and the marriage contract was faithfully fulfilled. This part of the wedding had been concluded successfully. Ahinadab and Paltiba'al embraced again, and descended from the platform, ready to lead their processions away. The combined household guards escorted all of the treasured items to Paltiba'al's treasury building. The musicians began to play again and the music mingled with the cheers of the crowd until the processions passed from sight. Everyone in the marketplace returned to their normal activity, but talk of the signing ceremony continued for days .

Preparations began for the prewedding ceremony. All attention was focused on the bride-to-be. The seven days before her wedding were the last days Melita would spend in the house of her father. There was much to be done, and she remained in the constant company of her mother and sisters, with her closest friends and servants. All of these helped her prepare for the wedding day, only one week away.

Dress makers arrived and Melita was carefully measured and fitted for her wedding garments. Her mother fussed over every detail like a mother hen with a newborn chick. Tally-ba'al thought she knew every detail of her youngest daughter's physical appearance. but in the days since the festival of Adon there were subtle changes that she was just noticing.

"Well now! Tallayba'al exclaimed. "Melita my darling, you have changed since your last fitting. You've always had a more boyish figure, with slender hips and almost no breasts. Now I see that is changing at last! Your lovely hips are getting a tiny bit wider, creating the beginning of an elegant curve at your waist. You now have a properly round bottom, which was almost flat before. And your breasts! They stand out from your chest perfectly; large enough but not too large. Like two ripe pears..."

"Mother! Really! You talk of me like I wasn't here in the same room. And your description would cause a sailor to blush! Please! Just keep such thoughts to yourself." This outburst brought peals of laughter from the other women. But her mother didn't join them. She grew quiet and pondered what her eyes were telling her. Was Melita pregnant? She could not have been with anyone but Aleon since her sacrifice to Ashtoreth. If Aleon had already made her pregnant that was awfully quick work. She kept this in the back of her mind and said nothing else. But she calculated the days since Melita's last red moon, and realized that she was overdue. Perhaps it was true. She smiled at the thought, but said nothing.

Chapter 74
The Wedding Day

At the House of Abdhamon

Seven days later, the morning of the wedding ceremony finally arrived, and the mood in the House of Abdhamon was frenetic. Before dawn, Melita's mother and sisters, with Sharia and other women servants, invaded her chamber to literally drag her out of bed. They took her to the rooftop of the House of Abdhamon where the family's shrine to the goddess Ashtoreth was prepared. Three priestesses from the temple were there to officiate at the bride's wedding sacrifice. A young goat was killed, its entrails examined for portents, and its flesh then burned on the altar of the shrine. Prayers to the goddess were offered by the three priestesses, who then pronounced blessings upon Melita and on the wedding ceremony. Offerings of fresh fruits and grain were presented and everyone partook of grapes, melons and other fruits while the grain offering burned on the altar. When the goddess was properly honored, the bridal party withdrew to the bath chamber in Tallayba'al's quarters.

Melita was given three ritual baths to purify her body of any and all evil. First, with water drawn from the sea, then with water blessed by the high priestess of Ashtoreth, and finally with water drawn from the sacred well of Gebal. For each bath the water had been carried from its source to the house in special vessels reserved for this ritual.

Melita stood naked in the center of her mother's bathing basin while the sanctified water was poured over her. She was rubbed from head to toe with fragrant soaps and rinsed with sponges dipped in rose water.

After the third bathing she was dried with heated linen sheets and all the hair, from her neck down to her toes, was plucked or shaved completely off. She was massaged and anointed with fragrant unguents and perfumed oils until her skin was as soft and smooth as butter. Her hair was oiled, braided and styled. A network of pearls covered and held her long tresses on top of her head. Against the dense, black braids, the pearls gleamed like a host of stars in a night sky.

While all this was done the excitement grew and grew. There was much laughter and friendly banter, with a great deal of teasing at Melita's expense. Wine flowed liberally, and as the morning advanced, many of the jokes bordered on crude or suggestive subjects involving the acts and positions of love-making.

Melita bore it all with good humor, sharing the excitement everyone was feeling. Her mother told stories from Melita's childhood, some humorous, some bitter-sweet. She became tearful at times, and clung to Melita's hand as she recalled special memories.

After the baths, massage, and hairdressing was done, Melita's face and body were coated with white powder. She then was dressed in a bridal gown, fashioned somewhat after a style made popular by the royal ladies at the court of the pharaoh in Akhenatan, but with some unique deviations.

In Kemet a gown like this was not specifically a "wedding garment".

The people of Kemet did not have formal wedding ceremonies. A woman was considered "married" the moment she moved into her husband's house.

But the women of Gebal liked to follow the styles and fashions of dress that were popular at Pharaoh's court. The elders and king of Gebal encouraged this, and themselves, adopted other customs of Kemet. It was seen as a way to demonstrate loyalty and solidarity with their most important patrons and overlords.

For her wedding, Melita's gown pushed the limits of Gebal's fashion to new heights, going far beyond the style of Pharaoh's court. It was cut in the latest Kemet fashion but boldly deviated by leaving the front open from neck to navel in the Kena'ani style. It was fitted to drape her otherwise naked body in a way that revealed every curve and detail of her form. It was made entirely of gossamer, a sheer, white, nearly transparent fabric. It was the most expensive single item purchased for the wedding.

Bejeweled gold broaches secured the sleeveless fabric at the shoulders, and a drape of pale blue gossamer fell across her back to form a long train. The forward corners were tied at her wrists so that the train flared with a wing-like effect whenever she moved her arms.

The body of the gown was secured at the waist with a golden belt set with precious gems. For the sake of modesty, a short, narrow golden apron, also bejeweled, hung down from the belt to mid-thigh at the front.

In keeping with the Kemet theme, she wore a broad, heavy, gold collar around her neck that was set with alternating rows of jewels and blue coral beads that extended from the base of her neck to just above the swell of her breasts. Matching earrings and a simple, crown-like headpiece of solid gold completed her accessories.

Finally, cosmetics were applied by Gebal's most celebrated beautician, the ba'alat Beshal, who was called upon to work her artistry for the second time in Melita's life. Kohl was used to highlight her eyes in the Kemet style, and pale pinkish powder was applied to her cheeks, creating a warm aspect to her face. It gave her the look of a blushing bride.

Henna was applied to her hands, carefully depicting prayers, charms, and spells written to invoke the favor and protection of the gods.

Then the orbits above her eyes were painted with powdered gold in a lanolin base. Instead of the usual red, Melita's lips and nipples were also painted with the same powdered gold.

When her makeup was complete, a pair of bejeweled golden sandals were set on her feet, and Melita stood radiant and fully adorned for her mother's inspection.

The attendants stood back to admire their work. Minutes passed. No one seemed able to breathe. Finally, tears began to well up in her mother's eyes, and she spoke in a quaking voice.

"My precious daughter! You are perfect in every way, and the goddesses will all be envious of you. For no daughter of Gebal was ever as beautiful as you are this day! My heart is full, and I have never been as proud of you as I am at this moment. Come! The noon hour is approaching. It is time to present you to your husband."

Chapter 75
The Pre-wedding Feast

In the great hall of the House of Abdhamon

While the bridal preparations went on in the upper chambers, the guests had been arriving at the House of Abdhamon for the pre-wedding feast. Aleon had been treated like a young prince by all of his closest friends and relatives for three days, and now he stood in the great hall of the House of Abdhamon, eagerly waiting for the presentation of his bride.

A steady flow of gifts, both great and small, came from the king, all the members of the council, and the elite families. Even the pharaoh's governor and other officials of Kemet who lived in the city sent gifts, as did representatives from other Kena'ani cities of the coast. Agents and ship's masters employed by Ahinadab, and some of the wealthier members of the lower classes sent gifts they could afford. Everyone wanted to honor the famous lion-slayer of Gebal on his wedding day.

Each gift was carefully cataloged and tallied by a team of scribes from both houses, under the watchful eyes of He-sham and Itthobaal. Notes expressing the couple's gratitude were prepared and the gifts were secured in the family's treasury. Aleon and Melita's personal wealth was growing

The great hall of the House of Abdhamon had been setup for the pre-wedding feast. Musicians with a variety of flutes, lyres, drums and horns played lively tunes on the landing above the great hall, to accompany singers who raised their voices in hymns of praise to the gods. Their songs drifted down as if they came from the heavenly realm itself. The lyrics were intended to encourage the bride and groom to be faithful to each other as husband and wife, to be good parents to the children that would bless their house, and to be loyal citizens of the city. Those virtues were considered a vital part of the success of any marriage and Paltiba'al had hired the best singers in the land for this occasion.

The guests were greeted as they arrived, and their feet were washed with perfumed water in the foyer. They were ushered inside and led to their places according to the order of their status. Each person was announced as they entered, and were acknowledged and welcomed by Paltiba'al. The men were brought to the right of the hall where they reclined on soft couches that bordered long, low serving tables ladened with all types of fine foods and wine. Likewise, the women were shown to matching couches along the left side of the hall. All were served by the household servants who kept their wine cups full and offered a variety of foodstuffs to pass the time before the bride appeared.

Aleon, his father and mother, Paltiba'al, king Rib-Hadda and the high-priests and high-priestesses of the temples were placed at the head of the hall, farthest from the entrance, on couches reserved for them. A separate set of servants waited on them there.

A joyous spirit pervaded the whole house as conversations developed and continued during the feasting. This was a very happy occasion for the entire city. When the appropriate moment arrived, Aleon rose from his couch and raised his wine cup. The conversation quickly faded, then stopped altogether as every eye turned to focus on the bridegroom. Everyone waited expectantly to hear how he would handle this traditional part of the banquet.

"I raise my cup in praise of my bride, the ba'alat Melita, who is worthy of all honor. My heart beats as one with hers, and so it will be always.

"My cup is also raised to honor the Lord Paltiba'al, soon to be my second father, for the excellence of his house, and for the gracious accommodations and the careful preparations he has made for this day. For all of these things I salute you, my lord and father!"

The room exploded with hearty cries of approbation as every cup was drained; the voices praised the appropriateness of Aleon's toast. His stature among the high and powerful of Gebal rose several notches with his gracious handling of this critical wedding custom.

As he resumed his seat, his toast was seconded, and additional toasts were offered by Ahinadab, by the ambassador of Kemet, and others. Blessings were offered by the high-priests and high-priestesses; each competing to glorify their own deity above all others.

The last to rise and bestow a blessing was high priest Ili-Rapih, who managed to outdo the rest, while also making veiled insults aimed at Ahinadab and Paltiba'al. He was wise enough not to avoid any direct insult to Aleon, knowing that the people of Gebal would look harshly on someone who cast a cloud over a man on his wedding day. That would be seen as an act of petty spite by the people who mattered to him. Those were the citizens whose support he needed in his quest for appointment as king. So, he chose his words carefully.

"Hear me, O lord Ba'al Šāmēm, ruler of heaven, lord of the sky, of the thunder and lightning! Hear me Yam-Nahar, god of the sea and all rivers. I call for your blessings on this wedding, and on the guests assembled here.

Let my words protect those who worship you, Ba'al Šāmēm, those who honor your name Yam-Nahar, and those who bring you offerings and make sacrifice at your temple. Cause their fields to be fruitful, their women to be fertile and their flocks to increase.

Hear me, O lord Ba'al Šāmēm, ruler of heaven, lord of the sky, of the thunder and lightning! Hear me Yam-Nahar, ruler of the waves and depths of the sea. Hear me as I cry out to you to bring destruction and ruin to those who hate you; to those who blaspheme your name and cheat you of the offerings and sacrifices that are your due."

There was silence when he finished with what amounted to a curse, aimed indirectly at Ahinadab and the House of Dan-El, whose patron god was El. Ahinadab had always been careful to send generous offerings to the temple of all the gods and goddesses, including Ba'al Šāmēm and Yam-Nahar. But it was generally understood in the city, that in the House of Dan-El, Ba'al Šāmēm was considered a lesser god, subject to his father El.

No one objected to this. After all, every man was allowed to honor the gods as he pleased within his own home. No one held Ahinadab's adherence to El against him.

In fact, the Kena'ani believed that El was the father of seventy gods or goddesses, and that each of them became the patron god or goddess of various peoples. To have a patron god or goddess was not at all uncommon among the great houses of Gebal. Since Ahinadab's ancestral home was Ugarit, and El was that city's patron, it was natural that El would be the patron of the House of Dan-El. So, Ahinadab's devotion to El was considered proper and admirable.

But Ahinadab dared to take his devotion further than anyone else would have. By magnifying and encouraging the worship of El beyond the walls of his house, his example had influenced many in the city, and through the far-flung activities of his fleet and his agents, it promoted and spread the recognition of El as superior to the other gods.

This influence offended Ili-Rapih deeply, as it diminished the status of Ba'al Šāmēm and Yam-Nahar, and weakened the high priest's personal power as their representative. More than anything else, this was the main source of Ili-Rapih's hatred of Ahinadab and his entire household.

Aderba'al's injury by Aleon on the night of Melita's sacrifice to Ashtoreth added them to the list of Ili-Rapih's enemies. Aderba'al had given his father a distorted version of the events of that night, insisting that Aleon had arrived late on the scene, after Aderba'al had already paid for Melita's sacrifice, and was about to enjoy it. He said nothing of his two cronies attempts to delay Aleon, and claimed Aleon's attack was unprovoked.

The high priest was no fool, and knew his son was not telling him everything. But it served his purpose to accept Aderba'al's version as if it were true. He would use it to counter any accusations that Ahinadab or Paltiba'al might make. But this was not the time or place to openly oppose the two houses, so Ili-Rapih limited himself to firing a few indirect curses in their direction.

The silence that followed Ili-Rapih's mixed blessing ended after a moment, with a loud exclamation from someone among the guests who shouted "Be it even so, as the high priest Ili-Rapih has spoken." The man who shouted was one of the lesser priests of Ba'al Šāmēm who had accompanied Ili-Rapih to the wedding.

A few quiet voices were raised in agreement, followed by louder expressions of the same; all orchestrated by Ili-Rapih beforehand.

But the moment passed with most guests keeping their thoughts to themselves. Soon the conversations resumed; some with whispered exchanges regarding the high priest's "blessing".

Paltiba'al face reddened slightly, but he remained otherwise unflappable; exchanging glances with Ahinadab who silently signaled his own exasperation. Both had the same private thought that it was right to have accelerated the plans for this wedding. It was clear that Ili-Rapih was ramping up his campaign against the two houses, and that some of the other houses were beginning to side with the high-priest. Today was not the day to fight back. Yet the harbingers of a coming storm were beginning to appear.

As the noon hour approached, the servants of Paltiba'al began clearing away the food, the tables and, finally, even the couches. Cushions were brought in for those who could not, or chose not, to stand for the wedding ceremony, but most guests were soon on their feet in the grand hall, waiting in small clusters for the wedding ceremony to begin.

Chapter 76
The Wedding Ceremony

In the great hall of the House of Abdhamon

Each day, as the sun reached its zenith, trumpeters sounded their fanfares from the roofs of the three major temples. This was the signal for the workers and slaves in the city to halt their labors for the mid-day meal. But this day, in the House of Abdhamon, the temple trumpets were drowned out by the horns of the musicians, who signaled the entry of the bride.

From the top of the stairway the bridal party descended. First came three maidservants who scattered flower petals before them. These were followed by the priestesses of the Ba'alat Gebal, who intoned holy hymns of blessing. Next came the bride herself, surrounded by her mother and sisters, and followed by her close female friends. As they advanced toward the head of the hall, the crowd of guests parted before them, and as all eyes followed the bride's movements, the gap closed up behind them.

The flower bearers, priestesses and all of the other ladies halted near the head of the hall. Only Melita advanced to stand before her father. Next to him Aleon waited, his face glowing with amazement as he beheld the radiant vision that was his bride. His breath came in ragged gasps, as if he had been running a race, and his heart pounded in his chest. This was really happening. He was going to marry the most beautiful woman he had ever seen, and it thrilled him to his core.

Paltiba'al raised his voice so all could hear him clearly. "Melita of the House of Abdhamon, and Aleon-Tabah of the House and lineage of Dan-El, you two were betrothed by your fathers as infants, and have been raised in the knowledge that this, the day of your wedding, would one day come.

Now it is time for you both to confirm that betrothal, and to take one another as husband and wife for the rest of your lives. Declare it now if you will be bound to one another in the sight of all the gods and these, your fellow citizens."

Aleon answered first, according to custom. Gazing directly into her eyes he said, more to her than anyone else, "Yes! I will be bound to you, Melita of the House of Abdhamon, daughter of lord Paltiba'al and ba'alat Tallayba'al! For the rest of our lives!"

Melita, her eyes glowing with love for her mate, answered, "Yes! I will be bound to you Aleon-Tabah of the House of Dan-El, son of the shofeṭ Ahinadab and ba'alat Nikkal. For the rest of our lives!"

"Then let us be bound together!" Aleon cried as her words sank deep in his heart.

It was the custom of the Kena'ani that when a man and woman married the groom and bride joined hands and had their thumbs bound together with a long strip of purple-dyed leather during their wedding ceremony to show that they were now one. This was usually done by the fathers of the bride and groom, unless, as might happen, one or both were dead or otherwise unable to do so. In those cases, the closest male relatives would do the binding.

Starting at the elbow of the bride's left forearm the leather strip was wound snugly, but not too tightly, down to her wrists. She placed her left hand in Aleon's right hand with their thumbs together. The leather strip was then wrapped around their two thumbs, around his wrist and all along his forearm to his elbow. The ends of the strip were tucked into the windings to keep them in place. With that completed, the two held their arms aloft for everyone to see. Cheers and loud applause broke forth from the guests, and the horns on the upper level gave a celebratory fanfare that was echoed by trumpeters on the rooftop. In this way the completion of the wedding ceremony, and the merging of the two families, was announced to the entire city.

The musicians began playing again and servants circulated with ewers of wine to refill every cup. Aleon and Melita, still bound together, circulated among the guest, receiving their congratulations, and thanking each one for coming and for their gracious gifts.

The tables and couches were brought back in and fresh food was set out for everyone to enjoy the customary post-wedding celebration. The music changed from the heavenly hymns to more earthly tunes, and dancers of both sexes appeared to entertain the guests, gyrating to the sound of the music in ways intended to excite the men, and please the ladies. Acrobats, jugglers and magicians also performed in turns, while the eating, drinking and entertainments continued throughout the afternoon and into the evening.

The attention of the men soon returned to their earlier conversations, with some discussing business affairs, the latest news, and reinforcing social or business connections. The women chatted and gossiped, about things that interested them. Every aspect and detail of the wedding ceremony, the banquet and the feast were discussed and critiqued. But the ladies quickly reached the consensus that the entire affair had been a tremendous success.

Tallayba'al, as hostess, drifted from one group of ladies to the next, joining in on their conversations and adding her own thoughts. Everyone congratulated her on the success of the wedding and offered well-wishes for the newly united couple.

Most of the women expressed their hopes for this to be a fruitful marriage, with many children to carry on the two families' lineages. It was all that Tallayba'al could do to keep from sharing her suspicion that Melita was already expecting. There would be a proper time to announce this, after it was confirmed, but this was not the right moment, and so she held her peace.

The guests began to depart at dusk. Those who were too drunk to manage on their own were assisted, or even carried, by their own servants. As the hall began to empty, the entertainers, musicians and singers were dismissed, receiving their payment from rab-tamkari Itthobaal, while the household servants began clearing away the remains of the feast.

When the last guest was gone, Melita and Aleon turned to their parents and thanked them for everything they had done to make their wedding day perfect. Then, as was the custom, the bride and groom left the House of Abdhamon and were carried to the House of Dan-El. Six sturdy slaves carried them on a special couch-like litter, similar to the ones used to convey the nobles of Kemet from place to place.

A procession, led by Ahinadab and Nikkal and accompanied by personal guardsmen of both houses, brought the couple to the home of the groom's parents. By custom they would live there for the first year of their marriage, or until Aleon had established a home of their own.

Years later, they would return to the House of Dan-El, when Ahinadab chose to turn over the leadership of the family to Aleon. But for now, the newlywed couple would occupy the large guest chambers at the far end of the upper floor.

The procession reached their home and the couple were descended upon by half-a-dozen female servants who were to help prepare them for their wedding night. But first the leather thong that tied their thumbs together was unwound by Aleon. Both were then disrobed, bathed, massaged, and anointed with fragrant oils and perfumes and dressed in silken sleeping garments.

The servants finished their work and withdrew, leaving the couple alone for the first time in days. Without the leather thong to restrict them, they embraced each other and shared a long, passionate kiss. This first kiss as man and wife was followed by another, and another, with their passion rising higher each time their lips met. Their arms embraced each other and their bodies pressed together through the thin layers of their silken garments.

"Take me to our bed my beloved!" Melita said in a voice husky with desire. Those were the last words that either spoke until morning.

Chapter 77

Plague

Spring, 1339 BC In the Nile Delta

One year before the wedding of Melita and Aleon, a pair of small, black, bead-like eyes peered cautiously from a clump of papyrus reeds along the bank of the Canopic branch of the Nile River, not far from where the waters emptied into Lake Idku. The sun would not rise for three more hours, and the owner of these eyes had waited until now to leave the safety of his burrow to search for food.

The eyes belonged to a small, fur clad creature with short, round ears, a keen sense of smell and a long hairless tail. He was a common brown grass rat; a type of rodent that was very familiar to the people who lived in the delta. His kind had inhabited the marshlands surrounding the many branches of the great river for tens of thousands of years and were adapted to feeding on the lush grasses that grew there.

For the people of Kemet, each year began with the season they called *Akhet*, the season of inundation. It was a season of massive storms in the mountains of Cush, far to the south of Kemet. The waters produced by these storms flowed into the Nile, picking up a heavy burden of silt. So much silt, in fact, that the waters appeared almost black. As the level of the river began to rise it overflowed its banks and flooded the farms and fields all along the course of the Nile. These fields were used to grow wheat, barley, flax, fruits and vegetables. There were also vineyards, groves of date palms, lotus, mulberry and other fruited trees. The annual flooding brought rich nutrients to renew the soil, ensuring an abundant harvest of all these crops.

The annual floods reached their maximum flow in the middle of the Akhet, and were vital to the people of Kemet whose existence depended on a good harvest each year.

But when the rising waters overflowed the river's banks, it forced rats, mice and other vermin to higher ground, bringing them into the areas where people lived. This annual invasion of their homes was one reason why cats were sacred in the eyes of the people of Kemet. Cats helped to keep the vermin population in check, and no household was complete without several of the sleek felines guarding their premises.

It was fear of cats that made the little brown grass rat cautious. As he waited for an opportune moment to leave his nest in the reeds, he was dizzy, and weak, and his legs trembled. But hunger drove him on, despite a growing illness that had worsened throughout the day. He could not have understood it, but he was dying.

The rat's imminent death was due to something else that the flood brought from the marshlands this season; something much more deadly than anyone could imagine or prepare for.

A certain strain of bacteria lived in the stomachs of fleas and normally coexisted with its hosts without harming them. But this year, as the bacteria reproduced inside one single flea, a mutation occurred that caused the bacteria to change in a way that made it deadly. The mutated bacteria reproduced at four times their normal rate, forming a thick mass that clogged the flea's throat. In order to feed, this flea first had to clear its throat by injecting some of the deadly bacteria into its host. These mutated bacteria were killing the small brown grass rat.

The bacteria spread throughout the rat's body, causing flu-like symptoms that sickened him, and as other fleas fed on him, they picked up the mutated bacteria. Now, three hours before dawn, several days after becoming infected, the little brown grass rat hesitated at the edge of a barley farm on the outskirts of the village of *Siuph*. His goal was a nearby granary where the remains of last year's harvest were stored.

The rat blinked its eyes and sniffed the air, alert for the slightest sign of movement or any scent of danger. But his keen nose was congested, and his sharp eyes were watery. So, in spite of his caution, he failed to detect the danger that lurked in his path. His furtive movements caught the eye of a gray cat that lay hidden in shadow beside the granary.

The rat never saw the gray cat as it pounced like lightning and caught the rodent in its jaws with stunning force. This cat enjoyed playing with its prey before killing and eating it, so with a shake of its head it opened its jaws and dropped the rat between its front paws.

But something was wrong. This victim made no attempt to escape. It didn't struggle or fight back. It merely collapsed and laid still. The cat was confused. The rat gave no signs of life. This was too easy a victory. There wasn't any fun in it. The cat nudged the rat with its paw, but the rat lay still. It wasn't paralyzed with fear or playing dead. It was dead. The cat was disappointed.

But having captured and eaten two other rats since sunset, the gray cat had a full stomach before this latest catch. It picked up this new victim and carried it into the farmer's house, intending to save it for a later snack. The dead rat was left lying on the floor of the house, near the basket the farmer had provided for the cat's comfort.

The rat's corpse had grown cold by the time the sun was rising, and the infected fleas abandoned it and went in search of new hosts. Several good choices were near at hand and soon three cats and four sleeping humans in the house were all visited by these tiny insect vectors of death.

Five days later the gray cat was the first to die. It suffered from painful swelling throughout its body with fever, vomiting and diarrhea. The swelling in its head and neck made it difficult for the poor cat to breathe. After four days, abscesses appeared on its skin, which ruptured and ran with pus. Its eyes were watery, and sores broke out inside its mouth. It stopped eating and was dead the next morning.

Within days all the other cats and humans in the household were also dead, having had much the same symptoms as the gray cat. A week later some of the neighbors who had tended the sick were also showing signs of the disease, and soon it spread to the entire neighborhood. A month later the plague had spread from the delta region to all the cities along the Nile where it killed over a thousand of the Kemet people. Before the plague ran its course six months later, it had taken the lives of four out of every twelve people.

Clearly, the gods were angry and the priests of Amun, whose rites and worship had been replaced by the pharaoh's new god, Aten, pointed to the plague as a sure sign of the old gods' displeasure. Daily sacrifices and prayers for mercy were offered at every temple and in every shrine throughout the land, but the gods were unmoved and the deaths continued. Even the palace of the pharaoh was not spared. The pestilence took the lives of several members of his own family. In the royal city of Akhenatan so many died that the corpses were heaped into piles and burned without embalming or ceremony.

Those who survived fled from the cities. Some going northward and away from the land of Kemet. The plague traveled north along the great caravan route that ran eastward, from Akhenatan through Paran, and northward following the King's Highway through the lands of the Edomites, the Moabites, and the Ammonites. In time it reached the lands to the north and east of Gebal. There it spread like wildfire through all of the Kena'ani cities that lay east of the White Mountain. It wiped out whole cities of the Hayasans, the Arameans, the Akkadians, the Mitanni, and the Luwians. It moved north and west into the land of the Hatti, where it wreaked havoc on the Hittite population. Then, in the capital city of Hattusa, it took the life of the Hittite king, Suppiluliuma the Great.

It seemed the gods of all these lands had turned deaf ears to the prayers of the people. Despite endless sacrifices, countless offerings, and the efforts of priests in all the temples and shrines of the effected cities, the gods were unmoved and so the plague raged on.

But the Kena'ani cities of the sea coast seemed at first to have been spared. For three years the plague had bypassed the coastal lands south of Ugarit while it ravaged the lands of Kizzuwatna, Mittani and Assyria. But tragically the favor of the gods did not last and the plague finally arrived in Gebal three years after its outbreak in Kemet.

Chapter 78
Desperate Measures for Desperate Times

Fall, 1336 BC in the City of Gebal

The first cases of the plague were discovered in the harbor district, by stevedores who unloaded the cargo of a ship from Ugarit. These men had worked in close quarters in the ship's hold, and noticed that some of the crew were very sick. The stricken men were too ill to continue their voyage when the ship departed the next day, so they remained in the harbor at one of the inns.

When these men began showing advanced symptoms of the plague, they were taken to the temple of Eshmun and placed in quarantine by the priests. Offerings to the god of healing were made on their behalf, and the priests gave them what comfort they could. But the disease was already beyond hope of a cure, and the men were all dead within the week.

Icy fingers of fear clutched at the hearts of the people when word of the deaths spread throughout the city. For the last three years, as news of the plague's relentless spread reached their ears, the people of Gebal had prayed that the pestilence would not find its way to their gates. Now the thing they feared had finally come among them.

For most, the first reaction was shocked disbelief that the gods would abandon them. It had seemed that the gods had chosen to spare them. People began to hope the plague would burn itself out without touching Gebal.

But within a few days of these first deaths, several of the stevedores who had unloaded the ship were also stricken. The people began to avoid the harbor district, and except for those who had to be there, the ports were nearly deserted. Fear gripped the city. Families stayed in their homes, huddled together in isolation. Taverns and brothels closed their doors. Workshops and businesses closed down and stayed shuttered and barred.

Those who could afford it, kept braziers of incense burning in every room day and night, in hope that it would ward off the pestilence. No one knew how the disease was spread, nor how it chose its victims. More deaths occurred without any noticeable pattern. There were victims among the very young, the very old, and those in between. No one was safe, whether rich or poor, strong or weak, devout worshipers or faithless fools. Entire families were wiped out in every quarter of the city.

When the number of dead and suffering passed one hundred, the council of elders met to decide what had to be done. They were determined to save their city from the fate that had overtaken so many other places.

For the first hour the council chamber was filled with hushed voices as the members waited for all to assemble. They gathered in small groups, sharing the latest news of the disaster and listening to each other's thoughts. Everyone had something to say. Gradually the groups coalesced according to their different factions and various proposals or ideas emerged from their discussions.

King Rib-Hadda arrived at the start of the second hour, followed soon after by Ili-Rapih. Seeing that the elders were now all assembled, the king called the meeting to order. Ili-Rapih was first to speak, as by custom he was expected to invoke the blessing of the gods for these proceedings. Two of his acolytes attended him, carrying braziers of burning incense.

One of the acolytes was Aderba'al, whose right arm had never healed from the damage Aleon inflicted on its tendons the night of Melita's sacrifice. He stood beside his father in sullen silence during the invocation with his ruined arm hanging uselessly at his side. Council meetings were closed to anyone but the elders, the king and the high priest, so the acolytes left the braziers and withdrew from the chamber as soon as the invocation was finished.

Aderba'al halted in a nearby hallway, close enough to overhear the proceedings. The other acolyte asked him what he was doing, but Aderba'al glared at him and told him to be silent. He knew it was wrong to eavesdrop, but he wanted to hear what would be said.

The king spoke to the elders from his throne. "My lords and ladies of the council, I ask that you give your whole attention to the emergency that has befallen our city. I speak, of course, of the long-dreaded plague that is now within our city walls." The king's scribes began to write down his words for the official record of the meeting.

"First, I call upon lord Zimredda, commander of the city guards to advise us of conditions in the harbor district."

Zimredda stepped forward and faced the crowd. "Five more deaths have occurred overnight, bringing the total to five score and six. Most of the dead are from the low-born inhabitants who had contact with the stricken stevedores, but as of this morning there have been two deaths among the servants of the noble House of Melqart'shama."

He was interrupted as these words left his mouth. There were gasps and cries of despair from the body of elders. These new deaths showed how close the danger was drawing to their own homes. Something must be done!

"Another nine score have also developed signs of plague. So many have been taken to the priests of Eshmun that the temple gates had to be closed. Inside its walls the grounds are full to capacity, with many lying in the open. The temple simply cannot accept any more of the sick until those already in their care either recover or die.

I was also told that it seems the pestilence takes three to five days to kill its victims, depending on the strength of each individual's constitution. So far none of the afflicted have survived longer than that."

This news was met with more outcries that threatened to totally disrupt the meeting. The king had to shout to restore order, and after several minutes the uproar subsided. Rib-Hadda thanked Zimredda for his report and addressed the council.

"We had hoped the afflicted crewmen from Ugarit were only a warning from the gods, but it is clear they will not spare us from this plague any longer. Now that the disease is established within the city, we must take all practical measures to limit its spread, and we must do whatever is necessary to regain the favor of the gods.

We have already ordered the city gates to be closed, and they shall remain so until the plague is over. Vital supplies and food from the outlying farm lands will be brought to the gates and left outside. When those who bring the supplies and the food have gone, the guards will briefly open the gates to bring everything inside, but no persons from outside will be admitted. Beyond that precaution, this council must decide what other measures can and should be taken."

"My lord king," said Abimilku, one of the elders who was a leader of the wine merchants' *kàrum*, a type of guild, "It is the opinion of the noble wine merchants that we must take immediate action to close the northern port. No ships that are now docked should be allowed to depart and their crews should stay on board in isolation. Only ships of the city's resident fleets should be allowed to enter the port. Foreign vessels must be turned away and kept away. Remember, it was a ship from Ugarit that brought the plague to us."

Ahinadab rose to respond, "My lord king, and members of this council, I speak for the fleet owners. Closing the northern port, though it will be costly to us all, is a wise move and we are agreed that it must be done. When the harbor was rebuilt, a great chain was added at the entrance to the port. It was needed to prevent attacks by enemy ships. The chain can easily be raised to prevent foreign ships from entering and lowered to allow our own ships to pass, if necessary.

At present there are fifteen of our ships at sea, belonging to four of our six fleets. Two of these left the port a day before the ship from Ugarit arrived, and are not expected to return for at least a month.

But this late in the year the weather will soon change to mark the end of the safe sailing season. Those two ships and any others still at sea when the weather changes must over-winter in other ports, or risk being lost in storms. We propose that any ships returning later this month be allowed to enter the harbor. The crewmen of returning ships will be quarantined aboard their vessels until it is seen that they are not suffering from plague symptoms.

But this does not address the southern port, which is mainly used by the fishing boats. The entrance there can also be closed with a chain, but if we prevent the boats from going out and coming in each day, we will lose an important part of the food this city relies on. It will limit us to dried fish and other stored foods to feed the people. How do the leaders of the fishermen feel about that?"

Lord Aziru, stood forth to respond for the fishermen's kàrum. "It will be a great hardship for us, and worse for those who rely on our daily catch to feed their families. There are no stores of dried fish that can last more than a few weeks without being replenished.

The fishing boats do not normally have contact with outsiders. They come and go with no great risk of contamination, unlike the ships of your fleet, lord Ahinadab. We do not agree to closing the southern harbor."

Even though Ahinadab had *not* suggested such a thing, Aziru spoke his piece with a sharp tone while staring directly at Ahinadab. A chorus of voices from the other fishermen underscored his points, and was answered by shouted replies from the other fleet owners.

"Silence!" king Rib-Hadda shouted, causing the crowd to calm down so that he could be heard.

"I see no reason to close the southern port, but we must be vigilant to guard against smugglers who might try to land cargo from other lands when they cannot enter the northern harbor. Lord Zimredda, I call on you to increase the patrols of your guardsmen and keep close watch on the southern harbor.

Now, what other measures should be taken?"

"Close the market!" A voice shouted from the back of the room. "We can't allow the people to gather there and spread the plague."

"What! That would be madness! What will people do to live? How will they eat?" shouted one of the merchants. "The market must remain open!" Other voices were raised in agreement, and others shouted for the market to be closed. The disagreement threatened to bring an abrupt ending to the meeting. Things were escalating quickly, and nothing could be accomplished in the turmoil. Disagreement turned to anger, with old feuds and jealousies being stirred up anew between the factions.

Once again, the king had to shout to be heard. "My lords, I will end this meeting if these outbursts do not stop at once! We have three important proposals to consider and resolve. It is time to tally those who are in favor and those who are against these three proposals.

First, shall we close the northern harbor, who says aye?" A moment later he spoke again, "Who says nay?"

The count was four score and two for closing the northern harbor, and only ten and three against. It was further decided that the north harbor would remain open for one week to give ships at sea enough time to reach the city.

The tally then was taken regarding the southern harbor. Here the count was unanimous in favor of leaving it open, with the provision that the city guard would detail extra patrols against smugglers.

Finally, the question of closing the markets was called and tallied. Here the vote was narrowly in favor of closing the markets, with a provision that food should be distributed to every house and home by the city guardsmen.

"So, it is the will of the council that the city gates will remain closed, except for vital supplies of food and medicines from the nearby farms and fields.

It is also the will of the council that the northern harbor will be closed to all but ships of the city immediately, and to all ships in one week.

The southern harbor will remain open for the fishermen to maintain their normal activities, with extra guards to prevent smuggling.

It is further the will of the council that the market shall be closed until the plague has ended. While it is closed, food stuffs from the city's emergency supplies and water drawn from the Well of the Lady will be distributed to every house by the city guards. Is that everything?"

After a brief pause, lord Paltiba'al spoke for the first time, "There is another issue we have not discussed. With the closures of the harbor, the market and the gates of the city, the stores of food normally kept against emergencies will soon fall short of the need, and we cannot be sure we will receive enough from the outlying farms. Those who work the land may be afraid to risk bringing their produce to the gates. I propose that we ration the food that is distributed by the guardsmen."

The king called for a count on this new proposal and the measure passed unanimously.

"Is there now any further discussion?" The council members looked around at each other to see if anyone would speak. There was shuffling of feet and a rustle of robes, but no one spoke for several moments.

"Then with no further matters to be discussed..." The king was about to close the meeting when he was interrupted by the high priest at his side.

"My lord king, and members of the council, there is a much more important measure that we must agree on. I speak to you from my authority as the high priest of both Ba'al Šāmēm and Yam-Nahar". His words had the effect he intended. All eyes turned to him.

"Speak!" king Rib-Hadda said. "We must hear what else the gods would have us do to protect our city from this pestilence."

Ili-Rapih knew how to influence a group of listeners and used all his skill to do so now. In his naturally deep, resonant voice he began speaking slowly and softly; his words rising and falling to emphasize key parts of his message.

"You all will remember how the father of our people, Kh'na, had a son named Phoenix. In the dark days before this city was founded, our people were suffering from a great sickness, like the one that has ravaged the lands all around and is now upon us. This sickness was sent by Anath, in her anger against Kh'na who had spurned her, and she sent it to destroy all of the people of Kh'na, who were his children, the Kena'ani that dwelt in all their lands and cities.

Kh'na was in anguish as his people began to suffer. He offered many sacrifices to all the gods, hoping to stop Anath's plague, but no mercy was found. So, in his grief he offered up his son, Phoenix, as a sacrifice to the god Yam-Nahar. Phoenix gladly gave up his life to save his father's people and built a great pyre of logs soaked in oil. He climbed to the top and set the logs on fire, which burned until all that was left were ashes.

His selfless sacrifice so moved Yam-Nahar that the god had pity on the people of Kh'na and blew his mighty breath to clear the land of Anath's plague. The Kena'ani people were saved.

Then Anath turned her anger on Yam-Nahar and the two battled until Almighty El commanded them to stop and restored the peace. El had pity on Phoenix and raised him from the ashes to live again, transforming him into a god in the form of a great red bird.

And you all know that, from the earliest days of our city, when threatened by enemies, famine or disease, we have found one among us to take the part of Phoenix, to intercede with the gods, and save us from catastrophe.

However, the years passed, and the people of Gebal multiplied until they became a great nation. A nation so large that sacrificing one of us was no longer enough to win the god's favor.

Instead, when the need arose, our fathers gave us the law that required us to offer up our firstborn sons to Yam-Nahar, to save the city!

Last night my lord Yam-Nahar showed me in a vision, that we must do this hard thing again if this plague is to be stopped! I say again, Yam-Nahar requires, as in times long past, that the elders must offer up their firstborn sons if the people are to be saved!"

The high priest's voice had risen to an awesome crescendo. From his place in the hallway, Aderba'al heard everything. He was surprised and amazed at the cleverness of his father. Obviously, Ili-Rapih had concocted his "vision" as a way to strike at the power of the elders. Especially his most hated enemies, Ahinadab and Paltiba'al. By eliminating the firstborn sons of all the great houses, including Aleon of course, the high priest would increase his own power and authority, while reducing that of the elders.

Most of the elders were older men, who, in a few years, would be surrendering their positions on the council to their eldest sons. These, the firstborn sons, had been groomed from birth to bear this responsibility, and their younger brothers, if there were any, would need years of training to be ready to take their older brothers' places. Aderba'al could see that eliminating the firstborn would give his father several years to influence the council to his advantage with little opposition. The younger sons would be like soft clay in his hands, easily molded to suit his will.

There was absolute silence when the high priest finished. No man or woman dared to breathe for the space of several heartbeats. All were deeply shocked at the words of the high priest. The idea of sacrificing their own children sent their minds whirling in panic.

Slowly, as the idea sank in, the elders turned to one another with somber faces. Each one wracking his or her brain, searching for some other way to stop the plague. But no other escape from this horror could be found. With tears in their eyes and cold sweat on their brows, the unthinkable gradually became the only alternative to the horrible, lingering, and painful death that threatened everyone in the city.

The king finally broke the silence. "In the chronicles of the city, this kind of sacrifice has only been done twice before, and not since the destruction of Thera has it even been considered. The chronicles tell us that it is only the firstborn sons of the houses of the council members who were sacrificed, and even so a substitute could be offered in their places."

Hope flared in the hearts of the elders on hearing this.

The king continued, "Members of the council number four score and seven. Five of these have no living sons. Exceptions are made for those already serving the gods or who are dedicated to the priesthood. Those who are lame, blind, or otherwise unfit are also exempt. Thus, those elders with sons that are subject to the law of sacrifice number three score and nine. That is the number needed for the sacrifice. Is that not so, lord Ili-Rapih?"

"You are correct, my king." the high priest replied, "But in my vision the god was most emphatic. It is his will that there be no substitutes, and only the firstborn sons of council members are acceptable to him, even if they are physically flawed.

Gasps of horror came from the throats of the elders. Hope failed at these words. Ili-Rapih moved on quickly as the shock set in.

"We must prepare for the sacrifice without delay. I have already had the temple potters make the necessary masks of unfired clay that will cover the faces of those who are sacrificed, and their family members. Linen shrouds that will cover their bodies will be ready soon. The altar of Yam-Nahar is prepared and a new-made bronze image of him has been installed over it. Wood has been cut and brought to the temple for the fire. All of this is now ready. The sacrifices must begin in three days."

"The council has heard the will of the great god Yam-Nahar!" said the king. "Now let us go to our homes and prepare our families for what is to come. As it has been spoken, so let it be done."

The scribes, who had recorded all that was said, added the last brush strokes to their scrolls as the meeting ended. Slowly, and with heavy hearts, the council members left the chamber.

Chapter 79
Aleon's Escape

At the House of Dan-El

The House of Dan-El was in turmoil. When Ahinadab returned home from the council meeting and shared the will of the council with his wife and family, their despair was overwhelming.

"How could the council agree to such a horrible idea?" Nikkal cried! She felt as if an icy hand had seized her heart. Her love for all her children was great, but the idea of giving her firstborn son to be sacrificed was unthinkable. She tore at her hair and could not even stand. Melita sat nearby, nursing her second child, a little girl, while her two-year-old son, Ahumm, played at her feet.

"I will never let my son be sacrificed! Yam-Nahar has no right to demand so awful a thing of us!" Melita said. She reached down to place a protective arm over the boy who had his father's eyes and his mother's raven black hair. Her little girl felt her agitation and stopped nursing and began to cry instead.

"You need not fear, Melita. Only the council members' sons are required, and neither you nor Aleon are members. But I am."

Ahinadab said somberly. Aleon was not at home, having business at the harbor to attend to. But everyone knew that he was the one on whom this doom would fall.

"And what of me!" Nikkal shouted at her husband. "How am I supposed to let my firstborn son, or any of my sons, fall prey to that scheming, misbegotten monster of a high priest? You know he is only doing this to magnify his own importance and to weaken the power of the other great houses. The loss of so many sons and heirs will leave a gap in the city's leadership for a generation or more. More than enough time for Ili-Rapih to work his schemes and gain even greater power! I will not have it, I tell you!"

"You are not the only one who feels this way, dear love!" Ahinadab replied, in a voice much calmer than his mind and heart would have warranted. He agreed with his wife's view of the high priest's actions completely, and thanked Almighty El that he had a wife with such an astute mind and quick grasp of the situation. This call for a sacrifice that would cost Aleon his life was also clearly one of Ili-Rapih's plots for revenge. It had been an especially crafty maneuver to wait until all the elders had spoken and voted on the other issues before he announced the "will of the god".

"Do not be troubled. I have been thinking of a way to avoid this. It is not without risk, and not without cost to us. But I have a plan that will save our son's life."

"Tell us what you mean!" Melita begged. He is my husband, the father of my children, and the hope of our two great houses for the future. I *cannot* lose him! We *cannot* lose him!"

"As you have said, so let Almighty El hear your words." Ahinadab answered. "The old custom was to allow for a substitute to be offered in place of a firstborn son, but Ili-Rapih has cleverly prevented that this time, claiming that the god told him only firstborn sons were acceptable, and no substitutes will be allowed. I am sure that Yam-Nahar would not have demanded that, and I have a plan to provide one anyway! There is some risk to us all, but if Almighty El is with us, my plan will work."

"Tell us more." Both ladies were focused on Ahinadab's voice. The spark of hope he had kindled now meant everything.

"I know of a young man who works aboard the *New Cabax* under Master Mariner Abirami. It is remarkable how close he is in height and build to Aleon. The two might be taken for brothers, if one didn't know otherwise.

This young man, Ahirom by name, is an orphan from a low-born house with no living family. Yesterday he began to show the first signs of the plague. I was made aware of this just before the council meeting. Abirami and I are the only ones who know of this, and he knows to keep his silence. Neither of us want the other crew members to learn that the plague has touched one of the ship's company."

He continued, "Ahirom knows he will die soon but through Abirami I have promised him that we will care for him and ease his suffering. I will have Ahirom brought here in secret after dark tonight. He is a strong young man with the vigor of youth to help him fight the disease. We will shelter him and give him what comfort we can until the day of the sacrifice, should he survive that long. If he lives, he will be given the milk of the poppy to make him unconscious as he is prepared. Once wrapped in his shroud and with the mask of joy upon his face, we will bring him to the temple of Yam-Nahar and offer him to the god."

"But what of Aleon?" Nikkal asked. "What if someone sees him or notices that a substitute is being offered in his place?"

"We must pray to Almighty El that the substitute is not noticed.

Aleon must remain in hiding until the sacrifices are finished. It is not safe for him to be seen anywhere in the city. I made arrangements with Abirami to take him on board the *New Cabax* after dark tonight and depart from the northern harbor before it is closed at the end of this week."

"But where will he go?" Melita begged. "I and my children must surely go with him!"

"That is not possible for now." Ahinadab said. "It will be hard enough to get him from the city without being seen. Abirami is to sail far to the west, to an island our master mariners know of, called Malet, the Haven, also called Malta. We have a small trading post there, although the people of that island have little with which to trade. They are a peaceful people, mostly farmers who live simply. Their island was discovered long ago by one of our ships that was driven westward from our normal trade routes by a great storm. Few ships go there, except to stop briefly for fresh water or food. Aleon will be safe at our outpost on Malet until enough time has passed for the plague to end and the memories of the sacrifices to fade away."

"But that will take years!" Melita cried. "I cannot bear to be parted from him for that long."

"It need not be that long before you can join him there with your children. As soon as it is safe to open the northern harbor again, I will have one of my ships carry you all there."

"Your plan is a good one Ahinadab." Nikkal said. "But is it right to sacrifice the life of another to save the life of our son? What will our god, Almighty El, think of us?"

"As I said, Ahirom knows he is dying of the plague. If he lives a few more days they will be a time of great agony for him. Better a quick death with the knowledge that he has saved another through his sacrifice. He will be given enough milk of the poppy to end his life. He will never suffer as the flames consume his body. He prefers this to the agony of death from the plague."

"Does Ahirom know he will take the place of Aleon?" Nikkal asked, "It is such an awful fate for one so young. Has he agreed to this plan?"

"Yes. He is willing to be Aleon's substitute. He knows our son and they have sailed several voyages together. Under the circumstances, Ahirom is glad to take Aleon's place. I have assured him that he will feel no pain."

"Then let us do what we can to keep him as comfortable as we can until the sacrifice." Nikkal said.

"It will take ten days to complete the burning of all the firstborn sons." Ahinadab said. "A lot was drawn and Aleon is to be sacrificed on the second day. That is five days from now."

Aleon returned home just as his father's plan was agreed to by his parents and wife. He was informed of the council's plans to protect the city, and the high priest's call for the sacrifice. Aleon's reaction was intense.

"This is an outrage!" he said, speaking of the latter. "I am your firstborn son, father! Am I to be sacrificed to Yam-Nahar? This is madness!"

His father explained his plan to prevent that, and Aleon saw that it could work, but was reluctant to flee the city. It seemed cowardly to him, until his father reminded him of his duty to his wife and children, and the two houses he would bear responsibility for. Still unsure, Aleon agreed.

"As soon as it is dark, take your black cloak. Not the purple one, used for formal affairs. Be sure to cover your hair and face and quickly make your way back to the harbor. Leave your necklace with the lion's claws with us. As soon as possible we will send it to you with Melita and the children. There is no other necklace like it in the world, and it will identify you to anyone who sees it. Hopefully no one will see you at all, but take care to avoid other people; especially the city guardsmen. You will have to slip past them to get aboard the *New Cabax*. Abirami and the crew are expecting you and will provide a distraction to draw the attention of the guards away for a brief moment. When you see it is clear, make haste and board the ship. Go into the cabin at once and keep out of sight. Here, give this pouch of gold and silver to Abirami. He will use it for any expenses or bribes that may become necessary."

Aleon hugged his father and mother, thanking them for the risk they were taking. Then he and Melita withdrew to their chambers, leaving the children with his parents. They spent the afternoon in each other's arms, making love for what they knew would be the last time in a long while. In Melita's heart she feared that it might be the last time she would ever be alone with him. Anything could happen.

Her greatest fear was that one of them might die before they were reunited. It was no idle fear with plague all around them and the uncertainty of life in general. The sea itself could be very dangerous, especially at this time of the year. These thoughts were also in Aleon's mind, and his heart was torn at the thought of leaving his home and family. But both knew this was his only hope of surviving and their only hope for the future.

So, they held fast to one another, finding comfort in the warmth of skin on skin, and flesh united with flesh. But the hours passed quickly and as darkness settled over the city it was time for him to go. Melita locked her eyes on his; those eyes that had so completely captured her heart. Tears ran down her cheeks and his as well. There were no words for the pain their parting was causing them. With a last, lingering kiss Aleon walked from their chamber and closed the door behind him. Melita collapsed on their bed and was inconsolable in her grief.

Aleon wiped his eyes and made his way downstairs. As he reached the main hall, he was met by old Yasha, the cook, who pressed a large pouch of spiced meat and bread, still warm from the kitchen, into his hands.

"Be well, young master! May the gods protect you wherever you are going and bring you safely home one day." Tears were in her eyes, and Aleon put down the pouch to embrace her warmly.

"I shall truly miss you Yasha! Thank you for all the care you have shown me and my family for so many years. I will not forget you, and will pray for your wellbeing."

"Thank you master Aleon! You are the pride of this family. I will look after your wife, ba'alat Melita, and the little ones."

"I know you will. I only wish..." Words failed them both.

Aleon took up the pouch of food, pulled his black cloak tighter, and walked the length of the hall and out of the house through the foyer. In the courtyard he passed by the stables, but did not take a horse. A rider arriving at the harbor would attract the attention of the guards for certain. On foot he exited through the main gate, with a salute from the watchmen guarding it, and made his way down to the harbor. The moon had not yet risen, and the shops and houses were all closed up for the night. He was not seen and encountered no one.

Abirami and his men were just about finished undoing the work that they had labored on for a week to ready the *New Cabax* for winter. They had worked all afternoon and into the night to open up the cabin and remove the decking. They retrieve the mast, spars, sails and cordage and brought the two great stone anchors up from the hold. Abirami stood atop the cabin and watched anxiously for Aleon to appear. When he caught sight of the young lord lurking in the shadows of a warehouse at the end of the wharf where the *New Cabax* was berthed, he signaled to four of his sailors to begin the planned distraction.

The four came up from the hold bearing a litter with the ailing Ahirom. To attract the attention of the guardsmen, the crewmembers on deck made a great deal of noise as the litter was carried down the boarding ramp to the wharf.

Guards were stationed along the quay, with one man every fifty paces. The commotion drew the attention of the two nearest to the ship and they alerted the next two guards beyond them. All four guards left their posts and converged to investigate the noise. As the sailors hurried the litter onto the quay and started toward the grand staircase. They were halted by the guardsmen who demanded to know what was going on.

"What are you men doing? All ships and their crews are quarantined. No one can come or go from the harbor. Get back on board your ship!"

"Our shipmate has been stricken by the plague! We must take him to the temple of Eshmun quickly."

"Our orders are to prevent any movement of goods or persons from the ships. Especially anyone who shows signs of the plague. Take him back on board at once!"

Five other crewmembers came from the ship and started to argue with the guards. "He cannot come back on board! We have been free of the plague until this man came down with it. We will all be at risk if he stays with us. He must be taken into the city, to the temple of Eshmun!"

"That will not happen! Take him back to your ship and clear this area!"

The crewmen continued to argue with the guards. And while the guards' full attention was occupied and their backs were turned to his hiding place, Aleon slipped behind them and crept on board.

As the argument on the quay continued and grew more heated, six guards from the House of Dan-El appeared as if from nowhere. They had been sent to follow Aleon at a distance, and show themselves as soon as he was safely on board the ship. They were led by Artros, the commander of Ahinadab's household guards.

"Who is in charge here?" Artros demanded. "We have been sent to bring this sailor to the temple of Eshmun on the orders of shofeṭ Ahinadab, without delay."

The guardsmen looked at each other in some confusion. "We have orders from Commander Zimredda that no one is to enter or leave any of the ships in the harbor."

"This ship belongs to the House of Dan-El, and the shofeṭ's orders are to remove this sailor before he spreads the infection to the rest of the crew. We will take it from here. Commander Zimredda will be informed of your diligence and cooperation."

Artros' men took up the litter and began carrying it to the grand staircase. The guardsmen knew that the shofeṭ was superior to their commander, and looked at each other and shrugged. They did not try to hinder Artros' men. Instead they turned back to the sailors, who were still standing on the wharf.

"Alright! You men get back aboard your ship. Now!"

An hour later the moon had set, leaving the harbor in complete darkness. The crewmen of the *New Cabax* untied their ship from its wharf in total silence and slowly eased it away from its berth. With muffled oars they moved their vessel past the great chain that lay slack against the sandy bottom of the harbor entrance. A fresh breeze from off the shore soon filled their sail and the oars were put away. The *New Cabax* soon was well away with Aleon safely tucked inside Master Abirami's cabin, hidden from human eyes, and hopefully from the eyes of the gods.

Before this, Artros and the household guards had arrived at the House of Dan-El with the litter bearing Ahirom. He was quietly ushered into one of the storerooms inside the house proper and given over to the care of the ba'alat Nikkal.

Nikkal had prepared for his arrival with a store of herbal remedies from her garden and kitchen. She had Honey, sheep's fat, milk of figs, frankincense, zinc, myrrh, theriac (a mixture of pureed snake flesh and opium), kalamos root and ginger root for fighting fever and inflammation. She would need all of these to treat the symptoms of the plague as Ahirom's condition worsened. He would be kept as comfortable as possible, for as long as he lived, or until the day of sacrifice.

Chapter 80
They Died Smiling

At the Temple of Yam-Nahar

The great bronze statue of Yam-Nahar stood on a raised platform in the inner courtyard of his temple. The god was shown in his normal posture, seated cross-legged on a cushion, with his body bare from the waist up and his arms outstretched in front of him. His palms were together, facing up and held out over a large brazier filled with a blazing fire. Thousands of small copies of this same image were enshrined in homes throughout the city. Others were installed on all the ships of the fleet, where incense pellets were burned to invoke his blessings. He was known for his benevolent, smiling face and kindly eyes. He was the god most beloved by the low-born people, second in their affection only to the goddess Ba'alat Gebal.

But Yam-Nahar had his dark side as well. If he was displeased, he could cause storms at sea to imperil ships and their crews. He could send drought or floods on the land, or hordes of locusts to destroy crops. But worst of all was his thirst for the blood of the firstborn sons of the Kena'ani. A hundred years might pass between sacrifices of this kind, but every Kena'ani man or woman knew, that in time, the call would come.

The people of Gebal, and other cities of the coast, knew Yam-Nahar could only be pleased if their children went to their deaths gladly, as did Phoenix, the son of Kh'na. To prevent the god from seeing anything less than joy, the victims' faces were covered by unfired clay masks with smiling features. To prevent them from crying out, the victims were strangled, smothered, or had their throats cut before they were given over to the god.

The parents and family members of these victims also wore the same smiling masks and sang songs of praise to Yam-Nahar while their children, one by one, were brought forward and dropped by the high priest's attendants into the red-hot hands of the god. Their linen shrouds would burst into flames almost immediately, and the smiling masks, made of unfired clay mixed with a generous portion of straw, would also burn and crumble away as the bodies of the children cooked, sizzled, and burned to ash in the god's hands. As the flesh was rendered by the heat, the skin on their faces would shrink and draw up into horrific smiles. Thus, it was said that they died smiling, even though in reality, they were already dead. When the bodies were completely consumed, the still smoldering ashes were raked clear of the god's hands and the next victim was brought forth.

With the smell of their own children's burning flesh filling their nostrils, the parents were expected to stand by without shedding a tear or making any show of grief, less the god be offended and reject their sacrifice. Many were so afraid of making any sound that they wore gags beneath their masks.

In the temple courtyard, the victims' parents and family members were surrounded by a large band of musicians. These played as loud as possible on their flutes, horns, drums, and cymbals so that no weeping or wailing from the crowd, should there be any, would ever reach the ears of the god.

The victims were selected by lot for each day's sacrifice. It would take ten long days for all the victims to be reduced to ashes. Some were full grown men and some were mere infants. Most were of ages in between. It did not matter, as long as they all were the firstborn sons of the elders.

By the end of the first day the sacrifices had become routine for the priests and servants of the temple. At sunset that day the remaining fires were extinguished, and the great brazier cleared of wood ash, charcoal, and any remains of the victims. Fresh wood and oil were brought and made ready for the start of the next day's sacrifices.

Before dawn the second day, Aderba'al arrived at the temple. He had been serving as a junior priest of Yam-Nahar, and had volunteered to attend the sacrifices. In the course of the first day's ceremony, he discovered a twisted kind of pleasure in the suffering he witnessed. Ever since his right arm was ruined by Aleon he had endured great pain from the torn ligaments, and he had learned to enjoy the pain of others as a compensation for his own misery.

He came to especially enjoy inflicting pain on the whores he visited. He found a sexual thrill in beating them severely before taking them forcefully. He would imagine that each one was Melita, who had escaped this very same treatment that fateful night.

He earned such a bad reputation that the priests of Ashtoreth banned him from the temple. No amount of gold could compensate the goddess for his abuse of her sacred prostitutes. He was forced to seek other victims in the brothels of the harbor district, and even there he was rapidly becoming unwelcome.

He had also become dependent on the milk of the poppy to mitigate his pain and make his life bearable. Bitterness filled his heart with a smoldering hatred for Aleon and Melita. Thus, while most of the other priests were reluctant to participate, he had strong reasons to volunteer his services. The lot had fallen on Aleon to be the third victim on the second day. Aderba'al made sure he was at the temple early, to enjoy watching Aleon burn, and Melita's hopes and dreams turn to ashes.

Ili-Rapih was disappointed in his son's weak character. But it stung him the way Aderba'al had been humiliated and crippled at the hands of Aleon. His own prestige and pride were as badly injured as Aderba'al's arm. That fed directly into the hatred he harbored for the House of Dan-El.

The plague had given Ili-Rapih a perfect opportunity to strike at that noble house, and those of the other high-born families that held Ahinadab and Aleon in such high regard. Since he was not a member of the council of elders, his own house was not required to sacrifice a son. But his son was a dedicated servant of the gods, and therefore doubly exempt.

The high priest smiled at that thought as he prepared for the second day of the sacrifices. Too bad Paltiba'al's only son, Bōdashtart, now served the god Adon, and was exempted as well. But it was common knowledge that Aleon would be the head of both houses in the future, so Aleon's death would damage both at once. Thus far, his plan was working smoothly, and this day would be devastating for his enemies.

The sacrificial fire had been rekindled at sunrise to begin the second day's ceremonies. Its flames had heated the hands of Yam-Nahar's image until they glowed red-hot. Ili-Rapih raised his own hands to quiet the musicians. With everyone's attention on him, he looked skyward and repeated the invocation of the preceding day.

"My lord, Yam-Nahar, god of the sea and maker of storms, lord of the fish that feed us and ruler of the rivers that water our lands, hear my voice. Your people are gathered in your temple once more, to offer up our firstborn sons for the glory of your name! We pray that you will stir up your mighty power and remove this cursed plague from our city and keep it far from our land!"

He paused, as if listening to the god's reply. Moments later he bowed his head and said, "So it shall be, Great One, so it shall be!" He turned to the crowd and cried, "Bring forth Sakarba'al, son of Adoniba'al of the House of Abiba'al!"

A pair of priests approached Sakarba'al's parents in the courtyard. Their 15-year-old son's body lay on a litter before them, wrapped in his shroud, with his face covered by the mask of joy. He had been strangled before dawn and his corpse was still warm despite the cool morning air. The two priests lifted the litter and carried it up onto the platform where the high priest waited.

The parents, wearing their own masks, followed and stood near the high priest. Their arms were around each other as they witnessed the horror being played out before them. No tear fell, no groan was uttered. The only sign of their grief was the quaking of the mother's knees as she watched her son's being offered to the god.

The high priest raised his arms to the sky again and said, "Here in your presence, Yam-Nahar, we offer up this son of our city with joy! We pray you receive him for your glory.

The musicians played and the litter was lifted above the arms of the great bronze image of Yam-Nahar. Sakarba'al's body was carefully rolled onto the glowing, red-hot hands. The priests swiftly withdrew from the heat as the shroud burst into flames. The mask blackened, its painted features burned away, and the clay crumbled; offering the parents one last look at their son's face before the body burst into flame.

Smoke rose all around them and soon filled the temple courtyard. The fire was so hot that an hour later only small pieces of blackened flesh still smoldered among the ashes of the corpse. Even the bones had been reduced to powdery white ash.

Aderba'al, with his ruined right arm bound tightly to his side, used a long-handled rake to remove what little remained of the sacrifice from the hands of the god's statue. Other attendants added more wood to the fire below. When all was ready, the next victim was called for, and this process was repeated.

About the fifth hour of the day the dreaded call finally came, "Let Aleon-Tabah, son of Ahinadab of the house of Dan-El, be brought forth!" Ahinadab and Nikkal followed the body of what everyone believed was their firstborn son onto the platform, they were outwardly calm, but inwardly apprehensive. Melita too, as the widow of the victim was permitted to join them there. If nothing went wrong in the next few critical moments their plan would work, with no one aware of the substitution. They all held their breath as the shroud-wrapped body of Ahirom, the young sailor, was rolled onto the hands of the god. He had died the night before, his passing eased by milk of the poppy. His body was immediately prepared for the ceremony, and no one outside the family knew the shrouded body beneath the smiling mask was not Aleon's.

A different kind of smile, one that was not from a mask, came over the face of the high priest as the body was rolled onto the hands of the statue. He looked directly at Ahinadab and the two women, hoping to see their calm facades slip. He wanted them to give vent to their grief, bringing shame upon their house. But they steadied themselves, straightened their backs and lifted their chins as the shroud burst into flames.

His cruel smile gave way to a puzzled look. His taunting expression had missed the mark, and did not provoke them as he hoped. Why not? The question bothered him and kept his attention on the couple.

"Well my dear, don't you make a perfectly lovely widow!" Aderba'al whispered in Melita's ear. He had moved close to her so only she would hear.

"You will need a new husband now. Perhaps I might offer your dead husband's father a chance to be rid of you. I'm sure that with his son gone he will have no great reason to keep you around. He may think an alliance with my family might have certain advantages. Think of that while we watch your husband's body burn!"

He said this with a sneer, and watched for her reaction. But Melita gave no sign of having noticed his taunts. He was disappointed and annoyed.

He turned his eyes back to the burning body. Something seemed wrong. What was it? He gazed into the flames, squinting from the smoke and glare, and it came to him. With the shroud completely burned away, the corpse was fully exposed. With a shock he saw the chest, which should have born the scars from the lion's claws, was smooth and unmarked! This could not be the body of the lion slayer!

Chapter 81
Sacrilege

At the altar of Yam-Nahar

Aderba'al grabbed his rake and rushed to the edge of the platform. With only one good arm he needed all his strength to pull the corpse up and out of the hands of Yam-Nahar. The heat was almost unbearable, and it took several attempts before he succeeded. In the process the mask was knocked aside as the smoldering corpse landed face-up on the platform. Aderba'al was frantic as he beat out the remaining flames that had started to consume the body.

The crowd below began to stir and the music faltered, then stopped. No one knew what was going on; least of all the high priest, who stood open-mouthed in shock as he witnessed his son's bizarre behavior!

"What is the meaning of this?" he shouted at Aderba'al. "What are you doing?"

"Look father!" Aderba'al cried. "This is *not* Aleon!"

Ili-Rapih stared at the corpse with a furrowed brow and quickly noticed the missing scars. Then his eyes fell on the face which had been protected by the mask and was clearly not that of Aleon. He registered the fact and quickly recovered from the shock. This could only mean one thing.

"What have you done?" He shouted at Ahinadab, giving full reign to his sense of outrage. "The god has forbidden the use of substitutes for these sacrifices! You have brought his wrath on us all with your blatant disobedience!"

Fear came upon the crowd below as they heard this, and some panicked and began to move toward the temple gates. Others fell to their knees and bowed to the image of Yam-Nahar. No one seemed to know what was happening.

Sensing that he was losing control of everything, Ili-Rapih turned and shouted for the temple guards. Five armed guards responded and were ordered to seize Ahinadab, his wife and Melita.

"Do you realize what you've done?" the high priest shrieked at Ahinadab. "You have defied the word of Yam-Nahar, and disobeyed my instructions as his high priest and representative! This sacrifice was to have won his mercy for the city. But that has been ruined by your act of sacrilege!"

Ili-Rapih turned to the crowd in the courtyard. "The ceremony cannot continue! We will begin again tomorrow. Those of you whose sons were not sacrificed as yet must return at daybreak!"

There were murmurs of confusion among the crowd. Few had seen what happened on the platform clearly enough to understand why the ceremony had been interrupted. Most only saw the body being pulled from the flames and the temple guards seizing the wife and parents. The confusion grew into anger.

Those whose sons had been chosen for this day's ceremony, but had not been burned, were ordered to return home until the next morning with the bodies of their dead sons. Through the long night they would have to endure the twin burdens of fear and grief, haunted by the loss of their loved ones. Then the next day, they would be forced to endure this grisly ceremony again. It was more than some could bear. Such things had never happened before.

The explanation filtered through the crowd from those who were close enough to see and hear what had happened. It didn't take long before the blame for all this disruption was fixed firmly on the lord of the House of Dan-El. The anger directed at him and the two women was great. The high esteem of the people that Ahinadab and the House of Dan-El had always enjoyed was washed away on a wave of shock and outrage.

Ahinadab's bodyguards had been forbidden entrance to the temple grounds, and had been waiting outside the gates for the ceremony to end. They were disarmed by the temple guards, and were met at the gates by a group of the city guardsmen. Ili-Rapih led the temple who escorted their prisoners to the House of Dan-El.

While his parents and wife were forced to wait in the inner courtyard outside the house proper, the guardsmen searched the entire premises and outbuildings, certain that they would find Aleon hiding somewhere. Of course, that search was fruitless.

"Where is your son?" Ili-Rapih demanded. "You must surrender him at once!" Ahinadab, Nikkal and Melita gave no answer.

Ili-Rapih signaled his guards and two men roughly grabbed Melita by her arms and thrust her forward to face the high priest. He stared intently into her eyes trying to intimidate her, to break her spirit so she would give up Aleon's hiding place. But nothing he did worked, and Melita looked him in the eyes and simply smiled.

"Tell me where Aleon is, or it will go hard on you and on his children! I'm sure Yam-Nahar would be just as pleased with the sacrifice of his firstborn son as he would be with Aleon himself!"

Her heart froze at this unexpected threat, but Melita gave no sign of the terror she felt. She reacted with anger, and spat her response back at him. "Aleon is gone where you can never reach him. But if you touch either of our children, I will kill you with my own hands!"

Ili-Rapih's anger boiled over. "You dare to threaten me?" he screamed. He raised his hand to strike Melita for her insolence. She stiffened in anticipation, but the blow never came.

"Enough!" Ahinadab shouted. "You have seen that he is not here. If the god will not accept a substitute, your suggestion would violate your own instructions. Aleon is not a member of the council. Therefore, his son cannot be sacrificed. Punish me if you must, but it is my right to demand that the full council rule on the matter."

"We will see about that!" Ili-Rapih said with a wicked sneer. "The god may demand an even greater sacrifice now that you three have desecrated this one.

Take the lord Ahinadab and his women into custody," he commanded his temple guards. "We will see what the will of the council may be regarding their punishment for this gross offense!"

Chapter 82
The Wrath of Yam-Nahar

At sea aboard the New Cabax

The off-shore breeze moved the *New Cabax* beyond sight of the harbor and city of Gebal. As morning broke, the late-night breeze freshened into a steady wind that provided fair sailing as the ship drove northwestward to Kit'ion on the island of Alashiya. The *New Cabax* reached this first stop on the long voyage to Malet in less than half a day. There had been no time to load adequate supplies of food and water for a long voyage before they left Gebal, so this stop was vital. It also allowed them to take on trade goods that would help pay for the trip when they reached their final destination. Abirami used some of the gold that Ahinadab had given him to buy all these things.

The next morning, they set out again at dawn, following the currents that ran westward along the southern shore of the island. Abirami plotted their course to cross open water from there to the port of Kommos on the south-central coast of the island of Kaptara. There was a minor trading post just outside Kommos that the Kena'ani had established there centuries before. By following the currents this passage would normally take almost four days. But this was not to be a normal passage.

On the third day out from Kit-ion the weather changed. Fair skies and gently rolling seas turned to rising winds with white-capped waves. The crew of the *New Cabax* lowered the sail and stowed it away. They manned their oars and began to row, without being ordered to, in the direction of the nearby island of the Telchines, or Rhodes. They hoped that the height of the island would offer them shelter from the wind and waves on its leeward southern coast.

At the urging of master Abirami, the oarsmen pulled as hard and fast as they could, with every muscle straining and bodies soaked in sweat. The wind continued to rise, driving the white-capped waves directly against the bow of the ship; alternately lifting and then slamming the vessel down forcefully.

Strong dry winds commonly occurred in this region of the Great Sea during the summer season, but rarely lasted more than a day. Though strong they presented greater danger to small boats but posed little threat to large ships like the *New Cabax*. But this unseasonal wind was not normal. It came at them on a day far into the harvest season, much later in the year than it should have. That did not feel right to the superstitious crewmen.

 If caught on the open sea, small boats and ships of shallow draft might capsize, but the *New Cabax* should have no reason to fear. The hardened sailors that made up her crew were doing the right thing, seeking the shelter of the island, still a good league to the north. Once they gained the leeward shore, they could anchor there until evening, when the winds normally died down. Then it would be safe to continue the voyage under the stars. There was no threat of foul weather, so there should be no problem.

But there were issues that troubled them beyond the usual challenge of battling wind and waves. For one, they knew that Aleon, who should have been sacrificed to Yam-Nahar, was alive and hiding from the god in the master's cabin. Their bond with the son of Ahinadab, had been forged over many voyages, and they knew him as one of them. They had gladly helped him escape, and they would fight any living man who tried to harm him. But fighting the god of the sea was another thing entirely.

Then a troubling omen had been found that very morning. The ship had been at anchor for the night, in perfectly calm waters. There had been only a light breeze, too faint to disturb the surface of the water, which had maintained a perfect reflection of the moon and stars. But the next morning when the watch was changed the statue of Yam-Nahar that normally stood in its niche in the bow riser was lying face down on the deck. There was no explanation for this other than it was a clear sign of the god's displeasure.

Now this unseasonable blast of cold, dry north wind, came roiling the waters and threatening their safety. It was all together too much for the crew to bear, and the earlier murmuring turned to expressions of real fear. These men were used to storms and winds and pirates, and other dangers that came with life at sea, but who could fight against a god as powerful as Yam-Nahar?

They pulled hard on their oars and prayed to all the gods to intercede and spare them from the wrath of Yam-Nahar.

But the seas rose even higher, surging over the bow and washing all along the deck, drenching the oarsmen and threatening to wash the tiller men overboard. The deck had been opened to extract the sailing gear, and the planking had only been partly replaced.

Water was pouring into the hold with every surge of the seas. The wind roared in their ears and they braced themselves against its strength. Every muscle was straining to reach the shelter of the island, and still it was not enough. Stroke by stroke, the oars should have moved them nearer to their goal, but the waves were pushing the ship back and away from the island. Master Abirami could see that they were not going to make it.

"Bring us about!" he shouted to the tillermen, his voice straining to be heard above the roar of the wind, "We must run before the fury of the god!"

The tillermen leaned against their long sweeps with all their strength and the ship, with agonizing slowness, began to turn its stern into the wind. It was a desperate maneuver, fraught with danger, but under the circumstances it was their only hope.

Halfway through the turn, with her port side facing the wind, a huge wave crashed over the ship. It knocked the oarsmen on that side to the deck and rendered several senseless. Only the lines that tethered them to the ship kept them all from being swept overboard. The ship nearly capsized but miraculously sprang back to right itself with the stern now facing into the wind.

Aleon had been thrown to the deck inside the master's cabin. His heart was breaking from guilt for bringing this incredible danger on his shipmates and their vessel. Hiding from the god clearly was not working. He picked himself up and staggered out the door, bracing himself against the rocking of the ship and made his way to Abirami's side atop the cabin's roof. Leaning in to be heard against the roar he said, "Master, how much more of this can we take!"

"That last wave almost did us in! The god's wrath is upon us!"

"This is all because of me! I am the one who has angered him. You, the ship and the crew should not be punished! I must make amends for cheating Yam-Nahar of his sacrifice. I must do the only thing that can satisfy him!"

With that Aleon offered up a desperate prayer to Almighty El, and stepped to the stern. Without further hesitation he leaped into the churning waters.

Chapter 83
Banishment

The Council of Elders

Once it was clear that Aleon was nowhere to be found, the council met immediately. The whole city was in turmoil, and people were demanding justice for the sacrilege at the temple. It was critical that the prisoners be dealt with at once. Ili-Rapih's order to resume the sacrifices the next morning was not obeyed, and the plague continued to claim more victims.

King Rib-Hadda opened the meeting. "Members of the council of elders, hear me! You all know why we are here. We must determine what to do about those who committed the sacrilege at the temple of Yam-Nahar this morning. Members of the House of Dan-El, namely its head, the shofeṭ Ahinadab, with his wife, the ba'alat Nikkal and the ba'alat Melita, wife of Aleon-Tabah, son of Ahinadab, have been brought to our chamber for judgement. These three conspired to aid the escape of Aleon-Tabah, the firstborn son of Ahinadab, and substituted another to be sacrificed to Yam-Nahar in his place.

Aleon-Tabah appears to have escaped the city, but is also to be judged with the others of the House of Dan-El. Who brings charges against them? Of what are they accused, and what shall be their punishment if proven to be guilty? These are the things we must decide according to our laws."

None of the elders had any doubt about who the accused were, or of what they had done. But there were doubts about how to respond. If punishment was in order, what should it be?

Many were filled with outrage at Ahinadab's attempt to save his son while they were not allowed to do the same for their own. Others thought what he had done was wise, and most of these would have done the same for their sons, had they thought of it. In truth, Ahinadab was not the only father who found a substitute for his son, but none of the others had been discovered as yet.

Most of the elders firmly believed that the plague could only be stopped by placating Yam-Nahar with the sacrifices. They were panicked by what Ahinadab had done. Others were not sure the sacrifices would be enough to save the city, but knew they had to do something. The people of the city were ready to riot.

All of them understood the seriousness of the situation. They looked to the high priest for leadership.

Ili-Rapih rose to his feet and said, "I charge Ahinadab, son of Nat'n-El with disobeying the call to sacrifice his son, Aleon-Tabah to the glory of our god, Yam-Nahar! I charge him with presenting a substitute in place of his son, in clear disobedience to the will of the god, and with full knowledge of the harm this sacrilege would cause. Furthermore, I charge him with profaning the holy fire of the temple with a corrupt and forbidden motive. I charge him with gross deception of the people, and behavior unworthy of a shofeṭ of the city!

I charge the ba'alat Nikkal and the ba'alat Melita, both of the same House of Dan-El, with conspiring together with Ahinadab to commit this same sacrilege, and aiding him in concealing these crimes from the people.

I further charge these three with aiding the escape of Aleon-Tabah from the city by unknown means, and I charge Aleon-Tabah with unlawful flight to avoid his solemn duty to our people. His act continues to cause deaths among us. The plague persists because of him.

I now call upon the council of elders to do justice in condemning these four according to the outrageousness of their acts."

When he finished the room was filled with voices loudly expressing their anger and shock. It was clear that most of the elders had already determined the guilt of the accused.

"And what punishment should they suffer for these offenses?" King Rib-Hadda shouted. His loudest voice could barely be heard above the noise of the crowd.

Ili-Rapih seized the moment.

"As the high priest of Ba'al Šāmēm and Yam-Nahar I say that the only fit punishment is stoning! The three in our custody should be taken outside the city walls and stoned until they are dead! Only then can we hope for the help of the gods in freeing us of this plague. Aleon-Tabah should suffer the same fate when he is captured."

Shouts of "Stone them, stone them!" rang out in the hall, echoing the high priest's harsh words. But a strong undercurrent of other voices cried out, "Nay! Nay! Stoning is too heavy a price to pay!" Those who were close friends of Ahinadab knew him as a man of character and were rallying to support the shofeṭ. Others who had gotten away with the same sacrilegious acts were concerned that his sentence might fall on them too, if they were found out.

Lord Paltiba'al rose to speak. "It is too soon to call for any punishment without first hearing from the accused."

His voice carried great weight with the elders. His words reminded them all of the importance of hearing all the evidence in any search for justice, and in this case that had not been done.

"Very well then," king Rib-Hadda said, "Let us hear from these accused. Bring forth the lord Ahinadab."

The city guardsmen who had been holding the accused trio in a chamber next to the council hall, brought them into the presence of the elders. Ahinadab stood before the king's throne, but turned to face the body of elders.

"Lord Ahinadab," the king said, "You are here to answer for your acts, and to explain your reasons. Speak now."

Ahinadab had anticipated this moment, and had determined what he wanted to say in answer to the accusations against him. He looked around the hall at the faces of the elders; men he had known for years. He quickly gauged the mood of each person and made a mental tally of who stood against him, and who was sympathetic toward him.

"Have you nothing to say, Ahinadab?" the king prompted him.

"My king, my lords and ladies of this council." Ahinadab began. "You all know me well, that I am honest even unto my own hurt, and will never lie for any reason. Many of you have seen my judgment of the cases that have come before my court, and you know my decisions are always fair and just. You have seen me always seek for the truth in every case. Hear the truth in my words now.

Throughout the history of this city there has never been a time more dire than this time of plague and pestilence. Nor have we ever been asked to sacrifice our sons to obtain the mercy of the gods the way we are doing now. We have been asked to give up our sons without the chance to find substitutes who were willing to take their places. Always in the past, so long as the substitutes were willing and not forced, they were known to be acceptable to the gods as sacrifices instead of our own flesh and blood. In fact, it is this willingness to be sacrificed for the good of all that the gods find most pleasing.

But now, for the first and only time since this city was founded, we have been told that the god Yam-Nahar will not accept any such substitutes. This unprecedented exception to the long tradition of our city was only made because we have been told by the high priest that the god willed it. Ili-Rapih, who told us he was visited by Yam-Nahar, and in a dream, claims he received this instruction.

There are no witnesses to this visit, so no one can confirm the high priest's words. With no disrespect to him, I raise the question if this was truly the will of the god, or if it was a detail the high priest added for his own reasons."

A murmur went through the room. Ahinadab had chosen his words carefully, and could see this argument was having some effect on the elders. They were used to following tradition and custom, especially when it came to the gods in their dealing with men. They were normally resistant to any innovation or deviation from the established ways and laws of their ancestors.

He continued, "It is true that I provided a substitute for my firstborn son to be sacrificed in his place, as was long the custom of our city, as practiced by our fathers. The substitute was a young man of low birth, with no living family. He was a shipmate of my son, and knew him well. He also was suffering the agonies of the plague and offered himself in place of my son, knowing that his own death was imminent.

But this one time in our history, the high priest decreed that no substitutions would be allowed. As I said, I have doubts about this, and perhaps you do as well. Ask yourselves, why would Yam-Nahar change his mind on this point? Why would he not have confirmed this by revealing it to other leaders among us? Oh yes, my brothers and sisters, I do have many doubts. Perhaps we all should!"

The murmuring increased. Some were nodding their heads in agreement with Ahinadab and their eyes fell on Ili-Rapih with suspicion. Ahinadab had remained with his back to the king and the high priest who stood beside him. He did not see the look of pure hatred that Ili-Rapih was aiming at his back as if it were a dagger.

"Why would the high priest add this requirement to his call for sacrifice? Can it be that the elimination of so many leading sons of the city is a way to enhance his own power and stature? Could it be that he covets the wealth of your noble houses, and knows that your love for your sons would compel you to offer generous gifts to commemorate their lives? Could that be the real vision he had?

I have made no secret of how the House of Dan-El has long enjoyed the special patronage of Almighty El, the father of all the gods, including Ba'al Šāmēm and Yam-Nahar. It is El that we revere in the House of Dan-El, and my trust is in his mercy and kindness. I believe he has given me, and this city, a great gift in the form of my firstborn son, Aleon-Tabah, whose life is not to be squandered on the word of a man of corrupt intentions like the high priest!

So, I have spoken. Let my words be so written! And so, let me be judged!"

As his final words thundered in the ears of the elders, Ili-Rapih could see that many minds were swinging in his favor. Ahinadab had turned the table to focus on his accuser's motives and character. The high priest was livid. It was all he could do to keep from interrupting Ahinadab, but he held his peace. Perhaps, he thought, the shofeṭ would go too far or say something to condemn himself. But as he watched the faces of the elders, he knew this wasn't what was happening.

"Enough!" Ili-Rapih shouted. "Do not listen to these lies! This is his attempt to blind you to the sacrilege he has committed! Do not let him succeed in pulling all this wool over your eyes! He deserves to die, and his punishment should be to die by stoning! Only his death, and the death of these women, will appease the god!"

The crowd, now thoroughly confused by Ahinadab's words and the high priest's outburst, were divided in their thinking. On the one hand, they had great sympathy for Ahinadab. He was still highly respected, but by his own words he confirmed that he had committed a sacrilege. The high priest, on the other hand, was a known schemer who had many times abused his authority to further his own house's interests. Many of the elders had come out on the short end of business dealings with him. He was not well liked at all among the city's elite families, and was despised by many.

But a significant number of parents of the boys who had already been sacrificed felt what Ahinadab had done was grossly unfair to them, and that he should be punished for it. Their anguish would not let them believe that their sons had died when they might have been spared.

King Rib-Hadda waited a space, then stood and said, "You have heard the words of the accuser and the words of the accused! What then is the will of the council? What should be done with these who have perpetrated this sacrilege? Who wants to see them stoned?"

Hands were raised and counted, for and against stoning. The majority were against it by a small margin, but those in favor of it immediately voiced their displeasure, and Paltiba'al could see that this would threaten the unity that was vital to the city's survival. Something else must be done.

"My fellow council members! Hear me, please!" he shouted. When he had their attention, he continued in a controlled tone, "Our laws allow us to stone those guilty of major crimes, and provides for lesser punishments in cases where there is a lesser offense. Since the council has not approved stoning in this case, I suggest that the most appropriate punishment might be banishment. May we consider this alternative?"

Murmurs of approval for this idea could be heard, and after some discussion the king called for a tally on the question. The count was nearly unanimous in favor of banishment.

The king spoke, "Lord Ahinadab, it is the will of the council that you and your household are banished from the city of Gebal for the sacrilege that you have committed this day. Therefore, before sundown tomorrow you must leave this city forever. You may take your fleet of ships with you, and all your personal possessions after making a payment of one talent of silver to each of the elders of the council as compensation for the damage done to them by this sacrilege. Your rab-tamkari may remain in the city to settle your accounts and arrange for your entire household to follow you wherever you may go. But after one month he must also leave and whatever of your wealth remains in the city will be forfeited to the temple of Yam-Nahar.

So, I have spoken. Let it be thus recorded in the chronicle of the city. This meeting is concluded."

The other elders had all left the hall, but Paltiba'al remained behind with Ahinadab, Nikkal and Melita.

"I am grateful to you Lord Paltiba'al." Ahinadab said. "You probably saved our lives, for which I cannot thank you enough. I am in your debt."

"Not so, lord Ahinadab. It was your excellent defense that changed the hearts of the elders, or at least enough of them. I must admit that I thought you would all be stoned, but you turned their thinking around.

I don't know what inspired the words you spoke. But now our first concern must be for your safety. You are free to return to your home for the night, but there are many who would still like to see you dead rather than banished. Powerful men who lost their sons to the fires of Yam-Nahar may move against you between here and the House of Dan-El. I sent a servant to summon your guards, and I will have mine accompany you as well. As soon as they are all here you must go."

"Your words are wise lord Paltiba'al. No man has ever had a truer friend than you have been. I and my house will always be grateful."

"I am just as grateful for your friendship Ahinadab. Our houses are as one through the marriage of our children. I will work with He-sham, to arrange your affairs after you leave the city. Together he and I will salvage whatever we can of your estate, and will forward it to you as soon as you are ready. I will pay the elders the required fines from my own treasury until you can repay me. Do you know where you will go?"

"I have interests in the city of Tyre, and a large warehouse there. I can find shelter for us within that city, with berths for my ships and space to store all our possessions until I build a new dwelling place for the House of Dan-El."

Ahinadab's household guards arrived and joined those of the House of Abdhamon to escort Ahinadab and his ladies, home.

"Goodbye my friend." Ahinadab said to Paltiba'al with unashamed emotion. "May Almighty El bless and keep you, and may the House of Abdhamon always prosper."

"We will meet again my friend." Paltiba'al replied. The two embraced and Ahinadab stepped back as Melita came forward to hug her father with tear-filled eyes.

"There now, my daughter!" Paltiba'al's voice was strained. "Take care of your children, and go with the blessings of Ba'al Šāmēm, and more importantly with the blessing of El. Your mother and I will say our final goodbye tomorrow at the House of Dan-El."

Chapter 84

Adrift

In the Sea of Kaptara

Abirami grabbed for Aleon as soon as he saw that he was about to throw himself into the sea. But he didn't react quick enough, and Aleon was over the side and gone in an instant.

He did the next best thing that he could think of; he rushed down from the top of his cabin, onto the deck and took up one of the spare oars. He looked out over the waves and franticly searched for the young lord.

There! Half the length of the ship away he caught a brief glimpse of Aleon struggling to keep his head above the water. With all of his strength he heaved the oar like a spear at the spot where he thought Aleon would be and prayed to El that it might be close enough to save him. It was all he could do. His full attention immediately returned to the peril that threatened to swamp the ship.

Aleon hit the water hard. The impact was almost as violent as a fall from a tall tree. It stunned him and forced the air from his lungs. He quickly regained his senses and tried to breathe but only inhaled water. Retching and coughing, he struggled to keep his head above the surface. He managed to clear his lungs and sucked in a mouthful of air just before a huge wave engulfed him. It lifted him, rolled him over, and smashed him down. The force took him deep.

He was completely at the mercy of the sea. He lost track of the surface. His vision was blurred by the water and his eyes burned from its saltiness. All he could see was a dim, murky impression of darkness all around. The wave pressed him further and further into the depths until its force was spent. He hung there motionless for a moment, then began to float upward.

His lungs were burning. He was desperate for air, but was rising too slowly. He began to kick and stroke his way toward the surface. There was a long way to go. Was this the moment he would die?

When his head finally broke the surface, he gasped and sputtered and took deep breaths of the crisp, clear air. He spotted the oar Abirami had thrown overboard and swam to it. His left hand grabbed onto it as the next wave hit. Before the wave could roll him under, he hooked his right arm over the oar and held on as if it were his life itself. The wave lifted him, but he stayed on top of it this time. He secured the oar beneath both arms and slid over the crest and down the wave's back as it passed.

From the crest he had caught a glimpse of the ship, battling the wind and sea in the distance. He could see she was riding low, and each wave that washed over her stern was taking her lower. She was taking on too much water. She was sinking. When the next wave carried him up to its crest, he saw a large wave strike her a fatal blow and he watched in horror as the ship was swamped.

Within seconds the *New Cabax* slipped below the surface and was seen no more. Master Abirami and all of the crew were tethered to the ship to keep them from being washed overboard. All were pulled under when the ship sank. Aleon was devastated and scanned the surface, hoping to see some part of the ship that was still above the water. He strained his eyes, hoping to spot some of his shipmates on the surface. But no matter where he looked, he saw only violent, white-capped waves.

Alone and adrift on the vast expanse of the Great Sea, Aleon was overwhelmed with despair. He had hoped he could save the ship and crew by sacrificing himself. With tears in his eyes he cried out to Almighty El for the crew's deliverance, but heard no answer except the roar of the wind.

The chaotic waves continued to toss him about, as if they were designed to rip him from the oar and take him down. It would be a simple thing to let go and surrender to their power. But he held on stubbornly.

His despair at the fate of his shipmates turned to anger and he cried out, "Hear me, Yam-Nahar! Why did you punish them for my offense? I offered myself to you, but you took them instead! You had no claim on their lives, so I reject your claim on mine!" He cursed Yam-Nahar and tightened his grip on the oar. He was determined to survive and, if it was the will of Almighty EL, he knew he would.

The sun was sinking when the wind began to subside. It became fitful at first, then fell off in low velocity bursts that finally gave way to faint zephyrs. The waves subsided; leaving the sea smooth and calm. Aleon was completely exhausted. He closed his eyes. and was startled to awake when his face slipped into the water.

It was nighttime, the full moon had risen in a cloudless sky, and he realized he had slept for several hours. He couldn't tell where he was, but felt himself drifting with the current. He looked all around in the light of the moon and stars. There was nothing in sight except empty water.

He thought of his family.

Melita's face came to mind, and then his children's. They would expect him to be waiting for them on Malet. What would they think when they learned he wasn't there? He thought of his father and mother. They had risked everything to save him. It would devastate them to learn their efforts had failed. His heart was breaking. These thoughts hardened his desire to live, and he called out to the god of his family.

"Almighty El, god of all gods, thank you for my parents and my family! Thank you for my life and the goodness you have shown us all. Although I do not deserve it, you have been kind to me all my days. I pray you will show me your kindness now!

I am lost in the grip of Yam-Nahar who seeks to destroy me, and you are my only hope, and the only hope for my family. You can free me from his grip if you desire it.

I pray that you will be merciful to me, and bring me through to safety. You are my god, and my trust is in you!"

A clear, calm voice rose from within his soul, with words that rang in his mind. *"Aleon-Tabah, do not be afraid. My favor is on you. You shall not perish this day. I am with you, even as I was when the lion attacked on the White Mountain."*

The memory of that day came to Aleon's mind. The lion rushed at him so fast! He remembered the flashing eyes, yellowed fangs and those cruel claws! He could almost feel the overwhelming impact as the beast crashed down on him, and the searing pain as those claws ripped through his flesh!

His thoughts turned to the strange dream he'd had while he lay wounded and near death. It returned to his mind in vivid clarity.

He had thought it was just a product of his fever. In the dream El had spoken to him. His body had been lifted up and he had floated through the air to the peak of Mount Zaphon, the dwelling place of Almighty El. Then the god had stretched forth his hand and blessed him.

Drifting there on the sea, the words of El from his dream came back to him.

"Do not be afraid. You are safe. Your father loves you and will protect you, and I love you as well. I have made plans for your life and I will be with you to see them fulfilled."

He was sure there had been more, but Aleon could not recall it now. He continued to hold fast to the oar and the current carried him south and west, away from the Telchines island of Rhodes.

Chapter 85

Captured

On the Isle of Karpathos

Four days later Aleon awoke, face-down on a rocky beach known as *Achata* by the people there. Though he didn't know it, he had been caught in the currents that flowed counter-clockwise in the great Rhodian Gyre. He had been washed ashore on the south side of the isle of Karpathos, half way between Rhodes and Kaptara, suffering from dehydration and exposure. Sores had broken out on his skin from prolonged immersion in salt water, and there were cuts and scrapes on his hands and feet from sharp rocks.

During the third night his ears picked up the sound of surf pounding in the distance. He couldn't see which direction it was coming from, but it grew louder and louder. Shortly before dawn, he could see the phosphorescent glow of the waves breaking on a shoreline close by. There was land!

Aleon let go of the oar and swam toward the shore. In the dim light he could see a small beach in a narrow cove, surrounded by high cliffs. He fought against the pull of the current that threatened to take him past the beach and away from the shore. His weakened arms and legs had just enough strength to overcome the current.

Near the shore he was caught up in the surf, rolling and twisting as the waves broke over him. He was forced down to the bottom and raked across small rocks and coarse sand. When he finally crawled out of the water, he collapsed just above the waterline, completely spent from his efforts. He lay face-down in the wet sand, his eyes closed, and he fell into a deep sleep.

Bright sun was shining when he came to his senses. Something hard and sharp was jabbing at his back.

"This one is alive!" someone shouted in the language of the Achaeans.

"Rouse him, tie him, and put him with the others." someone else replied in the same language. Aleon's studies included the languages he needed for his family's business, including that of the Achaeans.

"What place is this?" he asked, rising to his hands and knees. His mouth was dry and his tongue so swollen that his words were more of a croak than speech.

"This is the isle of Karpathos", said the man who had been prodding him in the back with what turned out to be the butt of a spear, "and you are our captive."

A water skin was held to Aleon's lips and he drank eagerly. It was his first drink in four days and he was grateful for it. But he drank too much, too fast and vomited up most of it.

"Take it slow." the same voice commanded, "Looks like you've been shipwrecked. What was your ship? How long have you been in the water?"

Aleon was cautious. He was trained, as all Kena'ani of the coastal cities were, to keep secret most things. He didn't want to say anything that he might regret later. Still, these seemed like harmless questions.

"Five...no, four days...I think. My ship was the *Ukral* from the port of Ugarit. She foundered in a great storm that took us off our course."

"Four days in the sea. Without water? You need to drink more. But slowly!"

Aleon did as he was told, only sipping the water. This time he managed to keep it down. It tasted better than the finest wine.

A second man joined the one with the spear. They grabbed Aleon's arms and lifted him to his feet, steadied him, and tied his hands behind his back. He was prodded along to where the cliff jutted out into the sea. His sandals were lost somehow after he went into the water, and the cuts on his feet made walking difficult. When he stumbled the butt end of the spear prodded him along.

An Achaean vessel was pulled up on the shore. It was painted black with a large pair of eyes and a shark's grinning mouth on the bow. Its sleek lines and shallow draft were ideal for fast raids on seaside villages or chasing down slow merchant ships. In other words, it was a pirate vessel, of which there were many operating in these waters.

Aleon was shoved hard against the ship's side and pushed roughly to the sand beside two other bound prisoners. Aleon did not recognize either of the two. One was a thin young man, about Aleon's age. Blood was clotted on the left side of his head. He looked dazed and unfocused. The other was a woman of child-bearing age with stringy black hair. Both had bruises, abrasions and bore other marks of abuse, probably suffered in their capture.

The woman had obviously been raped; her clothing was torn and hanging down from her waist to barely cover her genitals. Her breasts and ribs were bruised and a thin red cut across her throat still bled slightly. Her eyes were vacant and staring off into the far distance. The three of them sat there in silence, shaded by the shadow of the ship. Aleon studied the other two. Their condition told him all he needed to know about the situation he was in.

Looking down the beach, Aleon saw wreckage and what looked like bits of some cargo that had been carried there by the tide. About a dozen men were picking through this flotsam and collecting things that had value or usefulness. They didn't seem to be finding much.

A few dead bodies were scattered amid the wreckage, bloated and waterlogged. Some had been worked on by predators, probably sharks, that had found them before they reached this beach. Flocks of seagulls pecked away at the bodies, fighting over the bits of flesh that came away in their beaks.

The condition of the corpses made it impossible to tell who these sailors had been, or what ship they were from. Aleon's heart sank at the thought that they might have been his shipmates from the *New Cabax*. From where he sat, bound and held under the watchful eye of an armed guard, there was no way he could tell.

The pirates finished picking through the wreckage, having found very little. A tall, one-eyed man, flanked by two others, approached the captives. The tall one wore a linen band around his head that covered over his right eye. An angry red scar ran from his forehead, down across that eye and along his right cheek. Where his eye should have been the cloth had been decorated with a crudely painted, staring eye. He was dressed for battle, with a battered and tarnished bronze breastplate over a dirty gray woolen tunic. He wore a broad belt of leather, studded with bronze. A heavy bronze sword and a long knife hung from it. His arms were encircled with bronze bands above the elbows and long, thick silver arm guards covered his lower arms from elbow to wrists. He carried a boar's tusk helmet under his right arm and a round bronze shield hung across his back. The helmet was a rare thing and it marked him as the leader. It also marked him as a warrior of great importance.

The men with him were also armed; one with an old sword and the other with a large club studded with spikes. The rest of the pirates were similarly equipped, but none had weapons or armor that could match their leader's.

The two captives next to Aleon cringed and pushed back against the side of the ship as the trio approached. Aleon looked up, directly into the one-eyed man's good eye. That eye studied Aleon, assessing his condition as one would study a horse before purchasing it. Aleon heard him speak to the men beside him.

"Here is something different! Not the usual sort to be washed ashore by the sea. He's been well fed and aside from a few scrapes and sunburn he seems healthy enough. Look at his clothes. A fine black linen tunic with gold threadwork. Expensive no doubt, before the seawater ruined it. He is well muscled though, so he's not been pampered. Not some rich man's fancy boy. I'd guess he was from a wealthy family, but was expected to work at some business or other."

To Aleon he said, "What's your name boy, and where are you from?" He spoke in a stern voice that expected an immediate answer.

"My name is Palo of Ugarit." Aleon said, in the Achaean language. He knew better than to volunteer anything more than he had to, and to lie when necessary.

"Palo, eh?" the one-eyed man said. "That is a slave's name. It fits you well enough. You may keep it, as you are now my slave. But those are not a slave's clothes. Were you something else in Ugarit? And how did you find your way here, dressed like a rich boy?"

Aleon was thinking fast, improvising along the lines of these questions. He said, "I was not born a slave, but my parents died while I was young. My uncle raised me and saw to it that I was educated. That is how I came to speak your language.

When I was old enough, he sold me to a wealthy merchant whose children needed a tutor. This tunic is an old one of his that was given to me."

"Given you say? Stolen is more likely. I think you are a runaway slave that escaped your city by sea, getting this far before the winds swamped your ship and you washed up here. What else did you steal to buy your passage with?"

"Nothing, master!" Aleon replied, playing the part of a runaway slave. "I swear by Apollo, I took nothing. I paid for my passage by working as an oarsman. See my hands, they are blistered and calloused from the rowing."

The two men beside the one-eyed man raised Aleon to his feet and turned him so his hands, still tied behind him, were facing their leader. It was plain to see that these were not the hands of some soft tutor, but had done hard work.

"Good! We shall see how well you can row! We are short a few hands at present. If you do well, we may keep you. If not, we will sell you along with the others in the slave market at Rhodes."

Chapter 86
The Karcharias

*In the **Aigaíon Pélagos***

Six days later Aleon, or Palo as he was now known, was chained to an oar on the Achaean pirate ship, pulling hard as it left the harbor at Rhodes. The other two slaves hadn't sold for much, and they had traded the few things of value that had been found on the beach for salted fish and loaves of hard bread. Aleon had proven to be a good oarsman, and was too useful to sell. Now they were returning to their home, the island of *Skyros*, in the **Aigaíon Pélagos, the Aegean Sea.**

The sailing season had started out well enough for the crew of the *Karcharias*, or Shark, which Aleon quickly learned was the name of the pirates' vessel. In the opening weeks the sea was filled with merchant ships from the eastern coastal cities. The pirates, led by their leader, *Aniketos*, the Unconquered, of Skyros, had chased after five ships and had captured two, but as the season wore on their luck changed. They lost three men attacking the second ship and another two had sickened and died at sea. Four left the crew in Rhodes the first time they made port there.

That left the crew short-handed. So much so that, despite the speedy design of the *Karcharias*, they lacked the manpower to catch even the slowest merchant vessels that came their way. Instead, they started raiding small coastal villages of Ahhiyawa, Arzawa and Lukka, taking captive any villagers too slow to escape them, and raping, killing and stealing anything of value that hadn't been hidden away. The captives were sold in the slave market at Rhodes and the captured goods were traded for gold or silver.

The *Karcharias* kept in sight of land as much as possible on its northward passage through the islands that dotted the great bay that was the Aegean Sea. The Achaeans lacked the navigational skill and knowledge to risk sailing the open waters, except for short distances. They made slow progress, stopping at various islands for water and food when necessary.

For them, the sea at night was a fearsome place, full of monsters and unknown hazards that could destroy them. Thus, each night the ship was beached on some sheltered stretch of shoreline, where fires could be built and the men could stretch their legs. Aleon had earned a degree of trust among the crew, so was left unbound at night. He had given his word and sworn by Zeus and Apollo that he would not try to escape. He had been warned that his feet would be cut off if he were to break this oath. The left foot for Zeus and the right for Apollo. The threat was unnecessary. Where could he go? He had no knowledge of the lands surrounding this part of the Great Sea, and if he ran away on an island he would quickly be recaptured. He knew he would have to wait for a decent opportunity to present itself.

Aniketos was interested in this slave they had found on the beach. He was sure there was more to his story than he let on. When the crew gathered around the fire each evening, he made Palo sit next to him. He prodded the young captive for tales of his city, and the current affairs of the area. There weren't many opportunities to hear of events from beyond the limits of the few ports they visited, but Aniketos knew enough to tell if Palo's answers were truthful.

Aleon, as Palo, gave the pirate chief only the information a slave from Ugarit would have known. He drew on his experiences with his own teachers to be convincing in the role of a tutor to rich young children. But he was careful to leave out any details that might not fit well with his false identity. When Aniketos' questions got too close for comfort, Aleon would answer with vague generalities, and change the subject.

The pirate chief and his crew were starved for entertainment. It was easy for Aleon to divert the conversation away from the harder questions by peppering his answers with stories he'd heard from the crew of the *New Cabax*. As the pirates came to appreciate having this educated young man from Ugarit among them, his presence was welcome. By all that is, except for one.

Arion, the second in command of the *Karcharias* grew jealous and resented the attention Palo was getting. Everyone else seemed to like this slave, and each day the line between slave and crewmember was blurring more and more. This would come to a head as the ship neared its home port.

Chapter 87
The Truth is Discovered

En route to the island of Skyros

Aleon sat beside Aniketos one night as the evening meal of fresh caught fish was cooking. He bent forward to warm his hands and his signet seal slipped from within his tunic and reflected the light from the fire, catching the eye of Aniketos. The seal had remained on its leather thong, and had been hanging around Aleon's neck since his capture, hidden by the high neckline and folds of his tunic. He was so used to wearing it that he forgot it was there and no one had noticed it until now.

"Palo, what is it I see around your neck? Show it to me."

"It is nothing of any importance." Aleon replied, "Just a keepsake given to me by my father before he died." Aleon was hesitant to show it to Aniketos, and started to tucked it back inside his tunic.

"I said show it to me!" Aniketos shouted, drawing the attention of the other crewmen.

Aleon had no choice but to hand the seal to him. Aniketos held it up in the light of the fire and said, "A signet seal. How interesting. It seems to be made of carnelian, with symbols carved into it. An expensive keepsake!"

He turned the small seal over in the light, but couldn't make out what was inscribed on it. "Bring a torch!" he called out to a crewman standing watch by the side of the ship.

In the brighter light of the torch Aniketos studied the seal with his one good eye. That eye grew wider as he began to make out the inscription it bore.

"This appears to have been made by the *Phoiníkē*. I see the kind of writing those people use, although I do not read that language.

But I have seen these markings before, on cargo we took from a ship of Byblos. You say your father gave it to you when you were a child? In Ugarit? How did he come to possess the signet seal of a Phoiníkē merchant? Explain this to me!"

Aleon wracked his brain for an explanation. "I don't know." he said, "He was a merchant. Perhaps it came to him in the course of some business."

This poor response immediately raised Aniketos' suspicions. To his ears it didn't ring true. His one good eye narrowed, giving Aleon a hard look. "Are you telling me the truth?

Such a thing would not be given or traded away. A seal is the mark of its owner, and would be used to identify his property. As I look at the symbols carved here, I can see the image of a leaping lion with what looks like a spear or javelin thrust through its body. It is a signet I have only seen once before. I found it on the clay that sealed amphorae of garum in the hold of a ship we captured two years ago. This is the very seal that made those marks.

You say your father gave it to you when you were young. Yet someone used it to seal those amphorae just two years ago! You have not been telling us the truth! *Who are you?*"

Aleon's face reddened and his heart began to pound in his chest. There was no way out of this, except to confess and tell the truth.

"My name is not Palo, and I am not from Ugarit. I am Aleon-Tabah, the Lion Slayer of Gebal, or Byblos as you call it. My father is the lord Ahinadab of the House of Dan-El. That city is my home, but I can never return to it."

He went on to explain how he had fled the city to escape the sacrifice and had jumped from the ship to save his shipmates from the wrath of Yam-Nahar, only to watch as the ship sank a few moments later.

When he finished speaking there was silence. The entire company had been listening with intense concentration as his story unfolded. Aleon held his breath. He could not imagine what Aniketos was thinking, or how he would react.

After a few moments, Aniketos stood and paced about without saying anything. When he sat down again, he stared into Aleon's eyes with his one good eye. It seemed as if he was looking right through him. Finally, he spoke.

"So, you have been lying to us from the start. I sensed that there was something wrong with your story. But how do we know you aren't lying to us now?

We know this story of the Lion Slayer of Byblos. For years, that tale has been heard in taverns and marketplaces all around the Great Sea. Travelers and traders still spread the tale of the boy who single-handedly killed a vicious man-eater on the White Mountain. Some believed it, others think it is just a wild story. And here you are, claiming to be the one who did such a mighty deed. Forgive me if I have doubts. What evidence do you have to prove who you say you are?"

Aleon hesitated, as members of the crew crowded around with cries of "Proof, Proof, Proof!" and "Liar, Liar, Liar!" They were filling their hands with weapons. The situation was quickly going bad for Aleon.

In desperation he stood and shouted, "Here is my proof!" He slid his tunic down from his shoulders to his waist, exposing the scars on his chest and stomach. "These are the marks of the lion's claws, which nearly to killed me."

The crewmen had been on the verge of killing Aleon themselves, but what they saw silenced them. The braver ones reached out and touched the rippled scar tissue with amazement. Most had never seen a lion, nor understood how large their paws were, but here was the proof and it was a wonder to them that anyone could have survived such wounds. Gasps of astonishment replaced their angry shouts of a moment before.

"Hold your tongues!" Aniketos shouted. "Clear away so that I may see this proof."

He reached over to Aleon and put his hands on the scars, tracing the path of the lion's claws from neck to hip.

"So, it *is* true! You *are* the Lion Slayer of Byblos. The Aleon-Tabah as it is in your tongue. What am I to do with you now? I might sell you back to your father if you weren't a fugitive from his city. If, as you say, he helped you escape he would not want you to return. The danger to both of you would be too great to risk.

I suppose I could always sell you as a slave. But except for these lies, you have given me good service. You are strong and row well. You can fight, as we have seen when we attack villages. You have more value to us than selling you would bring. I can think of only one thing to do with you."

Everyone was breathlessly waiting for Aniketos' next words. He stood beside the fire and addressed his crew, "What say you, men of the *Karcharias*? Shall we have this fugitive, make this lion slayer, a member of our company?"

"Aye!" The shout rang out from the throats of every man. Except for one.

"Nay!" a loud voice bellowed. It belonged to Arion, the second in command of the *Karcharias*. "I do *not* believe him! He lied to us before and is lying now!"

"Then he must prove himself." Aniketos declared. "You two will fight, and the gods will reveal the truth by which one wins."

Chapter 88

Live or Die

Inside the circle in the sand

A few minutes later, stripped down to their bare skin, the two combatants faced each other across the sand. The fire had been built up to provide a decent amount of light, and a ring of ten paces in diameter was traced in the sand. The crew of the *Karcharias* surrounded the two combatants in a tight circle with torches held high for even greater illumination. Olive oil was brought from the ship, and the two men were rubbed with it until they glistened. No weapons were allowed for this combat. It was to be a wrestling match.

Wagers were made and odds were given that highly favored Arion due to his known fighting abilities, his greater height, and strength. Aleon was well muscled, but a head shorter than Arion and his wrestling skills were unknown to the crewmen. Still, he clearly had the favor of their god *Kronos*, who was known to the Kena'ani as El. How else could a mere youth kill a lion *and* survive a shipwreck?

A young crewman named Athos was helping Aleon apply the oil to his back and legs. He leaned close to Aleon's ear and whispered, "Have you ever wrestled before?"

"Not since childhood. I was never as good at it as some of my friends, but I know some good moves."

"Arion and most of the crew are of the *Dana'a'oi*, an island people, and their rules for wrestling are simple. The contest consists of three falls. The one who can take his opponent down at least two of the three falls is declared the winner. You may grapple, throw, strike with your fists, pull the hair or beard, choke, bite and gouge the eyes of your opponent, but you must never grasp, pull, strike or kick what hangs between his legs. That is an offense against the gods and you will automatically forfeit the contest. Should either of you suffer a broken finger the contest continues, but if an arm or leg is broken, or put out of joint, the match ends and the one with fewer or lesser injuries wins."

Aleon was surprised to hear how wide-open these rules were. In his childhood encounters, the boys would pull hair, kick, grapple and hit each other, but no one ever gouged an eye, choked or bit the other. Their bodies were not oiled and were usually not completely naked, unless they had just been swimming.

Athos finished his work and wiped his oily hands on his tunic. "Ready?" He asked. Aleon looked him in the eyes and shook his head in affirmation. His mouth was dry and his heart was pounding, but he was as ready as he could be. He squared off against Arion who had already taken his stance; with his arms spread wide the man seemed to cover almost half of the circle

"Begin!" Aniketos shouted. The crewmen cheered and hooted encouragement to the contestants, each in support of the one they had placed their wagers on. There were clearly more supporters for Arion than for Aleon.

The two men circled each other warily, their eyes locked. Aleon was tensed up, studying Arion's movements. Arion wore a condescending expression that bordered on arrogance, so sure he was of his superiority. He didn't seem impressed with Aleon's physique or attitude, and nothing he saw showed him that Aleon knew how to wrestle.

"This will be a short contest, lion killer! I will be merciful and finish you quickly."

Aleon tried to think of a retort, but as he searched his mind, he heard the voice of El saying:

"Trust in me. I am with you and will give you victory this day. My spirit will come upon you and replace your weakness with my strength."

With the words of El echoing in his mind, Aleon stopped circling. Arion saw this as his opportunity and rushed forward with his arms spread, prepared to grapple. As he did, an image flashed through Aleon's brain. The big man's pose seemed to be the same as that of the lion just before it crashed into him. Aleon dropped to his knees in a low crouch. Both arms were thrust forward with his hands locked together to form a single fist. He lowered his head just before impact.

Arion could not react in time and his momentum carried him straight into Aleon's out-thrust arms. His solar plexus crashed hard into Aleon's clenched fists. The wind was knocked out of his lungs, and his body flew head-over-heels above Aleon's crouching form to land flat on his back in the sand. The impact was so hard that, even on the soft sand, Arion's head bounced and his senses left him.

Aleon stood up quickly and spun around to face his opponent. But Arion wasn't moving. The men around the circle roared and cheered with approval. This was not the outcome they had anticipated.

Two crewmen rushed over to Arion's fallen form and sat him up. One slapped his face to bring him around. Finally, he shook his head and tried to stand. Pain shot through his midsection and a grimace was painted on his features. The crewmen helped steady him and lifted him to his feet. He was dizzy and still dazed from the fall.

"The first fall is awarded to the Lion Slayer!" Aniketos announced. "Let the contest continue!" There was a short period between falls to allow for more betting to take place. Arion used this break to recover his senses, but not his former arrogance. He was angry now, and would be more dangerous for the second fall. He would not be tricked so easily this time.

Wagers were paid off and new wagers made. The odds given were more even now that Aleon only needed one more fall to be victorious. Arion had to win both of the remaining falls or he would lose.

Aniketos shouted, "Begin again, and let the gods reveal the truth."

Arion stood with his feet planted and shook his head as if to clear it. He was breathing heavily, and his chest still throbbed where Aleon's fists had struck him.

"You were lucky that time, young trickster!" he growled at Aleon. "You will not be so lucky again!"

His confidence returned as he spoke, and Arion went into his wrestler's stance, but stood his ground. He was not going to fall for the same trick twice. He shook his head again, taking his eyes off of his opponent.

Aleon saw this as an opening and rushed forward. He hoped to bring Arion down again before he was fully recovered. He went in low and grabbed for the larger man's right leg. He could use the leg as a lever to flip Arion onto his back, winning another quick fall. He locked his hands around the leg and went to pull it forward, while pushing backward with his head and shoulders.

But he hadn't foreseen how slippery the oil made their bodies. His hands slid off the leg and Arion stepped back and to the side so that Aleon's unbalanced body shot past him. Arion continued to turn, spinning around and landing a solid punch on the back of Aleon's head. Aleon fell face-down in the sand, and didn't move.

This time it was Aleon's turn to be rolled over and helped to his feet by Athos and another crewman. When he opened his eyes, he saw bright specks of light, like stars, swimming in his vision. As his helpers stood him up, he shook his head to clear it.

"What happened!" Athos asked. "You were doing so well and now you let him even the score! I lost a third of my share from the season's profits on you both times! First when I bet against you and the second time when I bet in your favor. One more loss and my purse will be empty! Do not let me down again! Remember, you are the one who has the most to lose!"

Aleon was still groggy but responded, "Believe in me! Or better yet, believe in my god. Almighty El has a plan for me and it does not include my being sold as a slave."

"You are already a slave! And you can be sold anytime the crew decides you are more trouble to keep than you are worth at the slave market. But that is not an issue. The loser of this match forfeits his *life*!"

Aleon was stunned! The situation was more dire than he had assumed. His very life depended on him defeating Arion. There would not be any mercy for the loser.

More bets were placed, and the odds favored Arion again. All Aleon could think of was the promise of his god. Had he imagined it, or was it real? He closed his eyes to clear his mind and prayed softly and humbly.

"Almighty El, you are the god of my family, and you are my god.

Thank you for all your kindness and the blessings that you have showered on the House of Dan-El through all its generations. Thank you for the favor you have shown me and for your protection. Remember me my lord! I believe in your promise to be with me always. I know you will not abandon your promise now!"

The men nearest him heard the words of Aleon's prayer, and made more bets, just in case the god was listening to him.

"Let the contest continue!" Aniketos shouted, to begin the final fall.

Aleon's palms were sweating so he reached down and picked up sand in both hands. He rubbed it around from his fingers to his elbows. It stuck to the oil. Arion was already in his stance and the two began to circle each other. The tension in the air was thick and all cheering and hooting had fallen to silence as the crewmen waited to see who would make the first move.

Arion made a feint to his right; against the direction they had been circling in. But Aleon moved to his own right, maintaining the distance between them. Twice more Arion faked movements in that direction, and each time Aleon responded by adjusting accordingly. Then, having set up a pattern to make Aleon expect him to attack to his right, Arion came straight at him through the center.

Aleon side-stepped and spun around as his attacker passed by. As he turned, he threw his hardest punch straight into Arion's exposed left kidney. The blow glanced off without doing much damage. Still, it caused Arion to stagger slightly as he tried to spin to his right. It gave Aleon a split-second opportunity and he kicked out with his right foot into the back of Arion's left knee just as all the big man's weight was shifted to that side. Arion's leg buckled under him and he went down to his knees.

Aleon moved quickly to follow up with another punch, but as he did Arion grabbed up a handful of sand and turned, throwing it into Aleon's face, blinding him. As Aleon shook his head and tried to clear his eyes, Arion regained his feet and grabbed Aleon in a bear hug. He lifted the shorter man off his feet and squeezed him as hard as he could.

Aleon felt as if his ribs might break. He had one arm free and one wedged against his side. But for that, his chest might have been crushed. As it was, Aleon could barely breathe and knew he wouldn't last much longer if this kept up. He did the only two things he could think of.

With his free hand he reached out and grabbed a handful of Arion's thick black hair. The hair dripped oil, but the sand on Aleon's hand kept his fingers from slipping as he pulled Arion's head back and away from his chest. Then as Arion strained against the direction his head was moving Aleon released his grip and rammed his own head forward as hard as he could. His forehead smacked into the bridge of Arion's nose and the combined impact of their head-to-head collision shattered the bones of Arion's nose. Bone fragments were forced up and back into his brain by the impact.

The effect was devastating. Arion's grip relaxed and his lifeless body fell to the sand at Aleon's feet.

Epilogue

With the death of Arion, the contest was won and Aleon-Tabah of Gebal was accepted into the crew of the *Karcharias*, and became the pirate known among the Achaeans as the Lion Slayer of Byblos. His skill as a navigator enabled his ship to attack vessels on the open sea. The crew became rich from the precious cargos they captured, and the fame of the *Karcharias* grew among the other pirates of the Aegean Sea.

In time, when Aniketos of Skyros was killed in a raid, the crew of the *Karcharias* chose Aleon to be their chief. Eventually he became commander of a large fleet of Achaean pirate vessels and threatened the entire eastern half of the Great Sea.

He never returned to his wife and children, but they were always on his mind, along with his parents and the people of Gebal. He prayed that El would protect and bless them. In time he learned that his parents had been banished from the city, and had moved the House of Dan-El, including Melita and their children, to the city of Tyre. Shortly after that move, Lord Paltiba'al brought the House of Abdhamon there as well.

Aleon's enemy, Ili-Rapih, became king after engineering his own brother's death. He came to dominate the council of elders and ruled the city of Gebal like no king before him ever had. He oppressed the people, and those who could do so left the city to begin again elsewhere in the Kena'ani world. Before long, Ili-Rapih's fleet was the only one to make its home in the port of Gebal. Eventually, the great wealth that had always come from trade dwindled and Gebal declined in economic importance. Years later it would be important only as a center of the Kena'ani worship of their many gods and goddesses.

Aleon's hatred for Ili-Rapih grew into an obsession. He commanded his pirates to avoid attacking all Kena'ani ships of the coastal cities, except the merchant vessels belonging to the high priest and king of Gebal. Their success in this did much to hasten the decline of the city's commercial importance.

The fate of the House of Dan-El and the stories of Aleon-Tabah's descendants follows them from Tyre, to Jerusalem, Carthage, Spain and beyond. But those are stories to be told elsewhere.